Praise for *Kilmoon*

In her moody debut, Alber skillfully uses many shades of gray to draw complex characters who discover how cruel love can be.
—Kirkus Reviews

Lisa Alber's assured debut paints Lisfenora, County Clare, at the height of the local matchmaking festival, when the ordinarily sleepy village is crammed with revelers, cadgers, and con men galore. Amid mysteries and mayhem, Alber captures the heartfelt ache in all of us, the deep need for connection, and a true sense of purpose.
—Erin Hart, Anthony and Agatha-nominated author of *The Book of Killowen*

In the captivating *Kilmoon*, Lisa Alber serves up a haunting tale of Merrit Chase, a woman who travels to Ireland to sift through her family's dark past in search of a future seemingly fated to elude her. With exquisite craft and a striking sense of place, Alber serves up a rich cast of unforgettable characters and an intricate, pull-no-punches plot. Raw with grief and painful honesty, *Kilmoon* is a soulful and beautifully told tale that never lets up, and never lets go.
—Bill Cameron, author of the Spotted Owl Award-winning *County Line*

This hauntingly lovely debut mystery evokes the romance of Irish lore and melds it with the poignant longings of a California woman. When Merrit Chase seeks answers to her deepest heartaches and oldest questions, she slams into the eccentric souls who populate the village of Lisfenora, County Clare, and

at least one of them is a killer. Some residents hint at ancient wounds with shocking ties to the present, while others entangle her in their own disturbing intrigues. You will be charmed by this nuanced look into the eternal mysteries of the human heart.

—Kay Kendall, author of
Desolation Row—An Austin Starr Mystery

Moody . . . Engrossing . . . Lisa Alber weaves an intricate plot and vivid characters into a twisty story about betrayal and family secrets, redemption and love. A splendid debut!

—Elizabeth Engstrom, bestselling author of
Baggage Claim and *Lizzie Borden*

Full of surprises . . . Great Irish setting, compelling characters, and a tale full of passion, hate, and murder, told with style and craft.

—Ann Littlewood, author of
the Iris Oakley "zoo-dunnit" mysteries

What a beguiling start to this new mystery series! Clever, suspenseful, and complex—Lisa Alber is a consummate storyteller. I can't wait to read her next installment and neither will you.

—Michael Bigham, author of
Harkness, A High Desert Mystery

Lisa Alber's gripping debut signals the arrival of an outstanding new voice in the realm of crime fiction. Her dark Irish tale of family, love, murder, and matchmaking is a literary pot of gold.

—Jeannie Burt, author of
When Patty Went Away

kilmoon

 A COUNTY CLARE MYSTERY

LISA ALBER

Muskrat Press • Portland

Muskrat Press, LLC
Portland, Oregon
info@muskratpress.com or publicity@muskratpress.com

Publisher's Cataloging-in-Publication Data

Alber, Lisa.
    Kilmoon : a County Clare mystery / Lisa Alber.
      p. cm.
    ISBN: 978-0-9895446-0-3 (pbk.)
    ISBN: 978-0-9895446-1-0 (e-book)
    1. Family secrets—Fiction. 2. Murder—Investigation—Ireland—Fiction. 3. Fathers and daughters—Fiction. 4. Mystery fiction. I. Title.
PS3601.L3342 K55 2013
813—dc23

                         2013910968

Book design: Jennifer Omner

Printed in the United States of America

First Edition

In memory of
Joseph Anthony Alber,
who would have loved to have seen this

June 28, 2008

Northern California

Merrit McCallum rolled a plastic vial between her palms so that the liquid morphine sloshed against the sides. Red and viscous—like blood—the liquid coated the plastic on the inside of the vial while her slick palms left smudges on the outside. She was tempted to squirt the opiate down her own throat rather than contend with Andrew, who waited her out from his rolling bed. She no longer called him *father.*

If only he would shut up, but no, his whispered voice penetrated the leaden exhaustion that she had succumbed to weeks ago. "You know you want to," he said.

She turned away from Andrew's shrunken almost-corpse to gaze at a large framed photograph that hung above the fireplace mantel. A mist-enshrouded church stood among Celtic crosses. It was a nothing of a place, a moldering heap of rocks so old that without the crosses, it could be any artifact left to crumble in the North Atlantic rains. Andrew had insisted on hanging the image on this prime section of walled real estate. Merrit's mom, meanwhile, had banished it to the coat closet during Andrew's frequent business trips. All Merrit knew was that her parents had met in a village near the church. In Ireland.

She stared at the picture in an attempt to drown herself in the imagined sounds of whipping winds and pounding rains. It didn't work. Andrew's voice irritated like the fly that bounced against the window. The fly, like Andrew, didn't mean anything by its incessant buzzing. The fly, like Andrew, was nothing but a miserable prisoner inside this morgue of a house. Both of them irritant buzzes, no more, no less.

Just a buzz, she told herself. Don't let him get to you.

"I'm in excruciating pain," he said. "You hear me?"

She dropped the oral syringe onto the swiveling bedside table, now parked near the Barcalounger and far away from Andrew's bird-claw fingers. "It's too soon for another dose."

"Check my nightstand," he said. "You can read your mom's notebook for yourself. Then you'll see."

Notebook? What notebook? He'd never mentioned a notebook before. Or maybe he had. No, surely she wasn't so out of it that she'd forgotten something as important as words written in her mother's hand.

Merrit wished she could steady her voice, but it wobbled out of her, giving her away. "I don't understand what you're getting at. I'll see what?"

"Oh, you know."

But she didn't know anything except that Andrew exuded more energy now than he'd shown for weeks. Despite the morphine, he held her gaze with the steadiness of a combatant on the battlefield.

Merrit pressed trembling hands together and struggled to maintain her poker face. If only she could think straight. If only she hadn't been stupid enough to assume she could care for Andrew on her own. She'd forgotten why she'd insisted. Something about duty, or devotion, or loyalty. Now, six months after returning home to help him, her efforts felt pointless.

She fumbled for the cell phone that she'd left on the mantel, knocking over her inhaler in the process. It rolled under the Barcalounger. A worm of tension squeezed Merrit's lungs as she pressed in the hospice phone number. Unfortunately, sunlight barely lightened the eastern horizon. She'd have to leave a message with the answering service. She steadied her voice, requested a hospice visit, and hung up.

Merrit listened with her back still facing Andrew. She didn't need to see him to know the cracks of bitterness that etched his face. He'd been awake all night, restless and demanding, and with a strange light in his eye. She sniffed against the oppressive odor of illness in the stuffy room and eyed the knitting needles sticking out of a ball of yarn. For a while the new hobby had helped her cope. She'd even gifted Andrew with her first afghan, which now lay in a discarded heap beneath the bed.

"This pain," he said. "It's torture."

Slowly, she turned around. The glow from the bedside lamp illuminated his shiny head, which stood out of the murk like a floating skull. She knew about his pain. The hospice folks had explained it all, and it was horrible to witness. Yet, he didn't seem to be in that much pain right now. She stepped forward. And then again. Until she stood next to him. She reached out to adjust his pillow. Andrew's hand latched onto her arm. Merrit steeled herself not to flinch at the dried-up boniness of his fingers pressed against her skin.

"You're a coward," he said. "But then why should I be surprised. Runs in *your* family."

"What are you saying? Why now?"

"All those years your mother kept up the pretense that she loved me, not him," he said.

Patting her chest, Merrit retreated to the Barcalounger once again. She dropped to her knees and felt around under the chair for her inhaler. She pushed at the chair, but it was already wedged into the corner of the room. Worse still, she didn't have the strength to maneuver it over the edge of the rug and away from the wall.

Breathing hard, her brain fuzzy with exhaustion and distress, Merrit staggered to her feet. Andrew's insidious, creeping, rasping voice kept at her. His lips smirked. They pulsed, they pursed, they stretched around more words.

"Your mother was a lying whore."

No.

"She screwed a goddamned hippie freak—an *Irish* hippie freak—and said it didn't matter. Nothing but a mistake."

No. No.

Merrit grabbed the morphine syringe. She managed to gasp, "Just to sleep for a bit. Until the hospice nurse arrives."

"You're so weak. Look at you. Poor baby can't breathe."

Merrit leaned against the lounger, panting. White bubbles floated across her vision. She lifted the syringe and depressed the plunger the tiniest bit. One bitter drop of morphine landed on her tongue. Andrew's hand spasmed toward her and fell back. His voice wheedled up a notch, its incessant buzz pitched high.

"Your fault she died," he said.

NO.

Merrit acknowledged the truth of the matter: Andrew had never loved her, and he never would no matter how hard she tried to be the perfect daughter. Sobbing, beyond caring, just wanting to survive this moment, she dripped another smidgen of morphine onto her tongue. Calm down, lungs, please.

"If not for you, she'd still be alive."

NO NO.

White hot despair and guilt coursed through her, so molten that anger seeped in around its edges. She pictured her mom striding away from her, hurrying away really, because she'd wanted to flee her spiteful child. Merrit opened her mouth, but nothing came out except a painful wheeze.

"You should never have been born. A mistake."

NO NO NO.

Merrit clenched the morphine syringe, shaking. The fly still buzzed, louder than ever. Her vision narrowed into a dark tunnel through which all she saw was Andrew's caved-in face. His hateful face.

"The man your precious mom fucked right before she fucked me back in 1975? He never wanted you either. Ask him yourself. After you read the notebook."

Her head exploded. "Shut up!" she screamed.

The white hot rage subsided and Merrit's vision cleared. She blinked, disoriented and shaky with leftover adrenaline. It took her a moment to realize that she still held the syringe. She gaped down at the plastic vial—now empty—and then at Andrew's self-satisfied rictus of a smile, at his eyes focused on nothing. Depleted to her very core, she sank to the ground and let the syringe roll off her palm. The haunting image of the church gazed down at her as it always had, but now it also beckoned her. Come home to Ireland, it seemed to say. Find out the truth.

A trickle of longing surprised her. Yes, she'd discover the truth that had simmered beneath the facade of her parents' marriage, which was the truth that defined Merrit's very existence. Her mom died long ago, leaving Merrit alone with Andrew. Now Andrew was dead, leaving her—what?

Guilty. Lost. Possibly irredeemable.

She stared at the empty syringe lying beside her on the rug. The truth. From her real father.

· Part I ·

Friday, August 29th – Sunday, August 31st

"Better well-intentioned duplicity than truth's fallout."
—Liam the Matchmaker

Liam Donellan's journal

Ah Kevin, as you know, we Irish, closet superstition mongers all, find solace and hope in imagining faeries, in calling upon the spirits of the long departed in moments of stress, in deifying the woman who gave birth to Jesus. Whether the wood sprite at home in the local thicket or the Holy Virgin, we Irish, we tend to prefer our myths to daily realities. Hence, the fame of the Matchmaker of Lisfenora. Me.

In the '70s free-lovers traveled here in hopes of a good shag during the matchmaking festival. And you'd best believe I was the shag king who scoffed when a stranger proclaimed that my swagger masked kindness, the proof of which was my talent for creating happily-ever-afters. Matchmaking is the best part of me, true, but only a part of a flawed whole.

Here's what she said, this stranger: "You have something, whether it's an amazing knowledge of human nature or an uncanny sixth sense, I don't know. What do you call this ability of yours?"

She was an American journalist, you see, and she wanted a rational explanation for my success rate. So I said, "There are math and music prodigies, no one doubts that, so why not a—" and here I stopped for I didn't know what to call myself. A gut-instinct virtuoso? An intuition whiz? Bloody hell, an empath—that soulless word used in science fiction?

"Call me charmed for it," I said.

· 1 ·

For the seventh day in a row, Merrit sat on a plaza bench in Lisfenora, County Clare, Ireland. She sat with back straight and sure against the bench, and with bare legs stretched out and crossed at the ankle. Unlike most tourists—especially her fellow Americans—she wore flip-flops instead of sturdy walking sandals, and a skirt instead of hiking shorts. Day after day, she appeared to be waiting for someone. While she waited, she jabbed her knitting needles through blue yarn hard enough to skewer the poor sheep to death.

One of the locals, Marcus Tully, lounged beside Merrit with hands settled over his crotch. A fresh, unopened flask perched next to him. As usual, Merrit had invaded his self-assigned bench in the plaza with its centerpiece statue depicting an illustrious O'Brien of generations past. Fuchsia-lined walkways radiated from the statue like bicycle spokes. Sunlight cast a mellow glow onto colorful gift shops and pubs that pushed up against the sidewalks. All of it was bathed in an Irish heat, milky and cocoon-like compared with August in California.

Merrit stopped knitting to stretch out her fingers and gaze around the village. She reminded herself to be grateful that her journey had brought her to Lisfenora rather than to one of the nondescript villages she'd driven through after her red-eye flight. Lisfenora was only thirty-five miles from the Shannon International Airport, yet she'd imagined she was driving into the outback, Irish style. Drystone walls snaked for miles over the hillsides, delineating emptiness rather than relieving it. One-horse—or maybe that would be one-pub—villages rose out of the early morning mists and slid away as the green expanses took over again. The roads narrowed, and Merrit hugged the embankments as she drove, unsure of herself because of the left-handed road rules. She gripped the steering wheel and scraped along the hedgerows, predicting head-on collisions every time a car barreled toward her from the opposite direction.

Two hours after leaving the airport she had arrived in Lisfenora jet-lagged and frazzled, but also intact despite the scratches marring her rental car's paint job. One glimpse at Lisfenora and she'd heaved a soul-unburdening sigh. Charming, yes, and lively, and obviously historic. It was a far cry from the claustrophobia and trauma she'd left behind in California.

Lovely, all of it, and she'd absorbed everything from the *failte* welcome mats to the old-fashioned name boards and cheery shop fronts, trying to imagine what her mom had felt when she'd first seen the village. The fact that her mom had looked upon the same stained glass transom windows had amazed Merrit most of all.

Unfortunately, after a week, her amazement had long since faded. She was here for a purpose, after all, and her purpose had led her to pester every local she'd met to no avail. She'd given up cajoling information out of Marcus days ago.

"I'm after warning you not to waste your time," he'd said. "Liam's address and phone number are off limits to tourists. You'll have to wait for the matchmaking festival to start and stand in line with the rest of the love-starved wankers."

The problem was that Merrit wasn't just any tourist, was she? She'd bet Marcus would lead her to Liam the Matchmaker if she revealed she was Liam's long-lost biological daughter. But this knowledge was hers and hers alone.

Well, almost hers alone. Anxiety constricted her chest as she fumbled her knitting. She counted back the stitches along the shorter edge of the afghan and continued on with the trim that she'd begun earlier in the day.

"Yonder Ivan, one of God's own victims," Marcus said as a short man with jutting Adam's apple and red Albert Einstein hair rounded a street corner and disappeared from view.

Merrit waited, hoping for more, then shrugged away the knot in her stomach, or rather, tried to, but the same tension that disturbed her sleep prevented her from relaxing now. "I wouldn't call Ivan a victim. He seems savvy in his own way."

"And how would you be knowing that?"

"I've met him. At the Internet café."

Marcus's grunt came along with a wrist flick. He drank with athletic gulps as if his body needed replenishing—and fast. The silver vessel settled back onto his lap, discreetly covered by his hands. Merrit thought he'd doze, but he surprised her.

"I'm a bloody ghost for all I'm noticed." He nodded to himself. "Sozzled I may be, but I'm not deaf or blind. Oh, and here comes that Lonnie the Lovely. Bloody piece of shite. Who's minding the café while Ivan is at his lunch?"

Marcus sank into grumbles as Lonnie came abreast of them from the direction of the hotel that lined one side of the plaza. Merrit averted her gaze, trying to keep her needles clicking in steady fashion. Her knuckles turned white with the effort.

"Marcus, you manky old git," Lonnie said, "made your move on Merrit yet? Get on with you or I will."

"You'd like to try, wouldn't you then. Push yourself on her. That's your way, you damned—"

"Watch yourself, old man." Lonnie turned toward Merrit, smiling as if Marcus didn't exist. "Pleasure to see you again."

Lonnie in his tight Euro-jeans and linen dress shirt bowed to Merrit and strolled off in the direction of Internet Café, which he owned.

"You stay away from him," Marcus said. "He's a shifty sort."

Too late. Since Merrit's arrival, Lonnie had aimed himself at her like a money-seeking homing device. Within twenty-four hours of meeting her, he'd boasted of knowing that she was Liam's bastard daughter—and of knowing a few other things besides. What he might know about her had caused her lungs to spasm. She'd peppered him with the obvious questions. How could you possibly know I'm Liam's daughter? What *other things* do you mean? Other things about me, or about Liam, or both?

Unfortunately, Lonnie had only smiled and shrugged. "I'll let you dangle for a while longer. More interesting that way."

Slimebag.

Lonnie could sabotage her fresh start with a fresh parent. What a depressing, not to mention infuriating, thought. This was why she couldn't sleep, and why she sat here knitting an afghan when she could be out exploring the ancient sites her mom had visited thirty years ago, especially the church that had haunted Merrit from its position on the living room wall. Merrit longed to feel Atlantic winds chapping her cheeks and scouring out the ache that had shackled her since long before Andrew's death.

Instead, here she loitered, vigilant despite Marcus's insistence that before the festival started she'd sooner see a leprechaun than see Liam. She loathed the idea of Liam learning about her from a nasty piece of work called Lonnie O'Brien. Yes, he was one of those O'Briens, descended from the founding father himself to hear Lonnie tell it. And he was quite the talker when it suited him. She imagined gossip about her circulating the pubs, which was to say the village. Lonnie could say anything, and she'd had enough public speculation aimed in her direction to last the rest of her life. This was a good enough reason for her to pay Lonnie cash in exchange for his silence. For now.

She dropped her needles and slouched like Marcus. Meeting Liam wasn't supposed to be this difficult. She couldn't have predicted villagers circling the wagons around their celebrity, this matchmaker who'd put Lisfenora on the map, who'd managed to turn an annual festival into an event known to lovelorn singles all over Europe and North America. Unfortunately, the longer her quest took, the more apprehensive she became. The possibility of rejection loomed larger than she had expected now that she was actually in Ireland.

"Look there, will you?" Marcus said, interrupting Merrit's thoughts. "Now you'll be seeing how beloved is your Lonnie. That's Danny Ahern."

Marcus had brightened at the sight of the man named Danny, a detective sergeant, Marcus said. Perhaps this detective sergeant with the careworn facial stubble and graceful hands could help her out with her Lonnie problem.

"See there?" Marcus said.

Indeed, Danny had stiffened at the sight of Lonnie and then plastered a neutral—some might call it professional—smile on his face. The two men stood at the edge of the plaza near a row of parked cars, Lonnie doing all the talking and Danny all the nodding. After a moment, Lonnie walked on and Danny grimaced in Marcus's direction. "Cheers, Marcus," he called. "Have to get on, but you'll take care not to annoy our Lonnie, will you? Seems to think your presence might be throwing off his business."

"Piss poor shite I call that!"

A smile sparkled for the barest moment before Danny tossed up a wave and departed.

"Village life," Marcus said, yawning. "After a time, you'll recognize all its muck, sitting here. Not that Lisfenora's muck is special in that regard. That Danny's a good one though. A lifesaver to me, that's the truth. And like a second son to Liam, I might add. Quite the threesome, them."

Second son?

"The matchmaker has a son?" Merrit said.

"Indeed. Kevin. But he's not much about the village since last year's festival. Been keeping himself scarce you might say. As anyone might expect, truth be told."

Merrit waited, but once again Marcus lapsed into silence. That was the problem with Marcus—just when he started to open up, he stopped talking. Still. A son, a brother. Maybe she could get to know Liam's son first. She imagined a man similar to her, but younger—yes, surely several years younger—with reddish brown hair and a small bone structure. She'd always wanted a brother. How she used to pester her mom to have a baby, little knowing that her mom could no longer bear children after her own birth.

Her mom had loved children.

Marcus's head tilted onto his shoulder. His eyelids fluttered, and Merrit leaned closer, breathing in the smell of mint toothpaste and gin fumes. The bags under his eyes looked heavier today, swollen with bluish half circles. As ever, sitting next to him comforted yet pained her. She was drawn to his kindly father-figure presence, and it was this, precisely, that caused her heart to clutch with worry about his welfare. Marcus, a widower for many years now, had admitted to a daughter dead to him, yet he also appeared in clean slacks and button-down shirt. Thankfully, someone helped him out, and this someone probably provided the mint toothpaste, too. Unfortunately,

Marcus's patron didn't bother about Marcus's tatty sneakers painted with green and yellow stripes—some teenager's idea of a fun time while Marcus snoozed, so he said.

"Marcus?"

He harrumphed.

"Tonight I'll finish this afghan for you. It's the least I can do in exchange for invading your space all the time. You're my first friend here, you know."

"Off with you then. I'm that wrecked."

"OK, but I'm coming back later with food. I insist you eat something."

Merrit rolled up the afghan and tucked it under her arm. Despite Marcus's terse shrug, she spied the beginnings of a smile stretching his lips. He'd never toss aside one of her afghans like so much garbage, leaving her to wonder why she'd bothered.

· 2 ·

Merrit walked down one of the plaza's paved spokes, hoping to catch sight of Danny, the detective sergeant. From what Marcus had said, Danny was an honorary member of Liam's family. She could introduce herself, start a conversation, bring up Liam. She could try, anyhow.

The plaza sat like a bump at the top of the T-juncture where Burren Street ended at what the locals called the *noncoastal road*, which was to say that in either direction it meandered toward the coast through other noncoastal villages with other plazas. Turning right once she reached the noncoastal, Merrit headed toward the village church, which wasn't breathtaking— hardly St. Patrick's Cathedral—but in a certain light, like now when softened through clouds, the nineteenth-century walls reflected a peaceful yellowish glow.

The detective sergeant had disappeared into the throngs of tourists who strolled along in a carefree way, no doubt anticipating their future love connections. Merrit squeezed through a gaggle of Germans and pardoned herself past two Englishmen until she was forced to slow down behind a gang of women who turned out to be none other than Lonnie the Lovely's mother and sisters. Just her luck. She backtracked but not fast enough to avoid catching the matriarch's eye through their reflections in a pharmacy window.

"Well, here you are," Mrs. O'Brien said.

The women held fast, and the people stream parted around them. They gazed at Merrit expectantly, so she raised her shoulders with what she hoped was friendly confusion. In reality, she longed to duck into the pharmacy.

"I was after telling my girls that you plan to be here for a while."

Mrs. O'Brien's girls looked to be pushing their forties. In the rush of introductions and floral cologne, Merrit didn't let on that she knew them by name already: Mariela, Eloisa, Constanza. Why the Spanish names? she'd asked, to which Marcus had replied that Mrs. O'Brien fancied herself descended from Spanish high society—*aristocrats,* not deckhands, mind you—who had sailed to Eire and stayed. According to him, there was a reason they were all single, and that reason was their ghastly mother, who'd nag the devil out of hell itself. Merrit had avoided the O'Brien women because of Marcus's warning. "The mouths on them, you wouldn't believe. Gather flies, the lot of them. You'd better be sure Mrs. O'Brien will take an interest in you."

As if to prove his point, Mrs. O'Brien said, "You're staying in Mrs. Sheedy's upstairs flat for the month. She's the sort to watch over you, but she's hardly in a position to help you meet people. In fact, I have a brilliant idea."

Merrit had a nasty feeling about Mrs. O'Brien's so-called brilliant idea and tried to exit stage left, right, or backwards, but she couldn't because the daughters had her surrounded.

"I've got a prescription waiting," she said.

"We must visit my son," Mrs. O'Brien said. "He'll be the one to introduce you to the nicer elements of Lisfenora. You don't mind my saying that you ought to keep better company, and our lad, he's charming. I'm sure you've seen his business headquarters, the flagship as they say. Such an odd word really. Flagship. What could it possibly mean?"

Merrit caught herself patting her chest against tension gathering around her lungs. She drew in a deep breath as the women pushed her forward. "I need to run into the pharmacy," she tried again, but by then they had arrived at the Internet café.

"'Alloo," Mrs. O'Brien called as she opened the door.

Ivan sat behind the counter. At the sight of the women, he tugged on an earlobe and bolted into his workshop, but not without first aiming a tentative smile in their direction.

"The Russians are such a cowardly lot," Mrs. O'Brien said.

"He's Belarusian of Russian descent," said one of the daughters from behind Merrit. Which daughter, she couldn't tell. They all sounded the same to her. "Do the favor of getting it straight if you're going to malign him."

"Oh, do stop. Belarus, Russia, it's all the same. He speaks Russian and that's enough for me."

The powerful momentum of the O'Brien women propelled Merrit across the room, around the service counter, and into Lonnie's office. His monitor faced away from the door, but even so, he clicked his mouse once before stepping around the desk to greet them. "And what's this?"

"I implore you to rescue Merrit here from that Marcus," Mrs. O'Brien said.

Lonnie relaxed. A smile popped into place. "Just Merrit's luck to have met us then." He turned to Merrit. "As I recall, you're here for family research. Any luck?"

"What you'd expect." She matched his bland smile with one of her own. "No help at all, some people. In fact, some people aren't worth knowing."

"This is my point exactly," Mrs. O'Brien said. "People worth knowing. Remind me, Merrit—your surname?"

Merrit hesitated, glancing at Lonnie, then said, "Chase."

"Solid name but no Chases in this area. Unless you're here to look up your mother's lineage?"

Lonnie grinned. He knew well enough that Chase *was* her mom's lineage and that Merrit had officially changed her last name. Merrit rubbed her fatigue-laden eyelids. To think, she'd first entered this shop because she was having trouble with her wireless connection. Lonnie had suggested she leave her laptop for a few hours. His man Ivan would figure it out, he said, but just then he was busy. Lonnie's offer seemed kind at the time, but now she puzzled over how he knew within two minutes of meeting her that he'd find something interesting on her laptop's hard drive. She'd left laptops with technicians plenty of times and thought nothing of it.

"Well?" Mrs. O'Brien prodded. "Your mother's surname?"

Merrit spoke up against the daughters' side chatter. "My mom's side is well-documented back to the eighteen hundreds. They came over from County Cork, and every last family member emigrated."

"Oh. Cork. Now, where was I?" Mrs. O'Brien clapped her hands within inches of Lonnie's face. "Are you listening? Merrit must be your date to Liam's birthday party. How else is she going to meet the people who matter in Lisfenora?"

"What birthday party?" Merrit said.

"Quite the annual event for us, Liam being Liam. And best yet, this year his birthday falls on a Saturday. Tomorrow night, mind you. Over at the Plough and Trough. You'll have fun, I have no doubts, especially with my Lonnie to escort you."

Lonnie spluttered into a laugh, causing Mrs. O'Brien to aim an uncertain blink in his direction. "I don't know why this should be so funny. Everyone will be there."

"Of course," Lonnie said. "I had it in mind to get to know Merrit better anyhow."

Mrs. O'Brien patted Lonnie's cheek. "That's grand. You will escort Merrit."

Within seconds, the O'Brien women were gone. The electronic snore of dozing computers filtered into Lonnie's office. He fingered a thin braid that hung to his shoulder. Merrit longed to take scissors to the puerile affectation. Instead, she said, "Your mom's a real piece of work."

"And lucky fecking me." He settled himself on the edge of the desk. "Actually, this is a fascinating development. Mustn't disappoint Mother, mind, or she'll give me a bollocking for sure. What time shall I pick you up for the party?"

Merrit swallowed hard against galloping nerves inside her chest. This was exactly what she didn't want. Being railroaded. Not to mention the dubious distinction of being Lonnie's "date."

"Thank you," she said, "but I'll go on my own."

"Private party, only locals and their dates allowed. Old Liam's one stipulation, and even *you* won't get past the barricade." He held up a hand before she could protest. "Believe me, you won't. However, if you come with me, I'll announce you to Liam myself."

"You wouldn't dare."

He grinned. "Wouldn't I?"

"I'll introduce myself to Liam on my terms, not yours. And definitely not in front of the whole village."

"You and I both know you're itching to go."

She stared at him, loathing him for being correct. She was more than itching to go—compelled would be more like it. At the very least, she longed to observe Liam the Matchmaker from afar, to get a sense of whether he'd welcome or reject her.

"How much is it worth to you to ensure I keep my mouth shut during the party?" Lonnie said.

Merrit had considered scuttling back to California rather than deal with Lonnie, but that would have been yet one more sign of her weakness. Some might have called Andrew's end a death with dignity. But she knew different. Powerless against a tidal wave of fury and despair and exhaustion, she'd snapped. Now she had to live with the horrid truth of it: she was capable of taking a human life. Lonnie might or might not know something about the darkness that lurked within her. He might or might not decide to reveal her darkness to her real father just because he could.

"You are such a—" Merrit yanked her wallet out of her purse, then the cash out of her wallet. She threw the wad at him. "I'll go to the party with you, but you'd better keep your mouth shut about me."

Lonnie's smile turned gleeful just before he bellowed. "Ivan, fetch us coffee, will you?"

"Oh, that's right," she said, "we're such good friends. Screw you."

"Why so uptight?" he called after her. "You could probably do with a good shagging after all that."

Ten minutes later, Merrit reclined on her bed clutching a battered spiral-bound notebook with a psychedelic rainbow and "September 1975" on the cover. She'd found it in Andrew's nightstand just like he'd said. After reading it, her shock had been so profound that she'd barely survived the next weeks of funeral arrangements and legal turmoil. She was better now. She hoped. At the very least, she wasn't using her inhaler every ten seconds anymore.

She fingered the notebook's tattered cover. Above the

rainbow, her mom's precise block lettering spelled out "Ireland Article." Within the notebook, the pages revealed scribbles, cross-outs, and journaling that bore witness to her mom's increasing distraction back in 1975. Julia Chase had started out earnestly enough with initial research for her first big travel-writing assignment. Quite a coup for a woman, given the times, but the travel piece went unfinished due to the source of Julia's distraction. None other than Liam the Matchmaker. A man her mom had called *Liam the Lion*.

One sentence always filled Merrit with sadness. *I'm a coward, that's what I am, and all I can do is pack my bags because I hate myself for loving the man . . .*

Merrit's life, her mom's life—how different they would have been if Liam had fought for her mom. But he hadn't, and Merrit had to know why. Since childhood, she'd yearned to fill the void where the unsaid and the murky festered beneath her mom's smiles. Merrit couldn't recall when she'd realized that her mom was a woman who hid her unhappiness well most of the time. Nor could Merrit recapture the moment she first noticed that Andrew treated her like a houseguest who'd over-stayed her welcome, only that it hadn't mattered until after her mom's death. All she knew was that the answers lingered along Lisfenora's cobbled lanes, along which Liam had walked arm-in-arm with her mom.

Julia Chase's notebook

During the matchmaking festival, Lisfenora village is Liam Donellan's court. He reigns in a fur-trimmed, flowing purple cape that flaps around his knees. ~~Flamboyant and fashionable with his long hair and~~ *(My God, this is crap. Too bad the matchmaker is the best human-interest angle around.)*

Eccentric he may be, but he's the matchmaker, and each year September incomes grow along with Lisfenora's fame. Wives stockpile jars of preserves homemade from blackberries that grow along stone walls. Husbands invest in sheep to provide wool for hand-knit sweaters because the foreigners inevitably arrive underdressed. Children take up residence in living rooms thereby opening bedrooms up for lodging.

No one minds the inconvenience because the man is a bona fide tourist attraction. In this region where most villages molder under the debilitating effects of unemployment, little Lisfenora thrives. All, it's said, because of the matchmaking festival. (Need statistics here.)

Liam the Lion, as he's often called, plants himself in the plaza with a gigantic ledger on his lap. Gold leaf gleams under mild sunlight, and the calfskin cover creaks when Liam opens the book. Upon thick parchment he scribbles crucial data about each supplicant . . . (I need to get to the heart of this Liam character. What about his own love life?)

· 3 ·

Lonnie sipped coffee and grimaced at his computer screen. Christ, his mom together with Merrit, of all the sodding luck. But then, he couldn't argue with bringing Merrit along to Liam's party—good *craic* indeed.

He barked a laugh and settled back into moodiness. He tried not to picture Ivan out front wanking away on his laptop while twenty gleaming computers faced one another around the room's perimeter. They were on, but you'd never know it to look at them. They'd long since fizzled into energy-saver mode so nothing but darkened monitors graced his shop. By rights, his cyber café should be doing well. So why wasn't it?

In answer, Lonnie heard his father's supercilious voice. "What you have now, my boy, is the classic problem of demand not meeting supply. The good news is that you can create demand. Marketing plans, they're not just a dick-whipping exercise."

Marketing plans. Not to mention publicity and promotion and giveaways and tie-ins with the sightseeing companies and an actual coffee bar. The word *café* in the storefront name *Internet Café* was symbolic only, for feck's sake. Why would he serve coffee and risk damage to the computers?

So here Lonnie sat while down the road and across the plaza, his father, owner of the Grand Arms Hotel and a dozen other luxury accommodations along the west coast, perused numbers that glowed black as night at the end of each month. While he, Lonnie the Lovely—yes, he'd heard the words said behind his back—contended with digits that fizzled into the red even with Ivan's expertise to back him up.

The shop cat—Ivan's idea—nosed around Lonnie's feet. Idly, Lonnie scratched the root of its tail. And what about Ivan anyhow? Lonnie didn't dare fire him. Even this basic owner's privilege lay beyond his free will. The man was a genius with computers and had a global network of cyber-hack contacts besides. He could retrieve anything. *Any*thing. Which meant that Lonnie must tolerate Ivan and his dodgy personal hygiene for the time being. Lonnie's sideline into information nondis-closure services—INS, ha, ha—was temporary. Just until his business got going. Or maybe not, who knew?

"Ivan," Lonnie called through the closed office door.

Ivan poked his head in with fingers scratching deep into masses of red hair that fluffed out of his head like cotton. Lonnie shuddered. Could be anything under those fingernails.

"This place is a bloody morgue. Get the music, will you?"

"We could get disco ball," Ivan said, accent heavier than usual, a sign that he longed to sulk but dared not. "Hire women for sitting at the computers. They could be wearing almost nothing."

Lonnie stood. The slob might be onto something. He could rig up private cubicles and charge half-hour fees. He could spread the word through the pubs. Hardworking men straight in from their labors and not ready for home—of course not, what with multiple brats and nagging sow wives there to greet the poor bastards. They'd sit in the pubs with their mates then saunter down to Internet Café. Yes, these blokes hankered for a moment of privacy such as he, Lonnie O'Brien, budding entrepreneur, could supply. He could even provide a menu of recommended websites for their viewing pleasure.

"Brilliant," he said. "Ivan, you're the man. But I'm thinking we'd best cater to the ladies also, or they'll shut me down quick as a lad's prude girlfriend. We'll host women's-only nights to appease them."

"Your mother will love that," Ivan said with something other than enthusiasm. "She will be organizing everything like always."

Lonnie pushed Ivan backwards through the door. "We'll serve tea and biscuits, teach them how to use the Internet. It'll be a fecking social hour. Dear Mum will be useful when it comes to all that."

"Singles evenings too," Ivan said. "Maybe local dating service that we associate with the matchmaking festival. I can create password-aided program only accessible from our network. Our clients pay monthly fees to access our singles database and correspond through email—"

"Spot-on, you filthy Cossack, spot-on." Lonnie pointed across the street, where Kevin Donellan had just stepped out of the post office. "I tell you what, I'm not hiring that wankstain to build the cubicles."

"Cubicles?"

"You heard me, private cubicles."

Lonnie ground his teeth as Kevin strode away without a glance at Internet Café. "And he'd best not stick his prick into my business affairs again, not after last year. *Authentic* store-fronts, my ass."

He retreated back into his office. A moment later, one of those whiny American songstresses filled the air and worsened his mood. Fuck me, he thought, and pulled his special folder out from under his desk blotter. A desultory flip didn't yield magical revelations into fresh cash, though he couldn't help stopping at a marriage announcement and marveling at the mystery that was fate, or destiny, or some other bull.

Chase-McCallum

Timothy and Cassandra Chase of Boston are pleased to announce the engagement of their daughter, Julia Lane Chase, to Andrew James McCallum, of San Francisco, CA. Andrew is the son of Edward and Trinity McCallum of Chicago, IL.

The bride-to-be graduated from Vassar College and most recently worked as a travel writer. The groom-elect owns an international consulting and trade business headquartered in San Francisco.

Julia and Andrew met in Ireland. Their union is the result of an annual matchmaking festival held in Lisfenora, County Clare. The couple will move to California following their December 31, 1975, wedding, which is planned at St. Patrick's Catholic Church.

He'd already teased out every possible angle from this bit, including the all-important fact that Julia Chase was three months pregnant by the time she got married. He needed to step up his efforts because Merrit would have no reason to continue paying him after she revealed her identity to Liam. He needed more, more of everything: other people's secrets, other people's money. Not to mention a fierce shagging since he was drawing up a wish list.

Ivan poked his head into the office. "Customer," he whispered and by his hunched shoulders, the door chimes must have signaled a female of the good-looking variety.

"Go on then. I've got it."

Lonnie took up position behind the counter, taking his time and inhaling the sultry, slightly over-ripened scent that flicked by him on the breeze the woman brought in with her.

"No need to be shy. Come in," he said.

The woman stood just within the doorway. She was no local, to be sure. Lonnie hadn't seen a hip cocked that way since his last trip to Amsterdam.

"I'd say I'm in already, wouldn't you?" she said.

Ah, a Dublin accent. Jackeen in the western bogs and no wonder she looked as out of place as a whore in a nunnery. Beyond her, sunshine reached over the rooftops to lay bare cobblestone streets. Light silhouetted legs long enough to bow-tie around Lonnie's waist.

"My name is Kate Meehan. And you're Lonnie O'Brien?"

"At your service. Needing help with the Internet?"

"Hardly."

Kate strolled along a bank of computers, clicking each mouse so the blackened screens fizzed back to their colorful displays.

"Much better," she said.

She settled herself in front of the closest terminal and twirled the chair so she faced Lonnie. Her skirt slid up as she twisted to lift a laptop computer from the leather case still hooked over her shoulder. She pressed the on button, and turned the machine around to show Lonnie the blank screen. "I'm having a problem with the battery, only the battery is new so it must be the AC inverter." She waved a nonchalant hand. "You haven't a clue what I'm talking about, do you?"

"Not likely."

"I'll wait for your man's return then. He legged it out the back door just now. He's the computer expert, right? You're the pretty front man from the local rich family."

"Now, see here—"

"I could use a good servicing also." Her expression remained neutral. "For the laptop, of course."

Before he knew it, Lonnie was seated beside Kate, watching her sandal dangle then fall to the floor as she crossed her legs. Lonnie crossed his legs also.

"You're a man with connections," she said. "That much is obvious."

"Too true. Join me for a drink and we'll get started on the connecting."

"I'm here indefinitely."

He hesitated, caught off guard by her response. "Working then?"

"Call it a whim."

Kate wriggled forward on her seat. She had arctic eyes this one, and their icy haze pinned him as if she were an oracle— and a damned creepy, seductive one at that. Lonnie recrossed his legs, too aware of the itch in his lower abdomen.

"I might take you up on your drink offer," she said. "I'm curious about this village of yours. I hear there's a match-making festival each year."

"It starts on Monday, in fact. I can introduce you to the matchmaker. He's a most interesting old codger."

"I'll lay a wager on that." She closed the laptop with a smart snap. Harder than necessary it seemed to Lonnie. "No need for introductions though."

After that bemusing dismissal, Ivan returned, scalp-scratching as usual. He descended into earlobe-pulling as Kate explained her laptop's ailment. Her presence triggered a spasm in his English, much to Lonnie's chagrin.

"I must finding an AC inverter," Ivan said and fled into his workshop with the malfunctioning computer.

"Might be a couple of hours," Lonnie said. "The man's a pack rat."

"Fine. I'll be back in exactly two hours." She handed him a business card with only her name and phone number printed on it. "Call me."

Kate left, but her perfume lingered. No one settled in Lisfenora on a whim, this much Lonnie knew, and especially not a woman as calculated in her mannerisms as Kate Meehan.

One hour later, Lonnie bestowed a pat onto Ivan's back. After fixing the AC inverter, Ivan had bypassed Kate's security password—somehow, who knew how the techno-freak did it?—to reveal Kate's world on microchip, and what a scintillating world that turned out to be.

Tsk, tsk, a naughty one was our Kate. So much so that Lonnie thought she might be the perfect woman.

Lonnie chortled as he thought about nancy-boy Kevin again. Kevin didn't know shit about shit, poor sod. When he did find out, he'd pop a blood vessel for sure. That pleasure was for the future, however. For now, Lonnie must concentrate on his cash flow.

"I'd say a friendly chat with Kate is the order of the day," he said.

· 4 ·

On the brink of Saturday's dawn, Kevin Donellan hovered neither too close to his father nor too far away in case the stubborn old git lost his balance. Liam, as usual, sat on his favorite gravestone among Celtic crosses that marked the resting spots of people long dead. He wore a tweed newspaper boy's cap and matching sport jacket. The cap wobbled on his head, and the jacket sleeves hung past his wrists.

"You're sure about it then?" Kevin said.

"Quit harping. You're worse than the magpies. You think I don't drive myself into the village when you're at one of your construction sites?"

Kevin squinted against a hangover. Tonight he'd be after it again, the only difference being that he'd be buried alive by birthday revelers. He enjoyed his pints well enough, but he didn't look forward to the party. He never did, in fact, and this year would be worse than ever. One year ago today, he thought. Is that when things started to change?

"I made a decision here a long time ago," Liam said in a voice soft enough Kevin barely caught the words.

Liam's *here* was Our Lady of the Kilmoon, an early Christian church stained with mossy grime that had aged her past

31

her years. The relic was hardly bigger than Kevin's cottage but with a moody presence nonetheless as she watched over her graves. Her thatched roof had disintegrated long ago because only rock tolerated the Irish rainscape. Yet, even her hardy walls had started to succumb to the elements. Loose rocks littered the ground around her, half hidden by grassy tussocks. A drystone wall marked her territory, within which grave markers and Celtic crosses slowly sank into the ground. More walls bordered fields spreading green and lush in all directions. A few houses stood off in the distance. Out here in the middle of nowhere cows and sheep outnumbered humans.

In the neighboring sheep pasture, a pre-Celtic standing stone glowed orange in the growing light. The obelisk appeared more permanent than Our Lady, which was built a millennium later. It shared space with livestock and rock walls and blackthorn, while the church, though picturesque, usurped space as if she knew she didn't belong and must protect her parcel of land all the more for it. Kevin imagined the early Christians glancing at the standing stone as they entered the church and then secretly praying to the pagan gods the stone represented.

Despite the clash of old cultures, or more likely because of it, this was a sacred spot, which might be why Liam had started dragging Kevin along for what amounted to brooding sessions. No coincidence these sessions began the day after Liam had received a letter that he still refused to share with Kevin. When was that? Early July? Sometime after the rains finally abated for a short while, in any case.

"I decided to let myself fall in love," Liam said. "I felt entitled, you see. It was my turn, but I turned it into nothing but a harpy's burial."

Liam turned up his collar against the wind only to have a gust blow off his cap, which flipped three times and landed on one of Our Lady's windowsills. Kevin didn't understand how Liam's hats grew too big because surely his skull couldn't shrink. He retrieved the cap, fearing what Liam would say next. He preferred the Liam of old, who never spoke of his past.

Kevin handed the cap to Liam and stepped away to pluck at a bouquet of withered violets. To his way of thinking, the flowers were useless. The leftover bits of skeleton, if any, cared nothing about such niceties. They were already mutated into another life, another death, on and on through time like endless tiled corridors.

Off to Kevin's left, Liam pulled the irksome letter from his pocket to finger it for the thousandth time. With an annoyed grunt as prelude, Kevin began whistling against the sound of the letter sliding out of its envelope. A Beatles song, the one about Jude, who shouldn't carry the weight of the world on his shoulders.

"Why not let me match you this year, sonny boy?" Liam said. "Time's running out, you know."

Kevin squeezed the violet stems but caught himself before crushing them.

"You saw too much matchmaking in your youth, I suppose," Liam continued. "Took the romance right out of marriage."

A few minutes later, the sun officially breached the eastern horizon and bounced light off the Celtic crosses. Kevin remained close as they walked the lumpy path toward the lane and to Liam's sea-salt encrusted Corolla. Kevin took control of the steering wheel. The headlights highlighted a narrow lane lined with more rock walls. Hazel scrub and holly scraped the car when Kevin eased off the embankment.

"Let me help you with the matchmaking this year," he pushed. It was an old argument.

Liam scowled. "Enough discussion on the matter. I have the strength for one more festival at least. I'm not dead yet."

As he drove toward the village, Kevin struggled to imagine

Liam's prime as the swashbuckling matchmaker. Tales still circulated about the youthful Liam, cocky yet charming, with a mane of wild hair and vigor to spare. Liam the Lion he was called, though nowadays he looked about as leonine as a shorn sheep.

Despite this, Kevin could almost picture Liam the Lion striding through the village, which hadn't changed much since the 1970s. The hub still revolved around the plaza, and each Wednesday step dancing lessons still began at 7:00 p.m. in the Grand Arms Hotel. On the opposite corner, the market still stayed open into the long twilight to cater to the tourists. Too bad the new addition to their community, the Internet café, intruded between two gift shops. Kevin would like nothing better than to see the modern eyesore closed down for good, but the O'Brien family's bottomless coffers kept it afloat.

From the plaza, the Donellan homestead stood a few miles away off a series of rutted lanes. The Corolla's brakes squeaked as Kevin pulled up in front of a ranch-style house complete with bright green trim. Kevin had built it for Liam, all the while lamenting the demise of the white-washed cottages of old. Kevin pivoted out of the car and rounded to the passenger side to see Liam gazing at a sliver moon that still hovered near the horizon. His gimpy hand with fingers brittle as twigs lay curled on his lap. Kevin leaned over to hoist Liam to his feet.

"Hovering magpie, stop with you," Liam said. "I'm not arthritic. Only the hand."

"Old troll, don't forget the hip. Use your cane."

"Bugger that, I tripped last night, that's all."

The porch light clicked on as Kevin moved into its sensor range. Looking back, he caught Liam's eyes aglow, bright green and adamant. "I can handle the festival, do you doubt that?"

For a second, Kevin caught a glimpse of Liam the Lion, but the image faded with Liam's limping step forward.

"I don't understand vegans," Liam said when he crossed the threshold. "They're often judgmental and hard to match. Then there are the women who don't want children, and the men who'd prefer to stay home to tend them. It's all backwards I tell you." Kevin loitered in the doorway while Liam turned on the lamp next to his reading chair. "Even an old master like me has to let go. In fact, I've no choice. I made two matchmaking mistakes last year."

A draft slithered up Kevin's back, and for a second he froze in an attempt to comprehend the impossible. Liam never made mistakes. This was a law as universal as gravity. But then, there was a time when Liam filled out his clothes, a time when gray hair fine as a kitten's belly didn't ring his head, a time when Kevin assumed Liam would live forever. Just like there was a time—that sliver of time, still sharp after all these years—when he'd believed Sister Ignatius's answer when he'd asked how long God would love him. For all eternity, she'd answered in her hushed way. Kevin used to believe in eternity and forever.

"I'll have last say in the matter," Liam said, his tone defiant now.

"You always do. Now rest up for the party. I predict utter chaos."

Kevin's mobile vibrated from within his back pocket. He checked it, thinking it might be his work crew already bitching about something and the day not yet begun. Instead, he saw Danny's number and decided to call him back later. "That's Danny, probably checking on when we'll arrive at the party."

"He doing door duty again this year?"

"Doubtful. I get the feeling he just wants to relax."

"Ay," Liam confirmed. "I worry about that boy. His marriage—"

"I know it."

Kevin was almost out the door when Liam inserted his last

say for the moment. "No need to drop in for lunch. I'm fine, I tell you."

The door closed behind Kevin with a well-oiled click. He yawned up at the disappearing moon shadow and decided to walk the rest of the way down the track to the cottage that was his childhood home. He would return for lunch anyhow. This was what good sons did, check in on their fathers.

Liam Donellan's journal

The journalist didn't like my answer to her question, "What makes you so good?" At the time I shunned notions of "good" because they implied the existence of opposing concepts like bad, evil, and sin—which no matchmaker ought to consider for they're the death of empathy. After all, I, as matchmaker, can't pick the people who come to me with hopes of happiness. I've matched all manner of unsavory characters without judgment for they're in need of love too.

She had an empathy of her own, this journalist, which was why I allowed her to question me in the first place. It was true that I didn't think of myself as something so prosaically Catholic as "good." Even then, I believed good people—people like you, my son—fared poorly in life. They're too vulnerable to disillusionment, which is an unsuitable trait for a successful matchmaker.

In the end, disillusionment breeds resentment, which is a kind of hatred. A matchmaker must not hate his petitioners. This above all is taboo. However, I waged battle against this truism once, a long time ago. I thought I was superior enough to feel the fester without effect. There were no winners. In fact, the fallout continues, and when the toxic results of my life finally settle, and when you raise your head to take in the new view, I can only hope you won't detest me.

· 5 ·

At Patsy's, the restaurant across the street from Internet Café, Kate Meehan sat in a window seat with a cup of tea. She eyed the sandwiches on her neighbors' plates: cucumber with parsley, egg salad with sprouts, two-layer ham salad—all in various shapes of heart, clover, diamond, and circle, all with the crusts trimmed off. Next would come the deviled ham toasts and broiled cheese breads, the scones and currant brioches served with lemon curd and apple butter. And finally, the festive petit four tea cakes and strawberry meringues and peach sorbets.

It was enough to make her wretch. Really, who were these people?

Your average demanding consumers, that's what. She understood that much from her own business dealings. She also understood the shenanigans required of all small business owners, and she smiled as she eavesdropped on Patsy, who advertised her *official English-style high tea* with a sidewalk placard. "Our lemon curd is identical to that Queen Victoria herself enjoyed. The recipe came into my family through marriage. The head chef at the time married my cousin's great-grandmother. In fact, most of our recipes hail from Queen Victoria's royal kitchen."

Verbal vomit, Kate had long ago noted, was the inexpert liar's downfall. The opposite case—communicating just enough—was an art form. And the reason she was here in Lisfenora, when all was said.

Kate reached into her bra cup and pulled out the letter that had arrived back in July. What an exasperating day that had been. She'd been out of her mind with boredom, about to succumb to yet another bout of tepid sex with that fledgling porn queen, Becky Thatch, who refused to change her name to Elle Lure upon Kate's advice, and who insisted she wasn't queer. Not that Becky's sexuality mattered to Kate. Some relationships deserved cultivation, and some cultivation methods were more titillating than others. However, that day Kate had decided she was finished with Becky. Kate remembered the exact thought going through her head when the letter drifted through the slot. *If I have to explain to her one more time how the webcam works, I will poke my eyes out.*

She'd somehow become the diva of web porn, and along with the crush of website design work came the inevitable hand-holding of women too daft to know they couldn't aim the computer monitors at their beds like video cameras.

Kate fingered the letter now cradled in her palm. With a little ingenuity, she might find herself waving bye-bye to website design altogether. That cunt—that surprisingly resourceful cunt—Lonnie O'Brien might have sniffed out her profession and other bits from her laptop yesterday, but this letter's contents were all hers. She pushed the teacup toward the table's edge and smoothed out the stationery. The writing paper didn't fit the tone of the letter, as if the sender had grabbed the first sheet he'd come across. Subsequent research indicated that this was probably true. Kate rubbed a pink-tinted, scalloped edge. As usual, she perused one particular paragraph.

I'm sure you long to know why you ended up in an orphanage. For the answers, seek Liam Donellan of Lisfenora, County Clare. As an infant you had the oddest eyes.

No details there, so either a liar she'd take lessons from or a truth-teller with an ax of hate to grind. She leaned toward truth-teller because of that last sentence. Just the detail she needed to take the letter seriously. She'd been tempted to respond, *I still have those eyes.* Five simple words to show her for a kindred spirit. Unfortunately, by the time she figured out how to make contact, her window of opportunity had closed.

So here she was, in infuriatingly small Lisfenora with its second-rate village church and puffed-up sense of importance, contending with the likes of Lonnie. Despite his superior knowledge about the complication named Merrit Chase, Kate resented his intrusion into her private affairs, especially because she had no one to blame but herself. Her laptop's security firewall was a good one—not easily decrypted—so imagine her surprise when Lonnie insisted they chat in private about money matters. So much for underestimating the locals, especially bumbling little Ivan.

Kate sipped her tea. Nothing was happening inside Internet Café, but across the street and down half a block began the plaza, where Merrit sat on a bench with the village dosser. As Kate watched, Merrit rose and drifted in her direction. She had an ethereal quality about her that Kate found annoying, what with her flippy little dress and ballet flats. From afar, she looked inconsequential. So much so that Kate had laughed when Lonnie pointed her out earlier that morning. This was after Kate had all but shoved her first cash installment into the Lonnie fund up his nose.

"Take a closer look sometime," Lonnie said. "Her clothes are expensive, her teeth and posture perfect, and she takes in more than she gives away."

Lonnie had revealed keener perception than she'd assumed he possessed.

Now, Kate leaned against the window, intrigued, as Merrit stopped just shy of Internet Café's threshold and then about-faced to eye the restaurant. She trotted across the street, and Kate, who'd been about to leave, settled back in her chair. Couldn't be more perfect. There stood the waif pressing a hand against her stomach and reading the menu posted outside. Kate surveyed the filled-to-capacity room.

She signaled Patsy. "More tea, please."

"Brilliant." Patsy's gaze skittered toward Merrit now standing inside the entrance. "Oh, dear."

"I don't mind sharing my table."

While Patsy spoke to Merrit, pointed, shook her head, then nodded, Kate tucked the letter back into her bra, all the while continuing her assessment. Merrit looked like she'd been interrupted somewhere in childhood, that's what it was, and though her body had morphed, a part of her had remained behind.

"Hi," Merrit said, "you don't mind my sitting here?"

Kate leaned forward with chin on elbow on table, but Merrit was preoccupied with the menu. She sat sideways on the seat, fingering a large blue stone that dangled from a chain around her neck, and for several minutes she acted as if Kate didn't exist, which Kate found more interesting than insulting. Look at her, with no clue she's got a nasty surprise coming to her. Inform Merrit? Negative. No use giving up the advantage, after all. And why ruin her own fun besides?

After ordering her meal, Merrit turned to Kate with a sudden torso shift. Her hips followed next. Then her gaze like twin gun barrels. Again, fascinating, but hardly enough to intimidate Kate.

"You're Merrit Chase, aren't you?" Kate held out her hand. "I saw you in the plaza. I'm Kate Meehan."

"You know my name?"

"Small place."

Merrit rolled her eyes, but the attempt at nonchalance revealed rather than hid her discomfort. "So I've noticed."

Kate followed Merrit's gaze across the street, where Ivan exited Internet Café. She crossed her legs and let her toe tap Merrit's shin. "That Ivan, such an odd little man, don't you think?"

"I only know him enough to get my wireless going."

"Have to keep connected, don't we? I find it tedious, actually. The simplicity of communicating through email gives people license to blather all day long. It's a bloody leaky faucet. Drip, drip, drip, all day long."

"That, and cell phones." Merrit turned away from the window. "Wouldn't it be nice to disconnect from our lives for a while?"

Kate couldn't imagine anything more depressing, but she nodded as Patsy set down coffee, fresh tea, and the traditional sandwich selection. Merrit grabbed up her cup like an addict a syringe. After a long, slow sip she sat back with a sigh.

"I happened to be in Internet Café this morning," Kate said, "and Lonnie mentioned the matchmaker's birthday party tonight. You lucky thing, getting to join the fun."

Merrit raised an eyebrow. Her already direct gaze sharpened further. "Why do you keep looking at my chest?"

Kate almost laughed. There was more to Merrit than the bland and distanced friendliness, to be sure. "Not what you think. I was admiring your necklace."

Merrit smiled and the movement transformed her face. Her cheeks balled up just enough to fill in the hollows beneath her cheekbones. And fancy that, perfect American teeth.

"It looks old—family heirloom?" Kate said.

The smile disappeared. "My mother's."

Her mother's. Once again, lucky her. Kate felt a surprise jolt of jealousy, which didn't bother her except that it arrived with an unwanted companion: sorrow. She banished the feeling, but too late. Merrit's expression softened toward compassion. Kate warned Merrit off with a chilly smile and chastised herself for allowing her thoughts to show.

Merrit responded by biting into her sandwiches without finishing them. First the egg salad, then the cucumber, the watercress, and finally the cheese and tomato. All the while, she fingered the pendant dangling in the hollow between her collarbones. A bluish sheen slid across the surface of the stone when she moved.

"Moonstones enhance intuition," Merrit said after another coffee gulp. "At least, that's what my mom always said. She was intuitive. She used to say I was too."

"Too easy. I'm sure the necklace meant something more to her. That's the way these things work, isn't it? I'm not big on symbolism and sentimentality myself, but I notice that most people love that kind of thing."

"I'll bet you're all for what's modern and new anyhow." There went Merrit's twitching eyebrow again. "A minimalist."

Kate allowed herself a sociable laugh. Why, if the situation were different, Kate might actually like this Merrit. Kate hadn't suffered through one boring moment, which was unusual.

Patsy cleared away the sandwich plate and deposited a silver tray piled high with tea cakes. Merrit snapped her teeth shut over a pastel green confection and chewed fast. She nodded toward the cake tray, but Kate shook her head.

"You'll have to tell me how the party is tonight," Kate said. "From what I hear, the matchmaker was quite the predator back in the day. A right asshole always surrounded by his pride of females, hence the nickname Liam the Lion."

Merrit dropped the cake she was holding onto the tray. Behind the twin-barrel gaze, Kate spied pain, a soulful crackle from a buried place Merrit couldn't quite hide. Aha, got you.

"Do you know where the bathroom is?" Merrit said.

Kate pointed, and Merrit edged her way toward the far end of the room. Daft, letting Kate's comment get to her like that. She'd be five minutes in the bathroom at least, so under cover of a passing group of middle-aged fatties, Kate grabbed Merrit's forgotten bag from the opposite seat back. Holy hell, for a tidy thing she kept a filthy purse. Every kind of tourist pamphlet, yarn, knitting needles, gum wrappers, a notepad that Kate wished she had time to read, wadded Kleenex, a few scuffed aspirins, crumbs. In a side pocket, passport and money, just so. Deep into the other side pocket—she caught sight of Merrit with composure back in place. By the time Merrit returned, Kate was swinging her own purse over her shoulder.

"You should take care," she said. "You forgot your purse."

"Who's going to snatch it with you sitting there? Thanks for watching it." Merrit picked up her bag. "By the way, he was called *Liam the Lion* because he had a huge head of red-gold hair."

Smiling, Kate let her have the last word. Once outside and with polite goodbyes out of the way, Kate trailed behind Merrit. Instead of returning to the village dosser, Merrit veered left alongside the plaza, then left again into an alley that ran parallel to the noncoastal. Kate kept her distance and watched Merrit turn into one of the row houses. The reassuring press of paper against her breast reminded her of the letter's last line. *P.S. Watch for a woman named Merrit. She's your half-sister. She's sure to arrive in time for the matchmaking festival.*

Kate wasn't a woman to dwell on facts she couldn't control, but a sister for feck's sake? She needed a sister like she needed Lonnie's prying little bugger nose sniffing after her.

A most disgusting predicament. Sharing didn't come easily to her.

· 6 ·

The evening of Liam's birthday party, Ivan contemplated himself under fluorescent lights. His hair couldn't be tamed, his mother used to say. This was back in Minsk, in the days when he wore the frizzy mass long and backed into a ponytail. Too bad, his mother also said, he had the face of a man who *could* be tamed. A spineless face.

In the mirror, he watched his face crumple, first the sagging lips, then the slack cheeks, then the droopy eyelids. The contortion highlighted incipient wrinkles around his mouth. He didn't believe Connie when she said he'd age well. No going to pudge for you, she said. Then that laugh of hers, amazed that he should be interested in a fat old cow like her.

Ivan dabbed on aftershave. Little did Connie know he'd bought the scent because of—and for—her the very day he'd become aware of her apart from her pack of churchy do-gooders. On that first truly warm day in June, Connie had jutted her chin in a stubborn stand against Mrs. O'Brien's endless bullying about *plaza beautification*, and he found himself helping Connie down a ladder. She held his hand a moment longer than necessary and sniffed the air. "Lovely cologne." A furtive glance at Mrs. O'Brien, who stood nearby, another hand squeeze, and then she was gone. He had immediately returned to the pharmacy and bought the after-shave he'd sampled while buying a sweet for lunch.

Ivan smoothed down his hair with gel, grimaced, and stepped out of the bathroom. He'd never admit it to Connie, but buying that aftershave had set him back a week's worth of lunches. In letters home, he mentioned his *flat* above Internet Café. He described the back alley that dropped him off at the plaza opposite the O'Brien statue and his *business partner's* father's hotel. In reality, he lived in a storage area. He heated soup and water for tea on a camp stove. He showered in the moldy stall in the downstairs bathroom. He stored his perishables in the shop's half fridge, also downstairs.

Here he lived, a big brain with no money, few friends, no dependable business prospects, and no visa if Lonnie decided to cancel his sponsorship—which would surely occur if the business failed. Even Ivan's relationship with Connie was doomed because of Lonnie. Lonnie, who cultivated a braid of hair down to his shoulder as if that made up for a receding hairline.

Grabbing his one decent jacket, Ivan almost missed the sound of footsteps fading toward the storefront downstairs. He checked his watch: 7:00 p.m. Lonnie ought to be at the hotel primping for his fake date with Merrit Chase. A fetching woman, true, and more quality than Lonnie deserved, but a little too—he didn't quite know the word—unblinking?—for his taste.

Ivan knelt and listened with ear to the floor. Lonnie's computer chimed its start-up medley. Lonnie, working? Hard to believe, but it could be true. Ivan pressed his ear harder against the floorboard. Lonnie's mobile rang with the old-fashioned telephone sound. A mumbled conversation ensued, and then Lonnie's voice rose through the floor—"You heard me, another installment tonight"—then fell out of range again.

Would Ivan see a percentage? No, and this injustice was precisely why he needed a spine. He returned to his bed and the stack of crates that served as his nightstand. There, a newspaper clipping that he'd retrieved off the Internet a few days previously waited for the proper timing. His latest investigative haul, little did Lonnie know. Ivan slipped the article between the mattress and box spring, recalling the Chase-McCallum marriage announcement he'd handed over to Lonnie on the onset of Lonnie's new venture as blackmailer. If not for the announcement's mention of the Chase family name, Lonnie wouldn't have cared about Merrit—except to try to shag her, of course.

Ivan admitted, not without regret, that Lonnie's natural cynicism had led them toward a series of astute research inquiries. As Merrit's laptop had revealed, her last name did indeed link her to the Chase-McCallum coupling, proving Lonnie correct: her arrival had something to do with the enigmatic matchmaker. Still, to Ivan's way of thinking, Merrit's arrival was indeed a spooky coincidence in timing—much to her bad luck.

Kevin perused the Plough and Trough while stifling a yawn. Mrs. O'Brien and her band of women had outdone themselves this year. Posters featuring lions—everything from *The Lion King* Disney animation to twilit lion profiles on the Serengeti—plastered the walls. Streamers dangled from the ceiling, and a nasty-looking chocolate cake with licorice whiskers stood in the corner under the front windows.

"Ay, Kev, you were glad you weren't here for the preparations," Alan, the pub owner, said. Five pints of Guinness sat beside his elbow, their foam settling down to the perfect level for a topping off.

"I'd have been sick with it for sure, even more than I am now."

"The black stuff will do you well."

"Indeed, as it always does."

Along with Danny Ahern, Alan was one of Kevin's closest friends. The three of them had swallowed their share of Guinness together since well before cop life and family life sucked the juices from Danny, bar life leeched the color out of Alan, and concerns more intangible weighted Kevin's shoulders. The sense, for example, that he could no more control his life than he could the clouds overhead. Even this birthday party was out of his hands. Used to be that Liam's birthdays were cozy yet merry affairs. Kevin had fond memories of standing under Liam's elbow and basking in secondhand praise while Liam's friends traipsed in and out of their old cottage. It seemed to Kevin that the whole world had worshipped Liam the way those long-ago nuns from his early childhood had worshipped the father, the son, and the Holy Spirit. Only this worship began and ended with laughter, which made the Church of Liam a religious order Kevin could follow.

Now, the annual party was more gimmick than celebration, all to jumpstart the festival. Kevin had heard talk about making this day, August 30th, an unofficial town holiday. Matchmaker Appreciation Day. Pure bollocks, that. Kevin refused to discuss this cock's ball of an idea, given that it implied a posthumous tribute to Liam. When the topic came up, all he felt was an overwhelming urge to polish his specs.

"And where's Liam?" Alan said.

"He wasn't ready to come in yet. I wager he's walking around the plaza just to prove he can. Surprised Danny isn't here yet though."

"He'll be along as soon as Ellen stops messing him about. He could use a vacation from his life."

"Couldn't we all?"

"Now you're having me on—unless it's work, you haven't stepped foot outside the county in a decade."

"Maybe I'll surprise you one day."

"For shit, you are." Alan topped off one of the waiting pints, pushed it toward Kevin, and continued on down the bar, filling other drink orders.

Kevin arranged his glasses on the countertop. They reflected hazy light circles cast by the overhead fixtures. He slid his face into his hands for a moment of darkness, not that he wasn't without these anyhow, but just now, he didn't want to notice the dripping Guinness tap or the knick in the bar top that he'd left last year. All sights he'd seen too many times.

"Heads up, mate," Alan said, back again. He retreated to the other end of the bar.

Kevin raised his head to a pleasing world of blurred bottles. The fuzzy edges reminded him of the many times he'd stared at Jesus on the Cross through the spaces between his fingers. One of the hazy light circles in his lenses disappeared and Kevin turned around, unsure who he was expecting, but definitely not Emma.

"New specs?" she said. "Put them on, then, give me the pleasure at least."

So he did, curious despite himself. She reappeared in focus, and he watched her watch him for a moment before she perched on the stool next to him and let her legs dangle. She hadn't changed since a year ago, or at least not much. She still preferred dresses with elasticized waists, but now the elastic hung loose over nonexistent curves. She'd cut off her hair too. If she'd hoped to turn herself boyish, she'd failed. Vulnerability suited her.

"Your hair looks nice," he said.

"This was months ago. Has it been that long? How could it go so long in this place?"

He shook his head even though he did know. He'd made himself scarce since last year's festival, which was to say since Emma's rape. A year is nothing, he thought, looking at her, surprised by a fresh wash of regret and self-recrimination.

"I've been busy with the business—"

She brushed aside his excuse. "No need."

Right, no need to wax on about his construction projects, not to mention his pro-bono work. Good works bring you closer to God, so the nuns had proclaimed. He'd like to believe this. But did he have faith that he'd catch a glimpse of the bigger meaning if he volunteered to reshingle the Quinlan's roof; did he have faith that if not, his actions still had meaning; and again, if not, was it enough to be satisfied with the Quinlan's gratitude and the lamb roast they'd insist he take home to share with Liam?

And, if not, what then?

"Alan, top me off like the gent you are while I fetch Liam," he said.

Emma stood. "Don't you leave. I wasn't staying anyhow." She stared down the bar at nothing, or maybe at Alan's photos of his twice-ugly dog. "I wanted to reconnect, a little, just to—I don't know—to make sure you're all right. Today of all days."

He was already halfway to the door but turned back to catch Emma stealing a hasty gulp from his beer. She wiped her mouth with a hint of her old insouciance. Kevin stepped toward her and brushed a hand through her hair, its wiry feel he remembered. "Lonnie's sure to be here tonight," he said.

"And who will that wankstain be squiring this year? Feel for her, I do."

Kevin expected her residual anger but not what arrived with it, something he couldn't grasp but that hinted at her self-doubts, her conflicts. And her longing? Or maybe simple disillusionment at the injustice of it all.

Outside, but not fast enough to elude *his* leftover spite, he spied his father on Marcus's bench. Liam's chiseled profile appeared younger than Marcus's until Kevin stepped close enough to once again be startled by Liam's tissue-paper skin. He sat down next to Liam.

"I was admiring this fine blanket." Liam nodded toward a blue afghan that covered Marcus's lap. "Quite nice."

"And warm too." Marcus capped his flask and set it aside. With elbow hooked over the back of the bench, he leaned across Liam to capture Kevin in the conversation. "That Merrit Chase, there's another generous soul like you, Kevin. Made this for me herself, she did."

Liam's eyebrows rose in a motion so slow Kevin wondered what he was thinking.

"She's a tourist," Marcus continued. "Unmarried, I might add."

Ah, here we go, Kevin thought. Yet again with trying to marry him off. He tilted out of their conversation. Sometimes he forgot that Liam had a history that stretched beyond Kevin's existence. Liam had watched Marcus grow up, for example. According to Liam, young Marcus sang in the choir and dreamt of being the next great Irish rocker. Now Marcus was a faded version of his potential best self. But then, Kevin wasn't far behind.

"Let's get inside before the crowd gathers," Kevin said. "You're welcome to join us, Marcus."

Marcus raised his head from the dazed smile he'd aimed at the ground. "That Mrs. O'Brien, she'd nip the gin out of me flask before letting me in the door."

"I'll send out food," Liam said.

Marcus reached for his flask. "Oh ay, but I forgot that you can ask Merrit for a blanket of your own if you'd so like. Told me so herself she'll be at the party escorted by Lonnie the

Lovely. You'll have at saving her, good Kevin, just like your Emma?"

Kevin rounded on Marcus, but Liam held up a hand. "Let's hear what Marcus means to say. Marcus?"

To Kevin's irritation, Marcus shrugged and swigged from his flask. "Never mind then. Cheers."

· 7 ·

Liam's party was officially under way as confirmed by the people-buzz leaking into Merrit's flat from the Plough and Trough next door. Her flat wasn't much, just a box of a room with furniture pushed up against the walls and a tiny bathroom in the corner. Her landlady's lace doilies and runners sat under the lamps and over the sofa bed arms and along the coffee table. Merrit supposed the average tourist loved the Irishness of all this handmade lace, but all she felt was sticky-stuck in a spider web. Especially now, as she paced the length of her narrow confines.

Downstairs, her landlady's beagle howled, a sure sign that Mrs. Sheedy was about to cook up something with cabbage. Merrit opened the window above the sink to preempt the fumes. Outside, moonlight filtered through high cloud cover, and the breeze smelled of nothing, as if the currents that flowed over the Atlantic were more pristine than those over the Pacific. Merrit loved the empty smell, cool and clear as water. To calm her nerves, she inhaled until the breeze caught peat smoke drifting from the Plough's chimney.

Knuckles rapped on her door. The knob turned and Lonnie sauntered inside wearing a cream linen suit with narrow pant

legs and a black, collarless shirt. Nice suit. Too bad he looked
so slimy within it.

"Safe place, our Lisfenora," he said. "I'm glad to see you trust
us enough to keep your door unlocked."

"Not safe enough, apparently. Give me a second. You're early."

She stepped into the bathroom, wondering if Lonnie ever
felt a prick of contrition. Just one sharp little nudge. About
anything. But no—silly thought. She knew in her instinctive
way that self-reproach wasn't in Lonnie's emotional repertoire,
just like she'd known that the woman, Kate, hadn't invited
Merrit to join her table out of kindness. Something about Kate
fascinated Merrit, but she couldn't pinpoint what.

Merrit applied lipstick and put on her mom's moonstone
necklace. She opened the medicine cabinet's door so she could
watch Lonnie in its mirror. He tucked her latest cash "installment" into an inner jacket pocket. She'd left the money on the
telephone stand next to the door, ready to grab on her way out
the door.

"Just so we're clear," she said, "a party with hundreds of witnesses isn't the way I plan to meet Liam for the first time. So,
please, please, refrain from drawing attention to me."

Lonnie stepped out of mirror range. "Hello-o, what do we
have here?"

Rustling papers reminded her of the unmade sofa bed. She
hadn't bothered to tidy it because she'd planned to wait for
Lonnie outside. Worse yet, her mom's notebook lay on the
pillow. Springs squeaked when she landed on the bed and
made a grab for it.

"Aren't you the feisty thing?" Lonnie swung away from her
and flipped to a page at random. "*I need to get to the heart of this
Liam character*," he read. "Your mother, the intrepid journalist,
willing to do just about anything to get her story, was she?"

"Just give it to me. You got your money, what more do you want?"

Lonnie bowed and dropped the notebook onto the bed. "Nothing I don't already know, is it? Get on with you then, the festivities await."

Merrit pulled the rubber band out of her hair but didn't bother tidying the waves that fell heavy against her shoulders. "How about answering a question first."

"Ah, Jesus, *now* you're going to slag me? You'll be asking me how I could take money from strangers. If that's the way this evening is heading, I'll be needing a drink now." He opened cabinets in the kitchenette. Finding nothing, he trolled the fridge and pulled out a beer. Just like Marcus with the edge on him, Lonnie twisted off the top and downed it in one go. "Right, so here's your answer—I've got a hard-on for cash not linked to the family business. I've been told since this tall how lucky I am to have the hotels, a loving mother and affectionate sisters, and a father ready to be proud of me. And I could give a shit."

"That's quite the sob story. Seems to me you could go to Dublin, get a career."

"Don't go getting that pious look. You're a worse cock-up than I am, coming halfway around the world to find solace, or love, or fuck-all if I know, boo-hoo for you. Christ."

Merrit stepped into her sandals, trying not to let on that he'd driven his point home a little too well. A moment later she closed the door after them, and Lonnie in his shiny dress shoes tapped down the stairs ahead of her.

Inside the Plough and Trough, Merrit stood against a wall angling for a glimpse of Liam, who sat within a throng of well-wishers in the corner of the room. For the most part, she could see only the closest talking, laughing, and drinking heads. Lonnie wasn't among them, thank goodness. With a glance at his watch, he'd excused himself and disappeared into the crowd. She didn't mind if he never returned.

Merrit pressed herself against the wall as more people squeezed into the pub and the entire crowd shifted. The Plough was a genteel but shabby place, full of wood paneling and brass fixtures that used to gleam. The largest selection of whiskey bottles Merrit had ever seen hung upside down on the wall behind the bar. With fake nonchalance, Merrit sipped her two ounces of Bushmills and nodded at the old gents seated to her left. Wedged in good and tight between them and the gift table to her right, she felt somewhat protected from the buffeting crowd, somewhat invisible, somewhat safe to observe Liam in peace. She liked his kindly face, the type of face that invited intimacies of all kinds. She knew this well from reading her mom's notes, and now she witnessed it in action as he clapped a hand on a man's shoulder and laughed at something he said. A spasm of longing caused Merrit to cough on a sip of whiskey.

"Watch yourself there, love. You'll topple the presents," Mrs. O'Brien called as she pushed her way toward Merrit. Her voice pinned Merrit's eardrums like a couple of mounted bugs. "I swear I don't know what people think to give Liam. There's not a thing in this world the man needs except a woman around the house."

Mrs. O'Brien wore a shiny blouse left over from the 1980s. Shoulder pads and a large bow enhanced her doughy chin. With her overwrought teased-up hair, she reminded Merrit of a poodle with a bad stylist. Behind her, one of the daughters— Mariela? Constanza?—scanned the crowd with an impatient expression.

"Now, where's my Lonnie at?" Mrs. O'Brien continued. "My boy, he's social to be sure, has too many friends to keep count."

Merrit sipped, noting the way the daughter rolled her eyes and eased away from Mrs. O'Brien with a, "Right, I'm off then. Meeting a friend."

"And what friend is this?" Mrs. O'Brien said, but the daughter had already slipped into the crowd. "Really, I don't know what's wrong with her lately."

Merrit sipped to hide a smile, remembering what Marcus had said about Mrs. O'Brien nagging the devil out of hell itself.

Mrs. O'Brien added two presents to the table and began rearranging them, all the while talking to no one in particular and everyone in general. She blocked Merrit's view of Liam, so Merrit settled back to wait her out. She *uh-huh*'ed in response to Mrs. O'Brien's rant about inconsiderate children and stretched her neck to peruse the bar, where foreign currency papered a section of wall and hurling trophies lined the uppermost shelf. She caught Kevin Donellan angling for a glance at her through the moving heads. He directed a statement to the tall man next to him, who glanced over his shoulder and shrugged. Merrit recognized him as he returned to contemplating the whiskey bottles. Detective Sergeant Danny Ahern. Practically a brother to Kevin, Marcus had said. And it would seem so because the two men sat together drowning themselves in pints, not talking much yet looking utterly comfortable with each other.

Kevin glanced at her again. His blinks in her direction unnerved her even though, before disappearing, Lonnie had pointed him out and insisted that Kevin—Liam's *adopted* son, he kept repeating—didn't know her for anyone but Lonnie's date. That may have been true, but she was supposed to be observing Kevin, not the other way around.

"Can't stand the bastard." Lonnie had rubbed a finger along his perfect nose. "He landed me in the hospital last year because I dared shag his precious Emma. They'd broken up already, for

Christ's sake. Besides which, she was mad for it after his flaccid fumblings."

She'd barely heard him after the word "adopted." Liam's adopted son. She hadn't considered adoption, much less that the son would be about her age. She'd imagined Liam with a young wife, a woman he had met as he entered late middle age, a companion of sorts, but one who'd wanted one child before Liam got too old.

Instead, adoption. Given the way her mom had described Liam in her notebook, Merrit had assumed that back in the '70s he wasn't the fatherly sort. Yet, apparently he was. A nervous worm threaded itself around her lungs. Careful, she told herself. She mustn't clutch at emotional straws or succumb to the fear that she was unanchored in the world.

"I wager some of these gifts are beyond appropriate," Mrs. O'Brien said, rousing Merrit from her unwelcome thoughts. "Last year Liam received a gift certificate for a massage, and you know what that means. Oh, there's Lonnie."

Merrit's heart stuttered to a halt, and then pounded harder than ever. Lonnie hovered near Liam, and with a grin pointed in Merrit's direction. Liam straightened and sought her out through the crowd. Merrit ducked against the wall. A mini-earthquake spread among the presents. She grabbed the closest pile and waited until the lopsided table legs stabilized.

"Careful." Mrs. O'Brien's smile of pride never left Lonnie. "He's got a way with him, a truly delightful young man. Why, he's waving you over."

"Excuse me," Merrit said.

"Go on then. Meet Liam."

Like hell she would. Not like this. And Lonnie knew it. She'd given him the money out of her wallet to ensure he didn't pull this stunt. She tried to squeeze her way between the old gents to her left and Mrs. O'Brien in front her. A raised floorboard caught her heel, and she stumbled against the gift table. The gift piles swayed. Her lungs started their inexorable squeeze.

Merrit became aware of eyes flickering over her from all directions. She wasn't as invisible as she'd hoped, and it didn't help that Lonnie was waving her toward Liam. The worm around her lungs tightened. She was an intruder, and she never should have let Lonnie goad her into coming.

With Mrs. O'Brien barring her way, Merrit backed up against the wall again. There was nothing for it but to crawl under the gift table and get out fast before Lonnie yelled across the room, or, worse yet, forcibly dragged her to Liam. Before she could make her escape, a wall nail caught her dress and she yanked her arm so hard her elbow knocked into the gifts. Her tumbler let go a waterfall of amber liquid as it sailed to the floor. Dozens of gifts followed in a perfect arc of shimmering wrapping paper. She dropped to the ground but too late to save the glass from shattering against floorboards and a dozen gifts from landing in the whiskey and shards. A secondary crack followed as the last present landed on the floor. An amber stain soaked into wrapping-paper clown faces.

"I told you to be careful," Mrs. O'Brien said, her voice like a bullhorn. "Didn't I tell her?"

Merrit sat back on her haunches. There went her anonymity —such as it was—with the arrival of whoops and catcalls from the crowd.

"I'm so sorry." She held up the clown gift and heard an ominous clunk. "I'll pay for this. Tell"—she glanced at the card—"tell Patty O'Reardon I'll buy a new one. Will you tell her that?"

While Mrs. O'Brien sputtered, Merrit drew on the spirit of her mom to grant her enough poise to exit without further mishap. She crawled under the table, and grabbed at a jovial drunk's arm to pull herself up on the other side. Ducking and weaving through the crowd, she bumped into Ivan, who managed to appear both pissed off and fretful as he fought his own way through the crowd.

Lonnie's voice carried over the party chaos. "Merrit!"

"Why is Lonnie doing this?" Merrit gasped. "You must know."

"Maybe something annoyed him," Ivan said, "and now he takes it out on you. This is my experience."

"You tell him we're going to talk. Tomorrow bright and early. I'll come by the café."

Before leaving, she couldn't resist tiptoeing for a last view of Liam as she pulled on the door against the crowd's collective weight. Between the heads and shoulders, she caught sight of him tracking her with an intensity not meant for public settings.

He knew her.

He *knew* her, no dismissing the fact. Her lungs reignited at the thought that this humiliated retreat was her biological father's first impression of her. Gulping against the knot in her throat, she wedged herself through the door and into blessedly cool air.

Julia Chase's notebook

I'm unsure how to proceed with this article. It's well enough to write about the Burren, Cliffs of Moher, Aran Islands—highlights for the intrepid traveler—but Ramsey insists on his additional 750 words aimed at a wider audience. A fluff piece, he said. Human interest. So the matchmaking festival it is, and Liam the Lionesque, it is. Unfortunately, the more I ragtag with Liam, the harder this piece is to write. So much for objectivity. I'm a disgrace to my fellow travel writers.

However, that said, I think I've come up with a workable angle. Since I'm not distanced anyhow, I might as well insert myself into the story. I'll be my own experiment. Ethical or not, I'll let Liam match me—and apologies later to the man stuck without a bride. I can't think how else to write this piece because every time I meet with Liam, the article is the last thing on my mind—the way his long arms snake out of his cape, all small wrists and prominent veins and hands ready to grab mine.

· 8 ·

The morning after Liam's party, Merrit stumbled her way from the sofa bed to the bathroom and splashed cold water on her face. She opened her eyes to view her sorry reflection in the mirror. She was her mom's daughter for sure—at least with the greenish-hazel eyes and chin dimple— but try as she might, she couldn't tell whether she resembled the matchmaker. And, oh damn, the party last night. Dropping her head, she bumped it repeatedly against the mirror. No, no, no. Now she'd be the visitor who sat with the outcast drunk *and* destroyed birthday gifts.

Worse yet, Liam himself, the way he'd spied her out through the crowd, still sporting a good-natured smile, but also with a squint as if he were analyzing her fitness for daughterhood. Her hopes sank just thinking about it. Now she needed a less excruciating way to introduce herself to him than waiting around on the plaza until he caught sight of her. The possibility that he'd pass her over for one of the lovelorn made her queasy.

But, first things first: Lonnie and his grubby little machinations. He'd better tell her what he'd said to Liam last night.

Too tired to care how she looked, she grabbed the black party dress that she'd dropped on the floor before falling into bed, dressed, and left the flat. Downstairs, she eased past her landlady's side door and stepped into the narrow lane—more like an alley—that ran parallel to the noncoastal one block away. The cobblestoned lane smelled dank, and shadows held on against the coming day. Merrit paused, feeling eyes on her back. She glanced around, but the alley remained silent and still.

She peered left, toward the plaza, searching for but not seeing Marcus on his usual bench. A quick detour before heading to Internet Café was in order. She trotted out of the alley and into the plaza. In the fuzzy orange light cast by a rising sun, Lisfenora resembled a fairy tale village the way the storefronts shifted from canary yellow to purple to teal depending on the owners' tastes. Pretty soon, the *failte* welcome mats would appear, and, if not for drivers trying to maneuver around each other in the narrow lanes, Merrit might imagine herself back in the late nineteenth century when bonnets and gartered socks were all the rage.

Given her paranoid mood, the plaza was more like it: open and transparently cheerful. Even so, Merrit turned back to sight down the length of the alley and its double row of closed doors. Must have been her landlady, Mrs. Sheedy, spying on her comings and goings through lace curtains. As usual. The woman was almost as bad as Mrs. O'Brien.

On the far side of the plaza, Merrit found Marcus sprawled over the length of a bench with half the contents of an over-turned flask soaked into his trousers. "Wake up," Merrit said. "You'd better go to—wherever you usually go to sleep. Marcus?" She poked his arm. "Are you OK? Wake up."

He didn't move. Not a twitch.

Alarmed, she leaned closer. "Marcus," she said into his ear.

Marcus jerked awake with a sharp cry. His hands fumbled into the air, and then, seeing Merrit, he lapsed back into grumbles. "Sweet Mary and Jaysus fecking Christ, have you gone mental?"

"Maybe so, but Jaysus F. Christ yourself—I thought you'd gone and died on me. Here, sit up."

Marcus pushed himself up with a groan. With shaking hands, he patted down his hair and tucked his shirt into his soggy trousers. He felt under himself for the flask and tsked sadly when it came up empty. "Good *craic,* the party?"

"Hellish, more like," Merrit said. "And Lonnie only made it worse as you can imagine."

Marcus's stomach growled.

"One errand," she said, "and then I'll take us to breakfast."

Marcus muttered, shaking his head. "Could have sworn to a full dinner last night. Or maybe not, because we all know I'm not to be trusted, not even in thought. Even so, I'll take my gin-soaked vagueness, thank you very much. And maybe a bloody fecking pint for breakfast too."

"What's up with you? You seem more out of it than usual." She perused him with fresh concern. "Your shoes are untied."

He lifted his feet to view his graffiti'd green and yellow sneakers. "So they are."

Merrit cast about behind the bench. "Did someone take your afghan?"

"The afghan was on my lap. Cozy it was." Marcus's face crumpled. "Oh Christ, but then what? Such is the steaming load of shite that is my life."

"Don't worry about it," she said despite her disappointment. "I'm sure the afghan will turn up. Wait here while I tell off that Lonnie once and for all."

B ack in the alley, Merrit counted doors, passing her lodgings as she went. Fifth door down, this would be Internet Café's back entrance.

The door was the tiniest bit ajar, which was odd even by Lisfenora's safe standards. Merrit hesitated with fist raised against the shop's door. No way was Lonnie at work this early in the morning. Ivan had to be up and about then. She nudged the door open to see a shabby storage area. Stacked packages of printer paper leaned against one another, covered in dust, and a bathroom exuded a musty funk. A yellow tabby sidled through an inner door that must lead to the storefront. The little fellow mewed and brushed her legs. Merrit picked him up.

She carried the purring cat through the storage area and into the shop. Perhaps she could relay a message through Ivan to Lonnie. Something along the lines of, *Stop talking to Liam about me, or else.*

Or else what? She wasn't sure, but it was better than nothing at this point.

A squeal, or perhaps a moan, issued from Lonnie's office. Merrit froze. A moment later the rat-a-tatting of computer keys ceased and oaths in Ivan's native Russian took over. Merrit smiled. The minion up to no good in the boss's office. Now he'd see how much he liked having his personal life threatened with exposure.

On tiptoes, she stepped past computers and around the service counter behind which Ivan usually sat. Thankfully, the window blinds were drawn. No one could see her as she stepped toward one of two doorways marked "For Employees Only," only to freeze again, this time in the office doorway with the cat pressed against her chest. She knew death when she saw it. There was no mistaking its particular brand of stillness. Death had sucked the energy out of Lonnie's body, leaving it as bereft of life as a hologram.

· 9 ·

Merrit stood frozen for what seemed like forever while the cat squirmed against her clenched grip. In front of the desk, Lonnie lay on an Oriental rug that was too plush for what amounted to a converted storeroom. Scattered euro notes surrounded him, and for the first time since Merrit had the misfortune to meet him, his hair was natural in disarray rather than artfully arranged. He was almost a pretty picture in his cream linen suit. Except for the knife sticking out of his chest, of course. And the crimson stain around the wound. Even Lonnie didn't deserve that much bad karma coming back at him.

A fly buzzed, and Merrit knew it was only a matter of minutes before it landed on Lonnie to lay a few hundred eggs. She swallowed against stuffiness that hinted at the telltale and sweet beginnings of decomposition, and eased back a step. Ivan continued tapping away at the speed of desperation. Thankfully, the giant flat-screen monitor blocked his view of Merrit. Holding her breath, she eased back another step. To her dismay, the cat chose exactly that moment to thrust itself out of her arms.

"*Blin!*" Ivan shot up. "I see you. No, do not hide."

Merrit ran, but not fast enough. Ivan grabbed her in the murky storefront where darkened computer monitors yawned at them. Merrit yanked her arm, but as small as Ivan was, he was still bigger than she. "Let me go," she said. "I'll scream, I swear I will."

"How did you get inside?"

"The back door. Were you too drunk to lock it last night?"

Ivan pushed Merrit aside and sprinted toward the back door. Merrit grappled with the closed window blinds in search of the front door.

"You will not leave," Ivan said, grabbing her from behind once again.

She struggled, but he had the strength of desperation on his side. He half carried, half pushed her back into the office. She nearly stumbled over Lonnie when he let her go. Blocking the doorway, he surveyed the Oriental rug, the executive desk, the plank shelves that held nothing but old magazines. His skin looked clammy as the underside of a mushroom. "Please to listen to me. I do not care why you come this early."

Merrit steadied herself and tried to exude confidence. She pointed toward the blinds that protected them from view. Already, a few pedestrian shadows stretched along the slats. "I will scream."

"If you really thought I did that"—Ivan waved an arm at Lonnie—"you would already be screaming like typical woman. Could be you did this instead, but I do not care about this either because I only want to stay in Ireland." He rolled his eyes like an overloaded pack ass and pulled at his hair. "We do not have time for this talking. We help each other, yes?"

Ivan returned to Lonnie's computer to detach a thumb drive from the USB port. Merrit wavered, unclear whether self-preservation meant acquiescing to his request or calling the police. A notion spread through her like a malignant ink stain. Perhaps her arrival and Lonnie's death weren't a coincidence. Perhaps death had followed her from California.

"But you're tampering with evidence," she said. "I can't be a part of that."

"And you are not wanting me to tamper? Lonnie keeps all information you should know. I will be first suspect with the Garda—what you say *police*—and you will be second unless we minimize damage. My life that I thought could get no worse, just did. You are in same place, yes?"

He rubbed at goose bumps that had risen on his arms. "Stay there. I need sweater," he said.

At the threshold of his workroom, Ivan paused to assess Merrit. Her gaze, usually so witch hazel and wide, had turned inward. Hard to read, her, but she'd inched toward the front door while his back was turned.

"One word about you," he blurted. "Morphine. So you stay, yes? Or maybe *I* go to the Garda. I am sure you do not want them looking at you too closely."

"Did Lonnie know too?" Merrit said.

"Maybe, maybe not."

In an emotional about-face that startled—and gratified—Ivan, Merrit's face bloomed red and she patted her chest. She clawed through her oversized purse. Not finding what she looked for, she then exhaled in short huffs into the bag of her hands.

Let her stew on their predicament. Ivan continued into the workroom, chewing on his resentment once again. With Merrit standing there huffing and puffing, he couldn't even pinch the money scattered around Lonnie's body like confetti. He deserved compensation for his slave-labor hardships.

Worse still, with the matchmaking festival starting the next day, there would no doubt be extra scrutiny and scandal. And all of it aimed in his direction. Ivan knew how the system worked, no different in Ireland than in Belarus: tidy over local blemishes, keep the tourists happy and safe, find a scapegoat named Ivan, and boot said Ivan back to Minsk. He wasn't about to let that happen. *Blin*, no.

Not seeing his sweater on its usual hook, he grabbed a pair of latex gloves instead. He was already wearing a pair. He returned to Merrit. "Take these. If you did not kill him, and if I did not—"

"The big *if*," she wheezed.

"—we have to choose to trust each other, yes? I will not tell about you, and you will do same for me."

He balled his fists, waiting for her to catch breath enough to scream down the walls. Instead, she pulled in a shaky breath, put on the gloves, and fumbled a yarn ball out of her shoulder bag. With the distanced look of someone floating from the ceiling, she wiped down the door frame she'd grabbed to steady herself.

"When the Garda arrive," he continued, "explain that you walked in and saw me standing in doorway then you will appear truthful."

"And by association, you too?"

"Honesty by appearances. In Belarus this takes politicians far."

"The file. Where is it?"

Back at the computer, his fingers tapped the keyboard. His mind raced, trying to remember if he had erased everything that implicated him in Lonnie's blackmailing schemes. Damn Merrit for distracting him from his task.

"Hello, Ivan, where are the printouts?" Merrit said. "Lonnie showed me the file. It has to be here somewhere."

"I do not know where Lonnie stores the hard-copy file. I already looked, but you can try too."

Too many minutes later, Ivan was ready for the next phase of evidence tampering, and Merrit had given up her search for the file. "Now you help me with computer," he said. "And then we call the Garda."

· Part II ·

Sunday, August 31st – Saturday, September 6th

"Even well-honed instincts can come undone."
—Liam the Matchmaker

Monday, July 17, 1989   Gull's Hollow Community Gazette

Hero's Death Continues to Baffle Locals

Officials continue to investigate the death of local philanthropist Julia Chase McCallum. On June 7, McCallum was killed after her BMW collided with an oncoming Ford truck in the worst crash this area has seen in a decade.

The truck's driver, Chris Jones, 18, sustained massive head trauma and remains in critical condition at St. Joseph's Hospital. Sources close to the investigation say initial evidence shows McCallum drifted into the oncoming lane. McCallum's husband, Andrew McCallum, president of the privately held Mid-Pacific Consulting and Trading Company, headquartered in San Francisco, could not be reached for comment.

"Julia was an esteemed member of our community," said Mayor Danny Wyatt, "and we feel her loss immensely. This is a tragedy."

McCallum chaired the local equestrian club and was a show-jumping champion.

"Her expertise will be sorely missed," said Marilyn Cooper, cofounder of the Wine Country Equestrian Club. "She almost single-handedly raised the $20,000 sponsor-donated prize money for our first show-jumping competition."

McCallum has also been praised for her work with migrant families, especially in the area of literacy. "Julia loved children," said Sheila Ortiz, president of Migrant Worker Relief Fund. "I've always admired her commitment to literacy. She was not the type to lose track of her driving. She had too much to live for."

Inquiries into factors in McCallum's collision yielded nothing from her peers. The police won't speculate except to say that they are investigating all possibilities. Until the accident, McCallum had no record for traffic-related or other offenses.

McCallum was born in Boston, Massachusetts, on April 22, 1945, to Percival and Mary Chase, distant relations to the Chases of Chase Manhattan Bank fame. Prior to marrying Andrew McCallum and settling in Gull's Hollow, she worked as a journalist.

A memorial service was held at St. Rose Catholic Church in Santa Rosa, on Saturday, June 24, 1989, at 1:00 p.m. and was attended by more than 300 mourners. Her 13-year-old daughter, Merrit Lane McCallum, led the eulogies. In lieu of flowers, Andrew McCallum requests donations to the Migrant Worker Scholarship Fund established in his wife's name.

· 10 ·

The sun had risen high enough to reflect off the dirty dishes by the time Danny blinked his way to the sink to rinse out his coffee mug. Another four cups might rouse him, but the second brewing pot might also give him away. He pictured his wife drop-kicking him all the way to County Galway because he got ploughed at the Plough during Liam's party.

He plugged the sink and cupped his hands to drink while the basin filled. The water's metallic warmth went down easy.

"Do stop," Ellen said from behind him. "Do you want to set a bad example for the children?"

Mandy and Petey were outside, but Danny remained silent in hopes he wouldn't accidentally touch off his wife. Calm for the moment, she stood by the window overlooking the backyard where the playhouse Kevin had built no longer stood. Tangled blackberry vines seeped over the rock wall that bounded their land and overwhelmed the flower beds Ellen used to tend.

The children pressed funny faces against the outside of the window. Their church clothes were already dusty, and blackberry juice stained their lips. Danny stooped under the windowsill as Ellen moved away. Giggles turned into incipient hysteria. Just as the children were about to give up on him, he stood and pushed open the window. The smell of over-ripening berries rushed into the kitchen. He leaned out the window, grabbed each child in a one-armed tickle hug, and lifted them into the house.

Mandy, at eight, considered herself the expert on rules. "You're still in your bathrobe. It's too late for that."

She held one of Danny's hands in both of hers while Petey hugged his leg. "A deal then," Danny said. "I'll wash and change into my play clothes if you do the same."

Their identical smiles almost broke his heart. Mandy clapped her hands, then stopped. She approached Ellen, who had retreated to her spot at the kitchen table. "Mum, can we use your shower today, please? Instead of the bath? Please?"

Ellen's expression was lost to Danny, her head tilted as it was to gaze at her oldest child's freckled hand, but he knew its angled contours, the melancholy she tried to hide from their observant daughter, who now leaned close to Ellen and whispered, "Please, Mummy, I'll be ever so careful with Petey."

Ellen cupped Mandy's face. Danny shared Mandy's happiness for the kiss his wife planted on her nose. "Go on then. I'll be in to wash your hair."

"And Petey's too?"

"And Petey's." She sank back into a slouch as the children ran from the room. "You didn't miss anything at Mass today. The church was half empty, and Father Dooley talked about the body as temple even though he undoubtedly drank as much as everyone else at the party." She rubbed a finger through bread crumbs on the table. "How was door duty, by the way?"

Danny returned to the dirty dishes. Squeals and water gurgles issued from their master bathroom. "What you'd expect."

"Anything unusual this year?"

"By which you mean with Kevin. What's got you asking?"

"Just that I bumped into Emma outside the church. She looked awful, simply done in. All she wanted was to clear the air with Kevin. After a year, that's not so much to ask, is it?" She licked her finger. "For anyone but Kevin, that is."

Ellen liked to forget that Kevin might as well be Danny's brother. Danny opened his mouth to object and just as quickly Ellen shut him down. "Don't say a word, don't you do it. You always defend your men friends."

Ah, here we go then. Like clockwork a checkmate occurred, twice, three times a week. Danny's presence was all the accelerant Ellen needed to vent her despair, her anger, and her gripes against him, everything from the towel rack he hadn't repaired to his pittance salary.

Hoping to waylay yet another fight, Danny said, "You go splash, and I'll finish up the dishes. Then we ought to pick some of those berries. Petey's been pleading for tarts."

"You'll be here to make the dough—won't you? I don't think I can manage the dough today."

He nodded, relieved that her flare-up had dissipated as quickly as it had emerged.

"Mummy, Mummy, you're here," Mandy shouted a few moments later, and Petey in mimic, "You're here!" If anything, their delighted surprise depressed Danny, as did the abandoned garden, as did last night's drunkenness. He dry-swallowed aspirin, pulled flour out of the cupboard and mixed it together with the rest of the dough ingredients. Over the past few years, he'd become a decent cook much to his not-so-delighted surprise.

His mobile rang, displaying the number for his superior in the National Bureau of Criminal Investigation. He put the phone on speaker and continued mixing the dough. NBCI's Clare division superintendent, Eric Clarkson, worked out of county headquarters in Ennis. He didn't bother greeting Danny. "Problem out your way. The state pathologist and scenes of crime team have already left Dublin. You need to get on securing the scene for them, and do it well because I'm talking about Lonnie O'Brien here. Apparent homicide at his Internet café."

Danny froze with his hands in the dough bowl. "You're having me on."

"Indeed I'm not. Son of a friend, I might add."

A spurt of adrenaline drove Danny to hurry with the dough.

"I question whether you can handle this—" Clarkson said.

"Good call on your part, keeping this with me." Danny knew well enough that Clarkson was on the brink of calling in a more experienced detective. Any detective *inspector* out of Dublin would do. "The locals won't cozy up to anyone but their local lads. Plus, the matchmaking festival starts tomorrow."

"Ah, shit, that's right, isn't it? Just what we need, hundreds of bottom-feeders circling the action. Bloody nightmare. And mind you take care with the O'Briens. After last year's buggery, they'll want a quiet arrest. O'Brien Senior has an idea for a suspect. That Kevin fella we had trouble with last year."

But of course. Danny could have predicted that one.

From the bathroom, Ellen's voice called out for the children to hurry now. Danny patted the dough into a ball while Clarkson wasted precious minutes letting Danny know that O'Brien and Clarkson went back a ways and that Clarkson would be the one to keep O'Brien abreast of developments. Danny got the hint. Clarkson would receive the back slaps after he, Danny, solved the case.

"So O'Brien Senior found Lonnie?" Danny interrupted.

"What? No," Clarkson said. "Some employee of his did and called O'Brien."

Ivan. He was just the type to call the big man instead of the

Garda. Lately, Ivan had appeared more ratlike than usual as he scurried about Lisfenora on Lonnie's behalf, and now Danny wondered why. Ivan, who'd arrived just over a year ago, spoke stilted English, and lived above Lonnie's shop the last time Danny had checked.

Danny wrapped the dough in foil. He turned to see Ellen staring at him from the hallway with the children on either side of her. He held up the dough. "Work," he mouthed.

"That's convenient. You'll use any excuse to get away, even door duty, won't you?"

He covered the phone. "You like to remind me that I'm due for a promotion. So which is it? You can't have both the money and a house husband."

"That's the way with you then, push it all back on me."

Back on the phone, he begged Clarkson's pardon, ending with, "I'm on my way."

"You'd best be," Clarkson said. "And Ahern, no fucking about on this. You've had a rough go, but I don't want to hear any family excuses."

"Yes, sir."

He rang off. The children retreated to their bedroom, no doubt to avoid witnessing another fight. They took their plastic berry-picking buckets with them.

In a rental cottage that had seen better days, Kate Meehan peeled back her sleep mask. The clock read half nine, and normally she was not one to sleep past seven. Even so, she snuggled deeper into her body heat, closed her eyes, and luxuriated in a well-deserved lie-in. She still couldn't believe her luck and congratulated herself for her quick thinking during Liam's party. She fancied herself the only person with a bird's-eye view of the current drama, from 1975 to the present, from Liam to Lonnie.

She reached under her pillow to be sure of her souvenir and thought about how she might use it to benefit herself. She stroked its smooth surface—it looked so innocent from the outside—then let herself wallow in a self-indulgent doze. For once, she felt replete.

She'd come up with a plan. She always did.

· 11 ·

The scene that met Danny at Internet Café only half surprised him. He'd expected his men to arrive ahead of him and start securing the scene. He'd also expected Ivan, but he hadn't expected the attractive American who gawked at him as if he'd swanned in wearing a tiara. He shrugged off her reaction only to catch his reflection in the closest computer monitor. That was some slump to his shoulders. He looked like what he was—henpecked and hungover—which wasn't any better than wearing a tiara.

"Ivan," he said to the man whose hair stuck out in all directions except for lumps caked to his head with hair gel. Driving in, Danny had noticed a *Closed for Repairs* sign taped to one of the shop's windows and written in what looked to be a hasty foreign hand. Ivan's, no doubt, and what else had he touched along the way?

And feck if those weren't latex gloves on his hands. "Tell me Garda O'Neil gave you those, or I'll have to wonder."

"He was wearing them, all right." O'Neil nodded toward Ivan's cohort. "So was she."

The woman sat with O'Neil at the front of the shop while Ivan waited with Garda Pickney at the opposite end. In identical moves, the witnesses held up their hands and turned them over like magicians. Abracadabra, we're innocent, see?

Ivan pointed to one of two doors located behind the counter. "I keep a collection in my workroom. I am careful not to put finger oils on the computer parts. When I saw Lonnie—of course, I have seen the television shows. I know what I am to do."

He looked toward the woman for confirmation. "American cop dramas," she said.

These two, they reminded Danny of Mandy and Petey talking around each other to hide the fact that they'd pilfered the last biscuits.

"You still live upstairs, correct?" Danny said to Ivan.

A nod.

"Did you hear anything last night?"

A vehement shake. "I drank too much."

"And you didn't check the premises before going to bed I take it."

Ivan twitched. The movement might have been a shrug. "I never do. Lonnie does not pay me enough to be security guard."

"And you," Danny began, taking in the wavy hair floating over the woman's shoulders, similar to Ellen's hair.

"You're in charge of the case?" she said before he could continue.

"I'd say that's obvious."

"It's just that I saw you at the party last night. You were sitting next to Kevin Donellan at the bar. The matchmaker's son?"

Now he recognized her. "And you're the Good Samaritan who sits with Marcus."

"He's my friend."

Danny eyed her wrinkled party dress. "And you are Lonnie's

friend too? Seems like I recall that your date with him ended badly."

She grimaced. "As everyone knows by now, thanks to Mrs. O'Brien. You'd have thought I knocked over the presents on purpose. She thrives on drama, for sure."

O'Neil snorted. "That's putting it lightly."

"Tell me about your date," Danny said.

"It wasn't a date." Merrit crinkled her nose. "At least not by my standards of the word. Mrs. O'Brien butted her head into my social life, that's all."

"Mmm-hmm. What's your name?"

"Merrit Chase."

"And what brings you here this morning?"

"It's a habit of mine, to check my email first thing. Ivan heard me knocking on the back door—I'm staying just across the alley and down a few doors—and he let me in. I think I woke him up."

"I overslept today—how could I not?" Ivan said. "And I substantiate that she checks her email."

Pickney rolled his eyes toward O'Neil. "Hear that, he can *substantiate* Miss Chase's email usage. And I'll venture other habits as well?"

"We hardly know each other," Merrit said.

"For a couple of strangers, you seem to know each other well enough," O'Neil piped up. "Wouldn't you say, sir?"

"Maybe so," Danny said.

Danny glanced around the room at the quiet computers and dimmed overheads, then toward the noncoastal where Lisfenorans and tourists had started their rounds. Through the blinds, he could just make out flits of color as people passed the shop.

"Gents, hold on to our two witnesses while I take a look at our victim." He studied Merrit's tensed jaw and averted gaze. "Problem with that?"

She shook her head.

Garda O'Toole was already in Lonnie's office taking preliminary notes. A quick scan showed Danny nothing obvious except the knife in the chest and grubby euro notes littering the floor. Lonnie lay with eyes aimed at the door and jaw hanging as if he'd been in the process of saying something when the knife plunged into him.

"I know there's a cat in here somewhere," Danny said to O'Toole. "Before the day's out, grab it up and drop it off at the hotel. Mrs. O'Brien can take care of it."

"Yes, sir." O'Toole pointed to Lonnie's chest. "The knife is unusual."

"So it is." Danny bent over Lonnie for a closer look at the knife's inlaid wooden handle. "Shit."

"Sir?"

"Never mind. Thinking aloud, as painful as that is."

He crouched next to the body. In doing so, he caught sight of a white plastic canister under the desk. He swung himself into the other room. "Which one of you has asthma?"

"Not me, and neither did Lonnie," Ivan said.

"You?" Danny said to Merrit.

A purse the size of a backpack perched on her lap. Her hands twitched toward it and fell back. Something was off with her, but he sensed it wasn't the obvious. Criminals don't usually let themselves get caught wearing their latex gloves.

"No asthma," she said.

"Pickney, isolate Ivan," Danny said. "There's a storage room in back. Get his statement there. And Ivan, we'll talk about your brilliant move to call Mr. O'Brien instead of the Garda. Makes you appear guiltier than ever."

"I am not guilty of anything except healthy fear of the authorities," Ivan said as Pickney walked him away. "Of course I called Lonnie's father first. That is the proper respect."

"Respect, right." Danny frowned at Merrit, who sat prim as a schoolgirl with feet together and hands now resting atop her purse. Her eyes were a shade of hazel so light they appeared to glow, and her gaze hinted at depths she tried hard to conceal. "O'Neil, I need a second's worth of help with our illustrious dead man, then get Miss Chase's initial statement. Don't move, Miss Chase."

Out of Merrit's earshot, he directed O'Neil to watch Merrit carefully for signs of uneasiness or relief. "She's hiding something."

He returned to the corpse with a worsening hangover headache. Walking around the body, he noticed another oddity. Instead of the usual items found missing from a dead person—the gleaming watch, the wallet—it looked like Lonnie would be interred without his braid. Someone had snipped it clean away.

· 12 ·

On Sunday evening Kevin lounged with Liam. This was their last quiet evening before the festival chaos consumed them for the next month. Not that Kevin felt relaxed. He'd been tense for the past few weeks anyhow, and then this morning he'd woken up agitated by thoughts of Emma.

Kevin's recliner squeaked when he shifted, and the stink of beer sweat filled his nose. Meanwhile, Liam scribbled away, comfortable as could be in his stuffed chair with the turf fire roaring at his feet. Kevin turned his gaze from flickering fire shadows to his father, the true source of Kevin's tension. Something ailed Liam for sure. He'd been journaling since the bloody mystery letter arrived.

"Stop staring at me." Liam jabbed his pen down, a most emphatic period, and shut his journal. "I implore you, go out, have fun, have a life."

"Dusting," Kevin said. "How about that for having fun?"

Kevin fetched a damp dishcloth from the kitchen and began by wiping down the mantel above the hearth. He moved on to the shelves that lined the wall behind his chair. Shoeboxes and an eclectic assortment of trinkets lined the shelves. Kevin picked up a miniature painting of the River Seine as drawn by thousands of Parisian street artists. This one was signed, *Thanks to Liam the Matchmaker!*

He set aside the painting, began dusting the first shoebox, labeled *1969*, and continued on up the line of years. He could delve into any box and read thank-you notes from happy people everywhere. Liam's public history on view.

Liam's displayed life didn't amount to a piss in the wind though. "Why the sudden ache to record your life? The truth now."

"To leave to you, why else?"

Some consolation. Kevin tipped a box labeled 1975 off the shelf and heard a soft thunk from within. "You ought to hit the scratcher early. The first day of the festival is always grueling."

"Don't think I didn't see you eyeballing that Merrit lass last night at the party."

"Would you leave off about women, for Christ's sake?" Kevin said. "Marcus was the one to shout her out to us, but she didn't look to need saving from Lonnie after all that."

The truth was, something in her expression had disturbed Kevin. A furtive longing that she'd shot around the room like a searchlight only to land on Liam once too often.

"She reminded me of one of those lost dogs on the Battersea animal shelter commercials," Liam said. "Probably could do with a friend."

"Better she find someone else then."

Kevin whap-whapped the 1975 container with the cloth, hard, and watched dust plumes lose themselves among shifting fire shadows. Curious about the thunk he had heard, he lifted the lid to see a jewelry box with tiny hinges and a shiny black surface. Apparently, he'd never snooped as far back as 1975. He'd have remembered this item. He flicked open the box. A pair of earrings shone up at him. He held one of them up so that the firelight reflected through a dazzling blue stone that dangled from a filigreed silver ear clasp.

Liam squinted up at Kevin, who caught the sudden shock that rounded out his mouth. "What the devil?" Liam said.

"My thought exactly. Some special lassie missed her earrings. What's the story?"

"No story. I just don't care to see them."

"What's got you crankier than a rusted screw?" Kevin said.

"Oh me, that's rich. You've been acting the broody hen for weeks. I'm telling you, you need to get a life before I land feet up."

Kevin snapped the jewelry box closed and shoved the 1975 container back onto the shelf. He retreated to the kitchen, where he ground his fists into his temples and ordered himself not to feel so frayed and edgy. Maybe the time had come for a serious chat with Liam, something along the lines of, "Old troll, don't try to match me. Old troll, don't distract me with requests to befriend a stranger. Old troll, leave me alone to be your son for the years you have left."

"Holy hell," Kevin grunted and gave up the fight to stifle his frustration, not to mention his uneasiness. Liam had been acting sneaky. Hiding away a letter, writing in a journal, brooding on her ladyship Kilmoon's church grounds. *Sneaky.*

He yanked open the refrigerator. There stood the birthday cake he'd baked earlier that day while Liam napped. One cake for one year older, and he couldn't stand the thought. The way Liam liked to talk, next year's birthday party might be *en memoriam.* To hell with that. Kevin grabbed up the cake and exited through the back door. He clambered over a rock wall into the pasture he let the neighbor's sheep graze, took aim, and heaved the cake against the water trough. It splattered with a moist popping sound. He reclimbed the wall while soft hoof steps whooshed through the grass behind him.

Tomorrow it would be as if the cake had never existed, and he didn't feel any better for it.

Liam Donellan's journal

My magpie son, hovering over me, taking care of me, little knowing that all those years ago you saved me. That day is clear as crystal. My broken hand throbbed, and a tiny orphanage boy stared after the couple that had just rejected him. You were too young for that kind of heartbreak, and I knew this, too, to be my fault.

So I stooped and held out my arms for this little boy—you—and you picked up a red coloring pen on your approach. Maybe you saw despair you thought you could heal, pretending to be Jesus to whom the nuns prayed? By then, I was sitting on the ground. You perched on my left thigh and pulled the plaster cast that protected my hand onto your lap. The first thing you drew, a happy face. So simple. You looked up at me, hesitant and watchful, and of course I said, "That's lovely." Only then did you smile. A wavering and shaky attempt, to be sure, because the initial loss was still there and deeper than I could heal, but Christ was I going to try to erase the disillusionment, prevent it from appearing again. I'm still trying, all these years later.

Kevin, you're the one person in this world hardest to help. Maybe this is the tragedy of fathers and sons, I don't know.

· 13 ·

Danny parked his grumbling Peugeot in front of
Liam's house and heaved himself out of the car. He
stood for a moment, breathing in the scents of gaso-
line exhaust, damp sheep wool, and Atlantic tang.

Kevin rounded the corner of the house. "Thought I heard
your sorry excuse for a ride."

Tension pinched the skin around his friend's eyes and a
whiff of alcohol musk rose off him.

"You look like the bad end of a cow," Danny said.

"You don't look much better. Come on, let me pour us both
something."

Danny shook his head, then nodded. He sneezed as they
stepped into the living room. Liam's head popped around the
side of his head rest. "Ah, Danny boy, looking like you've been
ground under a butcher's mallet."

Too true on this crap of a day, which had started with con-
ciliatory dough making and ended with fingerprint powder
clouding Danny's vision, clogging his nose, and coating his
throat.

Danny stood blinking at the hearth fire, unsure how to
proceed. He thought about Kevin as Clarkson's—and the

O'Briens'—favorite suspect. Below the surface of him, Kevin was softer than a stuffed lamb. Brawling was one thing, killing quite another, not that Danny could say this to Clarkson.

"Ah hell, hit me with it twice then," he said and dropped into Kevin's chair.

Kevin retreated to the kitchen to fetch the whiskey.

"What's on with you? Is Ellen OK?" Danny read the misgivings in Liam's half-smile, then the decision to go ahead with the next query. "The children, they're fine?"

"I don't know what *fine* is anymore. Seems like time should have healed something between Ellen and me."

"For shite, that. Time could give a damn."

"That's a font of dire wisdom—thank you kindly."

"My pleasure," Liam said. "Always try to help."

Kevin arrived with a bottle and three glasses. He pulled up a dining chair from across the room and sat between Liam and Danny. The cozy silence the three of them usually inhabited felt estranged. His fault, Danny knew, for arriving with weighted conscience. He swallowed half the whiskey Kevin handed him, feeling Liam's gaze on him.

"I suppose I could use your advice, as usual. Only not about my marriage."

Liam settled back in his chair, sipping his whiskey. "Go on then."

"A case came in today not of the usual drug-addled sort. I should say an important case, and I could do with a promotion. Maybe if I progress in my professional life, Ellen will take heart and progress with her sadness. The good thing is that I'm in charge of the case—"

"Cheers to that." Kevin drank and poured himself another shot.

"The problem," Danny continued, "is that I already don't like the direction the case is going. You might say it involves family. You might say I'm torn between loyalty and duty. So what do I do?"

Liam and Kevin stared at him. They didn't utter a word, didn't drink, didn't move. Kevin's face reddened. After a long pause, Liam set aside his tumbler. "It seems to me," he said, "that we can only do what feels sane to do. It's unfortunate that sanity is a slippery slope."

Kevin reared back in his chair, almost toppling over. "Out with it already. Who's itching after my balls now?"

"Do you have something on your mind?" Danny said.

"I can tell you what's on Kevin's mind." Liam pointed at himself. "Me. He's as transparent as sunshine through spiderwebs, that he is. And, he's also worried he's made the neighbor's sheep sick."

Danny drained his glass and poured himself another dram. Liam and Kevin's relationship had always fascinated him. Their loyalty to each other was fierce, the kind that used up most of their emotional reserves. Whereas some ignorant pricks proclaimed Kevin bent, Danny had long ago ceased to rib him about his bachelor ways. The man didn't have the energy for a full-fledged relationship, not with Liam there to soak up his affection—and vice versa.

On the other hand, Kevin *would* marry someday given proper timing and nurturance, maybe even to Emma. He was a man who fared ill on his own, an orphanage boy through and through. Product of the nuns, even down to the way he glided when he walked.

Liam's caw of a laugh brought Danny back to the scene at hand. He'd missed their back-and-forth but now caught Liam's, "Did you think I wouldn't spy on you after you left the room in a sulk? Imagine, Danny boy, he fed my birthday cake to the sheep because I asked him to make nice with that Merrit lass. God forbid I help him with his rat-arsed social life."

Danny's ears stretched in Liam's direction. "You know Merrit Chase?"

"Not at all."

"Marcus seems keen on her," Danny said, "but I swear she's already wrecking my head. I'm fetching ice. Any for you?"

They shook their heads and waved him on with mannerisms so similar anyone would think they were biologically related. In the kitchen, Danny leaned into the freezer. Merrit Chase. In the plaza with Marcus. At the party. At the crime scene. He'd bet she had more to do with Lonnie's death than Kevin—little good that did his friend.

He checked the batteries in his microrecorder and made ready to tackle Kevin.

· 14 ·

Kevin recognized Danny's professional mask face when he returned with ice in his whiskey. "About to get to the point, are you?"

"Unfortunately. Let's go into the kitchen."

"You've nothing to hide, remember that," Liam called after them. The confidence in his tone comforted Kevin until Danny set a tape recorder on the counter. A sickening *déjà vu* enveloped him as Danny settled himself on a stool at the kitchen island.

"We're at this again? Why so official?"

"Because I need to be on this one. And I don't have an extra man handy to be my note taker. Better this way, actually." Danny fiddled with the recorder without turning it on. "Listen here, Kev, the shit's about to blow your way again. Lonnie was knifed in the heart sometime during the party."

"Holy shit. Why didn't anyone tell us?"

"Oh, I don't know—because of your temper?" Danny held up his hand to quiet Kevin's protest. "The news is already out. The journalists have arrived, and Clarkson has started his media games. He's already sniffing after you on the O'Briens' good say."

Unable to stand still, or sit, Kevin jerked open a cupboard. Of course the O'Briens pointed their fingers at him. It stood to reason, didn't it, because of his supposed jealousy, his uncontrollable temper?

He grabbed the cake and frosting mixes he'd bought before deciding to bake from scratch. Chocolate fudge, Liam's favorite. "I'd have been mad to kill Lonnie. Pure mad. And besides you were with me the whole evening." He yanked down a bowl, poured in the cake mix, and ruined two eggs in his attempt to crack them against the bowl. "Fucking hell."

"How much do you remember about last night?" Danny said.

"Is this the official interview?"

"Not yet. We're two friends, talking. Though you know I ought to treat you like any other suspect."

"Oh yes, duty." Kevin splattered another egg and bowed his head. "I'm grand. I did nothing. I have nothing to hide."

"I know that."

"Do you?"

"Yes." With quiet finesse Danny cracked two eggs into the cake mix. "The reason I ask about what you remember—" He shoved the bowl aside. "Listen, you went missing for a good thirty minutes."

"I did?"

"And I have to include this in my report. In fact, Mrs. O'Brien nattered on about it when she gave her statement this afternoon, so I'm sure others noticed, too."

"That cow can't help herself, always the busybody bitch."

"Still, I'm warning you, OK? I've got my men questioning the partygoers as we speak, and hopefully they'll find someone who saw where you went." Danny dipped his finger into the cake powder and licked it. "How many people do you suppose were in and out last night?"

"Three fifty? Four hundred? Your men will have more work than a ram in breeding season."

"But not nearly as much fun." Danny swung an arm around

Kevin's shoulder, the manly shake, and then his voice turned serious again. "Remember to answer with the minimum necessary. This is routine. We're asking everyone to run through their evenings."

"Not routine from your boss's point of view, I'd wager."

"And do not, I repeat, do not lose your patience."

"Good luck to that."

Memo of Interview

Detective Sergeant Danny Ahern questioning Kevin Donellan in the death of Lonnie O'Brien. Sunday, 31 August 2008, at 21.40, in the home of Liam Donellan at 94 Kilkany Lane.

DA: *Let's start at the beginning. What time did you arrive at the Plough and Trough Pub?*

KD: *Eight or thereabouts. People were starting to arrive.*

DA: *And what did you and Emma talk about?*

KD: *What's that got to do with the price of potatoes?*

DA: *Several people saw you talking with her early on.*

KD: *I bet they did—took a sorry interest in seeing us together, I'm sure. Last year, the relationship not even laid to rest, and she showed up at the party with Lonnie. Oh, and Lonnie made sure to swagger her around the room, acting as if he actually cared for her—*

DA: *You didn't grease this tin.*

KD: *(clanking) Anyway, last night Emma only wanted to be sure I was right in the head again, such as that goes.*

DA: *Were you angry last night?*

KD: *Angry enough to kill Lonnie, you mean? You can say it.*

DA: *Please answer the question.*

KD: *Talking to Emma saddened me, that's all. And honestly, maybe some residual guilt. That business was my fault. I left her high and dry.*

DA: *And last night?*

KD: *We said "hi," and then I fetched Liam. That's it. He was outside with Marcus. That was around eight thirty. I escorted Liam back into the party, and I didn't so much as wink at Lonnie the whole night.*

DA: *Did you meet his date?*

KD: *Of course not. I avoided him—and her by association.*

*Felt sorry for her though. Hope she didn't end up like
Emma. She didn't, did she?*

DA: No.

KD: *Besides, I was pretty well ossified by the end. I don't
remember much of anything.*

DA: *Then how do you know you didn't speak to her or
Lonnie?*

KD: *Because I'd remember that much, wouldn't I? Are we
done now?*

· 15 ·

After ten minutes of listening to Kevin rant, Danny clicked off the tape recorder. In that time, Kevin had managed to pummel the cake batter into submission, pour the batter into cake pans, and shove the pans into the oven.

"So much for not losing your patience," Danny said. "Plenty of people have seen your temper fly. This isn't exactly in your favor."

Without a word, Kevin added milk to the frosting mix. Danny, harking back to his own kitchen with Ellen, watched Kevin beat the frosting until sweat broke out on his forehead. Ellen, he predicted, had put herself to bed at the same time as the children, whose mouths and fingers were probably still berry-juice stained. If they went berry picking at all, that is.

The swinging door creaked behind them. "Ah, chocolate cake, I see," Liam said. "And thank you for that. I couldn't be bothered with the white cake Mrs. O'Brien supplied for the party. I detest white cake."

"And God forbid we sing happy birthday," Kevin said.

"I draw the line at that. I made a point of not going near the bloody cake in case Mrs. O'Brien saw me and rallied up a song.

Don't know why she insists on a cake. Give the people their pints and they're happier than two peckered dogs."

"She knows what she's doing," Kevin said. "More cake for her to gorge on at home."

"Silliness in any case. After the first couple of hours no one cares whether I'm there or not, and thank Christ for that. People having their fun, the way it should be."

It was the same conversation every year. In Danny's opinion, the only solution was to fire Mrs. O'Brien. Unfortunately, she prided herself on her party planning skills and fancied herself a festival sponsor because her husband's hotel turned a healthy profit during the festival.

"Since you're here," Danny said to Liam, "let's you and I have a round off the record. I'll send around a couple of men early tomorrow morning to get your official statement."

The two of them sat on stools at the kitchen island, inhaling chocolate fumes and drinking more whiskey while Kevin listened and tidied up.

"What did you think of Merrit?" Danny said to Liam.

"She seemed ill-at-ease, that's all, especially after she knocked over the presents. You can imagine Mrs. O'Brien in her element, making a scene when obviously the lass wanted to go unnoticed. She left soon enough after that with Lonnie yelling after her."

"Anything else?" Danny said.

"Lonnie came and went a fair bit. You'd best be sure I was trying to keep an eye on him after last year. I had a good view from the raised platform the band usually plays on. He had Ivan off in a corner for a bollocking."

"What time was this?"

"Just before Merrit fled the scene. The party had spilled onto the lane in front of the pub, and plenty of tourists had gathered around too. The usual gawkers. I've nothing more to add except that I drove—note this please—*I* drove Kevin home around one. I don't need bloody chauffeuring."

Kevin grunted on his way out of the kitchen. "So you say."

"I do say," Liam called after him.

A minute later, Kevin returned carrying a gift wrapped with silver paper.

Liam grinned upon seeing the present. To Danny he said, "I'd say we're done. You have more than enough to start with."

"That your honed instincts talking?" Danny said.

Liam winked and tapped his temple. "Still in good working order. This will be an interesting festival, you watch. Everyone enjoys a scandal."

Kevin snorted. "That's putting it lightly."

Liam took his time untying the ribbon and pulling apart the paper edges. His right hand fumbled. The second and third finger knuckles shone with scar tissue, whereas his other hand was oddly youthful. Danny had seen him use those hands—even the misshapen one—to excellent effect during the festival when he rested fingers on a nervous widow's arm or tapped a blustering drunk on the shoulder.

"This is brilliant work." Liam held up a bowl hand-turned from a solid chunk of reddish wood. "You made it down to an eighth-inch thickness. Light, isn't it?"

Liam handed the bowl to Danny. The wood gleamed. Black lines in the wood added the illusion of cracks, giving the bowl a fragile appearance.

"It's made from a type of conifer that's extinct in Ireland," Kevin said. "Over a thousand years ago a tree or two fell into a peat bog up Galway a ways. The black lines show where the boggy material seeped into the wood."

Kevin's brown eyes looked darker than ever as he waited

for a response. He rarely scavenged for compliments. Danny sensed that Lonnie's death had shaken him more than he'd let on. "You ought to get your work into galleries, Kev. You've got the touch with wood."

Kevin returned to the oven and pulled out the cake pans. "Oh-ay, maybe someday."

Danny rubbed a jagged black line near the lip of the bowl, regretting that he hadn't recorded his conversation with Liam. There was already a crack where a memory of something Liam had said should have lingered.

Julia Chase's notebook

I, in my new persona as festival participant, had forsaken my peasant skirt for a slip dress and my hair band for a chignon. I even wore lipstick and a bra. That evening Liam wore a crepe blouse with a wide neckline that split over his shoulders. I happened to be standing next to a dapper fellow who grunted with derision. "I wouldn't trust my happiness to a man who wears women's blouses and moccasin boots," he said.

This reporter had stumbled upon the only skeptic in the village. I felt it my duty to persuade this man to give match-making a try, if only for the fun of tracking the outcome.

(Not sure about including Andrew McCallum even though he is interesting for an opposing point of view. He said he's just passing through on holiday.)

Let's see.

The skeptic, Andrew McCallum, a thirty-eight-year-old businessman with sandy features, said he'd never found the time to marry. He has a reserved but attentive manner and the taut stance of a man used to controlling his circumstances. He didn't appear comfortable with Liam's newfangled take on an ages-old tradition. He said he preferred courtship and women who tended the home. Further prompting from me elicited a confession: he was supposed to have left days ago, but the festival atmosphere was "surprisingly engaging" despite Liam the Matchmaker.

Just then, a matron in sweater set and pearls took her leave of Liam, and Liam eyed Andrew. For the sake of this story, dear reader, I pushed him forward. "Your turn," I said.

· 16 ·

On the first day of the matchmaking festival, Merrit sprawled on her unmade sofa bed and flipped through her mom's notes once again. Unfortunately, the yellowed pages that started off so earnestly led to nothing but certitude that Merrit needed the other half of the story from Liam the Matchmaker.

Merrit rolled onto her back and stared at a ceiling crack. An image of her mom sailing over a tricky liverpool jump on Red Hot Glory, her champion Danish Warmblood, flitted through Merrit's head. Poised as always atop Glory's arching path, above polished hooves, tucked-up forelegs, and gleaming equine flanks, the same way she was poised as always in her everyday life, seemingly without a care in the world. Julia Chase McCallum had kept Merrit's life upright. The crumbling started after her death, when Merrit heard words whispered along school hallways (suicide suicide suicide) and realized with crushing distress that she'd never truly known her mom.

The day her mom died, Glory had landed the jump without faltering. Julia flipped a braid thick as nautical rope over her shoulder and aimed a smile at Merrit, who perched on the arena fence, sulking because she hadn't gotten a chance to ride. Her mom beckoned Merrit to climb on for the trek back to the stable. Sweaty saddle leather mingled with coconut-scented sunscreen as Julia's arm tightened like a seatbelt around Merrit's waist. Her mom had been clingier than usual, brushing Merrit's hair away from her face and kissing her nose. And Merrit had been the purest of adolescent horrors. Wanting none of it. Brimming for a fight.

Her mom's car crash later that day was an accident, it had to be—right? Otherwise, what could have compelled her to seek a definitive end to her troubles? What choice, if any, did she veer into on a smooth and wide road with the sun shining and her BMW humming to perfection? And, what part did Merrit, the bad daughter, play in upsetting the fragile balance her mom had maintained?

For years, these questions hadn't mattered. For years, Merrit had fought despair, anxiety, and anger—yes, anger—because her mom had left her alone with Andrew. For years, her only question had been: why did you abandon me?

As ever, Merrit's chest constricted when she remembered those harrowing months after her mom's death. She wasn't prepared for her body to turn into an alien creature; a creature with pimples, breasts, underarm hair, body odor, and, worst of all, excess blood; a creature that required too much maintenance. Without her mom, the simplest task—choosing a deodorant—overwhelmed and enraged her. Her mom was to blame for everything, including her traitorous body. Merrit had to live with the corrosive resentment, which only increased her guilt about her mom's death.

Banging from the first floor startled Merrit from her unwelcome reverie. She swallowed hard, telling herself that she had new questions now. More important questions. She wasn't that little girl anymore.

She slid off the bed, listening. After a pause, the thumps continued, and the thumps meant Mrs. Sheedy. The woman insisted on banging a broom handle against her ceiling rather than trek up the back steps to issue her landlady warnings: don't forget to turn off the porch light before sleep; don't use the outlet in the bathroom because it shorts the circuits; don't forget to set out the rubbish for Tuesday pickups.

Merrit sidestepped her suitcase, which was now pulling double duty as a dirty clothes hamper. Next to the fridge, a swinging door hid an unused dumbwaiter chute. Merrit batted the frayed pull rope out of her way and stuck her head into the echoing space. The pounding continued, but rather than call down, Merrit eavesdropped on the conversation in Mrs. Sheedy's kitchen.

"I don't have time—" said a man.

A woman's voice snapped something Merrit couldn't make out.

"She doesn't answer." Merrit recognized Mrs. Sheedy's voice easily enough. "She should answer. I know she's up there. There's no need for you to climb those stairs."

The man mumbled something, and then a head protruded into the square of light that marked the chute's opening on the first floor. "Miss Chase?" the man called before he noticed her above him. In a lower voice, he continued, "Could you come downstairs, please?"

Detective Sergeant Ahern. Or Danny, as Marcus had called him. Officer of the law and honorary member of Liam's family.

"Is this about Lonnie?" Merrit said. "I don't have anything to add to my statement. Like I told your officer, I left the party early, and Lonnie appeared to be into the festivities for the long haul."

Danny's voice remained neutral. "Come on down, please."

Best to get this over with. She had nothing to worry about, she told herself. She hadn't lied to the cops. Not exactly anyhow. Merrit hurried down the back stairs and along the narrow passage Mrs. Sheedy shared with the Plough's rear entrance. In her haste, Merrit bumped against the garbage can her landlady kept chained to the wall so that the pub staff wouldn't use it. The lid rattled beneath its lock, announcing her entrance into Mrs. Sheedy's kitchen. Danny leaned against a counter littered with the makings for a cabbage-something. He stood well over six feet but had the melted look of someone who'd lost weight in rapid fashion. She recognized this look, of course, from Andrew, but she sensed that Danny's illness was not of a physical nature. The weary film over his eyes didn't hide a lively snap just below the surface.

Next to Danny, Mrs. O'Brien stood with legs spread and fists on hips as if she were the police officer in charge. Merrit smiled to hide her confusion. "You rang?" she said.

Mrs. O'Brien's chin jutted in Danny's direction while chubby Mrs. Sheedy, who huffed when she did climb the back stairs, stood with a tea tray poised between Mrs. O'Brien and Danny. If Mrs. Sheedy's blinks were Morse code, they'd be signaling, God, help me remember every word.

Mrs. O'Brien pulled in her gut and smoothed down an elaborate black dress. Her eyes were swollen but otherwise she hid her grief well. "Merrit was my son's date. I insist that she must know something. Surely she saw that Kevin Donellan coming and going."

Danny nodded toward Merrit. "Did you see that Kevin Donellan coming and going?"

"Everyone knows I left the party early. What could I have seen?"

"You were there long enough," Mrs. O'Brien said. "And need I remind everyone about Marcus lurching about, and who knows what he was up to? Scaring the tourists at the very least."

"I didn't see him *lurching* about when I got outside," Merrit said.

"I suggest that you leave the questioning to the Garda, Mrs. O'Brien," Danny said. "Rest assured that we haven't forgotten Merrit Chase as a person of interest. Or Ivan for that matter. We must look at everyone, not just Kevin."

"Don't brush me off with your official-sounding nonsense, young man. Need I remind you that without my husband's good say you'd have been sacked months ago? Do you think we haven't noticed your dereliction of duties to our community, and that"—hand on chest, her voice thickened—"your utter drunkenness at Liam's party may have caused my Lonnie's death?"

The woman barreled on with suppressed emotion quivering her voice. "And while we're on it, you should have seen Marcus off to a facility long before now. His presence threatens our tourist trade, and I'd say you've let that wife of yours run you down to nothing besides."

"Leave Ellen out of this," Danny said, his voice stiff. "She does nothing but help you with your charitable church efforts."

"Do you know why she volunteers for every menial task that comes along?" Mrs. O'Brien took her time reaching for the tea that Mrs. Sheedy still proffered. "Because she tries to curry my favor on your behalf. She knows where the pull is in our family. Something needs to be done with Marcus, and as I see it, he's your responsibility."

Silence yawned between them while Danny set his full teacup in the sink. Merrit stepped toward the door. Despite being summoned, she had once again intruded where she didn't belong. Mrs. O'Brien had no right to ambush Danny that way, especially in front of an outsider. It wasn't right. Clamping her mouth shut, Merrit released herself back into sunlight and tourists' footsteps before she said something she'd regret. It wouldn't do to call Mrs. O'Brien a fat-cow bully who'd raised a slimy-bastard bully for a son. The last thing Merrit needed was Mrs. O'Brien swiveling her judgmental eye toward her.

Mrs. Sheedy didn't bother to lower her voice as Merrit pulled the door shut. "You mark me, there's something queer about that one, slinking out like that."

The festival was set to start after lunch, which meant that the plaza was already too crowded and too loud for Marcus's liking, not that he minded the older ladies who eyed him as they ambled past his bench, mistaking him for a worthy man.

He sat on the first bench along the walkway that led from the O'Brien memorial statue to the noncoastal. His position faced the Plough so he couldn't miss Merrit's approach from Mrs. Sheedy's place. She appeared impossibly young in baggy shorts, tank-top, and plastic thongs. Perhaps it was her eager wave or the heedless way she bumped into roving men with that bag of hers. Either way, she looked the same age as the teenager who collided into her, causing her to wince and limp the rest of the way toward him.

Marcus sipped quick and stored the flask inside his jacket. Now he wished he hadn't skipped his bath. It was just that bathing had felt a worthless effort after the weekend's uproar. Lonnie dead. Un-fecking-believable. Or perhaps not.

Merrit approached as fast as her limp allowed, and then she was upon him with flushed cheeks and ragged breaths. "What is it with this place?" Merrit propped her foot on the bench and fingered a reddened toe. "There's such a thing as too much community."

"Enough to make you mental."

"I suppose you saw Mrs. O'Brien arrive."

Marcus nodded. "And then Danny. Poor sod has to humor her because she loves nothing better than to lodge official complaints."

Merrit sat beside him and studied him in that strange way of hers—with eyebrow raised like an antennae receiving signals from a divine messenger. "How are you related to Danny anyhow?" she said.

Marcus fumbled for his gin and swallowed long. "Danny is my son-in-law."

"Son-in-law." She tapped a finger on his hand. "And Ellen, his wife?

"My daughter."

"I could have sworn you said you had a daughter dead to you."

He closed his eyes and tried to slouch out of her commiserating radar. "And so I do."

"Was it bad, what happened?"

He nodded at the same time a voice intruded with, "Excuse me."

Ah Kevin, arriving on those silent feet of his. Marcus threw a quick peek at Merrit, who had frozen with her mouth open. He was glad enough to see the end of her probes, well-intentioned though they might be. Kevin was a good-looking young buck and oblivious enough he attracted the lassies all the more for it. Merrit would do well to befriend a man like him, who looked after anyone he let into his world.

Marcus settled himself further into a sprawl with face aimed at the sun. "If you're looking for Danny, check Old Sheedy's place."

"It's Merrit I'm after," Kevin said.

· 17 ·

Kevin had the notion Merrit wasn't reacting well to his presence, which didn't make sense unless she, like most, wondered if he'd killed off Lonnie. Not that her opinion mattered to him. He'd introduce himself, inform Liam of the fact, and, with luck, satisfy the old troll's desire to expand Kevin's social horizons.

Merrit stared up at Kevin, clutching a large blue pendant, and then startled him with, "Did Liam send you to find me?"

"How's that?"

"Oh. Nothing." She frowned. "Just that I'm sorry about knocking his presents off the table. Can you tell him that?"

"Of course." Kevin eased himself down beside her on the bench. "I'm Kevin Donellan, but then it seems you know that already. I was on my way to set up an information booth for the festival when I saw you."

Merrit sat up straighter. "Oh?"

"In a way, I suppose Liam did send me because he thought you looked a little lost at the party."

"That was his word, 'lost'?"

"Indeed."

Merrit sagged back against the bench. "Oh."

Odd, this Merrit, taking the word "lost" personally. Most

people would be flattered that Liam had noticed them at all. Observing her up close, Kevin noticed how quickly she shuttered herself. Now her smooth expression said nothing but polite interest. How the devil Lonnie had landed her for an evening, Kevin couldn't fathom. Come to that, perhaps she'd hooked back up with Lonnie after the party. Perhaps she was the last to see him alive. Kevin opened his mouth, about to introduce Lonnie into their conversation, but changed his mind. Danny would sort her out.

He sat back to soak in the plaza hubbub and dozy sun warmth instead. For these brief and welcome minutes, he allowed himself to loll rather than to rush to the information booth, then to the construction site out Doolin way, only to turn around to escort Liam to the festival commencement, wait around, take him home, toil on the Quinlan's roof for a few hours, and finally, maybe, if he could keep his eyes open, retreat to his woodworking studio.

Another long day ahead of him. Better not to loiter here too long.

Beside him, Merrit opened her purse. "I'd like to send Liam an apology letter."

"Not necessary."

In Merrit's bag, he spied a travel-sized hand lotion, wallet, keys, lipstick, packet of Kleenex, knitting needles—and that was only on the surface as Merrit delved in up to her forearms in female paraphernalia. When was the last time he'd seen the inside of a woman's purse? Not since scrambling in an erection haze to grab a rubber from Emma's handbag. In other words, too long.

"I think a letter would be best, if you could give me his address?" Merrit pulled out a notepad and pen. "I see now that the plaza will be jam-packed all month long. Way too crowded and busy to speak to him in person."

"Ah, so you'd like a private matchmaking consultation, is it?"

The skin around Merrit's eyes tightened. "Don't assume I'm desperate and hard up because you saw me with Lonnie at the party."

Marcus's eyelids twitched along with the muscles around his mouth. "Check her eyebrow—that's when to know she's on to you."

Indeed, Merrit's right eyebrow was raised like a dainty pinkie finger over a teacup. Kevin decided Liam was drunker than a honeybee on mead to consider Merrit in need of his friendship. He took the pad and pen that Merrit held toward him. "Here's the address. Write your letter."

"Write my letter," she echoed, staring down at his scrawled words. With care, she closed the notepad and buried it at the bottom of her bag. "Thank you."

"Uh-oh, now we're in for it, innit?" Marcus settled his chin deeper into this chest. "Poor Danny, the load he carries."

Mrs. O'Brien had appeared with Danny not far behind her. She pointed in their direction and a minute later swept up to them with her teased hair and bagged bosom. Kevin held up his hand, ready to fend her off, but she glared at Merrit instead.

"Rude of you, running out like that. And imagine sitting here, proud as can be with Lisfenora's most notorious citizens."

"Being a foreigner, I haven't a clue what you're talking about."

"Sitting between two killers, that's what you're doing."

With a final accusatory squint, she pivoted and marched out of the plaza.

Danny had no idea who to call on first: Merrit, who blinked at Mrs. O'Brien's retreating back; Kevin, who bunched his fists and muttered oaths; or Marcus, most of all Marcus, who had shrunk into himself at being labeled a killer. How was it these three people with little in common

but a bench now headed up his ever-increasing list of complicated matters? Lonnie's murder had somehow brought them
together, but as yet he didn't know how. He watched Merrit lay
a hand on Marcus's arm, just that, and with the gesture Danny
adjusted his opinion. *She* was the unknown quantity. Figure
her out and the rest would likely come into focus.

"One word out of the lot of you," he said, "and I'm taking you
all in for official questioning. Give me nods and shakes, that's
all. Miss Chase, did you notice anything unusual about Kevin's
whereabouts during the party, or as you were leaving?" Shake.
"Kev, you calm?" Nod. "You realize I'm looking into everything
no matter what the O'Briens insist?" Nod. "Right then. You
two are dismissed. On second thought, Miss Chase wait for
me out of earshot. I have a few more questions for you."

Kevin left, and after a moment's hesitation Merrit followed
him.

Marcus patted the seat beside him. "What's it come to then,
Danny-boy?"

"It's come to the little things like why you didn't come
around for a bath and meal this morning. Ellen attended the
early vigil, as usual."

"Pointless. She'll never come around."

"One of these mornings Ellen will be in the kitchen to greet
you. You'll see."

Unfortunately, Danny didn't feel the hope he used to on
this score. By now, Ellen knew that he helped Marcus on the
sly, but she ignored the extra laundry and the leftovers Danny
wrapped in foil. She no longer insisted that Danny shun
Marcus as she had, and he no longer tried to persuade her that
Marcus deserved a home again.

"If I had the money," Danny said, "I'd rent you a room."

Marcus nodded with his gaze aimed at Kevin and Merrit.
They stood on the edge of the plaza beside Kevin's truck. Merrit

pressed her hands against her mouth and stared wide-eyed at the ground while Kevin spoke. "See Kevin there, telling Merrit everything about our wee Beth. Do you think she'll want to sit with me anymore?"

"Quit with Merrit already." Danny jostled Marcus's shoulder to grab his attention. "It worries me that during the party Mrs. O'Brien sees you larking about out here and then raises shite about scared tourists. She's all for me committing you for the duration of the festival, if not longer, and I've got fuck-all choice but to hear her out."

Marcus clutched Danny's arm with a soft-skinned grip that was a holdover from his previous life as an accountant. "A load of shite, that. I was on a bench all night."

"Why would she lie?"

"Doesn't need a reason, does she?"

"I suppose not."

"People always winding me up," Marcus mumbled, his gaze still aimed at Kevin and Merrit. "Like the bastard who painted my shoes last month."

Nearby, two men set up a small bandstand and sound system. By midafternoon the festival's full force would be upon them. A *welcome* banner hung over the O'Brien statue. Below it, the county councillor ambled through the crowd introducing himself and overseeing the placement of various refreshment and craft stands around the plaza's perimeter. He was another in Mrs. O'Brien's inner circle—her uncle to be more precise—and Danny knew well enough that unofficial local politics could land him unemployed just as easily as his boss Clarkson's official politics.

"I'll ask Kevin if he's got an empty house you can stay in for the duration. You can't lie around Carol Dooley's garage all day, kind as she is to let you sleep there at night."

"She fancied me once. Maybe she could again if I weren't bound for hellfire."

Danny took his leave before Marcus's self-loathing infected him. Beth had loved her quiet times with Grandpap Marcus up until the moment Marcus had turned away to pick up her discarded jumper and completed the circle to find Beth limp beneath the playhouse, her neck broken. *Just for a moment,* Marcus had repeated in an endless monotone until Ellen had given him the boot never to return.

How things change in the seconds we don't look, Danny thought.

As soon as he came within auditory range of Kevin and Merrit, Kevin's mouth stopped moving. Danny avoided Merrit's no-doubt sympathetic gaze. Thank Christ she had sense enough not to mention his Beth's death.

"It's best if Marcus makes himself scarce until this blows over," he said to Kevin. "You got a construction site that might do?"

With an imperious finger flick Merrit dismissed his question. "He can bunk with me. I don't care what my crabapple landlady has to say about it."

She returned to Marcus before Danny could oppose the idea. Kevin pulled off his glasses and rubbed them against his T-shirt. "Looks like Marcus is one worry off your list. You owe her a pint for that."

"I owe her something all right, but I'm not sure what. You get the feeling she wants to spite Mrs. O'Brien?"

"Not that, no," Kevin said. "But I'd give my right ball to know why she's really taking in Marcus. She must know something about Lonnie's death. I almost asked her about him. Maybe I will."

"Don't you go asking her for the time of day. Christ, first Mrs. O'Brien, then you—do me a favor and let the Garda do its job."

"No offense, but you lot are precisely the people I want off my ass."

Kevin grabbed a tool belt out of the back of the truck and

strode away. Danny strolled back to Merrit, feeling like a yo-yo the way this day was going. "You forget I wanted to talk to you?"

"Trying to." She threw a fetching smile in Marcus's direction. "Guess I'll buy us an early lunch, OK? Back in a few."

Out of Marcus's view, her expression turned sad. Danny didn't know whether to thank her for her generosity or order her to mind her own bloody business. "What didn't you find in your purse yesterday?" he said.

"In my purse?"

"Garda O'Neil took your statement at the crime scene, you remember, and he said you nearly broke the seams on your bag looking for a breath mint. So you said."

"So I meant."

"I thought you might be missing an asthma inhaler."

Merrit dead-stopped in the middle of the intersection, heedless of a tourist bus's screeching brakes. Her gaze, tawny and amber as stained glass, held his own. "I told you, I don't have asthma."

"So you keep saying. The inhaler I found in Lonnie's office is an American model. Quite the coincidence."

She marched the rest of the way across the street toward the corner market and spread her arms to encompass the plaza, the Grand Arms Hotel, and the view down the noncoastal toward the church and Internet Café. Tourists clogged the plaza and sidewalks. "Look at these people, it's all baseball caps and tennis shoes, are you kidding me? You'll find plenty of asthmatic American tourists."

"No doubt, but then none of them have inserted themselves into village life quite the way you have."

Liam Donellan's journal

Women were my drug of choice, and I continually surpassed myself in scoring a daily fix. I promoted happily-ever-afters, but I couldn't be bothered with that myself. Those days were a haze of women, yet the first time I saw Julia—the journalist though I didn't know this yet—is as vivid a memory as the first time I saw you in the orphanage.

That day, thirty-three years ago, Julia pushed her way to the front of the crowd to get a better look at me. She was tiny, and she sized me up with twisted eyebrows. She wore a boy's vest with a gauzy skirt. Brilliant she was, so lean and straight-waisted she didn't bother fabricating curves. One glimpse of her and I vowed I'd bed her before I matched her. Just another bird out for an adventure, I thought. And a saucy one at that.

This afternoon during the festival commencement the memory hit me like a felled tree. There stood Merrit, spying on me from the crowd just as her mother had. I'd seen Merrit at my party, but still, the sight of her caused me to stumble over my usual festival commencement speech with its usual rules of etiquette. (A little pomposity lends me credibility, I've found.)

Julia, I thought, and then Merrit blinked back into herself. Taller, quieter, and seeking me out just as Julia had—but for vastly different reasons. Julia's need to know led her to me, and in the end, took her away again. I can't help but wonder what will happen with Merrit.

· 18 ·

Eggs hissed and coffee perked, and for a moment Merrit reminded herself *of* herself from six months previously, when Andrew had still had an appetite. In fact, without realizing it, she'd broken the egg yolks the way he preferred. She tossed them into the sink and started again.

Marcus stood dazed but shower-fresh in clothes she'd purchased for him the previous day in Ennis. After a quick lunch, she'd surprised him with the field trip, and they'd returned just in time to hear Liam's commencement speech. A hush fell over the crowd when Liam stepped onto the bandstand. Even the kebabs at one of the food kiosks quieted their sizzle when he welcomed the crowd to the matchmaker's festival.

"Every one of you deserves to find your mate," he said, "and to the best of my abilities—which are profound as you surely know—I will do this for you. I invite you to confide in me, and then I invite you to enjoy the festivities. Every night you will find parties in the pubs, and dancing, and drink, and camaraderie. You talk to me, then you relax. I will find you, and I will introduce you to the match I've chosen for you."

He stood there looking Victorian yet bohemian in an immaculate velvet morning coat with long tails and a jaunty scarf tied around his neck. An Old World walking cane with an engraved silver handle and matching end cap completed his ensemble.

"However," he said, brandishing the cane, "there are rules, and I'm not afraid to banish anyone who disobeys me. So listen here all ye who wish to participate:

"Thou shalt not approach while I'm speaking with another participant.

"Thou shalt only approach me if I signal you to approach.

"Thou shalt not ply me with alcohol.

"Thou shalt not pester me for results after the initial interview.

"Most of all, thou shalt not request a match to the person of your choice."

By the end of his speech, Liam could have mandated urine samples from every last person in the crowd, and every last person would have nodded OK. Even his arrogance had a charmed quality to it.

Her dad, the smiling dictator.

Merrit pondered the spectacle of Liam as she finished cooking up Marcus's eggs. She had stood within the crowd as if cemented in place, mesmerized just as her mom had been. For brief moments at a time she'd seen what her mom had described in her notes: the swagger, the intensity, the charisma.

"I hear something," Marcus whispered.

"What? Oh, it's probably Mrs. Sheedy hoping to catch me in sin."

His hands shook. "Thirsty."

She knew the drill. He had to want to quit drinking. Even so, witnessing his dependency at close hand almost compelled her to nag, cajole, browbeat, or yell. Instead, she said, "Grab a beer to tide you over."

Merrit surveyed her chaotic domain as she tipped eggs over-easy onto a plate. The unfolded sofa bed bumped up against an equally messy cot, and Marcus's few personal belongings sat in a pile next to the bathroom. Most of all, there was Marcus himself, dribbling beer out the sides of his mouth in his haste to replenish himself. He seemed out of it this morning, probably because he'd been on his good behavior, drinking only beer when his body needed mass quantities of gin just to maintain.

She eased him onto a chair and served him the eggs along with brown bread and milked coffee. "Maybe you'll feel better with food. I'll be right back."

This being Tuesday, she grabbed up the trash bucket and stepped onto the landing that overlooked the plaza beyond the Plough's roof. Festival volunteers had dismantled the bandstand used during yesterday's commencement and replaced it with a caravan tent open on four sides. Beneath it sat a Victorian-style divan upon which Liam would peel open dreams and desires. According to the festival schedule, Liam appeared in the plaza from 10:00 a.m. to 4:00 p.m. and after a dinner break visited one pub each night in a rotating circuit. It could take him days, even weeks, to match a person, but according to the locals, he always found his couples from within the crowds.

Merrit leaned against the balustrade for a moment of rising sun, quietude, and wishful thinking. Please, no drama today. Please, just peace enough to work with Marcus and start a letter to Liam. Simple enough request, yet her neck pulled at muscles so tight they hurt.

In the passage beneath her, the chain on Mrs. Sheedy's trash can rattled. Merrit peered around the corner of the building and caught her landlady examining the garbage with her shoulders hunched in outrage. This wasn't unusual, but the sight of Danny with one of his men—O'Neil—most certainly was. Danny rubbed a hand over his mouth in a fierce movement that stretched his lips to one side of his face.

"And what was I after saying?" Mrs. Sheedy said. "This'll be why she hasn't brought down her bucket yet."

"Back inside," Danny ordered Mrs. Sheedy. "And keep this to yourself."

Good luck with that. Mrs. Sheedy was probably rolling her tongue around like a gambler with dice in hand, ready to let fly. Merrit watched as she scurried into the kitchen to perform her civic duty over the phone lines. Danny raised eyebrows at the grinning O'Neil, grunted something, and strode toward the back steps.

Merrit held up her trash bucket in greeting. "Trash day."

He squinted up at her, suspicion evident. "A little late, I'd say. Follow me."

He turned around without waiting for her. This didn't bode well. Mrs. Sheedy must have found something interesting indeed. Perhaps the guys at the Plough had snuck in a half-smoked joint, and Mrs. Sheedy would rather blame the outsider.

Merrit set down the bucket and pressed her granny nightie down against her stomach. It came to her knees and was conservative enough with long sleeves and a demure ruffle around the neck. So be it. She looked good enough for a trash can visit.

Danny was already waiting for her on the far side of the trash can when she arrived. His gaze flickered over her, lingering the barest second, before shooting back up to her face.

"Go on," he said. "Take a look, but not too close, and don't touch anything."

Merrit leaned forward from the waist to peer into Mrs. Sheedy's trash can. She grinned, relieved. "Marcus will be glad—he felt so bad."

"You knitted this blanket, correct?" She nodded. "Go on then, take a closer look."

Merrit bowed closer. She sucked in her breath when she spotted the telltale smudges and streaks. Against the blue yarn, they looked purple, and only something red—like blood—could make blue yarn look purple.

"Remnants from Lonnie, I suspect," Danny said. "Unless you have another theory."

She shook her head, remembering how addled Marcus had been the morning after the party. How he'd wilted as he took the blame for losing the afghan. She tried to imagine him plunging a knife into Lonnie with enough force to kill him, but she couldn't. Not that it mattered. She was the suspect here, not Marcus.

Merrit clutched at her nightgown, her breath hitching. Danny's unwavering brown gaze clocking her every reaction. O'Neil stood nearby, also watching her as he unspooled a length of crime-scene tape.

She bent over to catch her breath, inhaling a faint citrus smell that wafted up from the trash can. The guys at the Plough must have snuck in the lemon and lime rinds to rile up Mrs. Sheedy. The fruit rested in a festive pile near the dried blood. Someone—presumably the killer—had folded the blanket before slipping it into the container. The whole thing looked staged for a macabre still life.

"Well?" Danny said.

Merrit wavered, half turning away, rocking back and forth. The lung worm started its inexorable squeeze. Calm down, she told it like she always did, but once it started there was no stopping it. A pebble dug into her heel as she stepped backward. She sprinted for the stairs.

"Bloody hell, she's got a leg on her," O'Neil called after her.

Danny's footsteps pounded up the stairs after her. Breathless, she kicked her door shut, but Danny's foot was already inside. She twisted away from his grasping fingers, her lungs sizzling like the kiosk kebabs on the plaza. She knew this heart-attack feeling well, but familiarity didn't lessen the surge of fear that propelled her over the sofa bed and into the bathroom. She banged open the medicine cabinet and swept a shaking hand through her toiletries. Travel-sized containers of aspirin and Vitamin C fell into the sink.

Behind her Marcus mumbled, "Beth? Is wee Beth all right?"

Danny hushed Marcus and stepped into the bathroom behind her. He was too close, as gritty a presence as the dirt on the bottom of her feet. Panting now, her heart skittering around in her chest, she gazed around the bathroom.

Where the hell was it?

Marcus repeated his question, and Danny told him Merrit—not Beth—would be all right once he got her sorted. He reached out to restrain her, but she lunged away. She remembered now. Marcus had knocked her inhaler behind the toilet. She grabbed it and cowered inside the shower stall, the lowly addict desperate for her fix.

"What the devil?" Danny boomed. "Give me that."

Merrit pressed the nozzle and inhaled. She almost cried with relief as her lungs absorbed the blessed mist. Immediately, her heart rate slowed. She swiveled away from Danny and pumped her lungs again. And then again.

"Give it here." Danny pulled her around by the shoulder. "Now."

Merrit dropped the inhaler into a baggy. Her nerves vibrated taut as over-tightened guitar strings, but at least she could breathe and at least her lamentable weakness was under control.

Danny sealed the inhaler into the bag, tucked it into his pocket, and ordered her out of the bathroom. "You will have to reside elsewhere tonight. We need time to examine your flat. Get dressed. O'Neil will see to the details here."

"But, my stuff."

"You possessions will be safe."

"That's not right," she said. "I should be allowed a few minutes of privacy so I can pack."

"I'm sure you'd like that."

Danny picked up Merrit's oversized purse and rummaged through it with a vaguely disgusted look on his face. She winced, imagining his fingers touching everything she owned. She closed her eyes to prevent them from skittering around the room. She'd already given too much of herself away.

"Quite the stink coming out of there, just so you know," Danny said.

She opened her eyes and grabbed the purse. "Where will Marcus stay?"

"Bloody hell if I know. Right now he'll have to come along to the Garda station because he's implicated too."

"No, he's not."

"He was the last one to be seen with the afghan."

Marcus hung onto a chair. "I'll be needing a bottle first."

Later, in Interview Room 1, Merrit once again cursed her need for inhalers. In Interview Room 2, Marcus pictured *two* plates with food on the night of Liam's party. Two kind souls had thought of him while he sat on his bench watching the party from afar. If only he could remember who those kind souls might be. His attempt to pin down the memory faded into alcohol jitters.

· 19 ·

Kate felt lighter than she had since arriving in this bunghole of a village. So much so that the balloons tied to the benches looked cheerful rather than infantile, and the flower stand seemed a nice touch rather than tacky. Euphoric might be the word if she were one to wallow in emotion. Instead, she congratulated herself for understanding that life was all about positioning. Positioning, literally, in that she stood at the plaza's edge in view of Liam and, more importantly, in view of the lane from which a tall man who could only be Garda sauntered out with Merrit and her smelly sidekick.

Earlier Ivan had attempted just such a bland escape through the mingling crowds, but she'd caught him out with her wave. His usual twitchiness had settled into a cornered-rat stance when she stepped in front of him. "Was that your hefty squeeze I saw tiptoeing away from your squat earlier this morning? Not that she was light on her feet anyhow. You've got yourself a right weighty meal there, bad boy. Wait until news gets around."

He bared his teeth.

"And then there's your other friend, Merrit. Connie might be interested in how well you know her. Even if it was only because of Lonnie's illegal sideline, it could look a little dodgy. Best you take care which side you land on."

"I am my own side, nothing to do with you."

"You think?"

He nodded but appeared uncertain, as well he should.

"If you think it through—as I'm sure you will—your best option for remaining in Ireland lies with me, but I can't hire you as my technical whiz unless the Garda take you for Lonnie's innocent victim. Which you are, because how could you not obey him? He was all for holding back your wages, wasn't he? I, as a fellow victim, can vouch for this." She paused, entranced by the eager way he nodded. "Or not. It's up to you."

Too easy. In under two minutes Kate had positioned herself—metaphorically, that is—within Ivan's limited worldview. Dear little man, he was cute enough with his strung-out hair and wobbly Adam's apple, trotting away from her without a goodbye.

That was thirty minutes ago. This was now, in which Merrit ducked into the tall man's car and held out her hand for the drunk to follow, all of them trying to look invisible.

Kate hummed with satisfaction, inhaling the scent of overheated lamb and the more subtle fragrances that wafted in over the harvesting fields. September could be one of the best months of the year. The sunny afternoons and slow twilight, the snap in the air, the sense of all of summer's ultraviolet energy reaching a stored-up peak before the rain started in earnest.

She strolled toward the center of the plaza where Liam plied his trade. No playing it invisible for her. Promenading tourists brushed past her. They flirted; they mingled; they circled around Liam, hoping for their turns. She paused to eavesdrop on a reporter and a French tourist. The reporter was obviously looking for a dramatic statement about murder and matchmaking. Kate smiled at the tourist's comment. "This murder, it is interesting for now, but it is nothing to do with the festival."

She continued on, all too aware of the magnitude of Liam's importance to this community, and with that, his onerous responsibility. Stuck in this bog hole with everyone aware of his slightest sniffle. Stifled, surely, but what else did she have to inherit, as was rightfully hers, but this—this slice of power? This fragment of belonging that had eluded her since childhood?

Kate halted just within the no-hovering zone around Liam's tent. Conversation around her petered off as the congregants waited out Liam's next pick. He stood to scan the crowd, and Kate grimaced to see him looking dapper in an old-fashioned velvet waistcoat with long tails and gold buttons. He fooled them all. The gnawing she'd felt in her head since uncovering the truth of her orphaned status turned into maddened bites of anger.

She stepped forward and shushed a woman who admonished her for the trespass. Liam snapped his head in her direction, and for a dizzy moment Kate looked into eyes shaped exactly like hers. I know you, she thought, and nodded at him. He beckoned the woman who'd complained a moment before. Kate shrugged and stepped away to ponder Plan B. Meanwhile, she hoped Merrit was having a fine time with the Garda.

Memo of Interview

Detective Sergeant Danny Ahern questioning Merrit Chase in the death of Lonnie O'Brien. Tuesday, 2 September 2008, at 12.50, in Lisfenora Station.

DA: You told me previously that you don't suffer from asthma, yet this morning I witnessed you using an inhaler identical to the type we found at the crime scene.

MC: I told the truth. I don't have asthma.

DA: If not asthma, why the inhaler?

MC: Long story short, my mother died when I was thirteen and soon afterward I started having panic attacks, only the doctors thought it was asthma. By the time they realized their mistake, I was used to the inhaler.

DA: Tell me about the inhaler we found in Lonnie's office.

MC: I can't tell you what I don't know. If it was mine, then it fell out of my purse when I first saw Lonnie on the floor. I almost jumped out of my skin.

DA: Fell out and flew over Lonnie's body to land under the desk?

MC: Maybe Ivan accidentally kicked it under the desk.

DA: So you're saying this is a series of coincidences. That you happen to walk in on Lonnie's body, that your inhaler happens to be at the scene, that the afghan you made happens to be in your landlady's rubbish bin, stained with what appears to be Lonnie's blood.

MC: (no response)

DA: Mrs. Sheedy states that you know the combination to the bin's lock.

MC: (no response)

DA: *You realize that only Mrs. Sheedy and you know the combination.*

MC: *Someone managed to slip in the lemon and lime rinds. Obviously the trash can isn't that secure.*

DA: *Let's try this. You left the party around ten thirty, everyone knows that much. Where did you go after you left the party?*

MC: *To my flat.*

DA: *Witnesses?*

MC: *If you mean did I pick up a stranger, then no. But I bumped into dozens of voyeurs on my way back to Mrs. Sheedy's place. I can picture a few of them. A big, blond guy. A woman in a baggy cardigan. Another guy who looked like your officer, O'Neil. That's the best I can do for you. No, wait, Kate Meehan too. I'd met her that day. She also uses the Internet café, by the way.*

DA: *Your point being?*

MC: *That I'm not the only newcomer to become acquainted with Lonnie.*

DA: *But you're the one he invited to the party.*

MC: *(no response)*

· 20 ·

Stymied by Merrit's selective silence, Danny excused himself and entered the viewing room. He dropped into a chair beside O'Neil, who watched Merrit through the video monitor. She sat in the center of the boxy space with hands curved together on her lap. During the interview, she had settled her gaze on the wall and there it had remained until Danny had given up the attempt to shake the monotone from her voice. He'd have to ease his way past her defenses rather than batter them down. She apparently had experience with the latter.

"Did you see her outside the pub?" Danny said.

"Wasn't me she saw. I was inside the whole time." O'Neil fiddled with the volume control. "She's tougher than she looks."

"Except for the fact that she has panic attacks."

"Ay, funny that. You'd never know it to look at her."

Indeed. And no telling what else lurked beneath her wide gaze.

Merrit's panic attacks explained the lab's preliminary report. The inhaler found at the crime scene contained nothing but a saline solution inside it, and it wasn't inscribed with a prescription number. No way to track the inhaler, but then again, Danny would wager that Merrit was the only American in

Ireland carrying around useless inhalers. And odds were that the duplicate inhaler Danny had grabbed from her flat would reveal the same saline mixture.

Merrit shifted in her seat. She stared at the video lens as if she could see him. "Where's Marcus? Is he all right?"

Feverish and incoherent, that's what, but now Danny had a convenient entrée into his second go-round with Merrit. The door to the corridor opened as he reached for the knob. Clarkson poked his head in. "A word, Ahern."

Earlier, Danny had spied Clarkson's Volvo when he pulled into the Garda station with Merrit and Marcus in the backseat. The superintendent normally worked out of division headquarters in Ennis, the county seat, where he oversaw the four districts that made up County Clare. Unfortunately, him being a close and dear O'Brien friend, he'd taken to appearing in Lisfenora and remaining for most of the day.

"Let the tourist and drunk go," Clarkson said. "Marcus Tully is useless, and we don't know how bloody long that inhaler was under the desk. Merrit Chase knew Lonnie. She could have dropped it any time. But we do know Kevin Donellan had a grudge against Lonnie. You and O'Neil fetch him in tonight when it's quieter. I've had my fill of reporters for today."

"Yes, sir."

Danny foresaw a long afternoon of filling out paperwork and wading through witness statements from the party. There was nothing he could do about Merrit's flat until the crime scene techs arrived from Dublin, which wouldn't be until tomorrow.

· 21 ·

"I'm off," Kevin said. "I'll return at four to fetch Liam."

Constanza "Connie" O'Brien drooped onto a chair inside the festival information booth, pulling at a black skirt that stretched tight around her hips. She twisted a damp handkerchief through her fingers. "I'll be here. Better than anywhere else, I suppose."

"Thanks for showing up for your shift. I didn't expect—"

"Oh, I know. Mum will shout down the roof when she finds out." She smiled a little, but immediately wiped it away with the back of her hand. "Not that I care."

"I'm sorry for everything."

"Everyone's in shock. The hotel lobby is filling up with flowers and gifts. Dad sectioned off a portion of the lounge so the locals can congregate. I had to get out of there. I can't cope, I just can't. My brain is about to explode." Her tone turned stubborn. "And I have nothing against you, so why shouldn't I work the booth like I'd planned? I need a social life too."

Kevin didn't know what to make of that. He avoided working the information booth if he could help it. September was hell on his work routines. Without volunteers, Kevin would fall behind on his construction projects.

A skinny man wearing a matchmaking festival T-shirt

approached. Connie handed him Liam's pub schedule. Every year hundreds of men and women congregated to snatch up a bit of connubial happiness. Every year Kevin observed their love-starved antics as they waited for Liam to achieve their goals for them. They were needy, desperate, lonely specimens to Kevin's way of thinking, and every year they wearied him all the more.

It didn't help that every year brought its share of troublemakers, those who interrupted Liam's sessions or pestered him at every chance. One way or the other, the troublemakers made their presence too well known. The woman who now beelined toward them looked to be a prime candidate.

Connie stopped twisting her handkerchief to stare. "Slapper. Look at those shoes."

Kevin perused the long legs attached to the shoes. Stilettos, a rarity around here, and just the thing that would offend Connie with her thick ankles and arch-support shoes.

Connie's voice wobbled. "What's she after with the festival? She can have at any man. Not like me who'd do anything to hold on to one boyfriend."

In tears, Connie stumbled out of the booth with a mumbled apology about making it up to Kevin on her next shift. Bloody hell, it figured. But then again, he shouldn't be surprised. She was still an O'Brien—and a grieving O'Brien at that.

"Hello, Kevin, I'm Kate Meehan."

He threw down the volunteer schedule and straightened to his full height, which the stiletto-clad woman topped by an inch. Her black eyeliner, fringe of fake eyelashes, and pixie haircut seemed out of character, as if she wanted to beam herself back to the late 1960s from the neck up. And from the neck down? A right modern slapper, all right.

Kate glanced over her shoulder toward Liam. "He'd rather I left you alone."

"Excuse me?"

"You and I lived at the same orphanage in Limerick for a time, is all. I was nothing but an infant, and you were four. Still, we overlapped for a short while."

Beyond her, Liam half-stood. His jacket slid back on his shoulders, and he didn't bother to straighten it. Kevin's stomach tightened.

"Nice nuns at that particular orphanage. I don't mind admitting that I helped them with a bit of volunteerism of my own. They still tracked their adoptions the old-fashioned ledger-and-ink way, so I set up a computer database." She leaned forward and Kevin caught sight of a lace bra. "I couldn't help my access to their records and their documents, now could I?" She bent closer still. "Did you know that the day my adoptive family picked me, Liam started the process for you?"

Liam approached. The sight of the matchmaker abandoning a petitioner said everything; Kevin didn't need a neon sign to know that this woman was toxic. Worse still, Kevin spied Joe, the *Clare Challenger's* chief muckraker, bearing down on them with his reporter's pad on the ready.

Liam arrived and propped himself against the table with rigid arm and splayed fingers. "I've been expecting you, Kate."

"Lonnie mentioned me then? I'm not surprised. Couldn't trust him to leave without swiping the door hinges."

"I received word of your impending arrival well before Lonnie caught on."

Kate grinned, and Kevin almost collapsed to his knees when he recognized Liam within the upturned corners of her lips. He grabbed the table to steady himself.

"Too brilliant," Kate was saying. "You were manipulated from beyond the grave too. Bad luck Merrit was carted off by the Garda a little while ago. I'd love to round out our happy family reunion."

Kevin's mind froze around the word "family." The word echoed inside his head like the nuns' voices from the orphanage, with their hymns that used to scare him.

Kate's smile turned beatific. "Merrit is nothing but my half-sister, didn't you know?"

He choked on denial—two sisters, not possible—but denial was pointless because the truth of her statement was evident in Liam, whose skin had settled into a chiseled mask so tight Kevin's facial muscles quivered in response.

"Steady on, magpie," Liam said. "Stave off that Joe. He'd as soon report the truth as turn down a pint."

"Let him rot," Kevin said.

"Go on now. Get rid of him."

Kevin longed to kick Kate's stilettos out from under her. Instead, he stumbled toward the reporter. Around him, tourists stood about like moony eejits, crows argued from the rooftops, and clouds flitted in front of the sun. The normality of it all sickened him now that his world had tilted off its axis. He clamped down on questions, only too aware that he knew less than nothing; that he couldn't let himself feel the shock until later; that this was a moment he'd lose sleep over for months to come.

Kevin clasped Joe's bony elbow to maneuver him out of earshot yet still within view of Liam and Kate—Liam's *daughter*, his *sister*—fucking hell he needed a pint. He forced a just-one-of-the-lads tone into his voice. "You're after the gossip, I know it. If this is the start, I'm slobbering for what's to come. Something in the air this year, eh?"

Joe nodded. "And here I was thinking the same thing. Your candor does you proud."

"If I don't have it out with you now, next thing I'll read about is Liam's lover's spat with a lassy half his age."

Joe's gaze stroked up and down Kate's body at the same

moment she tapped Liam's bad hand, which curled in on itself like an anemone. Their similarities were eerie and obvious: the same attenuated height, the same in-your-face stance, the same slight Roman curve to the nose. Here was Liam's true bloodline staring them down, and Kevin could do nothing but distract Joe the Journalist before he jumped to the correct conclusion.

"Liam with that skirt?" Joe said. "Might do the old fella well enough, mind. The readers like that kind of thing." He paused. "But that's not what I—"

"No news here. Just a woman who's about to be banned from the festival."

"Yes, yes." Joe's pencil jittered to release its lead onto paper. "What's your thinking on Lonnie's death now?"

Kevin wrested his gaze away from Kate and Liam. A tourist sauntered past with a dripping Guinness, and Kevin thirsted after a sip to lessen the edge. The festival's unofficial logo—Liam's leather-bound tomb of a book—emblazoned the glass stein. Other tourists wore T-shirts festooned with the same image. *Matchmaking Festival, Lisfenora, 2008.*

"You don't know the latest news about the case?" Joe asked.

"Apparently not. But you need to talk to the Garda like the rest of your lot."

"Come on now, give your local lad a scoop over the Dublin bastards. They'll find you quick enough anyhow."

"What's that supposed to mean?"

"I have it from the source, old Sheedy herself, that earlier this morning she unlocked her bin for the collector, opened it up, and discovered a bloodied-up blanket."

Kevin couldn't keep his mind straight with Kate hovering so close to Liam. But now, thank Christ, she stepped away from him, her gaze leaking its iciness into her smile. Liam sagged but regained his composure with a chest-expanding breath. He returned to the divan and aimed a reassuring nod at his waiting guest.

Kevin regained Joe's eye and not a moment too soon. "What was the question?"

"What about the blanket? Off the record."

Kevin walked toward his truck, clutching his keys until they bit into his palm. Joe kept pace with him. "How the hell do I know? Besides, you think I'd trust you to sniff my shit and call it stinking after last year?"

Joe affected a wounded look. "What else could I do? There was no evidence to support Emma's allegations."

"Fucking hell if there wasn't. I saw the photos myself. I talked to her doctor. Lonnie raped her after last year's birthday party."

"Why didn't she press charges? Why didn't the DPP?"

Kevin slammed his keys into the truck, felt them dig into his palm a little more. Last year, Joe's impeccable logic had him suggesting that *perhaps* Kevin was the one trumping up the charge against Lonnie out of spurned jealousy. And *perhaps* Kevin later beat the living shite out of Lonnie to further his claim that Lonnie was a rapist.

"Not my fault Emma wasn't convincing," Joe said.

Kevin poked the man's chest with his keys. "The O'Briens had her so cowed she could barely talk—or were you too thick to grasp that? She took their money rather than face the shame in public. Certifiable, she was. Lonnie raped her because he could, and he did so to get back at me. Why else did he all of a sudden show interest in her and ask her out to Liam's party last year?"

"Yes, and there you were talking to her at the party this year, none too happy, and neither was she, looked to me. You think others aren't wondering about you? You were that lucky not to get jail time for the assault, full stop." Joe held up an arm as if to ward off a blow. "All I'm saying is that you're already the favorite, so give us some pleasure then. A quote about the blanket, no more."

"The O'Briens pointed the finger my way before Lonnie's body was cold. Nothing has changed. He gets away with rape, and I'm the sorry bowsie again a year later. There's your quote."

Kevin pulled the truck door open so fast it caught Joe in the thigh. He accelerated away before the urge to rip off Joe's writing hand overtook him. The booth would just have to stand empty for a while.

The rest of the day saw him stopping for a pint on his way to the first construction site out Doolin way. From there to the second site, another pint. From there back to Lisfenora to fetch Liam, a third. By that time, all he felt was bewildered and lost, a remnant of his little-boy self, the boy who'd shuffled toward candle glow that shivered with the exhalation of nuns' voices lifted in hymn. He'd squirmed under the hand that nudged him toward an echoing room redolent of candle wax, damp wool, and wood polish. "You're a big boy now, ready to join the others in the pews."

But he was never ready for change. Not then, not now. The alcohol wasn't enough to numb the sting of betrayal that assailed him at the thought of Liam entertaining not one long-lost daughter, but two, and of Liam secreting away his mystery letter all these weeks.

Back at the plaza at four, Kevin ushered Liam into the car for the drive home. "Don't talk to me, old troll. I might implode."

"I know it, but just so you know, Kate has some of her facts wrong."

"But not the orphanage. She was there too."

Liam didn't respond. He didn't have to. Not long after Kevin's first visit to the sanctuary, he'd heard Liam's voice for the first time. Liam had clutched a plaster cast to his chest, the same cast that Kevin would later decorate with crayon squiggles in rainbow colors. Cradling his broken hand, Liam gazed around the orphanage playroom. "Who's the patron saint of feck-all situations?" he'd asked, earning an admonishment from Sister Ignatius. Even now, Kevin recalled the answer: St. Jude, patron saint of desperate circumstances.

Liam Donellan's journal

Timing is everything, my boy, and the timing back in 1975 was abysmal. My poor Julia, she of the diabolical allure, care-free laugh, and sincere—and ultimately futile—attempts at objectivity. She didn't know what surrounded us until it was too late.

First, that pompous ass, Andrew McCallum. I never told Julia that he'd ordered me to match them together the night she pushed him at me for the sake of her article. Just like that, he'd decided on her. I denied his request—if for no other reason than because requests go against my festival rules—and assumed that would be the end of his impertinence. Little did I know that he was a man who loved nothing so much as winning the deal, out-strategizing the opponent, cutting out the middleman. He was money-making scum who chose the woman to best fit his lifestyle. No doubt she ended up an asset inside his gilded cage, God rest her.

Andrew and I were chemically repulsed at first sight, much like you and Lonnie. We'd have avoided each other with the territorial instinct of the great cats if not for Julia.

And there's more. As these things go, there usually is.

· 22 ·

Later that evening, still smarting from the day's revelations, Kevin stared at the bowl fighting to emerge from a prime piece of imported manzanita root burl. It spun on the lathe at a decelerating rate while he sucked on a finger. He'd been too distracted to take care with the chisel, and now the bowl's profile was irretrievably lopsided.

Sisters, two of them. The fact of them gnawed at him.

He loosened the screws that anchored the wood to the horizontally rotating faceplate and lobbed the block toward the rejects pile in the corner of the studio. It ricocheted off the closest set of shelves, causing Liam's plaster cast to fall. As automatic as a football goalie, Kevin leapt sideways and caught the ragged memento in midair before crashing to the floor.

He lay there still catching his breath when a footstep landed on the outside stoop. He turned over, expecting—no one, in reality, and certainly not Danny looking as wan as John the Baptist before the beheading.

"Sweeping the floor with your clothes?" he said.

Kevin held up the plaster cast. Danny had once asked him what it meant to him, this sad-sack souvenir that was nothing but a soiled tube of plaster in the shape of a skinny wrist. Answer: home.

"How goes the investigation?" Kevin said as Danny pulled him up.

"Tsk, against the rules to ask, but since you're asking"—he flashed his mocking grin of old—"I'll answer. Shittier than a backed-up bowel."

"Your men find anyone who saw me when I left the party? I was probably out back pissing with the other drunks. Better than waiting for the loo anyhow."

"There's nothing but alcoholic fuzziness so far. It will take weeks to talk to everyone who was at the party. It's bloody chaos. Walked through the village to check the crime scene, and I've never been more popular. And the tourists are photographing themselves in front of the café. Love, lust, and murder, what more could the skivers want?"

"Wish I could help you, truly."

"You're in luck. I'm meant to fetch you in for questioning, with your permission of course. Clarkson wants to watch the interview live."

"Now?"

"Riding us all hard."

Kevin twisted his torso back and forth with a back-cracking groan. "We'll have to drop Liam off at the pub first. He's on dinner break just now."

They trudged to Liam's house. Liam sat innocently enough at the dining table with its neat piles of mail. His matchmaking ledger sat before him. He'd already ticked off a few names with colored tabs. Under his elbow, a legal pad displayed other notes.

"I don't like the looks of you two," he said.

"Clarkson wants Kevin in so he can tell the O'Briens we're making progress," Danny said.

"Surely you have a better suspect by now," Liam said.

"Merrit Chase for reasons I'm not saying."

Liam's expression turned inward. After an unusual delay,

he responded with, "Ah, I see," and went back to scanning his ledger.

Kevin almost laughed at Liam's disinterested act. If Kevin could lay a wager, he'd have thought Kate the sister with the killer instinct. But then, what did he know? Merrit was the poster child for still waters and deep reservoirs and all that bollocks.

"No treating Merrit with the family-friendly touch then," Kevin said to Danny but with an eye on Liam, who frowned.

Danny waved his recorder toward Liam. "I need another round with you before we take off. Kev, take note so you don't fall all over your sorry self with Clarkson."

Kevin collapsed onto a dining chair. They ought to be laughing over stupid tourist antics and eating Kevin's specialty eggs with pork and parsley. Instead, Danny turned on the recorder, introduced the interview with Liam, and pulled a photo from his pocket. The image showed a wood-handled knife stained with blood. Kevin opened his mouth then closed it at a glare from Liam. Danny passed on his own silent warning. *Shut up and pay attention.*

"Mr. Donellan," Danny said for the benefit of the recording, "do you recognize this object?"

"I wondered where that had got to," Liam said. "I rather like that old knife. I bought it from a Galway man years ago. Fine work, isn't it?"

"This is the murder weapon."

"I assumed that, my dear boy. I used it to cut gift ribbon as you well know, and before you ask, yes, dozens of people saw me. Ask Sean and Brendan and Martin and Seamus and Raymond—the Harkin brothers. They gave me a blow-up doll, the tossers."

"So you or your son brought this knife to the party—"

"No surprise there. Kevin grabbed it off my desk before we

left. Alan never gives up his bar knives. The man's so stingy he wouldn't give you steam off his piss."

Danny rubbed a smile off his face. "Let's return to the provenance of this knife. It's well known that your son works wood. In fact, I wondered myself when I saw it at the scene. Was this hilt designed by your son, Kevin Donellan?"

"No, as I said, that's my knife, from Galway."

Relief passed over Danny's features, nevertheless, he continued with, "Some might say the woodwork bares a remarkable resemblance to your son's work before he began wood turning."

"Kevin used this old thing as a model, that's all. Mimicry, you know, that's how artists get started. In fact, I'll wager he designed dozens of such hilts in an effort to perfect his technique, then either tossed or gave them away."

"When did you notice this knife go missing at the party?"

"When indeed?" Liam frowned, thinking. "It was after eleven thirty by the time I unwrapped the last gift. After that, I don't know. The crowd was obliterated by then. No one was paying me any mind."

"So your son could have picked up the knife without your knowledge."

"By Christ, *anyone* could have picked it up without my knowledge. That's hardly a significant point against my son."

"End interview." Danny clicked off the recorder. A headache throbbed behind his eyeballs. "I'm walking a tightrope here, gents. I was supposed to bring O'Neil with me tonight for protocol's sake, and that's just the beginning of it."

Kevin fidgeted, then rose to pace around the dining table.

"Whatever else you do," Danny continued, "keep your temper with Clarkson. You hear me, Kev?"

"Oh, that's rich. Let's see you *keep your temper*—oh never mind—I need a drink."

Kevin disappeared into the kitchen. Oaths and slamming cabinet doors followed.

Liam closed the ledger and picked up his velvet coat. "At least he'll know how to answer your questions about the knife when you get him to the station. Bless you for that, good Danny. It does look similar to some he's made in the past, but it's my knife, and I'll swear to it again if I have to."

Danny stroked the leather cover that protected Liam's matchmaking lists. The giant book looked like a hand-me-down from Merlin the Magician, and it hadn't changed since Danny's childhood. The same cracked leather in dark green, the same binding that Liam unfastened as required, the same specialty paper stock with shredded edges and a vellum hue. Liam made it all seem so simple.

"He'll be all right," Liam said. "We'll see to it, won't we now?"

"Remember the tightrope."

They sank into silence, listening to Kevin stomp around the kitchen. Finally, he returned with flushed cheeks. Liam handed him a roll of breath mints from his pocket.

After dropping off Liam, Danny drove Kevin to the Garda station through a twilight that softened rock walls and turned silage bundles into silhouettes. From the backseat, Kevin's irate grumblings lifted into actual words. "It's no coincidence, you know. Lonnie's death. My sisters arrive at the same time but separately, and he dies not long afterwards. And Merrit Chase, your suspect. She's one sister."

Danny braked in surprise. "As in Liam's biological daughter?"

"Thought you'd like that." Kevin waved fingers through the air. "The wondrous symmetry of it all, like a macabre dance. We're pawns to the jig Merrit and some cow named Kate—the other daughter—are ringing around the lot of us."

"Merrit mentioned a Kate, but I haven't had a chance to follow up on her yet."

"There you go—things aren't what they seem. This Kate, she's a gem, believe me, and her gaze about shriveled me up to nothing." Kevin's voice whispered like a loss of faith. "There's no mistaking her resemblance to Liam."

A few minutes later Danny pulled into the Garda station parking area. The building stood on the noncoastal about a half mile from the plaza and with nothing to mark it as Garda except a small blue sign. The men sat while the engine ticked and dusky clouds lined up along the horizon. The wind was up, a sign of summer's passing.

Danny called O'Neil, who appeared a minute later from the pub around the corner from the Garda station. "You owe me one," O'Neil said with a good-natured grin. "Shall I do the honors?"

O'Neil positioned himself behind Kevin and propelled him forward by the elbow. Danny followed. Once inside, they passed through a door that unlocked with a code and dropped them into a realm of messy desks, stale coffee, ringing telephones, and on-duty guards. Clarkson loitered within the incident room, where whiteboards filled the walls and that morning's leftover pastries dried out on the conference table. He waved Danny to a stop and ordered O'Neil to escort Kevin to an interview room.

"How goes the investigation?" Clarkson said.

"Steady on all fronts."

Clarkson tapped a pen against the conference table. "Two days with exactly no progress in other words. Worse yet, today I learned from the O'Briens that you and our suspect are best mates in the pints."

"Which is not hampering the investigation."

"Is that so?" He waved a stapled sheaf of papers in Danny's face. "You mind explaining this then?"

He read aloud from Danny's original interview with Kevin.

KD: *I bet they did—took a sorry interest in seeing us together,*
I'm sure. Last year, the relationship not even laid to
rest, and she showed up at the party with Lonnie. Oh,
and Lonnie made sure to swagger her around the room,
acting as if he actually cared for her—
DA: *You didn't grease this tin.*
KD: *(clanking) . . . anyway, last night Emma only wanted to*
be sure I was right in the head again, such as that goes.

Clarkson let the memo of interview fall onto the table.
"Sounds to me like you warned your best mate not to implicate himself. And we'll not go into the efficacy of inter-
viewing a suspect without another officer present much less
while—what?—baking?"

"This was the best way to get him interviewed. He was on the
verge of refusing to be interviewed at all. And, sir, you know as
well as I do that there aren't enough officers to go around on
this one."

"I'll grant you the last, but you're stretching. What do you
have so far?"

"The blanket with blood plus an asthma inhaler, which
points to Merrit Chase as a suspect. Plus, I'm after learning
that—"

"Right. Merrit Chase, the tourist who knits, befriends
drunks, loses her inhalers, and checks her email. Motive?"

"Nothing on that."

"Whereas your best mate with the assault record hated
Lonnie. What have you got on Kevin's whereabouts when he
wasn't lobbing it back with you?"

"Nothing yet," Danny said. "My men are on it."

"Seems to me your relaxed attitude is interfering with the investigation."

Danny's rising blood pressure added its thump to his throbbing head. "You've got my reports about Ivan Ivanov and Merrit Chase. Plus, a new name cropped up today. A woman named Kate Meehan. I'm following up on all of them. Seems to me the O'Briens are running this case, and I'm the only person willing to consider suspects besides Kevin."

"That's your objective take, is it?"

"Yes. Sir."

"Time to interview Donellan," Clarkson said.

Danny turned to accompany Clarkson to the interview room, but Clarkson shook his head. "I'll see to him. Go home. Tomorrow first thing, drive to Ennis to see what came back on Lonnie's computer. Dublin bastards sent everything there instead of here."

So now Danny was an errand runner. "Fast turnaround," he said.

"Called in a favor." Clarkson paused. "After that task, you're off the case."

"I'm sorry?"

"You heard me. Off the case. You're too close to Kevin Donellan. And here I thought it would be your family problems that would sink you."

Clarkson departed, muttering about the techs in Dublin who best not have screwed up the chain of evidence.

"Damn the man," Danny hissed under his breath.

He was still standing in the middle of the room when O'Neil returned with a large stack of papers. "Clarkson's got Pickney manning the video equipment."

O'Neil settled down at the end of the conference table and started sorting through his pile. "This is for shit. We have to consider the whole damned village. Lonnie wasn't exactly Mr. Popular."

"Have you spoken to Emma Foley yet?" Danny said. "We need to confirm what Kevin said about their conversation at the beginning of the party."

"Not yet. Poor Emma though, speaking of people with issues. I asked her out a few months back, I don't mind saying, and she was having none of it. Still moons over Kevin." O'Neil slid a fax toward Danny. "Something for you. Internet Café's bank statement."

Danny squinted down at columns that represented Internet Café's cash flow. He perked up. This day had a positive end, after all. A way to proceed, a concrete inquiry based on numbers, lovely digits that didn't lie, confuse, or derail. "We haven't seen this report yet."

"We haven't?"

"No. And if Clarkson asks after it, tell him you'll follow up with the bank."

O'Neil, bless him for a few brain cells, caught on quick. "So much paperwork to track, it's no wonder a few items fall through the cracks."

"Good man."

Danny sat back, thinking. He hadn't forgotten Merrit's Tweedle Dee to Ivan's Tweedle Dum. In fact, he now wondered if their bumbling yet collusive behavior at Internet Café linked them to Lonnie's interesting financials.

"Tomorrow I've got an errand to run thanks to Clarkson, and then we're going to hunt down Ivan."

Liam Donellan's journal

Danny looked a sight too grim when he picked me up from the pub tonight while you languished at the station. Danny-boy, I said, you look worse than a week-old corpse. We stared at each other until he exploded with laughter. Would that be pickled and ready for viewing, he said, or too decayed for help? Seems he'll not be working the case anymore—except unofficially, of course. His tightrope broke, poor devil.

He mentioned Kate before dropping me off, hoping for insight about her possible guilt. I have my thoughts, but I'll keep them my own for now. I told Danny that she walks in the image of her mother—though in a harder version, my genetic contribution to the equation. At her core she carries Adrienne Meehan's knack for coveting the life she can't have, for stalking that life with a marauder's instinct.

Adrienne, she came along at the end of that September season and came to symbolize all that lay broken with my life, including the hand. You came along at the beginning of the next, the mending season. So it's said about blood, that it runs thicker, but I never preferred its viscous and sticky weight to the easy fluidity of water.

· 23 ·

On Wednesday morning, Ivan gripped Lonnie's pur-
loined mobile and paced around his rat-hole home.
He was about to fall into the first floor, he'd worn
the floorboards so thin. On the third ring, Connie answered
with a wary, "Ivan, that you? I can't take this secrecy when I
need you more than ever."

"I will make it OK, you will see, but right now it is urgent I
get help. A loan."

From downstairs, creaking floorboards stopped Ivan in his
tracks. "*Chert voz'mi,*" he hissed. "Someone's here."

Ivan slid the mobile under his mattress and locked himself
in the bathroom with his ear pressed against the door, hearing
nothing until his door banged against the wall. "Ivan Ivanov!"

Danny, no mistaking his baritone. Ivan imagined him brandishing a baton the likes of which Ivan hadn't seen since the
Soviet Union imploded. An extra-strength, blood-spattered,
steel-tipped weapon supposedly used for defense but more
often used for breaking down doors. His mother would say he
was more boiled than a turnip, which made good sense in his
native language.

Danny's voice easily penetrated the bathroom door. "Had
a feeling you'd still be here at what I like to call the crime

scene. Which shall it be, obstruction or good old-fashioned trespassing?"

Ivan opened the door to find Danny blocking the exit to the stairs. He stood in the center of Ivan's tiny domain, his head almost hitting the low rafters as he gazed around the dusty confines with scowl lines furrowing the skin between his eyes.

"I have no money," Ivan said. "This is only place for me."

"Ivan Ivanov, I'm in a foul mood, so you don't want to fuck me about. I want to know why Lonnie cornered you for a tongue-lashing."

"Lonnie cornering me? I remember no such thing."

"Trespassing?" Danny's voice was almost pleasant now. Ivan hated the pleasant voice. The pleasant voice was not good in times like these. "Hindering a murder investigation? Or simply export you back to Minsk? Your choice."

"Fine, you put it like that. Lonnie chastised me because I earlier left Internet Café's back door unlocked." He cleared his throat against his slippery English. "I did not know he would return to the shop to fetch the business credit card rather than use his personal one to buy drinks."

"Why did you leave the back door unlocked?"

Ivan felt his face flush redder than borscht. "A woman friend was to meet me later. That is all."

"And who is this *amor* of yours that I might be confirming your story?"

"It never happened so there is nothing to say on that, only that Lonnie did not like the door unlocked."

"Who was she?"

Ivan swallowed. "Connie, but do not tell. Her family does not know. I would appreciate the consideration."

"As in our very own Constanza O'Brien?" Danny grinned, looking too wolflike for Ivan's comfort. "You astound me. But at least you chose the nice one."

"It is not astounding. We love each other. It was disappointing that we could not meet. More than disappointing. Lonnie ruined everything, and you don't even know."

"Speaking of Lonnie," Danny said. "Sometime later in the evening he returned to the café again and died. Did he have his own *rendezvous* scheduled?"

"All I know is that the person who killed him was leaving the door unlocked when this person left because it cannot be locked without a key, which only Lonnie and I carry."

"You're doing me proud, Ivanov. Now that I've got you warmed up, time to get on with my real business."

"There is yet more? You cannot do this. This is harassment."

Danny waved him toward the head of the stairs, at the bottom of which loitered the officer called O'Neil. As Ivan descended with Danny right behind him, he eyed the padlock on the connecting door that separated the building's rear from the shop front. The yellow tape splashed across the connecting door was intact, as well it should be since Ivan had taken care not to so much as breathe on it.

Danny lowered himself onto a step and gestured toward O'Neil, who handed him a folder. "Sit."

Ivan sat beside Danny. A photo dropped onto his lap. The image showed a computer on a desk. Lonnie's computer. More images showed it packaged, then unpackaged in a forensics lab somewhere, and then with its innards on display. Pages of reports followed. In Belarus, such computer analyses took months, in fact more than half a year, which Ivan had counted on for planning purposes. He trembled with the sudden need to piss.

"Never mind trespassing," Danny said. "That's nothing compared to evidence tampering. Our head lab rat salutes you, Ivan. Made a fancy job of it, but he says this computer is too clean. I'm sure you know what that means better than I."

Ivan crossed his legs against pressure from his bladder.

"In other words, a mysterious someone *populated* a new computer with files. I read here, for example, that the computer doesn't contain any temporary files, which I gather accumulate automatically as computers are used." He tilted his head in Ivan's direction. "As do things called *cookies*—of which there are also none on this machine."

"Lonnie must have switched his computer for a new one. Or the murderer did."

"What did I tell you about fucking me about, Ivanov? I'm this close to frying up your balls and calling them round sausages. I suspect that you in your pretty latex gloves copied innocuous documents over from Lonnie's original computer to a new computer. Even I know that deleting files doesn't really delete them, so I applaud you for trying something new. Now, where's Lonnie's computer?"

Ivan squeezed his legs together. "There are many people having computer knowledge. All these tourists—"

Danny's jaw tightened and Ivan stopped. With a sigh, he nodded toward the storefront.

"Bloody Ivan. You'll have to show me, but don't touch anything."

While Ivan shifted from foot to foot, O'Neil and Danny went through the official maneuvers: donning gloves, calling for a scenes of crime team yet again, and unlocking the padlock. O'Neil ducked Ivan under the crime-scene tape after Danny. Ivan pointed toward his inner sanctum, where electronic bits and pieces spread across a work table like digital entrails.

"Congratulations, Ivan, a mighty effort. You copied over enough financial records, memos, invoices, and porn sites to confuse the lab techs for five seconds."

"I was desperate. I was not thinking straight. This, I can explain."

"I'm sure you can." Danny shot him a look that said but-I-don't-want-to-hear-it. "I have this straight from Lonnie's bank. In August, Lonnie made cash deposits that don't correspond to his negative business income. Was Lonnie dealing drugs with your help?"

"No, *blin*, no drugs, I promise." Ivan shook all the more as he grasped anew the magnitude of Lonnie's arrogance, not to mention idiocy. To deposit the blackmail money into his business account, it was too absurd. The donkey's ass deserved to die for that alone. Ivan wriggled against his aching bladder. "Can you excuse me?"

"The DPP—that's the Director of Public Prosecution in case you don't know—could press charges for evidence tampering, or maybe not, depending on what you tell me. So talk."

Ivan pictured Connie and Kate. They squeezed him from both sides to keep his mouth shut—lose Connie's love, lose Kate's potential patronage. And then there was Merrit. She factored in at zero squeeze potential now that Danny knew about the computer tampering. Time to grovel. This was survival of the fittest, and he'd apologize to Merrit later.

Ivan ran upstairs with Danny and O'Neil right behind him. He detoured into the bathroom. Surely the men could hear him piss well enough. They didn't have to be pounding on the door.

Ivan stepped out of the bathroom and, ignoring Danny's scowl, climbed onto the bed to grab a sheet of paper from its hiding spot in the rafters. He'd managed to find an obscure but fascinating newspaper piece about Merrit. Ivan shoved the printout at Danny. "Merrit is more suspect than you think."

Danny eyeballed the headline. "How did you find this?"

"That is tricky part. I"—he cleared his throat—"was looking for it? On the Internet?" Danny's scowl deepened. "I was unwilling participant!" Ivan yelped and then caught himself.

"Lonnie said he would shuck me back to Minsk like slimy oyster I am. He hired me on false pretenses. He was promising me partnership in the business, but I was only another immigrant slave who gathered information for him."

"Are you done?"

Out of breath, Ivan nodded.

"You're saying Lonnie blackmailed Merrit because of this article?"

"Not so exactly. I was keeping it to myself until Lonnie paid me my due."

"You're a model of discretion, Ivanov. What did Lonnie have over Merrit then?"

"Merrit is Liam's long-lost daughter, but she was not wanting anyone to know until after she approached Liam herself. She is private person. Very private."

"That's it? That doesn't seem too dire."

Disappointed that Danny wasn't suitably shocked and impressed, Ivan pointed to the printout. He struggled for the right words, words that would make sense of Lonnie's crooked behavior but not give anything else away. "Lonnie knew she must be hiding something more. He was like his mother that way, always sniffing for secrets." He tapped the article. "And see, Lonnie's instinct was true. She did have something bigger to hide."

"Indeed," Danny said. "*Local Woman Arrested in Father's Death*. But this doesn't explain how Lonnie first found out that Liam is her father."

"You are under the impression that Lonnie confided in me, yes?" Ivan hoped his voice conveyed beleaguered honesty. "That is wrong. All I am knowing is that one day while I was out, Merrit came in for help with her laptop, and then later Lonnie is getting money from her."

"So she lied when she said she checks her email here." Ivan

nodded. "Why did she come to the shop early on the morning after Lonnie's death?"

"Because Lonnie pointed her out to Liam at the party. Lonnie thought it was all very funny."

"So Merrit was angry."

"I'd say so, yes. She wanted to, what you say, 'have it out' with Lonnie."

"Let's backtrack. When did Merrit first come in with her laptop?"

"The 23rd? Yes, the 23rd."

Something lit behind Danny's eyes that Ivan didn't much like. "If you were such an unwilling participant why did you destroy Lonnie's computer?"

"Back in Minsk, we have saying that police are shining flashlight up your ass rather than finding truth." Ivan dug fingers into his hair. "I mean—"

Danny held up a hand. "Fine, for now I'll pretend you were a victim too. What did you not want me to find on Lonnie's hard drive?"

"Other articles I forwarded him about Merrit, financial records, and email messages between them."

"And that's all?"

"Of course, of course."

Danny stretched toward the ceiling. "By the way, you know a Kate Meehan?"

"No."

"Funny, when you copied invoices from Lonnie's old machine, you forgot to delete Kate's record. She needed an AC inverter, or did you forget?" His voice became expansive. "I suppose that's understandable, given all your many inner conflicts. Interesting the timing is all. Kate visited you last week to have her laptop repaired, and the next day Lonnie made a deposit. Fancy that."

Ivan fought himself to remain still while Danny pulled a sheet of paper out of the folder and jotted a line about Merrit's visit to Internet Café on the 23rd of August. "Why, look at this, a pattern. Lonnie also made a deposit the day after Merrit's visit. However, neither Merrit nor Kate explains Lonnie's bank deposits in the beginning of August—before they arrived."

DATE	ACTIVITY in CAFÉ	BANK DEPOSIT
12 Aug		500
17 Aug		500
23 Aug	Merrit asks for help with Internet	
24 Aug		500
27 Aug		1,000 (500+500?)
29 Aug	Kate orders new AC inverter	
30 Aug		500
31 Aug	Lonnie found dead with deposit slip	

Ivan sagged. The back of his knees itched where they wanted to buckle.

Danny waved the paper with enthusiasm. "It looks to me like Lonnie favored receiving many smaller payments rather than a few large ones. And it looks to me like he gathered money from *three* people. Kate, Merrit, plus someone starting on August 12th. I know Kate also claims to be Liam's daughter, which I'm sure interested Lonnie mightily. Think that might be why Lonnie blackmailed both her and Merrit?"

Ivan dug fingers into his hair again, hoping to pull something coherent out of his head, but all that came was an image of chopped turnips on the kitchen counter back in Minsk. He pointed toward the chart in hopes of a diversion. "What does that mean, *deposit slip?*"

"Lonnie had written up a deposit slip for Monday, September 1st for €3,000. We found it in his inner jacket pocket, impaled by the knife. Brilliant luck, that."

Ivan could swear he tasted the turnip's nasty tuberous funk, smelled its dirty stink that used to meet him at the door for every Wednesday's dinner, courtesy of his mother.

"If we surmise from my chart that Lonnie had three, shall we say *clients*, then we might imagine that he expected €1,000 out of each of them, and used the night of the party to gather it from them. As a matter of fact, this is my favorite theory because of the money left on the floor, which totaled €2,000. Apparently, Lonnie didn't get the chance to collect from his last client. I would imagine that he was meeting one of the three at the time he told you he was picking up his business credit card."

"I do not understand this at all."

"What intrigues me most is what Lonnie discovered that allowed him to up the ante from €500 to €1,000. He discovered something new sometime after he met Kate on the 29th. There's a fact out there in the world that three people want hushed."

Ivan didn't need to fake his confusion. Lonnie had managed to discover an important fact without Ivan's help? Something other than Merrit's arrest record? This was mind-boggling. It could only be something that came from Kate's computer.

"You knew nothing about the €3,000?" Danny said.

"Like I was saying, Lonnie was not telling me everything, and of course he would not mention extra money because he was supposed to pay me wages from money he made. He promised."

"You're the victim, all right." Danny handed the folder back to O'Neil, along with the newspaper article, which O'Neil carefully slipped into the folder. "I think we're done."

"We are?"

"Until I decide to arrest you, of course. But that all depends on how good a boy you are from here on out. Meanwhile, I need your key, passport, and paperwork—for safekeeping, you understand." He grinned. "Your secret girlfriend can help you with a new doss. Maybe even her daddy's hotel if you're lucky."

Friday, July 11, 2008   Gull's Hollow Community Gazette

Local Woman Arrested in Father's Death

Officials took Merrit McCallum into custody on charges that she facilitated the death of her father, local entrepreneur Andrew McCallum.

Andrew McCallum died June 28, 2008, after a long battle with liver cancer. He was known locally as the founder of Mid-Pacific Consulting and Trading Company, which recently moved its headquarters from San Francisco to Santa Rosa. Merrit McCallum stands to inherit assets, including the privately held business, worth an estimated $30 million.

The investigation into Merrit McCallum began at the behest of the senior McCallum's hospice nurse, Elaine Smith. Smith claims that she should have reclaimed a high quantity of the elder McCallum's prescription painkillers after his death. "I found nothing," Smith said. "Nothing at all."

By law, hospice care workers who tend patients in the home must retrieve unused drugs after the death of their patients. In this case, Smith referred to liquid morphine and Vicodin. According to her, Merrit McCallum knew how much and how often to administer the drugs in a fashion termed "comfort care," which aims to keep terminal patients as comfortable as possible in lieu of subjecting them to the often painful life-prolonging procedures used in hospitals.

"The end stages of liver cancer can be excruciating," said Dr. Brent Opell, oncologist at Santa Rosa General Hospital. "In addition, the patient is likely to suffer from increased mental agitation if the cancer spreads to the nervous system."

According to Opell, morphine is often necessary to keep the patient calm as well as pain-free.

"My client was a devoted daughter," attorney Jacob Roth said. "She put her life on hold for six months to care for

Andrew McCallum. Anyone who has tended a dying family member knows how traumatic and exhausting the experience can be. These charges are ludicrous at best."

Whether the experience was traumatic and exhausting enough to cause McCallum to administer extra morphine is not the only question for investigators.

"It would appear she had something on her mind," Deputy Chief of Police Larry Werner said. "At the time of her arrest, she had already consolidated the various trusts left to her by her mother and was considering two competing bids to buy her father's business. We know she was preparing to leave the country."

Sources close to the case quote Smith as saying that she was suspicious of Merrit McCallum because she did not get along with her father.

McCallum was released on bail, and the arraignment is scheduled for next week.

· 24 ·

Merrit sniffed at the fermented smell that emanated from her purse. A knitting needle pricked her elbow as she rooted around for the source of the offending odor.

"Why don't you dump it out like any sane one?" Marcus mumbled from the neighboring bed. He lay under the drab hotel comforter fully clothed.

"Are you kidding? Never. I prefer not to see my junk by the light of day."

Marcus chuckled and Merrit found herself following along, only to feel troubled by the foreign feel of the sound in her throat. At the bottom of her purse she came upon a plastic bag and recalled the blackberries she'd picked the previous week.

"Disgusting." With a toss, the baggie with its mushy cargo landed in the hotel room's tiny garbage can. "Now to find my inhaler. There's got to be one in here even if Danny didn't find it. Maybe I should thank the blackberries for offending his sensibilities."

For the millionth time, Merrit considered her love-hate relationship with her inhalers. On the one hand they provided comfort; on the other, talk about a painful reminder of her weakness. The panic attacks had plagued her since her mom's death, sometimes less frequently, sometimes more, and all despite years of therapy.

"I brought four inhalers with me," she said. "I always carry extras."

"Like my spare flasks. Don't feel safe without them."

She must have lost an inhaler the previous week, the one that had somehow landed under Lonnie's desk. Perhaps it fell out of her bag the day that Mrs. O'Brien and her daughters hijacked her off the street. Then, Danny kidnapped the second inhaler to use as evidence, which left her with two more that if not in her purse, could be in Mrs. Sheedy's flat, under a plaza bench, anywhere.

She burrowed into a little-used side compartment and with a *voilà*, waved the third inhaler at Marcus. She tucked it into her jeans pocket, pondering where the fourth one could be. She glanced around the room, but, of course, her suitcase and most of her belongings were stranded in Mrs. Sheedy's flat until further notice. Her stuff, scrutinized by the Garda. But she mustn't think about that. *That* would panic her for sure.

"If this inhaler was always in my purse," she said, "where did the one at the crime scene come from?"

"How do you know you didn't have two inhalers inside that thing at some point? You're messy, so I've noticed."

"I know. It's awful." She flung the purse onto the floor. "Oh, never mind. What about you? Is the night of the party still a blur?"

"Enough, yet not." Marcus's gray and watering gaze wandered to the bottle perched on his stomach. "I'm troubled, troubled indeed. Who untied my shoes? I think of the shoes, I think of cake. Bloody nuisance."

"Start with the last thing you remember clearly then."

"Liam. He said he would send out food from the party." He blinked at her in earnest concentration and sat up on his elbows. Merrit snatched up the gin before it sloshed onto the comforter. "He must have sent out food later in the evening, but I don't remember for shite. He fancied the afghan you made me, I do remember that. You'll be having to knit a longer one for him though."

Merrit perked up a little. Liam had liked her afghan. "You think he'd want one?"

"Ay, why wouldn't he?"

Merrit set the gin on the nightstand next to a draft of the letter she planned to send Liam if she could think of the perfect way to apologize, officially introduce herself, assure him of her benign intentions, and suggest they meet. She'd thought to keep it simple, something along the lines of, *Sorry about Lonnie and the gifts. I am indeed Julia's daughter. Can we meet, just to talk?* But that seemed shabby somehow.

Marcus had a better idea. Maybe she could offer to knit Liam his own afghan. That might be a nice way to start a conversation, because she wasn't about to interrupt Liam's festival duties on the plaza, not with the festival participants surrounding Liam's caravan tent all day long. Marcus hadn't done justice to the festival when he'd told her she could stand in line with the rest of the tourists. A line implied order. Instead, the crowd churned on hormonally charged undercurrents, flowing toward Liam and then ebbing away when he chose a new person to interview. She'd bobbed along with everyone else, fascinated by the way Liam absorbed the crowd's energy. He cut a dashingly antiquated figure in his velvet tails, with his matchmaking ledger on his lap. He was a love conjurer, invoking the spirits of a lost world, a world in which matchmakers were magicians, and magicians were mercurial creatures, as likely to spurn you as to bless you. She hadn't seen him spurn anyone, but she had a feeling he could be ruthless if put to the test.

So, she'd held back, unwilling to be spurned. After all, not all fathers cared to meet their bastard children. This was a fact of life, and it was silly to think otherwise. Liam hadn't sought her out since his birthday party. He was busy, of course, and no doubt exhausted at the end of the day, but this didn't change the fact of his apparent ambivalence.

"Yes," Marcus was mumbling. "I think Liam did bring me dinner. He went so far as to walk me to the other bench so I could eat in peace."

"I'm sorry, Marcus. What was that?"

"There's some get plastered and like to fuck me about. Better to sit out of view of the pub, Liam said."

"He's kind."

"That's so. Always was with me."

"What else?"

"Nothing else. I was well and truly ossified by then." He grabbed the bottle off the nightstand and swallowed. "Passed out and didn't notice a thing. I'm sorry."

Merrit rolled to the edge of the bed and stretched to grab a beer from the mini-fridge. She had hoped to have a fact to take to Danny with his tired eyes and loose suits. He'd obviously forgiven Marcus for his daughter Beth's fall from the jungle gym, which said a lot about him. He could be reasonable. Maybe.

She longed to ask Marcus about his estranged daughter— Danny's wife—but refrained. Danny was a cop, not her friend. His family problems were none of her business. "Tell me more about Kevin and Lonnie's feud."

Marcus settled back into the pillow and closed his eyes. If Merrit understood nothing else about him, then it was how coherence and chaos could exist side by side, sometimes within split seconds of each other. So, she waited patiently for Marcus to steer himself away from chaos.

"Daft, really," Marcus said a few minutes later, "but Lonnie couldn't let it go. A year ago this past June he accepted bids on the remodel for his shop. Wanted it bright and shiny for the festival, that he did. He favored a solid wall of plate glass windows and a neon sign."

Marcus issued a spitting sound of contempt and then continued. "Kevin raised hell about keeping the old storefronts authentic, eloquent he was, out there on the plaza with a sign. Lonnie backed down, of course. Even he wasn't eejit enough to risk more ridicule." He swallowed another mouthful of gin. "There, then, that's what started the conflict between them and why Lonnie later went after Emma the way he did. He raped poor Emma, that he did, the bastard."

"*Raped* her? Oh my God. I had no clue it was that bad between them."

A knock on the door jerked the next question out of Merrit's head. She stood and straightened her shoulders. No need to cower. She opened the door to find Ivan holding a suitcase and cowering for the both of them. "Before you ask, Mrs. Sheedy did not mind telling me where you are. She said to tell you that she does not appreciate having Garda officers trampling overhead all morning, and that she has had about enough of your overnight guests."

"Always was an ogre, that one," Marcus said.

Ivan yanked at his hair. "Speaking of the Garda, have you heard from Danny yet?"

"Yet?" Merrit pulled him inside the room. "I take it I'm about to become vexed with you."

His pinched lips were little solace to Merrit, who fingered the inhaler in her pocket. Ignoring Marcus's presence, Ivan relayed the news that Danny had caught him out with the computer tampering and promised him trouble if he didn't shed light on Lonnie's interesting financials. "I promise it was not to be helped. The Russian instinct for self-preservation overtook me. I told Danny about blackmail and gave him article I had stored away about your arrest in California."

Merrit's heart skipped ahead a few beats. She collapsed onto her bed, now clutching her inhaler. "At least you have the courtesy to warn me."

"Yes, but I must go now. I need new place to live."

Despite her racing heartbeat, Merrit spoke carefully, well aware that Ivan spooked easily. "I keep coming back to Lonnie's missing folder. There were quite a few pages in there besides the ones that he pulled out to show me when he started in with the blackmail. Someone took it the night Lonnie died. You must have an idea."

Ivan's eyes darted back and forth. "Women," he finally exhaled. "I tell you this, and then we are even for me giving away your arrest record." He blinked at her with what Merrit interpreted as watchful curiosity. "There is another woman in town. Lonnie was blackmailing her too, because she also is— that is, she is also secretive person like you."

"Don't tell me, Kate Meehan."

"How did you know?"

"Call it intuition." She remembered the day she met Kate and the way she had retreated into chilliness when Merrit caught her out in a soft moment. She'd also seemed well acquainted with Lonnie and Ivan. "What about her?"

"I think that Lonnie met Kate in his office the night of the party to receive more money from her. Lonnie told me he went to the shop to get his business credit card." He pulled on his earlobe. "Why did Lonnie want €1,000?"

"He just did. Isn't that the way blackmail goes? Start small and turn the screw?"

"I am supposed to believe that, I do not think so."

"Believe what you want. At least I know that Kate was in Lonnie's office that night. Where is she staying?"

Ivan shifted the suitcase from one hand to the other. "I would not tell you even if I knew. Do me a favor, do not mention me when you find her. She will skewer me alive."

The door shut behind him. Jittery, Merrit considered pumping her lungs but stopped herself. No, she was OK. She simply had to make a move. Now. Before Danny arrived to once again escort her to the Garda station.

"McCardle Cottage," Marcus said.

"What was that?"

"Where that Kate bird is staying. Overheard Mrs. Sheedy one day—she's that nosy she keeps up with the local rentals."

Merrit grinned at the man who wavered between homelessness and institutionalization. At last, a way to proceed. "You're a doll, Marcus, you know that?"

· 25 ·

Merrit and Marcus sat inside Merrit's car, catching their breaths after their successful foray into breaking and entering. An hour earlier, Merrit had parked in an unnamed turnout that led to nowhere except a jagged terrain of limestone hills. Vast rock terraces stepped up the hillsides. They were oddly symmetrical and graceful, like remnants from a lost civilization. Drystone walls undulated from the terraces, snaking over the lush pastures toward the Atlantic. The moon cast an otherworldly glow over stark rock and obsidian-like ocean, but even so, she was unprepared for the deep dark that was west Ireland at night. Froth from Atlantic waves coated the air in a moist chill that sank into Merrit's bones when she hooked arms with Marcus. Together, they stumbled across a pocked rural lane and toward the only sign of civilization for miles, McCardle Cottage, Kate's home away from home.

They'd waited until dinnertime, figuring Kate would be out playing the *femme fatale* in a pub. Marcus demonstrated how to jiggle the ancient casement windows into submission with the help of a penknife, a trick he'd mastered as an errant teenager.

Inside the cottage, Marcus kept watch at the front window

while Merrit tiptoed around with a nervous-giggly catch in her throat. Cupboards, cabinets, and closets revealed Kate to be a woman who prided herself on efficiency. Her powdered foundation was also a sunblock and concealer; black basics mixed and matched with various colored tops and accessories; grab-and-go health bars and individual yogurts sat in the fridge. Unlike Merrit, Kate kept her domain tidy to the point of anonymity. Outside the storage spaces, almost nothing showed of the woman except a toothbrush in a glass and a novel by Nuala O'Faolain. Merrit considered the book for a moment, then set it aside with a soft pat.

"Nothing in her garbage either," Merrit called. "Just one cotton ball in the bathroom and a yogurt container in the kitchen."

If she hadn't lifted the garbage can out from under the kitchen sink for a thorough peek, she'd have missed the weight discrepancy—heaviest yogurt container she'd ever encountered—and thus Lonnie's errant folder. Kate had hidden it at the bottom of the bin, beneath the plastic liner. Merrit flipped through the pages, fast at first, then slowing to a stop. She returned the folder to its hiding spot, wheezing with the effort to remain calm.

Now safe in her leased Nissan, Merrit held three deep breaths in succession. It would be OK. She didn't know all the facts yet. No need to panic.

Beside her, Marcus fondled an unopened gin bottle and gurgled in triumph. "I didn't need a sip either. That was a jolly time."

"I'm glad." Merrit forced a smile and gave his stubbly cheek a light pinch. "You were great. Shall we go?"

Merrit dug around in her pockets for her car keys. She almost missed Marcus's widening stare. "Jaysus H. Christ, it's the woman herself."

She caught a ghostly flicker in her side-view mirror. Adrenaline shot through her with such force that her fingertips tingled. Instinctively, she made a move for her inhaler but stopped herself from pumping up with a preventive dose. The last thing she needed was Kate witnessing her weakness. Fighting the urge to squeal away on burning tire rubber, Merrit told Marcus to stay put and exited the car. She dug her shaking hands into her jacket pockets. Her heart felt like it was about to burst out of her chest, but she gathered a long, deep breath of chill Atlantic air into her chest and held her ground.

A few feet away, Kate bent to rub her ankle above a high-heeled ankle boot. She looked as sinuous as a cat burglar in slim black pants and snug top. However, the effect was marred by a slash of red scarf across her neck. "Hope I didn't sprain it. Treacherous walking out here."

She didn't sound outraged. Merrit relaxed a little, but just a little. She didn't trust her voice yet, so she remained silent.

"Came over the hill, and there's your white car glowing in the dark. I recognized it from around the village and figured you were up to no good, so I parked and walked on down in hopes of catching you in the act." A wry smile flickered over her features. "I don't usually talk in clichés, so there you go. Congratulate yourself on surprising me. This is unusual, you know. Find anything?"

Kate also didn't sound worried, which worried Merrit. Maybe Ivan had it right to be fearful of her—especially if she did kill Lonnie.

Play it cool, she told herself. "Just a novel about the exorcising of personal demons."

Kate leaned against the car's hood, favoring her right leg. "Ah, another cliché, one we all share. Did you have a happy childhood?"

She had asked the question as if she already knew the answer. Merrit hesitated. "Up to a point."

"And how old were you when your childhood changed?"

"Thirteen. My mom died."

"Me, ten. From the good life to disaster when I was too young to control anything. That's not good for anyone's development."

Kate gathered herself and stood. Just like that, the coolness Merrit had noticed at the tea house returned like a hard coating. She watched Kate hobble her way back up the hill toward her car. Anxiety sweat soaked Merrit's T-shirt, but she waited. Five minutes later, Kate's high beams flashed as she passed them and parked. She entered her cottage with a jaunty backwards wave. Light illuminated the front window. Kate appeared. She watched them for a moment, shrugged, and snapped the curtains shut. Her shadow drifted away from the front window.

"By Jesus, that woman is scary," Marcus said when Merrit slid into the car.

"She's something all right."

Merrit fingered the printouts she'd removed from the folder before returning it to the garbage can. On the top page, four grainy people gazed up at her from a blurred image. There was dashing Liam, complete with the cape described by her mom. To his right, a woman with a remarkable resemblance to Kate held an infant. Her grin looked forced as she held the infant's arm in a wave toward the camera. On this woman's other side stood Andrew, the man her mom married.

Merrit swallowed hard and picked up the printout to view him clearly. He didn't look harsh so much as serious with his wide tie and slicked-back hair. He peered past Kate's mom and Liam toward Julia, who leaned in from the left to tickle the infant. Andrew focused his gaze on Julia, yet there they stood on opposite ends of the lineup. The caption read: *In the plaza*

Liam the Matchmaker socializes with his fans, (left to right) journalist Julia Chase (USA), Liam, Belfast native Adrienne Meehan with daughter Kate, and entrepreneur Andrew McCallum (USA).

Merrit dropped the printouts and started up the car. "Do you think Danny is still awake?"

"Danny-boy? Ah no, can't be going there."

"You can stay in the car while I talk to him. I have to give him something else to think about besides me as his favorite suspect. Do you think he'll forgive the little fact of our break-in?"

Marcus twisted hard to open the gin bottle. The paper seal crinkled and then his swallowing sounds filled the car. Merrit pulled the bottle away from his mouth. "I promised myself I wouldn't lecture, but I've grown too fond of you. You are a dear man, and the alcohol only distances you further from your family."

"Ellen will never be letting me near Mandy and Petey again anyhow."

She held his hand, felt it shake. "One thing I know, you'll never get the chance if you're still drinking."

With a gentle yank, Marcus took back his gin and settled it between his legs. "There goes your eyebrow, higher than ever. Now leave off, will you?"

She kissed his cheek. "Ellen is lucky to have you for a father."

Marcus lowered his head to hide his smile.

After his long day dealing with Ivan and Lonnie's mashed computer, not to mention Clarkson, Danny had longed to read the children traditional tales about Fionn and the salmon of knowledge, Deirdre of the sorrows, and King Lir's swan. Reading aloud to Mandy and Petey never failed to ease the tension from his shoulders. But, he'd missed his chance and now sat in the dark looking out their bedroom window. With the end of his work day had come the end of his investigation into Lonnie's death. Officially, at least. O'Neil had agreed to keep him in the loop on Clarkson's progress, not that that would amount to a piss in the wind.

Mandy mumbled and bike-pedaled the covers off her bed. Danny tucked her back in, and then adjusted the stuffed pink flamingo that threatened to smother Petey. By rights they should have converted Beth's nursery into a bedroom by now, but Ellen wanted none of that. They were two years past, and he rarely entered the baby's room anymore. More like a mausoleum now, a heavy presence within their midst that Ellen entered most evenings for prayer.

Unsettled, Danny rose and eased the bedroom door closed behind him. He hesitated on his way to the sofa for yet another back-aching attempt at sleep. On Sunday after working on Lonnie's case all day, he'd returned home to find a note taped to the unused blackberry tart dough. He'd be on the sofa until further notice.

Light from the big bedroom lit a line under the door. Hoping for a reprieve, he knocked and entered. Ellen sat on the rocking chair staring into space with a brush in hand. She'd pulled on her hair hard enough to straighten the waves.

"I have a new idea about Lonnie's death," he said. "He had issues with others besides Kevin."

Ellen parted her hair into three sections. Danny trembled to take on the task of braiding that she'd allowed him in the good days. He thought about the way Ellen's hair used to shine, the way she used to laugh with her head thrown back when Marcus played horse with the children.

"Should you be talking to me about the case?" she said.

He opened his mouth, about to confess that he wasn't on the case anymore anyhow, but Ellen interrupted him. "Best to stop then. Can't take chances on the promotion. All the hours you've been putting in have to lead somewhere. Indeed, anywhere but here."

He retreated, knowing it was futile to point out that the *here* Ellen detested was the *here* she revisited when she insisted on sitting vigil for Beth in the church and when she prayed in the nursery. The *here* that was her discontent, her misery.

He pressed thumb pads against his eyelids and held his breath to the count of ten. On the last exhale, he opened Beth's door, stepped inside, and closed it again. "Here you are, my sweet, but here we must part."

There wasn't much to the room. A toddler bed, dresser-changing table, toy chest, and low shelves packed with hand-me-down plush animals and child-safe toys. The furniture had to go. Mandy required a grown-up girl's room. He must force his family forward if only to lessen his sense of inadequacy, just as he must continue his investigation if only to produce enough conflicting evidence to cast Kevin's supposed guilt into doubt.

Headlights flashed across the animal alphabet poster. Danny trotted to the living room expecting Kevin looking to unload his shite. Clarkson had let him go earlier that day, but Danny hadn't had a chance to talk to him. Danny didn't recognize the white four-door that rolled to a stop. Sometimes tourists lost themselves on the back roads, but closer inspection had him muttering, "holy hell." He hurried outside and knocked on Marcus's window. Marcus obliged him by rolling it down.

"Have you gone stone mentaller?" Danny said.

"Listen to Merrit. We're after doing your job for you, that we are."

Merrit arrived at his side. She wore her hair in a loose ponytail. Tendrils danced around her face. Danny followed her gaze to Marcus—who was now waving like a maniac—and from there to the nursery window. Porch light outlined the recesses under Ellen's eyes, cheekbones, and jaw, and reflected glints off her eyes as she stared at Marcus. She retreated back into the shadows.

Marcus attempted to open the car door, but Danny leaned against it and directed his words to Merrit. "This better be worth the lashing I'm in for."

She held out two pieces of paper. "Read these. Ivan told me that Lonnie was blackmailing Kate also"—Danny grunted, annoyance increasing by the second—"so we went looking for Lonnie's missing folder at Kate's place. Seemed logical."

"Breaking and entering? Brilliant move." An unreasonable impulse to shake Merrit came and went. He grabbed the two sheets of paper she still held toward him. "What missing folder?"

"This proves that Kate has an agenda—"

"I realize that Kate is here for the same reason you are. The agenda being Liam. I'm not about to get roped into your sibling rivalry. You and Kate enter that ring on your own."

Merrit's determined expression withered. She rubbed her chest and dug into her jeans pocket. Danny waited her out as she pumped saline mist into her lungs once, twice, then three times. He understood that she needed a second or two to regain her calm with this fake medicine of hers. However, as he watched, she began to gasp.

Marcus jabbed Danny's thigh with his gin bottle, and Danny stepped aside. His father-in-law tumbled out of the car in a waft of gin fumes. "I've got you, Beth." At the same time, lamplight from within the house fanned toward them when Ellen opened the front door. "Who *is* this woman?" she said.

Merrit's chest jerked as she fought for breath. Her complexion drained of its healthy glow, and she stumbled forward onto all fours. Danny shoved the clippings into his pocket and knelt beside Merrit. "Ellen, grab her keys and get the car going." He tossed her his mobile. "And call a neighbor to come watch the children."

Marcus prodded Merrit, whose head hung between her arms. Her spine showed through thin cotton as she fought for breath, back arching with the effort. Marcus's plaintive cries for Beth tore at Danny as he pushed Marcus back onto the passenger seat. Within seconds, Merrit's limp form hung in his arms. She was so slight, hardly bigger than a teenager. He lowered himself into the back seat with Merrit still in his arms.

"Go. Ellen, drive."

Ellen sat stiff, staring back at him through the rearview mirror. "But I can't, not with *him* here."

"Don't do this, Ellen. Not now. Just drive."

Ellen shook her head and dashed the back of her hand across her eyes.

Danny struggled to keep his voice low. "Get your head on straight. This isn't about you."

On his lap, Merrit's respiratory efforts slackened. She quivered and gulped in shallow breaths, which scared Danny more than her gasps. She stared up at him with no expression except a mute fear of death—which was expression enough for anyone.

"Drive, woman!"

As Danny knew she would, Ellen focused her indignation into managing the steering wheel along the narrow lane, almost hitting their neighbor, who waved and called out that the children would be fine. Danny grabbed his mobile off Ellen's lap and called the local emergency number. He yelled at a triage nurse to send an ambulance out to them. "We're on our way to Ennis. Have the ambulance meet us on the road. We'll high-beam him to stop. I don't care if this is irregular. We're thirty miles away from the hospital, for Christ's sake. That's too long to wait."

By the time they screeched to a halt in front of the emergency entrance at Mid-Western Regional Hospital Ennis, the emergency services technicians had stabilized Merrit. One of the technicians snapped at Danny to keep out of the way and waved two hospital orderlies with a gurney toward the ambulance. Quickly, they lifted Merrit onto the gurney and ran her inside the hospital, leaving Danny alone in the parking lot with his fractured family.

Danny hovered halfway between the emergency entrance and Merrit's Nissan, out of which Ellen had shot the moment she'd turned off the engine. The supernatural glow from the outdoor floodlights veered her pale complexion into the green zone. Ellen with her tousled braid stood barefoot in a summer nightgown. Dirt on her feet. Dainty crucifix flipped over her shoulder. A woman Danny didn't know anymore.

As Danny turned to face Ellen straight on, Marcus heaved himself out of the car. In the silence after the hospital doors swallowed Merrit, Marcus's voice erupted as a wail. "I turned my back for a second, only a second, and she was on the ground."

A sound echoed against the hospital walls as ethereal and earthy as an animal's death cries. Ellen keened with two years' worth of grief. Marcus backed into the car door and stretched for the bottle. Danny held his ground, for once unwilling to mollify Ellen, protect Marcus. Oh please God oh please God, he whispered to himself.

Ellen's despair softened into heaves not unlike Merrit's. Then she was around the car and face-to-face with her father. She thrust out her chin. Marcus gazed at her almost in wonder. This was the closest they'd stood since Ellen tossed him out of the house.

"Don't you drink," she said with depleted voice. "Don't you soften your misery. I've carried it for the both of us so don't—you—dare—drink—from—that—bottle."

Marcus raised his hands in mute supplication. His lips quivered. He raised his hands a little more and gin sloshed onto Ellen's feet. She thrust herself at the offending bottle and smashed it against the car roof.

"You think I feel sorry for you? I don't. You've had it easy. You haven't had to live under Beth's roof, you haven't had to face Danny every day knowing that"—she choked to a stop and lowered her voice—"knowing that he ought to hate me."

She stepped away from Marcus, swaying. On a long inhale she straightened herself, her nightgown, and her necklace. "Take me home," she said to Danny. "*He* can remain here to wait for his friend."

During the drive home, Ellen leaned against the window and stared at herself in the side-view mirror. Danny hoped to Christ she saw herself clearly. He braked in front of the house. Their neighbor waved the OK as he closed their front door and went home. Ellen blinked and roused herself. "What does that woman want with *him* anyhow?"

"Say his name."

"With Marcus, my father, satisfied?"

"Not enough, I'm not."

Ellen's nightgown billowed around her knees as she strode toward the house. Danny considered dashing after her to apologize, but for what? He couldn't keep begging forgiveness for everything—his inability to keep up with the housework plus obtain a promotion; his close relationship with Kevin and Liam; even his faith in Liam's matchmaking skills despite their marital problems. "This mess is Liam's fault," Ellen had ranted on many occasions. "Why did he think we were a good match? He's a fraud."

But Liam was no more magician than Danny himself. Liam couldn't have predicted Beth's death, or Marcus's disintegration, or Ellen's inability to forgive, or Danny's imploding life.

He turned Merrit's car around for the return trip to the hospital.

Julia Chase's notebook

We most often meet at Our Lady of the Kilmoon at night, which is fine by me because the insomnia is back. It never seems to stay away for long...

I often wonder how to write up the private Liam, the mighty lion undone by a silver moon. Last night, light softened the edges of all it touched, and the air scented us with dew-laden grass, livestock, sea salt, and the overheated-engine smell of peat smoke. Kilmoon Church stood in genteel isolation, open air to the night as if shrugging off its Christian ties and embracing a more benevolent lunar goddess. The church seemed to watch us, indulging us our frail humanity and our unseemly trespass. We strolled around the site, taking in the uneven stones and skinny windows, the crumbling gravestones and tall Celtic crosses. We then stepped over a crumbling wall and piles of sheep dung as we approached the Celtic standing stone, which to me represented Liam and his nouveau-old ways.

Liam spoke little. He was preoccupied with Andrew, silly man, not understanding that Andrew is only a subject for the article—the skeptic—and nothing but a familiarity from my childhood. My world was filled with old-fashioned gents like him. My father, uncles, all of them expressed their affection through bank accounts and a kind of chauvinistic chivalry. In fact, Andrew reminds me of the stifling life I left behind. Contrary though it seems given Liam's career, Liam is the New World to Andrew's Old.

· 26 ·

Kevin parked alongside the plaza, hardly aware of the drive from home much less the half bottle of Jameson's he'd just sucked down. Across the street and half a block down stood the village church and between him and the church, two pubs. Tourists and locals alike drifted between them. Lonnie's death hadn't lessened the festivities in the plaza. In fact, Michael, the bakery owner, had set up his sound system, and dozens of couples swung around in time to tinny-sounding Celtic jigs.

Kevin imagined the inevitable whispers, curious glances, and stilted *'allos* that would follow him on his rounds. By now, everyone knew that he'd been questioned about Lonnie's death. What they couldn't know, of course, was the way Clarkson had almost pestered Kevin into confessing to Lonnie's murder just so Clarkson could call himself a hero and suckle his way that much closer to the O'Briens.

A pub crawl wasn't a grand idea, after all. Kevin angled out of his crooked parking job and drove on to the church. Deacon Fitzgerald's cottage sat in back of the parking lot. Kevin knocked, paused, and then continued knocking until a light ignited the pane above the door. Fitz's double-chinned, cherubic face appeared in the door crack. "Holy Mary, you're a sore on the eyes. Do you know it's after midnight?"

Kevin was tempted to offer him a swig of whiskey. Instead, he nudged the door open to reveal Fitz in blue flannel pajamas. "Have you the grace to let a sloppy, disillusioned man into the church?"

Fitz tilted his head back to view Kevin through his bifocals. "What's got you in this state?"

How to explain that he—who considered the gospels a genius stroke of propaganda perpetuated by the early church and who looked on Liam as the closest thing to a deity he could believe in—would like to idle awhile in hopes of absorbing generations' worth of faith that had soaked into the cool, stone walls.

"Solace for the sinner?"

"Cheeky." Fitz grabbed the bottle. "You'll not be taking that in with you, and you'll not be telling anyone about this either."

Fitz strutted ahead of Kevin with keys jangling. He clucked like a discontented hen. "Mary, mother of God, Kevin Donellan, you're fit to be laid out in a drunken stupor. Just see to it you don't do it on one of the pews. The bottle waits for you outside the side door. God bless you, son."

The church welcomed Kevin with stones set firm as arms crossed over chest, its cavernous silence the only embrace. In the faint light that filtered through the windows, the altar saints looked inconsequential while they waited for their vigil candles and tears. Crucified Jesus's crossed feet and thin legs faded into the loin cloth that faded into the dark. Kevin slipped into a smooth oak pew, genuflecting as the nuns had taught him.

Foolish to think Liam could live up to Kevin's expectations. No one was that good, not even the saints themselves who had foundered on their vices until they supposedly wised up.

With faith, he might learn to accept the current changes in his life. But his was the road to balk at change whatever its form, especially when it came to not one—bad enough, that—but two sisters. No doubt they had arrived to battle it out over Liam and the rights to his bloodline. He imagined them in fisticuffs. He imagined them punching each other with left hooks and upper cuts. He imagined them cartwheeling into chop-chop kicks and whizzing their arms around like blunt sabers.

"Oh Christ," Kevin said just to hear the words bounce back.

Footsteps sounded behind him. "Is that the sound of prayer I hear?"

Father Dooley's low and sonorous voice drifted along the saints' alcoves. Kevin crossed himself instinctively and stood to face the priest, who wasn't much older than Kevin but wore the smile of a soul with wisdom to spare.

"May I sit?" Father Dooley said.

Kevin nodded, hoping the whiskey hadn't started to ooze out his pores yet. The rustle of black fabric soothed him, and he relaxed down beside the priest. "Forgive me, Father, for I have sinned."

"Chronic ailment then?"

Kevin shrugged in response to the jesting—or was that sardonic?—tone in Father Dooley's voice. "Deac-Fitz knew you were in here, did he?"

Father Dooley nodded.

"I suppose I could use an ear. Confidence of the confessional?"

Father Dooley nodded again.

Kevin stared into a darkened corner where a St. Patrick statue stood ankle deep in snakes. "Liam lied. He said the knife that killed Lonnie was his, but it's mine. He said he bought it from an artisan in Galway, but I worked the wood myself. He said he opens letters with it, but I store it in my shop. He said he needed it to open birthday presents, which is true, but I brought it along because Liam is loath to admit to weakness. He lied to the bloody Garda, and I went along with it to save my hide against false accusations."

A leathery whoosh dipped toward them and away. The belfry bat. "That's your sin?" Father Dooley said.

Kevin slouched so his knees hit the pew in front of them and his bum slipped off the bench. He leaned his head back to stare into the gloomy interiors where gothic-style arches looked like ribs and a bat slept upside down. "Isn't that sin enough?"

"Hmm," Father Dooley said with the open-ended signal that Kevin remembered from his youth.

"I'm selfish. I don't want to share them with Liam."

"Hmm?"

Kevin related his family's 200 percent growth spurt. Kate and Merrit. Merrit and Kate. He angled his head to check on Father Dooley's expression. But no, the man was adept at his job, and besides yet, he'd heard worse. "I'm envious of them. That's the sin of it. I covet their blood ties."

Father Dooley cleared his throat, and in the murk Kevin thought he saw his eyelids flicker. "Envy is the signal that there's something you're to learn. Given your conflicts, I almost dare not say this, but have faith. Liam and you are father and son. God meant this test for reasons you may never know."

Kevin righted himself with a groan and leaned forward with elbows on the pew in front of them. "Do you believe in fate?"

"No. I counsel on the choice we have to sin, or not. Fate implies that choice is an illusion. It implies an untrustworthy and fallible God. He doesn't play that game. His will allows for choice and change."

The whiskey felt like acid in Kevin's stomach. He swallowed against the ache. "You believe God meant Liam and me to be father and son. How's that differ from fate?"

"One involves faith, the other doesn't. One offers hope, the other, nothing."

Out of the gloom a silver flask similar to Marcus's appeared.

"Shame on you, Father." Kevin accepted the offer. "Ah, Jesus, what is that shite?" he sputtered a moment later.

"Cognac. The finest there is so don't you be lifting your nose at it. I often have a quiet nightcap or two here when I can't sleep."

Father Dooley stood. He kissed his fingertips, moved his hand in the sign of the cross over Kevin, and disappeared into the gloom. "Don't go hiding behind the philosophical questions. Go deeper. What scares you so?"

"What indeed?" Kevin whispered, and then louder, "Cheers, Father."

"God bless, and watch where the whiskey takes you."

At the side door, Kevin retrieved his bottle and stood for a long moment inhaling the scent of dew about to form. He wavered, listening to tinny tunes echoing from the plaza, then started walking.

· 27 ·

lease ring doorbell on your left and wait, the sign said. So
Danny did. Five minutes later, an Internal Care Unit
nurse opened the door, glanced at him with bleary eyes
and sighed. "No, Detective Sergeant, she is not awake yet."

She shut the door in his face.

Danny returned to the second-floor waiting room with its
blue plastic chairs and garishly pink walls. He squeezed in next
to Marcus on the sofa seat. Marcus dozed with head angled to
the left, arms crossed over his stomach, and feet pigeon-toed.
No one noticed them, just two more poor souls waiting out
an illness as the early morning light filtered through a high
window. Danny had decided to sleep in the hospital rather
than return home to Ellen's wrath.

When the sunshine, weak as it was, reached Marcus, he
jerked awake and doubled over, retching. A passing nurse
paused and two steps into the room stopped in her tracks. All
she had to do was sniff to know Marcus's ailment. Danny drew
her back into the corridor with its yellow walls and dingy floor
tiles.

"Can you help him with something to ease the shakes?"

The nurse's hair net slipped as she strode away from him.
"I'm sorry."

"Surely there's a medicine you can give him?" he called after her.

To revive himself, Danny fetched Cokes and Cadbury Dairy Milk bars from the machines located inside the first-floor waiting room. The sun cast an ever-shorter shadow across the bubble-gum walls while he and Marcus waited. After two Cokes and a Cadbury, Danny told himself that it was no use leaving now only to turn around again when Merrit woke up—which had to be soon. Besides, he had nowhere to go. Not home. And the only thing calling him to the station now that he was off the case was unfinished paperwork.

He drummed his fingers against his thighs, knowing he had to do something. Anything. He couldn't take this waiting anymore. Waiting for Ellen to return to the land of the living. Waiting for his career to grind into the proper gear. Waiting for the bloody doctor for that matter.

"I doubt Ellen and I will make it," Danny said, the words like an emergency warning test. "Unless I finally do something. And even then, who knows? The children are growing stunted under the affliction that is our household. Ellen refuses to do anything to help herself—counseling, antidepressants, I don't care what. It's been two years. I'm not looking for miracles, but I do need her to try for Mandy's and Petey's sakes."

Beside him, Marcus gulped at his Coke. A sickly sheen covered his face, and he squirmed with feverish, eye-darting anxiety.

"Time to squeeze out the infection. At home I'll start with Beth's room. Here and now, I begin with you."

Marcus shook his head. "Ah, no, Danny, no."

Danny beckoned another passing nurse, this one with hair so short she didn't need a hair net. "Do you have a place for people with alcohol problems?"

"There's a treatment center up the coast. Just outside Ballyvaughn. The owner refurbished the old family home herself, so I hear."

"A bit rich, is it?"

"Payment plans if you're eligible."

"I ought to be. Fetch me the number, will you?"

He followed her away from the waiting room and jabbed at the Internal Care Unit button another ten times. The craving for progress of any kind felt like a sore tooth he couldn't yank out.

"Stop that." The nurse with short hair had returned. She waved him away from the ICU door. "Believe me, everyone knows you're out here."

She handed Danny the treatment center's phone number and strode away. He returned to Marcus and his expression of hurt-dog betrayal.

"I'm not leaving," Marcus said. "Merrit needs me."

"You're going to a treatment center, and when you're sober you'll have the den back. If Ellen and I fail it will be because I did what's right." He handed Marcus a Cadbury. "What do you really know about Merrit anyhow?"

Marcus spoke in a whispery monotone. "She has a crooked pinkie finger and looks a sight too snobbish and dainty when she's knitting—the way it pokes up. Broke it jumping her mum's horse—right after she died, this was—Christ, my head—the same day her father shipped the horse off to auction—just like that—one morning, fresh from crying all night, Merrit rode for solace and broke a finger but decided not to tell. Truth be told, she was that scared of him, she was—his anger." Marcus unwrapped the Cadbury, sniffed it, and set it aside with a gagging sound. "Later that day she came home from school and the horse that reminded her of her mum—gone. And her da never noticed the finger or the endless crying—imagine that—this is what I know about Merrit. And that she'd never send me away either."

"How would she help you then?"

Marcus shook his head against the cushion. "Piss off. Go find your bloody doctor."

But Danny at long last didn't need to because Doctor Timms entered just then. "Miss Chase is still asleep," he said in a harassed voice. "As I said earlier, a nurse will fetch you when she's ready for visitors. Might be awhile yet. I haven't seen an asthma attack like that—"

"I told the first doctor that she's not asthmatic."

Dr. Timms pursed his lips in a prissy scowl. The skin around his mouth had the soft, withered look of powdered old ladies. "She was diagnosed with a severe attack. We don't commonly take the word of amateurs, Detective Sergeant."

This man hovered in his late thirties, like Danny. This man probably made five times Danny's salary and didn't fret about money, didn't fret about promotions, didn't fret full stop. This man was a puke.

With a fortifying breath, Danny began again. "Merrit Chase is under investigation. As such, I confiscated one of her inhalers. It contained a saline solution. She's prone to panic attacks. Care to explain how she's suddenly become asthmatic?"

"If, as you say, she's not asthmatic, then we have a problem."

"Bloody right we do. Don't you yobs talk to each other? The inhaler she used last night should already be at a lab somewhere with a rush order to analyze its contents. One of the emergency docs, a Dr. Patel, said he'd see to it himself. Check it, will you?"

Doctor Timms returned to his imperial world removed from the amateurs.

Kevin entered the waiting room and spotted Danny on the only comfortable seat. Danny drooped over his knees with head in his hands, apparently as knackered as Kevin felt after his night of whiskey and no-good deeds. Kevin had woken up at about eleven to find himself on a lumpy mattress with Father Dooley's words about looking deeper repeating themselves like a bad mantra.

Best to get the confession off his chest then. Kevin shook Danny, who shot up with whites rimming his eyes. "Whah?" He goggled at Kevin. "What the devil are you doing here?"

"Good morning to you too."

Danny fumbled for a Coke, drained it, and let his head sink again. "Jesus God, I've gone and done it now."

"Fancy that, so have I." Kevin pulled up a chair and propped his feet on the cushion beside Danny. "You first or me?"

"You've got nothing on me. I'm just after bullying Marcus into treatment, only you need to be a bloody millionaire to afford the place so I'll be borrowing against the house without notifying Ellen, who won't accept Marcus back anyhow."

Kevin decided now wasn't the time to reveal his drunken escapade. "Where's Marcus now?"

"Upstairs on a twenty-four-hour hold. He'll be transferred to a place called Callahan House tomorrow afternoon." Danny jiggled his empty Coke can. "What brings you here?"

"Liam, who else? I woke up too late to drive Liam to the plaza—he drove himself, unfortunately. So I caught up with him at the festival, and he asked me to check on Merrit's status. I almost refused but a good deed might serve me well about now. Nice of you to wake up Liam last night, by the way."

"Not me, the hospital. The hospital-admitting lass asked me if she had family here." Danny straightened. "And since you're lucky enough to be family too, you can get us into the Internal Care Unit."

Kevin grimaced. "If it will help you liberate me from Clarkson, fine."

"Fat chance, that." Danny stood. "What did you want to tell me?"

"Nothing that won't keep."

Liam Donellan's journal

It had to happen that Julia met Adrienne Meehan, who loved nothing better than perambulating her infant girl with pride, assuming I would make a family out of us. I'd just finished my afternoon session on the plaza when Julia spotted Andrew with Adrienne on his arm and fidgeted to know who had captured his fancy. But I knew better. That was no romance. Those two had found each other by that accursed cosmic conspiracy called fate. Andrew was only too happy to forge an alliance with Adrienne after she claimed that I was Kate's pappy. Adrienne, likewise, knew a kindred spirit when she met one.

The sorry truth of it was that I didn't remember Adrienne when she first appeared on the plaza. The previous year, she had traveled down from Belfast for the festival. Adrienne and I shagged once, and she left after the festival. She was just another randy lassie. One of many. And I was one of many for her too—or so I thought.

Another sorry truth: I didn't care. I was the matchmaker!

If I had revealed the truth beneath the charade—which is to say, if I had trusted Julia—perhaps I'd not be here writing this tattered tale, this old man's journal of remorse. Perversion this mess has become, a perversion of love at my hands.

· 28 ·

Ivan stared around the monastic room with a crucifix above the bed and flat pillows on top of it. Connie had cajoled Father Dooley into lending Ivan the guest quarters used by visiting clerics, and Ivan's proximity to so much Catholic goodness chafed at him, especially now as he felt around under a mound of clothes for the laptop he'd managed to sneak out of Internet Café. His laptop. His only worldly asset, little did Danny know.

Danny wasn't entirely heartless. He could have kicked Ivan to the ground when he'd asked for a chance to pack his suitcase before being escorted from Internet Café. Instead, Danny had granted Ivan ten minutes. While Danny hovered, Ivan threw in his clothes and toiletries. He didn't care about the clothes, only the suitcase itself. He owned an ancient hardshell affair with many compartments, one of which had hidden his beloved laptop.

Ivan carried the laptop to the bed. Of course he'd kept copies of everything he'd gathered for Lonnie. This was practical for backup purposes if nothing else.

His goal then and now remained the same: stay in Ireland. Now more than ever, he must. For Connie. To do so, his best bet was trading information for leniency. Danny would surely welcome insights into the cash that Lonnie had collected the night he died, cash that implied Lonnie had stumbled onto a super secret. And if Lonnie the Lovely could figure it out, so could Ivan.

He depressed the laptop's power button and contemplated Lonnie's blackmail scheme, the truth of which Ivan had kept from Danny because it was one thing to nose around in outsiders' business—like Kate's, like Merrit's—quite another to mess with everyone's favorite local, Liam the Matchmaker. If word got out, Kevin himself would weigh Ivan down with bricks and sink him into the black horror of the nearest bog.

He shivered and forced his thoughts away from suffocation by mud, starting with Liam's arrival one morning in early August. "Never thought I'd see you grace my threshold," Lonnie had said, to which Liam had replied that there was no help for it. "Kevin will have my head as a traitor if he finds out, so keep it to yourself—and no gloating. He's too busy, and I need to learn something about this Internet."

Lonnie took time from his oh-so-busy schedule to teach Liam the basics. Then the old man shooed him away and typed in searches that were easy enough to recover afterward: *Andrew McCallum death, Andrew McCallum funeral, Andrew McCallum obituary*.

Ever nosy in true O'Brien fashion, Lonnie had ordered Ivan to look into this Andrew McCallum. Ivan's research hadn't led to much, admittedly, until he found the Chase-McCallum marriage announcement that mentioned the matchmaking festival. A few days later, in the newspaper archives over at the *Clare Challenger* office, Ivan uncovered a gossip snippet that hinted at amorous conduct between Liam and Julia Chase, soon to be Julia McCallum. "Hard to fathom, but our Liam lost at love," Lonnie said with a smack of lips. "But I wager it's more than that or he'd have asked Kevin for Internet help.

Pure bollocks that bit about Kevin being too busy—it's all the sod lives for, being a bloody saint."

Though Ivan wasn't privy to their conversation, he imagined Lonnie had tested the waters with the finesse of a blunt-force kick to the dangly bits. "What are you hiding from Kevin? How much will you pay me to keep my mouth shut?" That Liam bothered to pay money over something as mundane as an old love triangle hinted that sharks lurked beneath the surface. This much was too obvious, even to Lonnie.

Liam was well settled into Lonnie's payment plan by the time Merrit visited the shop. So like an American, she'd introduced herself as if they would care. Unfortunately for her, the moment she said her name, Lonnie danced up on his toes as if he'd like to whirl her around in a pirouette. A few chatty questions about her hometown in the States, a glance at her passport for "identification purposes," and Lonnie's eyes had glazed over with something bordering on arousal. "How many Merrit Chases could there be from fecking Gull's Hollow," he'd chortled after she left. "And born six months after Andrew McCallum married Julia Chase. I'm telling you, pretty Merrit is the fruit of Liam's randy loins. This is too beautiful."

Yes, beautiful for Lonnie, but not so beautiful for Ivan. It was just his luck that Lonnie died before Ivan had a chance to barter Merrit's arrest record for a cash bonus. Not that it would have mattered because by then Lonnie had had his eye on Kate.

Kate, with her sharp shoes and sharper gaze. Succubus. Satan's slut. Siren of death. Hell's spawn with tongue that could slit his throat—

A scratch of a heel on the outside stoop levitated the hairs on the back of Ivan's neck. At the sound of Kate's voice calling for him to open the door, please, he shot off the bed and shoved the laptop into the closet. He'd accidentally called Her Darkness from her lair.

"Ivan, come on now. I don't bite—unless you want me to, of course."

He opened the door to behold the woman nearly a foot taller than he was in her strappy sandals. Kate looked almost demure in a sheer white blouse with long sleeves and high neckline, except of course for the skimpy purple push-up bra and hint of nipple that displayed when she turned into the light. She stepped past him and took in the thin mattress and Holy Mary shrine. "Cozy."

"How did you find me?"

"Your rotund girlfriend. Found her at the hotel, and she was eager enough to point me in your direction when I mentioned potential employment for you." Kate leaned against the tall dresser, favoring a swollen ankle. "You told Merrit where I'm staying."

"She asked me, but I did not tell her because I do not know."

Her freakish blue gaze never wavered. "No matter. Merrit's thievery doesn't change anything. In fact, I would have done the same in her place."

"Thievery?"

"As in information about certain people gathered in a certain folder."

Ivan twitched away from her, closer to the window in the back of the room. He'd dive through the glass if need be. "So you did take Lonnie's folder. I was not sure."

"Of course. Who else?" She widened her eyes in mock surprise, then jumped at him with fingers outspread. "Boo!"

Her laughter filled the room, and a more joyfully mocking sound Ivan had never heard, not even from his dear old mother. He collapsed back on the squeaky bed. "Bygones. Just please do not maim me or pull out my eyeballs."

Kate picked up the Holy Mary statue that sat atop the dresser. She appeared to be considering how best to smash it. Instead, she smiled and set the statue back in its precise spot. "I adore you, Ivan. You're too precious."

She blew him a kiss and departed. Through a hole in the curtains, Ivan watched her stroll away. He found himself thinking about Connie as if with nostalgia, as if their fragile relationship had already imploded under pressure from her family, his spinelessness, and now Kate's oozing presence. To think, Connie hadn't inspired a second glance—*blin* no, she was an O'Brien after all—until she had single-handedly foiled her mother's petty dictatorship. Back in June, he'd sat at his usual lunch spot near the O'Brien statue, not far from Marcus. Little had he known that Lisfenora's founding patriarch, Patrick O'Brien, had been due for his annual cleansing courtesy of Mrs. O'Brien's ladies-in-waiting. Mrs. O'Brien arrived in rubber work boots and directed her minions to the dirty work of bird-shit cleaning. Poor Connie was forced to climb the ladder, but then Connie, she had stood atop that ladder in baggy overalls and girlish pigtails, peeked into the statue's crown, and said, "Stop with the water. There's a nest up here." While Mrs. O'Brien fumed, Connie stood with pigtails shiny as black corn silk, an avenging angel for all bird-dom and other underdogs. Ivan had been hooked.

Unfortunately, Kate now had her hooks into him. He must find a way to cut her sponsorship noose. No use evading deportation only to fall under the Evil One's command. She would suck him dry, and not in the good way.

A moment later Ivan had the laptop on his thighs, more determined than ever to discover Lonnie's super secret, the one that was worth €1,000 chunks of money. Then, possibly, hopefully, he'd know how to banish Kate. He closed his eyes, remembering Lonnie's smirk when Kate exited the shop that first day. Ever the one to hump a money-making idea to death, Lonnie had insisted that Ivan explore Kate's hard drive. Everyone has something, he'd said to Ivan, and I smell slag with a capital *S*. Lonnie knew his slags, this was true. And Kate's hard drive didn't disappoint. Not only did she design websites for strippers and porn stars—much to Lonnie's delight—but she also spent a good deal of time obsessing over Lisfenora's charismatic matchmaker. Lonnie had about leaked into his linen trousers he was that excited. In fact, Ivan had chosen that moment to leave the room because with Lonnie you could never be sure.

It was too funny. Merrit and Kate. They couldn't be more different, yet they had both come to collect on Liam's paternal obligations.

Ivan propped his head on the two flat bed pillows and moved the laptop onto his stomach, ready to acquaint himself with the data from Kate's computer. Unfortunately, Kate's archives consisted of endless newspaper articles about Liam. Mostly human-interest pieces that were too dull. Lonnie hadn't paid him enough to troll through all of them. Ivan had simply transferred the lot to Lonnie's machine, kept copies for himself, and tried not to think about the money Lonnie wasn't paying him. Already bored, Ivan started with 1975, the year in question. One by one, he opened files and scanned their contents. They were bleary, no doubt scanned into Kate's computer from photocopies, and they appeared with stock photos of Liam sitting on a rock wall with his matchmaking ledger. This concession to publicity showed in his tight expression. The caption read, *Liam the Matchmaker at rest from the masses at his favorite scenic spot, historic Kilmoon Church.*

Thirty minutes later, he cut short a yawn and jerked up into a sitting position. "Holy *chert*."

Our Lady of the Solace Catholic Orphanage
By the Order of the Cloister of St. Mary's in the Field
Limerick, County Limerick, Ireland

Preliminary Enrollment for Succour

Dated, this day, 28 September, 1975, I, Novitiate Evangeline Sarah, swear on my faith and my oath to the Holy Roman Catholic Church that the information below is true, and that with regards to my conduct, the named child did not arrive through any means morally, ethically, or legally dubious to the cause of this Order.

Child's Name: Kate (from infant necklace)

Age: Can roll over so three to four months

Reason for Succour: Left on our step

Mother's Name: Unknown

Father's Name: Unknown

Comments: I was on duty early this morning, after Prime, when a man rang the bell. He took pains to keep to the shadows, but even so I couldn't help gasping because one of his hands was mangled to a pulp. He was tall, thin, red-haired, and held the hand against his chest as he staggered away. He ignored my call and stepped into a waiting vehicle. I didn't see the plate number, or whether the driver was male or female.

Special Care Instructions: The child is in good health and of lively disposition. My initial opinion is that she was not abused or neglected though she was hungry when she arrived. She's not taking well to a bottle so I've requested a volunteer nursing mother from Father Gerald's parish.

· 29 ·

While Kevin waited next to the locked Internal Care Unit door, Danny lassoed his thoughts back around the case that wasn't his anymore. From his jacket pocket, he pulled out the clippings that Merrit had nicked from Kate's place. The gossip snippet ran with a photo that showed baby Kate in the midst of these shadowy parties from yesteryear. Charismatic Liam. Julia Chase, his lover. Adrienne Meehan, his ex-lover. Andrew McCallum, the unknown factor. The photo unnerved him, but even worse was the second clipping, a confidential orphanage memo that could only be construed as evidence that Liam had abandoned Kate. The notion made Danny's head hurt. And what would it do to Kevin?

Kevin appeared. "Off your arse. The door has opened."

Shoving the papers into his pocket, Danny approached the ward with Kevin. A doctor stood in the entrance. She wore a stethoscope around her neck and nodded at Kevin. This doctor, a Dr. Greene, appeared fresh, young, and attentive. Just what Danny liked in a medical professional.

"A severe asthma attack," she said, "as we initially diagnosed."

"I already told the—" Danny started.

"Please. Do you know anything about asthma?"

Danny shook his head while Kevin said, "Just the usual."

"I'll be as plain as possible then. Think in terms of two types, mild and severe, and we're not concerned with severe in this case. Mild asthmatics need rescuing every now and then, and their inhalers normally contain a broncho-dilator called Salbutamol, or Ibuturol in the States." She smiled. "Good thing Dr. Patel was here last night. He's a dear man and was interested in Miss Chase's case. Just now, he rang up with the findings that came from his friend at the lab. I take it Miss Chase began with a panic attack and used the inhaler?"

Danny had assumed that this much was the given. "She pumped herself up and still couldn't breathe. In fact, the attack grew worse."

"Exactly. Panicked, couldn't breathe as expected, more panic still. Her adrenaline levels spiked, which can cause much cardiac stress on top of everything else."

"She could have died then."

"A slight possibility, yes. How many times did she inhale?"

"Five or six."

"Precisely."

Exactly what? Precisely what? Danny's confusion had to be caused by sleep deprivation. He glanced toward Kevin, who appeared equally puzzled.

"That's more than enough to cause a crisis," Dr. Greene continued. "She'd have needed Salbutamol to reverse the effect of the attack. Here's the kicker. Doctors can test for asthma by administering ever increasing amounts of a drug called Methcholine. This drug induces bronchial spasms—asthma attacks—and is only found in controlled medical settings."

"What does this have to do with anything?" Kevin said.

Dr. Greene squared her shoulders. "Miss Chase was poisoned."

"Poisoned?" Kevin said loud enough to cause a man with a head bandage to stumble as he passed them in the corridor.

"Shocking, isn't it?" Dr. Greene turned away. "Come along."

Danny lagged behind Kevin and the doctor. For all he knew, Merrit's poisoning had nothing to do with Lonnie's death. Given her presence in Ireland, either she was found innocent of euthanizing Andrew McCallum or the case was dropped—all of which said nothing about her guilt. Unlikely though it might be, someone could have wanted a little revenge and slipped her a bad inhaler before she left the States.

"Hold up, Doctor," he said. "You're saying that Merrit sucked on an inhaler that contained this Methcholine drug, which *causes* asthma attacks and is hard to obtain."

"Right. It's not as if you can buy Methcholine on the black market and prepare a handy mixture. Your culprit has a contact within the medical community here in Ireland."

"The inhaler I handed off last night wasn't an American model?"

"No."

So much for his unlikely theory.

Dr. Greene directed a sympathetic gaze to Kevin. "We'd best get on with it then because Merrit is awake but drugged. She might fall asleep on you. Ready to go?"

Kevin's silence stretched on for a second too long, so Danny took over. "Excuse him, that would be a yes, he's ready to see his sister."

Kevin frowned in response to the word "sister" but nodded agreement. They stopped in front of a door. Dr. Greene entered first, telling them to wait a moment.

"Maybe," Kevin said in a low voice, "Merrit overdosed on purpose to prove herself innocent of Lonnie's murder. Maybe she was willing to go that far."

"Nice try, but she wasn't faking the initial panic attack, and I should know because I let it slip that Kate is her sister. I assumed she knew."

"Brilliant, Sherlock."

Dr. Greene waved them into the room and departed with a warning that they had five minutes. Danny stepped ahead of Kevin to get a good look at Merrit. Her skin looked thin enough to crack, and her lips were cracked already. She contemplated the ceiling without glancing in their direction. "Just so you know, I'm not drugged up enough to confess to something I didn't do."

"Your confession can wait," Danny said.

"Kind of you, I'm sure. If I were Blanche DuBois I'd say something about the kindness of strangers, but lately strangers haven't been so kind." She caught Danny's eye. "Kate—she's really my sister?"

"Apparently."

"Everyone knew but me." Merrit rolled so her back faced them. Her huff sounded like half a yawn. "I don't understand anything, I guess."

Danny waved down Kevin's spasm of impatience. "There's a question about your inhaler."

"I must have received one with medicine inside it by mistake. It tasted funny but I didn't think to question it."

"What the devil is she talking about?" Kevin whispered.

Merrit heard him. "The inhalers I use are placebos for medical testing. They're filled with saline, which tastes like nothing." A shoulder blade appeared out of the covers as she shifted further away from them. "Psychiatrists can get them for their patients. By the time my childhood doctor figured out I was prone to panic attacks, not asthma attacks, I'd gotten used to the ritual of inhaling to calm myself down. Understand now?"

Kevin rolled his eyes and circled a finger near his temple. Danny shot him a warning glance, but unfortunately, Kevin could restrain himself no longer. "What do you want with Liam?"

"Just to meet him. Nothing earth-shattering."

"That's utter shit. You're here for the same reason Kate is—"

"Oh? And why is Kate here?"

"Kev, don't answer," Danny said. "That's not the point."

"Maybe it is," Merrit said. "Kate bears watching."

"And you don't?" Kevin said.

"Detective Sergeant, you listen then." Merrit waited while he dragged a chair around the bed and sat down. "Last night, the folder I mentioned? Lonnie stored his—research materials, I guess you could say, in it. Kate managed to snatch it before you locked down Internet Café. This proves she was at the café twice that night. The first time she paid Lonnie his €1,000, but he would hardly let her walk away with his folder, so she must have—"

"This entire mess is about sibling rivalry, after all?" Kevin interrupted.

"Danny said the same thing." Her eyelids drooped and she rubbed them open again. "Why do you both say rivalry?"

"Because you two are each a bead short of a rosary?" Kevin said.

"You'd like that." Sleep softened the edges of her voice. "Kate though, she—"

"How's that?" Danny said, but too late. The men watched her drift to sleep.

"I'm not buying her lost-little-lamb act," Kevin said.

Danny stood. "She's holding back is what she is. But then, so is Ivan."

A light knock jerked Ivan out of a doze. His stomach tightened, and he held his breath. One dose of Her Evil Darkness per day was already too much for his nerves.

"Ivan?" Deacon Fitzgerald called. "You there?"

Grunting with relief, Ivan opened the door to behold his

new neighbor carrying a black cat. "Take care of her for a few hours, will you? She's on a new medication or I wouldn't ask. I've got to run off to a parishioner's house—family emergency." He draped the cat over Ivan's shoulder. Claws dug through his T-shirt. "Her name's Bastet."

Ivan closed the door on convivial festival sounds and lamb curry aromas wafting out of the plaza. The cat crawled over his shoulder and landed on the bed with a low growl. Scooting the cat over, Ivan reclined with the laptop on his stomach. Bastet licked a dainty paw then drew four bloody lines across the back of his hand. Within a second she was settled next to Ivan's head and purring in his ear. Just like a typical woman, he thought. Drawing blood one second, fawning the next. He missed his shop cat, his even-tempered *male* shop cat, and hoped Connie was taking good care of him.

"Where do I look next, cat?" he said.

Ivan had found the *Preliminary Enrollment for Succour* for infant Kate easily enough. It was one thing to hold an orphaned daughter over Liam's head, quite another to threaten publicizing that Liam was the one to abandon her. Could be Lonnie used this information to increase Liam's, maybe even Kate's, payments to the €1,000 Danny had mentioned, but why would Merrit cough up extra money?

The answer was that she wouldn't and this wasn't the super secret. Lonnie must have discovered yet something else. However, novitiate Evangeline's report brought up an interesting question: how did Kate confirm the tall, thin, red-haired man was Liam? The mangled hand was interesting, true, but still, the description was generic enough to fit thousands of Irish men. It wasn't likely she'd come to Lisfenora on a hunch, not Kate.

Curious, Ivan looked up the creation date for the orphanage document. Kate had scanned in the document four years previously. Four years she'd searched for a tall, thin, red-haired man, possibly with a gimpy hand. That was diabolical dedication.

"I suppose that does not matter to me," he said to Bastet. "Except for Connie, you females are treacherous. Devious. In fact, you must be Kate's familiar sent here to curse me." The cat nipped his earlobe.

Ivan returned to Kate's archives. He'd already perused the 1975 folder, so he opened the 1976 folder. Ivan scanned the contents and found nothing but the typical boring publicity. He continued on, folder by folder, dozing and then shaking himself awake. What seemed like hours later, he opened the 1980 folder. More of the same. The substance of the articles changed little from year to year. *Lisfenora Boasts Largest Turnout. Mr. Marriage Matchmaker.* Ivan had only to read the first few sentences to know he'd find nothing interesting.

A file titled *Zero Hour* caused him hope, then ennui, when he opened it to read the full headline: *Zero Hour Pressure for Matchmaker.* Reporters manufactured drama to camouflage the same old facts.

He yawned, dozing off again. Bastet, who'd been chewing on his hair, chose that moment to pounce on the keyboard in a flurry of black limbs. She wrapped her forelegs around one of Ivan's hands. Her back legs scrabbled against his arm.

"*Chert voz'mi,* get away from me!" Ivan flung out his arm. Bastet sunk her teeth into his thumb and let go. Bloody wheals covered his arm and hand. He'd probably die now like in that American song "Cat Scratch Fever."

Ivan was about to toss the cat into the bathroom when the word *dead* snagged his attention. Feline antics atop the keyboard had caused the computer to scroll further into the document. It took him a moment to understand that he was now gazing at a second article that Kate had imbedded into the file so that it followed the *Zero Pressure* nonsense. Dead crafty, that Kate.

"Ah," Ivan breathed and wondered if Lonnie had jumped for joy when he landed on this treasure. Ivan clicked once to close the file, his thoughts whirring through Lonnie's likely thought process—painful as thinking must have been for his ex-boss—until he was satisfied that he knew what Lonnie had believed, which in turn must be what Kate still believed.

Ivan jumped to his feet. He, Ivan Ivanov, now had data that he could use to bargain for his sorry life. So could he, Ivan Ivanov, not act for once? But how? And who did he think he was? The pitiful fact remained that who you knew set the course for your life. In Soviet Russia, then independent Belarus, and now Ireland. The same all over again: buggered for lack of status.

Unless.

Ivan returned to the laptop. "If I were the Internet café owner, what would I do to turn profit?" he asked Bastet.

For a start, sell coffee. Ivan tapped lightly on the keys without depressing them. He set his brain to turning over the matter, all the while hoping that O'Brien the Elder maintained a pragmatic view of business. After all, better to keep Internet Café going than to close it down. Business was business, money was money, and Mr. O'Brien was an expert on both. Maybe Mr. O'Brien would like to know what Lonnie had discovered. Maybe he would like to keep Lonnie's schemes from becoming public knowledge. Maybe he, Ivan Ivanov, could remain in Ireland without Kate's hellish patronage and, best yet, remain with Connie too.

Julia Chase's notebook

When it comes to the business of matchmaking, Liam focuses with an attentiveness that invites you to spill your deepest truths. He leans in, crosses his legs in your direction, and touches your shoulder with the hand he drapes along the seat back. He writes notes in a leather-bound book whose heyday disappeared with the Dark Ages.

He insists there's a method to his madness. "I must get at what's quirky or difficult about the person for, ultimately, the people we're most compatible with are those with whom our personal demons or weaknesses find the most solace. I think of it in terms of music taming the wild beast. A truly compatible and loving couple are each others' music."

Liam does have an eerie way of honing in on our fragile essentials. He's insightful and kind with his petitioners.

More crap. I can't concentrate, and I'm delirious with exhaustion. Today Andrew McCallum showed up on the plaza with a woman named Adrienne Meehan. The first thing she did was raise her sweet baby to Liam's face for a kiss. I felt a tad jealous, I'm not sure why. Could be my maternal instinct kicked in, or, could be I'll miss Andrew's comfortable attentions. (What girl wouldn't?) Could be I didn't like Adrienne's playfulness with Liam. Now, thinking about it, I'm uneasy.

· 30 ·

Two hours after talking to Merrit in the hospital, Danny sat at his desk in the Garda station, enduring sidelong glances from the uniformed guards. No one had ventured so much as a fart in his presence. Danny's men were out canvassing the partygoers as far as he knew, and to his relief, Clarkson was nowhere to be seen. He considered the stack of papers sitting in his in-box and rolled away from the desk.

Since Merrit was indisposed, he decided to tackle Ivan again. The little maggot was still holding back. Danny rang Connie O'Brien, who tried her best not to tell him where Ivan was holed up. Across the room, the door to the waiting area opened, disrupting the low-key buzz within their bullpen. Voices trailed into the room. At the sight of Clarkson and O'Neil hauling in Kevin, the room erupted in a louder buzz. Danny hung up on Connie.

Kevin wore handcuffs. He caught Danny's eye and grimaced. "Long story."

"Shut it." Clarkson sounded harassed yet oddly content. "O'Neil, get him into an interview room." He scanned the room, ignoring Danny. "Pickney, help out the men at Merrit's flat. Need new evidence gathering. Make sure there are no mistakes. O'Toole, bring the landlady in. I want her statement all but embossed in gold."

Clarkson strode toward the office that he used when he visited the Lisfenora station. No doubt to report to the O'Briens and to call the media in hopes of getting a quote in the papers.

While Clarkson was occupied, Danny visited the video monitoring room where O'Neil fiddled with the equipment. "Tell me in as few words as possible."

"Breaking and entering, that's what."

"Ah, Christ." It was a bloody epidemic. First Ivan, then Merrit and Marcus, now Kevin. "And?"

"And Clarkson's happy to arrest him for that while he works up the homicide charge."

"Don't turn on the video yet, and keep an eye out for Clarkson."

In the interview room, Kevin sat with one knee jangling and eyes closed. "What the holy hell did you do?" Danny said.

Kevin peeked at him with one eye and closed it again. "That something I meant to tell you in the hospital this morning? It's a brilliant tale. Sometime in the wee hours of this morning, in a whiskey-induced attempt at genius, I broke the crime-scene tape and the flimsy lock on Merrit's flat to seek a few answers on my own. Seemed like a sound idea at the time, but all I got for my efforts was a spiral notebook taped behind the headboard before I passed out on her bed. This morning Mrs. Sheedy rode me with her broom stick all the way into the plaza. The notebook is still in my truck if you want it. You know where the spare key is."

"You daft prick." Danny rubbed at his face, too exhausted to chide Kevin further. "I'll see your truck gets home."

The audio system hissed to life with O'Neil's voice. "Clarkson."

"Better go kiss his hairy arse," Kevin muttered.

So Danny went, mindful of the tension spreading down his neck. In the corridor Clarkson stood rocking back and forth.

All he needed was a hand tucked into a red coat to turn him Napoleonic. "You're not to even sniff in Kevin Donellan's direction, am I clear?"

"Yes, sir. You should know that the other suspect, Merrit Chase—"

"Speaking of Merrit Chase, get one of the officers not on festival duty to round her up so O'Neil can get her statement. Most of her belongings appear to still be in the flat. We need to know if anything went missing since you escorted her off the premises."

Oh, there was something missing all right, and Danny would bet his last few pennies that Merrit wouldn't mention the spiral notebook when she made her statement.

Danny stared at a cherry birthmark covering half of Clarkson's hand and stretched for a neutral tone. "As I was about to say, Merrit Chase is in the hospital. She had a severe asthma attack."

"Fine. Let me know when she'll be up for questions. But that's it. No interference out of you." He stepped away, then paused. "By the way, her flat was clean. Nothing there to incriminate her."

"Except for the inhaler I bagged yesterday." Not to mention the notebook Kevin had found that might contain a few hints about what hid beneath Merrit's calm demeanor.

Danny wonderd at his sanity even as his next words fell out of his mouth. "I'll wager you on Kevin's guilt. When it comes to light that Kevin isn't guilty, you'll forget any disciplinary action."

Clarkson barked a laugh. "You're playing with your career, you know that, don't you?"

"So I've nothing to lose."

"I can almost respect that if nothing else at the moment."

With that, Clarkson disappeared into the monitoring room, leaving Danny to wonder if Marcus's treatment expenses would have been better spent on a loony bin for himself.

· 31 ·

Kevin's pulse echoed against his eardrums. He resisted the urge to pace the interview room. He'd refused to talk, or even to call a solicitor, so Clarkson had left him to stew for the past few hours. Kevin reminded himself to neither avoid nor glare at the video camera lens.

Behind him, the door opened. "Donellan," Clarkson said, "I'm allowing you a visitor. Hopefully she'll talk you into calling your solicitor."

"Kevin?" came the familiar, soft voice.

Emma approached and waited for him to invite her into a seat, for she was polite. Had always been, to the point she'd sent him a thank-you note for believing that Lonnie had raped her after Liam's party last year.

"I heard," she said. "News is already circulating. You were in that American woman's flat—the one who dated Lonnie?" She shook her head, agitated. "Never mind. It's none of my business."

With a vague sense of disquiet that had nothing to do with his current dilemma, Kevin motioned to a desk that sat along the wall in front of him. She didn't meet his gaze until she'd settled herself, and then when she did, her careful expression cracked.

"I'm so sorry, this is my fault, and if not for me, you'd be fine."

Kevin quieted his jouncing legs as a wave of regret washed over him. He remembered how many times she had hugged him only to have him yield for a stiff moment and then pull away.

"I was hoping we'd get a chance to talk this week. After the party, I thought—" She lapsed into silence, then tried again. "Don't you remember?"

Kevin blinked. They'd chatted early in the evening—she'd stolen a sip out of his beer—but surely she wasn't talking about that. "I was beyond plastered. Why? Did we talk later in the evening?"

Kevin could always tell when Emma was tired. Her left eyelid drooped. It also drooped when she was upset. Like now. But then he didn't know what it meant to be raped and judged partially to blame by her fellow Lisfenorans, only to face the attention again a year later.

"Never mind. It doesn't matter." She stood in a swift and graceful movement. "Just call me a class A screwup. Please call a solicitor, will you?"

She knocked and the door opened. Kevin jumped toward the door, knocking over his chair in the process, but he was too late to grab the knob before it clicked shut. "Shit," he shouted. "Shit shit shit." Then lower, "I'm sorry too."

He stumbled back as the door reopened. Clarkson stepped inside.

"Congratulations, Romeo, you sent her away in tears."

"You get your wank up on voyeurism?"

"Watch the tone. If you're not going to call your own solicitor, we'll have to wait for one from the court to arrive. Meanwhile, shall we talk anyhow?"

Hell no, Kevin knew better than that. He'd landed himself in trouble enough last year, supposing that honesty—"Sure

I pummeled Lonnie after he raped Emma. Sure I was angry when I saw them together at Liam's party, who wouldn't be?"— would paint him in a better light.

Instead of talking, Kevin righted his chair and let himself sag with head on chest.

Liam Donellan's journal

This evening at the Slanty Shanty Pub, Kate stared me down. All through my conversations with the shy, the lonely, the insecure, there she sat. Kate, she drained my energy what with her tilted lips and cocked head. I finally beckoned her, which was, of course, what she wanted, stalker that she is. She smelled of bruised apples, and she lowered herself to my side like a cat.

"You'd best scribble something, hadn't you?" she said.

So I did: Unmatchable.

"I'm in a quandary about Merrit."

No doubt, *I wrote.*

"It's too crowded in your house."

Indeed, *I wrote. "*Insightful,*" said I.*

What, I ask myself, is the solution to the current state of chaos? I must think carefully as I didn't back in 1975. I must account for the unexpected as I didn't that last evening within her royal Kilmoon's shadowed embrace. What a fine night that was too. The remnants of the day's sun and harvest on the breeze, and a moon big and bold near the horizon, lighting my way and shining off Kilmoon's rock walls. Kilmoon shone like I'd never seen her, already prepared for me it seems now.

· 32 ·

On Friday morning, Kate sat like a dutiful sister beside Merrit's bed in the Internal Care Unit. She had only wanted to peek in at the waif, ask a question or two about her condition, and return to Lisfenora. All she'd had to do was tell the truth—novel, that—and mention their sisterhood. Thank Christ the waif was dead-asleep under the influence of narcotics. Kate had taken advantage of the nursing staff's preoccupation with a patient in another room to pull up a chair.

The moonstone necklace that Merrit normally wore was missing, probably removed when she was admitted to the hospital. Kate opened the drawer in the bedside stand, but the necklace wasn't there. Too bad. The precious gift from Merrit's mother matched Kate's eyes perfectly.

"Tough blow, your mom dying," Kate said in a voice low enough not to wake Merrit. "But at least you knew her. As for me, when I was ten, my adoptive parents found themselves pregnant. Talk about a surprise. From then on, it was the ugly-stepchild syndrome. I was the free nanny and housekeeper. That's it, pretty simple really."

Except that it was never that simple. She'd loved her parents to distraction and gladly played their serving wench in hopes they'd return her love. She might not have existed anymore, not truly. The day she realized this was the day she realized she could depend only on herself. Self-sufficiency was her catchword. For good, for ill, it didn't matter. She preferred herself as she was now to the groveling puke of a girl she once was.

Merrit snuffled and rolled toward the wall. Kate tensed until Merrit's even breathing resumed. Best to leave. She felt too much like the little puke girl in this place, just another hushed voice no one heard.

Instead, Kate settled deeper into her chair. The movement was a reflex remembered from childhood. She had too much experience with medical settings and their antiseptically controlled chaos. Almost a second home, in some ways. All those hours, waiting, simmering.

She found herself continuing her one-sided conversation with the waif.

M errit rolled onto her back and stared at the cracked ceiling tiles after Kate departed. Kate's low voice and her words were corrosive. They'd eaten away at Merrit while she pretended to sleep. A portly nurse with pink lipstick and two orderlies appeared just as Merrit pressed the call button.

Merrit cleared her throat against foul slime stuck to the back of her tongue. "Can I have a Percocet or whatever you give out here?"

"Are you in pain?"

Yes. The worst. "Well—"

"Then no." She rattled the IV drip. "Nice to have visitors, at least when you're awake. Like those two handsome men yesterday. I don't mind saying that the taller one was nice looking."

Detective Sergeant Danny Ahern, yes. With Kevin. Some visitors. They were about as compassionate as Kate. They must have practiced their good-cop-bad-cop routine before arriving, though she'd have imagined Danny as the hard-ass; Kevin, the patient listener. But then, maybe not. Kevin now detested her on principle it seemed. Come to that, was there anyone in the village who liked her besides Marcus?

What a lonely, useless thought, here in this sterile, foreign hospital with a nurse chattering on about how wonderful it was to have visitors.

The nurse emptied Merrit's pee bag and announced that she was ready for the female medical ward on the first floor. One orderly wheeled in a chair while the other lifted her out of the bed. Merrit didn't notice her surroundings again until a new, skinny nurse tucked her into a new bed. "There now. Better?"

High ceilings, Pepto Bismol colored walls, and floral curtains around the beds. "Better," Merrit agreed.

The nurse with the pink lipstick peeked around the curtain. She handed Merrit a message slip. "Almost forgot that a phone call came in for you. I couldn't make out everything but hopefully enough."

Merrit read the note and struggled to sit up, only to fall back again, still too weak to be much use yet.

· 33 ·

Many miles north of the hospital, Merrit stood before Callahan House after a long and expensive taxi ride from the hospital. North Atlantic tides breathed in and out along the rocky shore a few blocks away, reminding Merrit of the hiss of Andrew's oxygen tubes during his last days. She shook her head against the memory and peered up at Callahan House. The grand old home from a bygone British era resembled the B&Bs tucked along the Northern California coast, except sturdier with deep gables and short chimney stacks. Irish winters kept adornment to a minimum, but even so, the deep blue trim and removable planter boxes comforted Merrit.

She had understood Marcus's garbled telephone message well enough, but she'd had to ask a nurse what "Callahan House" meant. It had taken her all day to gather up the strength to walk out of the hospital. Now, her limbs required a few seconds to catch up with the impulses her brain sent them as she teetered toward the entrance and then through it. Entrance chimes prompted the arrival of a woman with protruding collarbones and a name tag that said Sandy.

Merrit hoped her voice didn't betray her shakiness. Her

lungs and heart felt like sore muscles. "My father, Marcus Tully, left me a message this morning. He said he needed to talk."

Sandy jutted out a chin as sharp as her collarbones in response to Merrit's voice. "From the States then."

"We were estranged until recently. I grew up with my mother in California."

"Ah," Sandy said as if familial estrangements were her stock in trade. She considered Merrit. "His son-in-law filled out the paperwork though. You would be related how?"

"The son-in-law is married to the daughter from the second wife. I'm from the first. Like I said, estranged."

Sandy continued to scrutinize Merrit, who held her gaze easily enough. She was too weary to do anything else.

"I'll make an exception this time."

After thoroughly searching Merrit's purse and pockets for contraband, Sandy led the way up the main stairs and down a hallway with thick carpet and amateur paintings. "From previous participants of our program. We have an art therapy class that is a wonder." She stopped before a door and explained that the facility didn't allow visitors or phone calls within the first two weeks. However, since Marcus had arrived under more than the usual duress and Merrit had traveled so far, well, she saw no harm in a visit. "Frankly, our doctor couldn't make sense of him. Something about a birthday party, so we let him have the one phone call."

A pager attached to Sandy's belt buzzed. She glanced down at it and frowned. "I must go. A crisis with one of the other patients. Have Marcus ring for me when you're ready to leave."

The door opened on a room designed to soothe raw nerves. Walls painted the color of sea foam surrounded shaggy hand-woven area rugs, Irish landscapes, and quilted pillows. Marcus stood before the window. He didn't turn around until

Sandy left, and then it was with a shy downcast expression. His hands shook.

Merrit had a feeling that he was unsure how to relate to her as a sober man, so she decided to treat him as usual. "Nice bathrobe."

Relief cleared the wrinkles from his forehead, but he didn't smile. "I feel like a queen, and I'm not talking Nefertiti either."

He was far more clean and presentable than Merrit but also diminished somehow, as if having choice taken from him—even one so self-destructive as drinking—had left him with nothing but his clammy, greenish skin.

Marcus scanned her up and down with a dubious crinkle between his eyes. "A return call would have been fine. I was only that half-cracked to be here, and I wanted to check on you besides. Had to throw a fit to get the phone call."

"The staff wouldn't let my call through for some reason, so here I am instead. I snuck out of the hospital and cabbed it. Danny's still got my car as far as I know."

"Ay, he'll keep it safe, that bugger." His voice rose. "Danny didn't sign my life over. He doesn't have the right. I could leave anytime."

Merrit approached the bed and ventured a hand across the quilted duvet. Exhaustion dulled her senses. She longed to sleep her tired body and mind into a fit state again, if she could recall what that fit state might be. She'd like to return to the horses of her youth. Perhaps she would again someday.

She sat on the bed as Marcus said, "I could leave right now with you."

"You could leave at the same time as I, but you'd be leaving on your own."

A depressive scowl settled over Marcus's face. "That's just words. It amounts to the same bloody thing."

"No, it doesn't. I'll visit you whether you're on a bench or in this clinic, but I'm not taking you anywhere else with me. First my flat, then the hotel, then Kate's cottage, then your daughter's house. I haven't been good for you."

"Oh, but you have at that."

"If so, then it follows that Callahan House is good for you since my interference landed you here."

He pointed at her face, more specifically at her raised eyebrow. "You're a fair prize, aren't you? You could turn the conversation around on a politician."

Merrit leaned back on the pillows, feeling her body sigh. She forced her mind to stay alert. "So, you called?"

Marcus chewed his lower lip. "I'm hard by thinking clearly but seems like that night isn't such a blur now. I can't help the thoughts—have to ponder something besides how much I hurt. The medicine they gave me in the hospital helped settle me, that it did, and reminded me that I hadn't felt easy since the party. I was off me head, but at least Liam was a true friend." Marcus rubbed his hand in sure mimic of the matchmaker. Merrit recognized the kneading movement. "He brought me dinner and a double hot toddy the likes of which I'd not tasted in years. Ah Christ, for another one now."

Marcus pulled up a rocking chair and sat down. "That toddy was like to put me out cold. Later I woke to the shivers and cake."

"Cake?"

"That's what I've been saying. Two plates of food. The second being a fat piece of cake. I says to myself, Jesus, where are my shoes and then noticed the cake." He paused. "Isn't that an odd thought? Where are my shoes."

Merrit bunched up a pillow behind her head. "Your shoes disappeared?"

"I wake up shivering without my shoes but with a piece of cake, then I wake up again with my shoes but no piece of cake. Could that be right?"

"Cake brought before or after you lost your shoes though? Your mystery friend could be a witness and not know it."

"Bother this, I'm just a drunk. Can't believe what I remember, can't remember what I believe."

Merrit leaned over the edge of the bed to observe his feet encased in slippers that matched the bathrobe. "Fancy."

Marcus blushed. "Chills you know, coming off the gin. I've been sicking up chunks of my stomach too—can't eat a thing. Thank Christ for the drugs. Old pisser like me can't go cold turkey. I could keel over, so they say, but I'm not about to believe that. They just want us docile until we're in our right minds again." He pressed trembling fingers against his temples. "Nothing makes the headache go away though. What were we on about?"

"You have a big set of feet. Who'd want to steal your clown shoes anyhow?"

"Who indeed? Ugly as sin, my shoes." He bent into a coughing spasm then sagged back. "Sorry, not fit for the hosting, but you look the worse off so you sleep a spell."

"That woman Sandy wants you to buzz her so she can see me out."

"Don't you fret. She's always busy. I'll toddle down and tell her I walked you out. I'll pretend to be exploring and showing an interest. She'll like that."

"I told her I was your long-estranged daughter."

He patted her arm, but his gaze didn't meet hers. "That'll be easy enough to fake. You sleep."

Merrit couldn't resist the invitation even as she felt a warning tug from something Marcus had said.

Julia Chase's notebook

I can't help myself—I'm worried. It's been a week and Liam hasn't matched me to anyone for purposes of my article. My editor is losing faith, and I've dried up. Even out here at Liam's favorite spot overlooking Kilmoon Church with its charming churchyard and community of Celtic crosses, I find no inspiration. Yesterday I took a ferry to Inishmore where I encountered endless rock walls and locals who spoke only Irish. The barren limestone terrain could have been the inside of my head, and the salt air biting my cheeks didn't revive senses lost these past weeks.

Is this what love does? Debilitate? I simply cannot concentrate or sleep. I want myself back, but I fear I'm lost, which frightens me because I might be the one in for the disappointment. Adrienne hovers, and Liam tenses, and Andrew smiles. And me? What do I do? Try to write an article that means nothing to me anymore.

· 34 ·

A click woke Merrit out of a sound sleep. She opened her eyes to view a dimly lit coastal print on the wall and a fringed lamp on the nightstand. Her head felt fuzzy, as if she'd woken from a coma instead of a nap.

"Marcus, how long have I—?" She rolled onto her back to find Danny standing over her with a bleary but penetrating expression. "Oh, come on," she sighed.

"Need your inhaler?" he said.

"Funny, ha-ha. Give it time. I'm not awake yet."

"Come with me. Let's let Marcus sleep."

He pointed to the ground beside the bed, where Marcus curled on the floor, hidden from hallway view by the bed. He still looked clammy but at least he slept.

In the hallway, a night attendant with long sideburns and a patch of hair under his lower lip hopped to with an unabashed grin. "I see how it is then. An unauthorized visitor. Now to call Mrs. Callahan—she owns the place—so that we can perform the lock-down and room check."

Danny landed an arm around the man and lowered his voice. "Calm down, Leonard. This one's American. Pretty but clueless. You understand. Give us five minutes."

A few more minutes of hushed conversation, and Leonard agreed to stand watch while Danny retreated with Merrit into the closest empty room, which happened to be the women's restroom.

Merrit gargled water and splashed her face, trying not to let on how vulnerable she felt in Danny's presence. "What time is it anyhow? And how did you find me?"

"Four in the a.m. Last night I went to the hospital to check on you only you'd scarpered. Thank you for that, by the way. You caused quite the furor. We've been looking for you ever since. One of my men finally got wind of the incoherent phone call you received at the hospital. Could only have been from Marcus, especially because Liam was about his matchmaking duties at the time of the call, and Kevin was in custody."

"As in arrested?"

"Which is why I'm here. He broke into your flat. You'll be glad to know that the eejit was drunk, no more than that."

Merrit leaned against the counter, renewed weariness over-riding the effect of the cold water that still dripped down her face. Kevin, then the Garda, had rifled through her flat. Hope-fully they hadn't found her mom's notes. She inhaled against tension around her lungs and tried tapping her fingers against the counter to drown out everything except the self-protective drill sergeant who ordered her to stay calm.

"We need a statement about your belongings so I'll need to bring you in to the station," Danny said.

He leaned against the bathroom door with crossed ankles, making no move to escort her to his car. Merrit didn't like the looks of the leather portfolio he clutched beneath his arm.

"I'm curious about why you paid Lonnie at all—except that you have something to hide, don't you?" he said.

"My arrest in California, yes, but you know that already, so why ask?" She mustered a smile. Damn Ivan once again for his blabbermouth. "The charges were dropped for lack of evidence, by the way. The DA's principle witness—a hospice nurse—was snitching meds from her patients and selling them on the side."

"You still wouldn't want your arrest to get around so you paid Lonnie those first €500 allotments—"

"In hopes that he would leave me alone, not delve further, mind his own freaking beans, say what you will. I'm all about my privacy, and I didn't want Liam to overhear secondhand gossip before I'd had a chance to meet him."

"And what kind of privacy did the jump to €1,000 buy?"

She tapped her fingers on the counter. "Liam's. I caved, this time to keep his business off the streets instead of mine. Lonnie said he had something, to quote him, 'wicked juicy' on Liam."

"He didn't tell you what?"

"No, but I decided to believe him anyhow because something happened with my mom back—" Danny appeared to be reading her mind. He nodded in agreement. Dusky as the bathroom was, Merrit felt the lights as pinpricks of pain. She tested her breathing. Doing fine, just fine. "Lonnie said he'd reveal all at some point, contingent on more money."

"Ah, so it wasn't so much that you were coerced out of €1,000 as that you'd entered into negotiation with him. Interesting."

"Think what you like. Besides, why else am I here but to know Liam—however that may be?"

"Fair enough. Now, about Kate."

The pinpricks of pain poked a little harder. "Kate?"

"In the hospital, you were about to reveal something about her, but you fell asleep."

Merrit caught her tapping fingers with the other hand. "You're trying to rattle me, but it's not working."

His smile said that he observed otherwise. "Kate?"

"I don't remember what I was going to say about her. I was drugged up."

A quick knock and Leonard poked his head into the bathroom. "I'll need to be calling in Mrs. Callahan and seeing to the proper procedure."

Relieved, Merrit stood. "Yes, we're done. And I'm so sorry—"

"Do what you need to do," Danny said to Leonard. "We'll finish our conversation in the meanwhile. Won't be too much longer."

Leonard shrugged. "Old Callahan screwed up good, not checking that Marcus's guest had really left. Can't wait to see her prune face when she arrives."

His chuckles retreated down the hall with him.

· 35 ·

Danny gazed around the bathroom that was grander than his at home. In fact, it was roomy enough to allow for two dainty chairs, a pedestal table, and an antique armoire. He opened the armoire and tossed Merrit a fluffy towel for her face. Marcus had best pilfer a dozen of them, the rates the place charged.

He beckoned Merrit to one of the chairs and sat down opposite her, unsettled by the film-noir feeling within the underlit bathroom. All he needed was a fedora and cigarette; all Merrit needed was skimpy lingerie. But this was the best opportunity he'd get to pry information out of her without Clarkson getting wind of it. She didn't need to know that he was off the case.

Voices and footsteps paused outside Marcus's room. Leonard's procedure had begun.

Danny set his leather portfolio on the table, noting the way Merrit's gaze darted toward it and then away. "What about Lonnie?" he said.

"Lonnie?"

"You've forgotten this mess began with him?"

Merrit shook her head and then nodded. Knowledge flickered behind her eyes. She lifted her hands out of her lap, tapped her fingers against the tabletop. Watching her from under his eyebrows, Danny sensed that she'd veered off in a new direction, away from her previous focus on establishing her innocence. It was as if she didn't care what he thought about her guilt anymore. He could almost see the wheels grinding inside her skull as her eyes bounced along with each tapping finger.

"What about Marcus had you rushing out of the hospital?" he said.

"I'm his surrogate daughter until your wife comes around."

And for the time being, Marcus was her surrogate father. That much was obvious, but bloody well beside the point—as were most of her responses.

In a sudden movement, Danny pressed his palms onto her fingers. He squeezed her hands and pulled her toward him. Film noir indeed, he thought, as she locked her elbows against his drag. "Marcus called you because he remembered something out of the gin fuzz. He's not talking to me at the moment, so what did he say?"

The bathroom door banged open to reveal a skinny woman who could only be Leonard's "prune-faced" boss, Mrs. Callahan herself. She glared at Merrit.

"Detective Sergeant," the woman said to Danny without taking her eyes off Merrit. "May I have a word?"

"In a moment."

The door closed with another bang. He turned back to Merrit, who jerked away from him and rose to stand before the bathroom mirror. She frowned at her reflection. "I need a toothbrush."

Danny waited. After a moment, her gaze returned to his. Slowly, he pulled her mom's notebook out of the portfolio. "Your mother. She never got over Liam, did she?"

Merrit stared through the mirror at the frayed notebook cover with its psychedelic rainbow. After several seconds in which nothing moved except Merrit's chest, she heaved a breath with such force Danny dropped the notebook and grabbed her shoulders to help steady her as she bent over. "Inhaler?"

She stood stiff, battling her breaths. Her breath hiccupped with each painful sound. "I—I—am—f-f-f-ine."

Danny retreated to give her space. His surprise attack had backfired, not that he was surprised. He had retrieved the notebook out of Kevin's truck, read it, and by the last page understood one thing: he'd never unravel the bandages that lay over Merrit's heart—or anyone else's for that matter. The truth was, he was just starting to pick at his own.

Warm air hissed through the Peugeot's vent, but Merrit shivered. Fatigue lay on her like a fog layer, and her body ached anew after her mini-attack in the bathroom. If only she could think straight. If only she could talk to Liam. Now.

Danny knew her for a liar, that much was obvious, but she refused to alleviate his frustration. Since Lonnie's death, the truth had become even more momentous and personal, especially when it came to her mom. Surely Danny grasped this now that he'd devoured her mom's words.

"Can I have my mom's notes back, please?"

"You made it through a panic attack without an inhaler."

She should be happy for what her doctor would call a breakthrough. All she felt was breached and sick to her stomach.

"Pages back," she said. "Please."

"Not yet. They're evidence." Danny pointed out the window. "That's the Poulnabrone Dolmen."

They passed a three-legged table-top tomb that glowed in the dawn and dwarfed grazing cattle. Low clouds diffused pink and orange hues over an already dappled terrain of mixed limestone and fields. They were miles from anywhere, certainly miles from Liam's house.

"Over five thousand years old," Danny continued, "and the slab lying over the three legs weighs five tons. Amazing prehistoric feat of engineering." After a few more silent miles, he said, "Back to the blackmail."

There he went, circling around her again with his astute blinks, ever closer like a vulture that had caught the whiff of death from miles away.

Danny's mobile chirped before he could continue. He snatched up the phone. "Ahern here. O'Neil, that you? You sound like shite."

Merrit rocked forward when Danny braked and pulled into a dirt lane. His *uh-huh*s ground out between increasingly clenched teeth. "I have Merrit Chase with me. I'll have to bring her along, and then we'll figure it out from there. Thanks for calling me."

He clicked off and threw the mobile into the back seat. "Son of a bitch." His palms smacked the steering wheel. "Son—of—a—bitch. You've a good instinct, Merrit Chase. I might not need to cajole the rest of what you know out of you, after all."

Outside, lowing sheep and hectoring magpies answered for her. A farmer rounded the corner of the house at the end of the track and paused to stare at them with hand shading his eyes. Danny ground the car into gear.

Merrit rolled down the window and stuck her head out, watching rock walls and sheep and a castle keep speed past. She pulled her head in when Danny accelerated away from Lisfenora and further into the countryside, toward the coast.

"Where are we going?"

"A crime scene." He spared her a businesslike glance. "I don't like what's going on here, but I'd say you're a lucky one."

She held her breath.

"Kate Meehan is dead."

Julia Chase's notebook

Sometimes I wonder who I think I'm fooling. My mother? Even she doesn't buy my career aspirations. Her latest letter includes this: "Did you know that Erica Wallace—you remember she went through a 'commune' phase—announced her engagement with the most lavish afternoon party I've seen in years. And to David Mitford, no less. He always pined after you, but too late now! As ever, I patiently wait for you to come to your senses (as you will!)," etcetera...

Her letter had me so infuriated that I welcomed Andrew's appearance outside the post office and our subsequent respite from the crowds in a nice little pub over in Doolin. He's an interesting man, what with his experience in the Far East. I didn't catch all the details because I was thinking I could solve my writer's block by pretending that Liam had matched me to Andrew. Pure fiction, but what does it matter? When I broached the topic in the middle of our second pint (maybe I was a little drunk), Andrew positively beamed.

We moved on to other topics, but on the return drive, he said, "You'll see yet. This Liam, he's not the man he seems." I had to laugh at his gallant certainty. Mother would approve of a man like Andrew McCallum. He's just her type.

But Andrew, he'd never take me against a standing stone or under Kilmoon's watchful eye. He'd never run amok with me, scattering sheep before us. He'd never toss me into the air like a beach ball again and again until I about faint with laughter. He'd never breach his finely wrought decorum to kiss my callused feet.

· 36 ·

Danny parked and ordered Merrit to stay put. Before he'd finished his sentence, however, she was out of the car and rushing toward a break in the hawthorn through which one of his men had just disappeared. Danny caught up with her as she stumbled to a stop with a sharp intake of breath. Following her gaze, he saw Kilmoon through the hawthorn branches, looking as broody as ever. The church stood off the roadside, and the overgrown hedgerows had hidden her from view.

Merrit stared at Kilmoon's cracked facade, patting her chest, her expression settling somewhere between dismay and horror. "Kilmoon Church," she said. "Of course. It had to be."

Before Danny could pursue this most interesting statement, O'Neil appeared to block her path. Worry lines appeared between his eyes.

"Excuse me, sir." He sneezed. His nose and eyes were red. "Clarkson is stuck in a meeting, but he said he'd be here in about two hours. Meanwhile, the scene needs a superior officer—"

"Did Clarkson tell you not to call me in?" Danny said.

"No."

"Then we're covered, but I still plan not to be here when he arrives. Hold Merrit in my car." Merrit still stared at the church behind its drystone wall perimeter. He thought he could hear her lungs rattling with each breath. If Danny hadn't been with her since early on, he'd have suspected her of killing Kate. In fact, he still suspected her of something, he just wasn't sure what. "Switch that. I want her in my sightline at all times, but off church grounds."

Danny made his way toward Kate's body while O'Neil led Merrit around the outside of the drystone wall that surrounded the church.

Kate Meehan could be a pictorial for high-fashion demise in her black skirt and silk blouse. Makeup stark against death's pallor looked as if she'd taken care. And her arm in arabesque, hip tilted toward the bent leg—such grace. She wanted only for a hint of a smile to achieve aesthetic perfection. Her macabre beauty displayed in a graveyard rendered the scene all the more grotesque.

"Oh, she's a fresh one, this one," said the state pathologist, also known as Benjy the Bagger. A spry old bastard, he'd been around long enough to watch his hair fade to silver and his peers succumb to politics. Danny liked him for his irreverent outlook. A moment later Benjy didn't disappoint.

"Chee-rist, no Sunday confessionals for this one I'll be betting."

Danny retreated to let Benjy get on with his examination. He felt Merrit's watchfulness grinding into his back. Unorthodox her presence may be, but all the better to see her reaction to these events. He shifted so that he could view her. She appeared subdued but not exactly stricken with shock.

Benjy peered at a grave marker so weathered no epitaph remained. Over the centuries half of it had sunk into the earth so that what appeared above ground was a triangle of limestone sharp enough to do serious damage. A camera flash from one of the scenes of crime officers illuminated blood on the headstone then flashed again to capture Kate's broken shoe. Benjy dropped a stiletto heel into a bag and handed it off to the exhibit officer. Next, he crouched on his hands and knees and lifted Kate's head to peer beneath it.

"Almighty beauty that one. I wager I'll find a fractured skull, intracranial bleeding." He hummed under his breath. "Heard Clarkson's riding you harder than a rutting bull."

"And I'll be taken off this case once it's linked to Lonnie's death. Clarkson's sidelined me well and good."

"You seem sure."

"That I'll be packed off to lesser duties or that the two deaths are linked?"

"Both."

"Of both, I'm sure. Call it a rumbling from my gut."

Benjy crawled toward Kate's legs and pressed latex-covered fingers into the flesh around one of her ankles. "She injured her ankle within the last few days, not bad, but enough she'd have been wobbly." He shook his head with a tsk. "Who the devil wears shoes like hers anyhow? And take a look at this." Benjy slid open Kate's blouse to reveal a smooth pane of white skin, a push-up bra, and a perfect circle of a bruise.

"Hey!" O'Neil shouted, and Danny pivoted to see Merrit climbing over the rock wall. She stumbled over a gravestone and ran toward Kate as if the church grounds were nothing but a bloody obstacle course. Danny caught her by the arm. Breathing hard, she stared at Kate with a hand pressed against her mouth.

"O'Neil!" Danny said at the same time the sheepish detective arrived with apologies about a coughing fit. "Get her out of here."

Danny rubbed his hands over his face and felt its unwashed, stubbly surface. His eyeballs itched from lack of sleep. He should have known Merrit wouldn't stay passive for long.

Benjy returned to humming, while around them, various officers combed the grass for evidence and dusted nearby gravestones for fingerprints. Danny swiveled away from Kate. Her stiffening corpse disturbed him in a way that Lonnie's hadn't. It was the perfection again, this time in timing. She'd granted everyone the favor by dying, especially Little Miss Scene Compromiser.

Danny weaved his way toward Merrit, whose wilted posture hinted at something, but, once again, he wasn't sure what. "Someone did you a favor."

A worry-wrinkle appeared between her eyebrows, but she banished it fast. "Really, is that what you think?"

"I suspect both Lonnie and Kate would still be alive if you hadn't come charging into our fair village like one of the four horses of the apocalypse. Now come with me."

· 37 ·

S till clutching her inhaler, Merrit followed Danny as he led them toward an old standing stone that stood sentinel over the cow paddies. First Danny, then she, then O'Neil, stepped over the stone's shadow that pointed like a grim reaper's finger back toward Kilmoon Church. You started this, it said. Our Lady held her ground against the accusation, unyielding, and Merrit vowed to remain likewise. She hugged herself as closely as the church did. She visualized strong walls. All she needed were defenses like Kilmoon's for a little longer. All she needed was to keep her cool with Danny.

In reality she longed to sink to the ground, gnash her teeth, and wail with childish abandon. This church, Kilmoon, with its weathered walls, looked just as it had on the living room wall in California. Its impenetrable window eyes followed her just as they had when she was a child. I see you, they seemed to say. I know something you don't know.

Danny gazed at her with his own brand of impenetrability. "Earlier you said something about Kilmoon Church—'it had to be.' It had to be what exactly?"

"It's nothing. Family stuff."

"And your family stuff is why we're in this shit storm." He swung his gaze toward the church. "She's a mighty relic, that one, and you seemed mighty comfortable jumping her wall. Been here before?"

"Believe me, I wish I'd never seen this church before today."

Danny raised his eyebrows with a look that said he was willing to wait all day and that he would.

"Fine," she said. "I feel like I know this place because we had a picture of it in our living room while I was growing up. As soon as I read about Kilmoon Church in my mom's notebook, I knew it must be the same place." Danny nodded for her to keep going. "I've been meaning to visit it, but it's not listed in my guidebook—"

"It wouldn't be. And?"

"And the reality of it is more—I don't know—alive than it should be. Like it's been waiting for me. Idiotic, I know, but—"

She clamped her mouth shut before revealing her mom's sadness and Andrew's insistence that the picture remain on the wall. "Call me sentimental," he'd say, "for the site where our relationship truly began."

"And you're saying you've never been here before today?" Danny said.

She nodded.

"Why did you trespass the crime scene?"

"I had to see Kate up close." Merrit recalled the red splash of Kate's scarf on the night she had caught Merrit outside her cottage, and her low voice in the hospital as she revealed secrets. "She was my sister, after all."

Which had made this Merrit's last chance to view something of herself in Kate—slant of bone under skin, arch of eyebrow, curve of lip—but all she'd noticed was the color red like a blinking light unsure whether to stop or beckon. Between Kate's lipstick, sandals, and belt, the color completed her ensemble. Unfortunately, the color also tinted her bruised ankle, discolored her hair, and stained the headstone.

Guilt leaked through Merrit's strong walls. The problem with Danny was that he had hit too close to home when he'd said that she was the lucky one. A part of her had wanted Kate gone, and now she had her wish. Perhaps she *had* caused Kate's death. Somehow. Danny was certainly staring her down as if she had.

She took a seat where Danny indicated. He was the person she feared most at the moment, not because he might consider her the puzzle's key—which she wasn't, because if she were, she'd have all the answers—but because his presence was too warm. "I wish you'd give me time to sort things out for myself."

"Why, do you think she killed Lonnie?"

She shrugged and hugged her purse, where, if he insisted, Danny would find a folded sheet tucked into her passport holder, safely hidden away along with Liam's precious address. The folded sheet hid the third article she'd swiped from Kate's cottage, the one Merrit had not shown Danny because it led to conclusions that Merrit wasn't ready to examine closely. And she wasn't about to remind Danny about a news item that was published during his childhood, back in 1980. Now that Danny had read her mom's notes, he might just jump to the same conclusions that she had about Kate's motivations.

D anny watched Benjy cinch paper bags around Kate's hands and over her head. Then he straightened her limbs so that her remaining bit of humanity disappeared. Now she was a cadaver. A team of crows settled on a church wall in hopes of fulfilling their part of nature's plan. Beside him, Merrit gripped her purse like a stuffed animal.

"Danny," Benjy called, "we've got a missing puzzle piece over here."

The crows ruffled themselves in a gust of wind and then resettled. Something Danny couldn't make out dangled from

Benjy's fingers. "Watch her," he ordered O'Neil, who sneezed in response.

"Didn't you tell me this was missing off Lonnie O'Brien when I worked on him?" Benjy said when Danny arrived at his side. "I found it under the deceased's shoulder."

The six-inch braid that used to touch Lonnie's shoulder hadn't held together well despite the rubber band someone had wrapped around the snipped end. Benjy grinned. "Clarkson will like this. He'd like to close the case of the dead O'Brien heir."

"Kate had motive enough, I suppose."

"Ay, and by the looks of her broken shoe, that wankstain Clarkson will declare that our deceased beauty accidentally fell and hit her head. Two cases closed for the price of one."

Danny bagged the braid and handed it off. "Easy answer."

"My point exactly. We know all about Clarkson back in Dublin—notorious ass kisser and politician, he is." Benjy gestured toward the men who systematically combed every inch of Kilmoon's grounds. "We'll see if they find anything that points to answers, and I'll see what I see when I cut her open. That's all I can do."

Danny sat back on his haunches for a last look at Kate before Benjy body-bagged her. He pulled out his mobile. "There's one person who needs to witness this scene. Grant me this last shot at answers before Clarkson arrives."

Julia Chase's notebook

Liam doesn't want to see me after tonight's pub crawl. We sat in his car before his evening session, enjoying the view of the Burren's limestone terraces receding toward the ocean. Upon unveiling my brilliant idea to use Andrew as my surrogate match, he revved the car into gear and careened along narrow lanes, nearly colliding into oncoming traffic, and never mind the wending cliff-side dangers, he never slowed, and all this with hands lax upon the steering wheel while I yelled that it was only for the article, that this relieved him of the task of matching me, that there was no reason to be jealous.

He drove until sweat dripped out of his hair. He drove until we completed a roundabout circuit back to Lisfenora and pulled up in front of my hotel. Balled muscles gathered along his jaw. "I'll not have it," he said

"Not have what?" I replied. "Andrew's seeing Adrienne anyway."

"Like hell he is," he snapped and then caught himself with a head shake. He kissed me on the forehead, saying that after the evening's activities he'd sojourn, alone, to Kilmoon Church, his favorite thinking spot.

Liam has grown distant, but Andrew always seems to be about, hovering in his courtly, slightly claustrophobic way. As I walked into my hotel, there he was, seated in the lobby. There's something you need to know about Liam, he said. Can you meet me later tonight?

I trust Liam, I do. But I want to hear what Andrew has to say. I want to prove Andrew wrong.

· 38 ·

The second day of Marcus's internment at Callahan House found him rocking in the so-called drawing room, a room filled with worn chintz-covered chairs and sofas. He tilted the rocker back and let it tip forward. The repetitive movement soothed him because it was similar to the drunken sensation he used to feel while sitting still. Television chatter issued from the sitting parlor next door and cards slapped against the game table. Despite these little comforts, he could still walk out, yes, he could, and it might be that he would tonight when everyone was at dinner. Too many jitters in this place for his liking.

A door creaked and Mistress Callahan herself called out, "Team A, group therapy in the blue room. Team B, stress management in yellow. Team C, you're stretching and breathing in purple."

Murmurs and footsteps receded as the other inmates filed out with varying degrees of disgruntlement. Marcus opened his eyes. A lank-haired teenager and her dolly stared at him.

"They get this team stuff from the States. Big in the States, all this." She nodded to herself and rocked on her feet. "You're in my chair, by the way. That's my chair."

Mistress Callahan appeared again to beckon the girl. "Come, Poppy, Dr. Frank will see you now. Marcus, you troublemaker, you're next. Afterward we'll assign you to a team."

Marcus slipped back into a rocking lull and tried to ignore the tingles that poked the tips of his fingers, not to mention the stretched-out-ear-drum sensation inside his skull. A moment later, trotting steps roused him. "I'm after seeing a woman in the lobby," the girl, Poppy, said. "Asking after you. Said your name, that she did."

Marcus rose to his feet and clutched at a paneled edge of wainscoting until his vision cleared. Merrit back so soon? He steered himself toward the lobby through a series of connecting doors that led from the drawing room to the sitting parlor to the visitor's lounge, each room more frilled than the next. Merrit might like the curio cabinets.

In the lobby, however, he was met by a mirage. He had to be around the bend to conjure his own daughter. Raving, that's what, and he'd continue to think so if she didn't just then pull fingers through her hair in an impatient gesture he recognized. Ellen, his Ellen, who'd gained a stone but still stood with dignity. Maybe it was her haste to see Marcus that had her pairing one of Danny's wool sweaters with a cotton skirt. Not that Marcus cared. His Ellen. Here. Danny had always said to give her time. He blessed himself and patted down his hair, ready to tap her shoulder.

"No message for him." Her voice snipped at the attendant. "I'm simply verifying my husband's utter disregard for my feelings."

Marcus shuffled backward, hands limp at his sides.

"We called because you're listed as the emergency contact person," the attendant said. "Obviously, a mistake."

No mistake. That was Danny assuming the best out of all circumstances—that there'd be no emergency, but if it should so happen, that Ellen would open her heart. Mad foolishness. Marcus peeked around the doorframe for a last look at his Ellen.

"Everything is fine now," the attendant said. "We calmed him with a light sedative, and he'll be seeing a counselor today." At Ellen's snort, the attendant's tone dropped to careful sympathy. "It's always difficult to—"

"His overnight guest—long reddish-brown hair?"

"Yes. And she looked none too good herself when I arrived to help Mrs. Callahan."

"I'll bet." Ellen glared around the lobby with an observant eye toward the varnished stair rails and antique copper plate pictures. Marcus ducked back when she turned in his direction. "Hand me over a copy of your fee schedule, if you please."

Holy Mary, help Danny now.

A derisive laugh erupted from Ellen. "You'd better be serving lobster and caviar for this price, and my father better graduate fully recovered. If he so much as sips cough syrup in his lifetime, I'll see to it you're forced to take him back at no charge. Relay that message to whom it may concern. Otherwise, no other word of my visit."

The front door slammed shut, followed by muffled oaths from the attendant. Marcus stepped into the lobby.

"Got a tongue that would clip a hedge, that one," the attendant said.

Marcus peered out the entrance window. Ellen bounced her car off the curb with a squeal of tires. Pessimism settled on him like a tired reminder. Try as he might to imagine a life without alcohol, he couldn't. Even before his slide, he'd liked his pints as well as the next bloke. "You tell me, what else is there to drink in a pub anyhow?" he muttered.

Mistress Callahan appeared before him in that uncanny way of hers. Her blouse sagged where breasts should prop up the crinkled silk. Too bony for his taste, but a kind smile she had when she chose to bestow it.

"Water, soda, coffee, juice, but you're a long way from that." She held out a manicured hand. "Come. Almost your turn."

He let her drag him past bulletin boards filled with schedules, memos, and thank-you notes. She talked about the counselor, Dr. Frank, but Marcus stopped listening. In truth, the deal was done. Now that Ellen knew the course Danny had set for him, Marcus had no more choices. None that made sense anyway. After seeing her hunched over the reception desk, her resentment bristling, he at last understood that she'd never let herself heal until he gave her reason for hope.

· 39 ·

The Mazda with sunroof and leather interior sat on tractor ruts in the cow pasture adjacent to Kilmoon Church. The car sat well off the road as if Kate had wanted to avoid notice. Danny stepped aside when the scenes of crime team lugged their equipment over from the church. Benjy followed them, grumbling about needing to get Kate's body onto a slab.

"My surprise guest should be arriving in a few minutes," Danny said. "And then I plan to be gone before Clarkson arrives."

Benjy pulled a cigarette out of his pocket, sniffed it with a sigh, and tucked it away again. "Forgot about Clarkson. I'll be needing to wait for him anyhow. My sorry luck."

The men started in with photographing and gathering evidence. O'Neil arrived with Merrit at his side. "What do I do with her now?" he said, and sneezed into a soggy handkerchief.

"Barricade her in my car until I'm done here."

One of the men snapped a picture of Kate's purse, which perched on the driver's side seat, and another of her keys in the dirt beside the car. "Car doors were unlocked," he noted. Then he pulled a power cord from the back seat. He let it dangle before dropping it into an evidence bag.

"I didn't see her computer the night Marcus and I visited her place," Merrit said as O'Neil dragged her away. "Just so you know."

Danny wondered at her current calm. She still drooped, still looked pallid, but compared with their previous encounters she appeared panic-free. O'Neil walked her along the tractor ruts toward the lane where their various vehicles were parked. Benjy followed, striking up a cigarette and inhaling with a pleasured groan. Danny lost sight of them as they disappeared behind the hawthorn. A moment later, one of the scenes of crimes men popped open the Mazda's trunk to reveal an empty laptop bag, which bloody well figured. He wouldn't be surprised if Ivan had gotten his hands on Kate's laptop and saved it for himself. Bloody Ivan.

Benjy's voice called out from the lane. "Danny, come see to your guest!"

Speaking of the twitchy little devil. Danny checked his watch. Clarkson would be arriving any time now. Danny trotted out to meet Ivan, who had been escorted to the site courtesy of one of Lisfenora's finest uniformed guards. Upon seeing Danny, the officer waved Ivan out of his vehicle and reversed down the lane.

Ivan's self-pitying expression went along with frizzed hair and an inside-out sweater. "I am not appreciating the Garda showing up outside the deacon's house—it is not right. And you should know that you cannot harass me. Mr. O'Brien agreed to take over my sponsorship. In fact, I am to manage Internet Café, make proper business of it."

"How did you manage that one?"

"Mr. O'Brien, he has his family reputation to think about. He was shocked when I told him how Lonnie earned his money. It was my duty to warn him, and to offer my computer services to him. It was logical business arrangement since I already know so much. About the business I mean."

"You're a model citizen, Ivanov."

Ivan puffed up with a pleased smile. "Thank you. And when he knows me, he will see that Connie and I are perfect for each other. But that is just between you and me."

Danny led Ivan toward Kilmoon Church, surrounded by her Celtic crosses and buried dreams. After haggling with the lead forensic technician, Danny signed himself and Ivan into the scene. They were safe to walk a precise path behind the technician toward the corpse, but only after they had donned the requisite white suits and booties. Danny would have hell to pay if Ivan turned out to be involved in Kate's death. But then, Danny was already on Clarkson's shit list. Why not truly tank his career by escorting a civilian into the crime scene?

Ivan had better make this farce worth the ass whipping Danny was in for.

They rounded the backside of the church. Blue harebell blooms dotted the grounds, and in the distance heather shimmered at the start of its autumnal turn to purple. A breeze sent whispers through the grass, and on the hillside, the standing stone pointed its shadow straight at enshrouded Kate.

Ivan squealed when he caught sight of the body bag.

Danny lunged after Ivan's retreating form. Ivan's bony shoulder shrank under this grip. "Guess who this is?"

"Liam, it is not Liam, is it? I swear this is not my doing. Just because I am wanting that my part in Lonnie's schemes be quiet does not mean I do something like this. You must to believe me. All I wanted ever was to stay in Ireland. Why do you think I went to Mr. O'Brien? And even if I hated Lonnie, you know I am not killing him, so why would I kill Liam? I promise on this consecrated ground that Liam had no bad will for me."

Ivan squirmed in Danny's grip. Wiry fellow, Danny allowed, as he adjusted his fingers around Ivan's arms. "Why would Liam have a grudge against you?"

Ivan's squirming stopped. He stood still as one of the Celtic crosses that surrounded them. "*Blin*," he muttered.

"Go on, then."

"Remember your theory about a third blackmail victim?"

At Danny's nod, Ivan whispered something.

"What was that?" Danny said.

"Liam! It was Liam. But I swear on—on any of these graves that Liam knew I was not to blame!"

Now it was Danny's turn to go still as medieval stone. Goddamned Ivan. He wanted to throttle the little twot. "Why blackmail Liam?"

"His paternity issues, what else?"

"What else is what I'd like to know."

"Nothing else."

"And you told O'Brien Senior about Liam paying Lonnie?"

"Of course. No word can get out about that. Liam is too beloved. Would be too much scandal on the family. I have deal with Mr. O'Brien now."

Danny stared at Ivan, thinking about how O'Brien Senior might go about ensuring that the reporters didn't snuffle their way to this juicy bit of news. Promoting Ivan to manager ensured his silence, but then there was also Clarkson, who was sure to help O'Brien in any way he could. "And you're telling me you haven't tried to shake money out of Liam too?"

"You think I am continuing with that after getting good with Mr. O'Brien?" Ivan's voice went up an octave. "I plan to marry Connie. Become a citizen. I cannot help you if that is what you are thinking. Why kill Liam, this is not making sense to me." He yelped as if surprising himself. "Kate did it. She resented him more than healthy resentment. She is—she is—" He caught his breath. "*Blin*, I am upsetting by Liam's death, I forget my English. She is a crazy—a nutter, that is what, and I am betting that if Liam was not giving her what she wanted—"

"Which was?"

"What do I know? I am not knowing. This is guess. And with Lonnie out of the way she was free to do what she wanted without trouble from him. She did not like Lonnie knowing Liam's secrets. They were only meant for her to use. This is what I think anyway. She only paid Lonnie to keep him nice to her."

"Tell me about Kate, and I might cut you some slack."

Ivan raised his hands and let them fall. "That woman is wanting everything, so what do I know in specifics?"

"A lot more than you're letting on." Danny pointed toward the body bag. "You want to view Liam? Say a prayer?"

"Not on my life, no."

Danny nodded to the technician, who hovered next to them, silent but attentive. The technician bent over the bag with hand poised above the zipper. Ivan flapped his arms, and Danny caught a whiff of his clammy body odor. Slowly, the technician pulled down the zipper. Ivan inched closer, apparently curious despite himself, and then reeled back when the plastic parted to reveal Kate's icy half-lidded gaze. He bounced against Kilmoon's wall, jostling a stone loose. He staggered back, tripping over one of the many other stones that had fallen over the years, and finally landed up against a tall Celtic cross. He glared at Danny. "Why did you not tell me it was Kate? You let me go on like idiot."

"Nothing like a little shock treatment to bring out the truth. So, tell me, why did you kill Kate?"

Ivan's squashed his hair down beneath his hands and shook his head. "I cannot believe this. This is impossible. I did not kill Kate. How could I? She would have eaten me alive if I even blinked at her wrong."

"It's obvious you didn't like her."

Ivan shrugged. "And so what? No one did. And besides, the

same goes for her as it did for Liam. Why would I kill her when I had made good with Mr. O'Brien? I did not need Kate for a visa sponsorship anymore. I would only be her slave hacker like I was for Lonnie, but for Mr. O'Brien I am more than that."

The technician pushed the zipper back into place, signaling that their time was up. He led them out of Kilmoon's territory. Back on the rural lane, surrounded by official vehicles and hawthorn, Danny continued his questions.

"Tell me why you thought Kate would kill Liam. If she wanted everything as you say, I don't see her killing him in such a hurry."

Ivan pulled on his earlobe. If anything, his twitchiness increased. "I don't know about that—I am confused—but I do know about Lonnie. Before the party, I was in my flat. I could hear him on the phone in his office. 'The next installment, tonight,' Lonnie is saying. I put my ear to ground and heard Kate too. She was spitting, never heard a woman sound like that, not even my mother. I was not catching all of it, but Kate told him he better watch his bogtrotter hide or she find a way to skin and dry it herself. She was threatening Lonnie before the party. That is all that I am knowing."

"If Kate killed Lonnie, how did she get her hands on Liam's knife? She wasn't invited to the party, if you remember."

Ivan wriggled. "That would be easy for her. She could get any man to invite her into the party. She is diabolical."

"Convenient, isn't it, that Kate isn't here to defend herself. You and Merrit are operating on the same wavelength."

"But you believe me about hearing Kate and Lonnie fight?"

"This is just the fact you'd tell me at your convenience, but I wouldn't say I believe you, no. You'll need to give a statement at the station anyhow."

"I will do that. That is no problem. I am here to help."

Danny's mobile tweeted. A text message arrived from

O'Neil, who stood farther down the lane next to Danny's Peugeot. Clarkson was ten minutes away. Danny hurried Ivan out of his white suit, slipped out of his own, and dragged Ivan to the Peugeot. He'd have to take the long way back to Lisfenora to avoid passing Clarkson.

"Tell me about Kate's laptop," he said. "It's nowhere to be found."

"You blame me for everything. I see how this goes. Just like in Belarus."

Danny aimed Ivan into the backseat next to Merrit. "Make good with Clarkson," he said to O'Neil. "Tell him I arrived, figured this case was related to Lonnie's death, and left."

O'Neil snorted and sneezed. "Toeing the line."

"Just so he thinks so." He rolled down the window as he pulled away. "And get your arse home. You'll cause a contagion."

On the road to Lisfenora, Danny watched Merrit and Ivan through the rearview mirror. Merrit with a troubled frown, and Ivan biting his lower lip. Tweedle Dee, Tweedle Dum, each clutching what Danny suspected was the final fact of the matter, the fact that would explain everything.

Julia Chase's notebook

What I overheard from inside lovely, diabolical Kilmoon's walls. It can't be. But it is. It was. Stupid, stupid, not to have realized the obvious about Adrienne's baby, not to have seen beneath Liam's engaging facade, not to imagine worse betrayals. All because he cast faerie dust in my direction.

Andrew and I hid inside the church walls. Sound travels far in the silent Irish night, and we heard two cars arrive. First, Adrienne's, then Liam's. My heart pounded so hard I thought I'd be sick.

I can't bear to think about the noises, but they won't go away. Their voices rising in a kind of sick passion, the wind whistling through the church's medieval windows, the pounding, the squealing, the damp fall of their bodies to the ground, a breathless sigh.

You take yourself back to the hotel, Andrew whispered. There's a girl. I'll let Liam know it's over between you two. You never have to talk to him again.

I fled with Andrew's car keys like the fake I am.

I'm a coward, that's what I am, and all I can do is pack my bags because I hate myself for loving the man anyhow. But I won't be betrayed by love again, which means I'm doomed to become my mother's daughter. Perhaps it won't be so bad—safe at least.

· 40 ·

In Interview Room 2, Kevin slouched over his knees in an attempt to fight off a fluorescent-light headache. He shifted to ease a kink out of his back and listened to the buzzing overheads. Frenzied activity earlier that morning hadn't roused him from his state of dazed listlessness, not even when he recognized Clarkson's strident voice through the walls. Kate Meehan. Dead.

And all he'd thought was, thank Christ the Garda had his alibi on record. No way could they blame him for her death after putting him through a sleepless night and another long day of questions.

Kevin tensed as a knock sounded. The door opened to admit Liam not-so-fresh from a day on the plaza and looking thinner all of a sudden. He stepped toward one of two desks that sat near the front of the room. He laid out brown bread and white cheddar, and beckoned Kevin to scoot his chair toward the food. "Where's the solicitor?" he said.

"In, out, useless." Kevin shook his head. He didn't care anymore. "How's the hip? You were limping as you came in."

"Stumbled again." Liam gazed around the room. "Why the devil did Clarkson call me in?"

Kevin plucked a chunk of bread out from the middle of a

slice and dropped it into his mouth with no more thought of food than of Aegean vacations. Upon swallowing, however, hunger overtook him and he broke up hunks of cheese to eat with the bread while Liam looked on with an absent frown.

"Saw Emma while she worked the booth today," Liam said. "She said she came to check on you, and Clarkson was kind enough to let her through."

"Kind, my ass. We both know he wanted to wind me up about Lonnie. I'd wager he was hoping I'd let something slip."

"How did your chat with her go?" Liam said without his usual teasing glint when it came to women.

"Not well."

Through the long, flickering night and long, flickering day, Kevin's thoughts had strayed back to Emma. In fact, he'd have driven his head against a wall by now if not for the fleeting but penetrating sense that something good had passed between them the night of the party. Within the cozy shadows of a shop doorway, in a darkened lane away from the festivities, whispers he remembered, and if not what they'd said to each other then at least the distant comfort of sound like waves within a conch shell.

"Out with it then, what did Emma say?" Liam said.

Clarkson entered the interview room before Kevin could answer.

"Unfortunately," Clarkson said, his tone clipped, "under Section 4 of the Criminal Justice Act of 1984 we no longer have enough to keep Kevin. You are free to haul him away, Mr. Donellan. At the moment, we have no men available to chauffeur your son home."

"Why the sudden reprieve?" Liam said.

"New developments. Let's leave it at that." He frowned at Kevin. "You're still on the suspect list, but the DPP is unwilling to make a case against you at this time. You are free to leave."

Kevin stood. "Hell, yes, I am."

"The DPP has yet to decide on the breaking and entering, so don't get too cocky."

Kevin retrieved his belongings from the duty guard and trotted ahead in his haste for fresh air and natural light. Lowing cows, a yell, and a honk from the nearby cattle crossing sounded like heaven to him. He preferred the bovine aroma to the Garda station's conditioned air. He tilted his head toward the sun and closed his eyes to savor late-afternoon heat just this side of cool. He'd always loathed being cooped up. One of Liam's greatest kindnesses upon adopting him was to let him run wild outdoors until he dropped from exhaustion. In that respect his life hadn't changed much since childhood.

"You drive." Liam landed a light swat to the back of Kevin's head on his way to the passenger side. "But take note that I drove myself here without a hitch."

They got caught in tourist traffic as they approached the plaza. A few satisfied couples already strolled arm-in-arm, no doubt ready to share their successful experiences with those still pining. Liam smiled and waved as if he hadn't a care in the world.

Kevin thought back to Julia Chase's journal, which had revealed half the story from 1975 and without a proper ending at that. It seemed to him that Liam had been the one to let his guard down the most, falling for her with what amounted to childish bravado. How quickly he must have matured when she suddenly refused to see him anymore. Surely Julia Chase wounded him in ways that penetrated deeper than the busted hand.

"Are Merrit and Kate why you started blathering on about retiring from the matchmaking?" he said.

"Not exactly, no."

"Then it's about the letter you received, isn't it?

"Not exactly, no."

Liam splayed his bad hand as if taking stock of the damage done. Kevin remembered Liam's scabbed fingers sticking out of the plaster cast, and he now knew from Julia's notes that she'd left Ireland just days before Liam's arrival at the orphanage. His hand must be a constant reminder of his loss.

"Odd as this may sound," Liam said, "for a while there I thought to pass the matchmaking reins down to you." He smiled. "Then you hit adolescence."

"Miserable little shit, was I?"

"That, but more importantly, you're not wired for matchmaking, and I realized soon enough that it can't be taught. I can sit with a person and concentrate until I feel their shoes on my feet. It's a gritty sensibility, and you, my son, overthink instead of trust your intuition. You grow impatient. You need physical outlets to ground you. Also, you've got too much of the Catholic in you. You're all twisted up inside about what to believe."

"You've never told me this or a fuckload more besides. There's so much I don't know about you."

"You know the two most important and best things about me. Everything else is—everything else, simple as that."

"That a fact? The matchmaking is one of the two, of course."

Liam's searching gaze warmed the left side of Kevin's face. His hand settled over Kevin's with skin aged soft as well-washed jeans. "Hovering magpie."

"Old troll."

"But you're still needing to marry. Don't think I'm off that track."

They settled back into silence as they passed the plaza and Kevin spied Emma closing down the information booth for the day. Ignoring Liam's glance, he nodded in response to her hesitant wave.

· Part III ·

Monday, September 8th – Tuesday, September 9th

"Never mind old age and illness, regret is the true enemy."
—Liam the Matchmaker

Clare Challenger   *17 Mar 1980*

Kilmoon Church Unburies its Dead
Garda Seeks Information About a Missing Woman

In a shocking discovery in our quiet midst, the skeletal remains of a woman were found in the local historic site called Our Lady of the Kilmoon Church. Official inquiries began last week after torrential rains, the worst in decades, uncovered what appeared to be a human knee joint.

"I was about my business with the dogs," said Tommy O'Donnell, local shop owner. "Give them a bit of a run through the pastures at the end of the day. We cut through the churchyard. The ground was soggier than a baby's nappy, that it was. Couldn't miss the bone because I stumbled over it."

The investigation remained hushed until today so that officials could rule out grave-raiding, vandalism, and cultlike activities before the news went public.

Today, officials revealed details in the hopes that locals might shed light on missing persons. The remains appear to be those of a Caucasian female in her twenties who most likely went missing within the last decade.

Officials would not reveal the cause of death.

Anyone with information that might lead to the identification of this missing person should contact Detective Inspector Sean Mallory through the Garda station at 7 Priory Lane.

· 41 ·

At last, Merrit stood before Liam's front door. It was a nice door with green trim and an owlish sprite for a knocker, a solid mass of an entrance that hung square on its hinges. Merrit inhaled until her chest and stomach expanded. So far, so good.

She'd parked down the lane and walked the rest of the way to the house so that Liam wouldn't hear her car. She told herself she wanted to surprise him, but the truth of it was that she wanted an easy out in case she lost her nerve at the last second. Now, on a long exhale, she raised her hand and grasped the knocker. She concentrated on calming images such as the empty lane behind her, and the bleating sheep, and the smoke plume rising from the chimney. The setting sun lengthened her shadow toward beveled glass panes and settled an orange glow around her like a floating expectancy. She'd never written Liam the letter. The time for letters was past.

From inside the house a crash plus muffled oath preempted her knock. A vision of Liam's inert form compelled her to try the door. She wasn't surprised to find it unlocked. She stepped into a room infused with the smells of peppermint, lemon-scented cleanliness, and cozy peat warmth. Liam faced away from her, staring down at a soggy teabag and china shards. His walking cane also sat near his feet. She was struck by the sight of the sturdy length of wood, but then again, she didn't need to see this evidence of his weakness to know that Liam wasn't who he appeared to be to his adoring public.

"Hello?" Merrit said.

Liam huffed up to his full height and turned with an awkward twist that, even so, hinted at his youthful self, the man who had entranced then devastated her mom. His eyebrows shot up in surprise.

"Walk in on faerie feet, do you?" He stared at her for a moment, then caught himself. "It's a grand pleasure to meet you at last, Merrit Chase McCallum. You take your time for a lass who's come thousands of miles. I've been waiting for you."

Merrit's heart skipped a beat. She had a sudden sense that he was a spider, patiently waiting for her to entrap herself in his web. She blew out a hard breath. "You could have visited me anytime in the village. Everyone knows where I'm staying."

"Oh no, this is your journey, after all." His tone turned self-mocking. "Besides, don't you know I'm an arrogant SOB, and I'm used to people coming to me?"

Liam held out his hand, perhaps as a peace offering. His hand was dry and lumpy against her own as they shook. She read welcome in the parentheses around his upturned lips, and she relaxed. A little.

"And how are you feeling after your hospital stay?" he said.

"I slept for two days straight. Thanks for asking."

Thanks for asking? Merrit felt heat gathering in her cheeks. She pulled her hand away and waited under Liam's scrutiny, scanning the room rather than meeting his piercing gaze. Finished wood floors glowed around the edges of a rug woven with a foliage motif. Shelves behind a well-worn armchair held dated memorabilia boxes and an odd assortment of trinkets. This was a real home. But then what had she expected, a wizard's lair—dark, unsettling, tinged with danger?

Unfortunately, Liam's serene home didn't ease her nerves. Her stomach churned and a wash of seasickness overwhelmed her. Slippery tides, standing here. Maybe this wasn't such a good idea, after all. Maybe she didn't want to know the whole truth. Maybe she wasn't strong enough.

She scrabbled in her purse for her inhaler. She clutched it hard in an effort *not* to pump a preventative measure into her lungs.

Liam ignored her distress and instead murmured that he would clean up the spilled tea later. He pointed her to an easy chair. He spoke in a reassuring tone. "I take it by your appearance today that you got wind of my new schedule. Kevin's doing, blast him. For the first time in my career, I shall be taking Mondays off. It's a blow to my ego, to be sure."

"Kevin—" she said. "He's not here, is he?"

"He'll be in his studio for a while yet."

Which meant that Kevin could walk in at any time and start his badgering like at the hospital.

With a grunt, Liam bent toward the fire.

"Let me," Merrit said.

She took her time wrestling the lid off a wrought iron canister, using the moment to steady herself. Fresh peat pellets roused the flames into a small firestorm that smelled of subterranean depths—dark, oily, secure. Merrit lowered herself into the chair he indicated. Liam's malformed hand lay inert upon his armrest. Merrit tried not to stare at it.

Liam smiled. "Ready, are you?"

Merrit realized she was still clutching her inhaler. She set it beside her on the chair cushion. "I'm not sure."

"Well, I'm ready. Have been for a while now. I've got a story to tell, and, like it or not, it's a story of hatred."

This didn't bode well. Here Merrit had thought to surprise Liam by launching into his past straight away, but—no. Instead, something was going to drop on her. She could feel this something deep under her diaphragm, the way it wanted to shove itself up against her benighted lungs.

Liam blinked toward the flames. His voice turned introspective. "I have my reasons for choosing to trust you. Think of it as payment in kind for what I'm eventually going to demand."

Merrit swallowed disappointment. "I didn't come here to be manipulated, just so we're clear."

"Believe it or not, I hope you'll at least tolerate me, which is another reason to tell you the truth." He smiled. "Besides, all social interaction is manipulation of one kind or another."

Great, Merrit thought. In other words, his truth was suspect.

With a heave and a huff, Liam pushed himself toward the front of his armchair. He stretched hands toward the fire and his words melted into the hiss of the peat pellets. "Andrew and I were too much alike, which is the only way that I can rationalize Julia's feelings for him. That said, it was really Kate's mother who set the course for all of us."

"Yes, I know. I *know*."

Liam's head cocked at her tone. "How do you know about Adrienne Meehan?"

"My mom's journal from that time together with a newspaper clipping about skeletal remains—a woman—found at Kilmoon Church in 1980. I found the article at Kate's rental place. Given my mom's journal, it seemed pretty obvious that the body belonged to Adrienne Meehan, and it seemed pretty obvious that somehow Lonnie had figured it out also. He must have been holding her death over someone. You."

"With enough dots, the line gets connected?" he said.

Liam stood. Merrit rotated with him as he circled behind her chair. She crouched backwards with knees on the seat and elbows on the head rest, watching as Liam picked up an abalone shell with a *Thank You, Liam!* scratched into its opalescent sheen. He set the memento aside and reached for a small marionette complete with purple cape and a tuft of bright hair. Liam jangled the marionette in front of Merrit. "Look at this. I used to detest it. Me? A puppet on a string? Never."

He set it on the shelf among the other trinkets and continued along the wall, tapping the dated boxes as he went. His fingers stopped at a box marked *1975*. Merrit stretched an arm toward it. Let me see, she wanted to say. I want to see what's inside, please? She leaned so far over the head rest that the chair clicked backwards into its reclined position. Liam nudged her upright, and by the time Merrit resettled, he was seated with the box on his lap. He dropped the lid on the carpet and pulled out a stack of handwritten notes in envelopes of every color, some bright as tie-dye, others creamy and elegant.

"Letters from people I matched that year. Even Andrew sent me a snide note that I burned upon receipt. It's the cruel gestures that keep hatred stoked through the years."

Liam gazed into the box, the interior of which Merrit couldn't see from her position across the hearth. His fingers dangled over the rim. "Just like you, Lonnie thought he'd connected my dots. I suppose I'm to blame for his ignorant assumptions because I've said nothing all these years."

Liam lifted out a small black box. He stretched toward her, and Merrit caught the box in her cupped hands. "Go ahead. Open it."

Tiny hinges squeaked when Merrit flipped up the top of the box. "Oh," she said, saddened more than she could express in words. Instinctively, her hand went to the moonstone that dangled at the base of her throat. Inside the box, a matching set of earrings glimmered blue-gold in the firelight.

Liam nodded toward the necklace that Merrit wore. "It's said that if you give your lover a moonstone on the full moon— which I did—you will always have passion for each other. Also, it can reunite lovers—so I was told."

"Oh," Merrit said, faint with understanding. Her heart swelled with sadness for the love Liam and Julia might have shared, for the childhood she might have had. "Mom only wore the necklace when Andrew wasn't around."

Liam sagged back into his chair. "Christ, there's something to be said for ignorance."

Merrit brushed thumbs over the earrings' pearly surfaces and listened to Liam's story of hatred, starting with a fateful night in 1975. From his rendering, she imagined a moist chill that presaged winter rains and a low-slung moon hovering before finally crossing away from daybreak. A romantic kind of evening except that Liam had blown off Julia hours earlier so that he could meet Adrienne, Kate's mom.

Sadness crept into Liam's voice. "Julia had the bright idea to pretend that I'd matched her to Andrew so that she could write up a funny little piece about the matchmaking festival. Andrew must have planted the idea in her head. So there was Andrew on one side, and then on the other side, Adrienne, who had cornered me earlier that day, making me promise to meet her at 2:00 a.m. at Kilmoon Church.

"I'd been simmering for days anyhow, trying to keep a lid on my fury over Andrew and Adrienne. To put it plainly, I was in a pisser of a mood by the time I met Adrienne. She insisted on goading me about Julia while I wanted to set her straight that there'd be no marriage—not to me anyhow. She laughed as if it were the most enjoyable game. Unfortunately, she also brought Andrew into the conversation. 'You arrogant prick,' she said. 'You think your American will like finding out about my baby girl, your daughter? Besides, she fancies Andrew as much, if not more. They are peas in a pod those two.' "

Liam shook his head, lost in thought for a moment. "I still wish she hadn't said that."

Merrit tightened her grip on the box as he continued his story of hatred.

Liam Donellan's journal

That first meeting of rock wall and fist—I didn't feel a thing. I kept on like a bare-knuckle boxer crazed with the need to win. Why didn't I take a breath, count to ten, anything? If only I'd acted with compassion and financed Adrienne a fresh start as a widow. Instead, I saw a world of hurt if I let her have an inch's sway. I saw Julia smiling but in the end drifting away as Adrienne slow-stewed my freedom into mush. I saw red.

I hope you see my dilemma. I was in love with Julia. Simply that. I'd finally understood the yearning that I saw in the eyes of the people I matched, and there stood Adrienne thinking she could take it all away. There's no logic in a fist whether it be against a rock wall or Lonnie's smirking rapist face. This, my boy, is precisely why I never asked you to explain yourself. I remember the red haze too well, and Adrienne, she knew her own brand of jabbing. Straight at my Achilles heel, you might say.

"You as much as admitted that you'd bastardize my child in exchange for your little Julia. Wouldn't the gossips love to spread the news that our matchmaker goes straight for the money. So much for your integrity and reputation."

She dared to try to control me through my best self, my role as matchmaker. That's when I shoved her against Kilmoon's wall hard enough to unleash a tumble of rocks. Kilmoon herself had entered the fray to protect one of her own. Adrienne soon enough lay on the ground with clouds in her eyes, sightlessly peering beyond her own small life. I didn't notice my blood smeared on Kilmoon's wall until the pain lit me like dried tinder, the blood a red reflection of my despair.

· 42 ·

Merrit blinked fiercely, recalling her mom's last entry in the spiral notebook, her numbed resignation, her inability to relive the whole truth even while writing to her private self. Until Merrit had read the article about the skeletal remains, she had thought her mom had overheard Liam and Adrienne having the kind of passionate sex that bordered on violence. But still, just sex.

"You killed her," Merrit said.

"I did."

"But it was an accident." Merrit couldn't help the urgency that leaked into her tone. "Right?"

"Technically, yes, but I should have stopped with the pounding. I should have noticed that a few rocks had already landed around us."

Merrit understood. She'd battled her own red place with Andrew and lost.

"Picture the scene," Liam said. "Adrienne in a lime green dress, me still in my matchmaking regalia. We stood out in the middle of nowhere, surrounded by limestone and pastures and gravestones. Adrienne leaned against Kilmoon's wall with an elbow hooked on a recessed window ledge. Kilmoon, that sacred lady, she warned us with a groan or two of shifting rock, but we were beyond noticing. I stood in front of Adrienne, not so much leaning as bracing myself against the wall. The more enraged I became, the more time slowed down. I remember the way Adrienne's fake eyelashes trembled as she blinked in time to my pounding. The way the rock wall began to squeal. Kilmoon practically announced her intent, but I didn't heed her until one of the chunks of falling limestone cracked against Adrienne's head. The sound of it—it was disgusting. Wet. Soft. Final. All I could see through my red were Adrienne's eyelashes, their final trembles before she fell.

"Only then did my body, mind, and soul turn into the broken hand, a massive pulsing pain that voided out the world until I came to, I don't know when, to find myself on the ground next to Adrienne and too late to save her. I made it back to the lane thinking I'd knock down the door of the closest house a quarter mile away and call the Garda, but there leaning against my car, whom did I see?"

Merrit pressed a hand against her chest. "Andrew."

"Oh yes, and as pleased as a rutting pig. He boasted about his and Adrienne's agreement to help each other achieve their true hearts' desires. If he ensnared Julia, then I'd be free for Adrienne. He and Adrienne had planned for her to goad me into admitting that Kate was my child and that I wanted nothing to do with her. Show me up for the despicable cad that I was while Julia listened."

Liam stared into the fire and kneaded his bad hand.

"In the end," he said, "Andrew won the jackpot, but even he couldn't risk being associated with Adrienne's death. He'd been seen around the village with her, so he offered to help me bury her. I was in so much pain, I went along with him. And, sad to say, no one remarked her absence. Just another tourist who left the matchmaking festivities early. Andrew took care to mention to a few people that Adrienne had had second thoughts about being there with her child." Liam glanced at Merrit with hostility sparking green glints in his eyes. "He could afford to be magnanimous because he had what he wanted: Julia."

Liam flexed scarred fingers as if the residual ache lessened the pain of his memories. A sympathetic throb pulsed in Merrit's hand as he went on to describe a delirium of pain and rage and grief. Somehow, he managed to drive home for shovels while Andrew watched baby Kate, who'd been asleep in Adrienne's car the whole time. Halfway through the digging Kate seemed to sense that her mother no longer lived. She didn't cry so much as keen and whimper.

"The sound haunts my dreams," Liam said. "There was a prominent Catholic orphanage down in Limerick. Mind you remember, Ireland, Catholic, conservative. Children out of wedlock? Still a scandal. In those days, you could drop infants off on orphanage steps and the nuns gladly took them in. So that's what we did. Andrew drove my car. I settled Kate in her bassinet on the stoop, knocked on the door, and fled. Then Andrew dumped me and my car at the hospital and somehow found his way back to Kilmoon before dawn. He said he'd drive Adrienne's car over the border, abandon it, and hitch back. What I remember most of all is my self-loathing as I left my fate in his hands." Liam tucked his weak hand into the folds of the strong. "That was the first and I vowed last time I'd land myself in such a passive position. I'd broken half the bones in my hand, and all I could think about in the hospital was how to salvage my tie to Julia. But there was no way. For the first time in my life, I'd lost at something that, also for the first time in my life, truly mattered."

Merrit hugged herself to lessen the chill that had invaded her bones. Such a waste, the whole wretched mess.

"You trust me not to go to the Garda with the story?" she said.

"Bah, at my age the Garda are the last thing on my mind. Besides, trust isn't the issue. You deserve to know how I ruined Julia. The last time I saw your mother was the next day on Andrew's arm. I had insisted that the doctors do a quick job of repairing my hand so I could get back to my duties. Julia looked as beautiful as ever while watching me at my match-maker's business, but her spark was gone. She'd already left Ireland behind. It was as if she woke from a long dream and realized that her efforts to be other than a well-bred, upper-class girl would always end in heartache. Andrew must have convinced her to leave it all alone—don't go to the Garda, don't worry herself over baby Kate, she'd be fine." Liam shoved the 1975 box off his lap as if its memories sickened him. "I'm sure he was persuasive."

"You could have fought for her," Merrit said. "She would have stayed with you, I know it."

"It was too late." He leaned over as if to pat her hand, but stopped himself. "No sweet family of three. It wasn't meant to be. I'm sorry."

Merrit closed her eyes against an image of Andrew's fevered gaze aimed at her from within sunken eye sockets. He'd always known how to get what he wanted.

"I don't know how I made it through that day or the next or the days that followed until the end of the festival," Liam continued. "All I thought about was Julia and what she heard from behind the wall. What it must have sounded like." He pointed to the jewelry box that Merrit still held. "Those earrings were the only thing I had left of her. I'd planned to surprise her the next day."

Merrit eased the lid shut. Her fingers left sweaty prints on the box's shiny surface. If only she knew what her mom had been thinking the day she died, when Julia had walked away from her spiteful, spoiled daughter. She now knew part of the story, the missing bit not included in the notebook, but she sensed yet more lurking beyond her grasp.

The flames had all but burned the peat back to its gritty origins. Merrit hurried to pile more chunks on the fire. Liam took the opportunity to retreat down a hall that Merrit presumed led to bedrooms. Merrit leaned her head against the fireplace bricks, reminding herself that Adrienne Meehan's death was an accident. An accident.

Liam returned, holding a worn envelope. "So you can see the extent to which the past has influenced you. I received this letter back in June."

One look at the letter's salutation and Merrit's hands began to shake.

· 43 ·

Three boxes under the window carried their labels like weak proclamations. Danny hadn't bothered to use a permanent marker, just a blue ballpoint pen that skipped over the corrugated lumps. His penmanship appeared weak-willed. *Donation*, read the first box, then *Refuse*, then *Storage*. His daughter's life partitioned into three categories no more personal than bins at a rummage bazaar. It was enough to send him out of the room, except that he'd committed himself to this final agony.

Danny reached into a dresser drawer without looking. His fingers knew this cool, smooth memento. The purple piggy bank with chipped snout. Beth had placed her first pennies into the slot on its back. Sad little piggy, time for donation. He pulled a sheet of day-old newspaper off the pile next to him, noting the headline, *The Haunted Church*.

Kilmoon Church had had her share of stories over the years. He wondered if the kids still dared one another to spend the night under her stern eye. He'd spent a frightful night or two out there himself.

Danny wrapped the piggy in newspaper and set it in the donation box. A creak and a footstep sounded from the hallway. He turned to see Ellen standing in the doorway with a footstool hugged to her chest. Without word, she positioned herself on the stool in the corner farthest from Danny. At least she wasn't yelling at him. Now, instead of calling him an untrustworthy bastard or an inconsiderate ass, she hovered with mouth closed and knees knocking together over pigeon-toed feet.

Several minutes passed in silence. Their deadened hush echoed into the rest of the house and returned shadow sounds of emptiness. An ache of wood, a tic-tac of magpie steps on the roof, the hum of the icebox. With the children visiting play-mates, the house became a morgue. It occurred to Danny that even the most corrosive comfort was hard to relinquish. Like perpetual sadness, for example.

"I saw Kate Meehan in the village," Ellen said.

Danny tensed. So this was why she'd decided to linger in the same room with him. She had something to say, and by Christ, she would.

"I couldn't help staring at her, wondering who she resembled." Her snort said all there was to say about Kate Meehan. "Of course that would be Liam. Now that the gossip's gone around about his illegitimate offspring, it's too obvious Kate takes after him. She walked around with the same air of imperious-ness about her, as if her existence justified her actions."

"Kate took after Liam in some ways. At least from what I've heard, but—"

"But you adore Liam so how similar could they be? It's almost as if you have to revise your opinion of him—just a bit, mind—to make sense of their similarities."

She was on a roll now, and the train of her words accelerated toward the wall between them. Danny dropped his hands to his lap and waited.

"You're trying to rearrange your thoughts around Liam," she said, "given the fact of this daughter. And maybe the other one, too. Merrit. You don't want to but your sense of fair play won't let you not. And if Liam isn't really the village's resident saint, could it mean that—" she hiccuped over breath stuck in her throat. "Could it mean that—"

"This isn't about our marriage, by Christ. That's you. Your doubts are your own."

"You doubt too."

"Not until lately." He pulled a wooden caboose out of the drawer. "Liam's not to blame if we've changed over the years or if events caused us to change. He's just a man."

"My point exactly," Ellen said. "He's just a man."

"Stop it."

"You forget that I still know you." Ellen spoke with quiet conviction. "You got tossed off the case—"

"How did you know?"

"Mrs. O'Brien, who else? Saw her at church yesterday. Couldn't help herself, going on about your loyalties to Kevin and Liam over doing your job." She spoke fast, not letting him respond. "So you got tossed off the case, but you can't stop yourself from investigating against Clarkson's orders."

Danny glanced down at a paper scrap anchored by a rubber ducky that no longer floated. "I guess not."

"You're willing to bankrupt us to help Marcus and lose your job to help Kevin. Turn us into paupers. All because you must do the right thing—"

"It's not that simple."

"—without regard to how I might feel. Even this, Beth's room—without my say." Ellen popped into his line of sight long enough to grab the paper scrap out from under the rubber ducky. "And what's this, more secrets?"

"Go on, read it aloud and tell me what you see."

Timeline at the party:

8.00	*Kevin arrives at party with Liam.*
8.30	*Kevin fetches Liam in from Marcus's bench, talked about the afghan.*
9.00	*Danny Ahern arrives, at bar with Kevin.*
10.15ish	*At party, Lonnie chastises Ivan for leaving back door unlocked. Lonnie just in from errand to Internet Café—received €1,000 from Kate.*
10.30	*Merrit leaves party.*
10.45	*Kevin gone for 30 minutes.*
After 11.30	*Liam opens last present using the knife that killed Lonnie. Last knife sighting.*
1.00	*Liam and Kevin leave. Liam drove.*

"Of course that's not the last time Liam saw the knife—" Ellen shook her head and leaned her head back against the wall. "Bloody hell."

Hairs danced a jig on the back of Danny's neck. "Mind telling me what's going on?"

"I was there that night if you must know. Thought I'd make some amends—I don't know for what exactly—and keep you company at your post. Only, you weren't exactly on door duty, were you?"

"That can rest a moment, don't you think?" Danny spoke in the low monotone he reserved for banishing the children to their room without dessert. Only this was his wife, and this went beyond the daily dance around her moods. He felt around under a pile of frilly socks until he found his pen. "Go on, take it."

Ellen grabbed the pen. She hunched over his timeline. Danny couldn't watch her. While the pen scratched, he matched up the socks as if his hands had brains of their own. A sick certitude washed over him. This was the end of something, right here, right now.

Ellen handed him the timeline with her blocky printing squeezed between his scrawled lines.

Timeline at the party:

8.00 *Kevin arrives at party with Liam.*

8.30 *Kevin fetches Liam in from Marcus's bench, talked about the afghan.*

9.00 *Danny Ahern arrives, at bar with Kevin.*

10.15ish *At party, Lonnie chastises Ivan for leaving back door unlocked. Lonnie just in from errand to Internet Café—received €1,000 from Kate.*

10.30 *Merrit leaves party.* Around this time, I bump into Emma outside pub, frantic to talk to Kevin. I send someone in to fetch him out for her.

10.45 *Kevin gone for 30 minutes.*

11.00 Liam visits Marcus with plate of food and escorts him to new bench.

After 11.30 *Liam opens last present using the knife that killed Lonnie.* ~~*Last knife sighting.*~~

12.00ish Liam cuts himself piece of cake with knife. You look drunk. I leave.

1.00 *Liam and Kevin leave. Liam driving.*

Hands shaking, Danny read the list through twice and carefully folded it in half. "You were spying on me. Worse yet, you knew we were talking to all potential witnesses yet you withheld information—why?"

"I haven't had a clear thought in what seems like ages."

"You seem clear enough when you're bollocking me, and you seem clear enough now." Danny grabbed up the rubbish box and upended its contents on the floor. "You can't keep using Beth's death as an excuse. Not anymore."

He carried the box into their conjugal bedroom with its big bed, one side tidy, the other rumpled from Ellen's tossed sleep. Ellen followed him.

"When Marcus recovers," he said, "he's moving back into this house. You'll need him."

June 24, 2008

Mr. Matchmaker, you cocksucker,

Pardon my pinched penmanship. I bullied Merrit into running a useless errand, and now I'm finding it hard to maneuver the pen around the oxygen tube. Yes, I'm on my last gasps, and all I think about is your clinging presence in my life. It's my death's bed wish to have the last say—at last. Call this a tug from the other side because I'll be dead by the time you receive this.

I know your daughter Merrit well, but how could I not after years of observing her. Merrit's was a difficult birth. Julia was so tiny, she couldn't carry my children afterward. You can imagine my disappointment.

I drift, but without apology. To reiterate, I know Merrit, and she can't handle conflicts that impact her most cherished notions, especially about her mother. I've already furrowed the seeds by asking her to help me die. She refuses. She maintains a daughterly sense of duty despite my indifference, even rancor. But then, I haven't yet pushed her past her infernal panic attacks. What shall I say to breach her meticulous boundaries, to push her past the brink of sanity, you ask?

I imagine if I tell Merrit that my dear Julia was a whore and that Merrit was a colossal, unwanted mistake, she would see me off to the land of morphine easily enough. This, Liam, is how I plan to have the last word.

All these words come down to this: I am sending your daughter to you. I'm sure you'll have no trouble recognizing her. She's not the end of the fun, though. Behold, an act worthy of a standing ovation:

Kate Livingston, a.k.a. Kate Meehan, a.k.a. your other bastard daughter. Money buys much information, and I have found her for you. I've seen pictures of her, and she's all yours. With the letter I just finished, Kate will come find you. Believe me, she will, because my private investigator tells me she tried to discover your identity through that orphanage we dumped her at. In fact, seems she's ruthless when it comes to getting her way. Genetics, a natural miracle.

I trust this summer will bring you a joyous family reunion. You have much to answer for: daughters without their mothers. I'm sure they'd like to know why.

Now, I sign off as these letters must leave with the hospice nurse, Merrit none the wiser.

Have yourself a nice summer,
Andrew McCallum

· 44 ·

Merrit let the letter drop from her benumbed hands, which had shifted from sweaty to icy in the space of a minute. This, she hadn't expected. Not this sucker punch straight from the grave. She could see Andrew now, the way he'd lain there with alert eyes on a face that had started to cave in on itself, knowing how ripe she was for a meltdown after months of caretaking and days filled with verbal abuse. So methodical and relentless the way he'd used her panic attacks against her. She'd sniffed then as she sniffed now against tension building behind her nose and pushing up against her throat.

"Oh boy," she said and felt a sting as if she'd inhaled water. She dug her inhaler out from beneath the seat cushion.

Liam rose and retrieved the letter from Merrit's lap. "Think about what you want to ask me while I see to tea. Strong, black tea."

Merrit squeezed the inhaler between her hands and concentrated on her breathing. There had to be a purpose for all this—what?—this mess of entangled lives and feuding male egos. At the very least, a purpose for her.

On the positive side, she'd survived reading such a letter. She hadn't cried. She hadn't used her inhaler. And, after

reading such a letter, what more could there be, right? Surely
the universe had no more tricks up its sleeves. Maybe now she
could relax. A little at least. She hadn't forgotten Kevin with
his quick temper out in his studio.

By the time Liam returned five minutes later, Merrit had
her game face on again and was ready with a question. Still, her
voice quavered as she asked, "Why didn't you retie Marcus's
shoes when you returned them?"

If surprised, Liam didn't show it. He busied himself with tea
bags and hot water. "Connected more dots, did you?"

"Marcus's dots actually."

"Ah Marcus," Liam murmured, "the man no one but you
would care to believe. And sobriety, the one factor I never considered." He passed her a cup, then the cream and sugar. "Your
turn to talk. I'm curious about your dots."

She sipped her tea, starting slowly. Liam nodded now and
then as she explained how she worked through her confusion. Did someone really make off with Marcus's shoes only to
return them later? Or did a prankster merely untie them? Did
a slice of birthday cake really appear then disappear? Finally,
that morning, after waking from a long sleep, she had decided
to take as fact all of Marcus's ramblings. Clarity had arrived in
short order.

"I was thinking so hard about the disappearing shoes and
cake that I failed to see the significance of something else
he'd mentioned. Earlier you had brought him dinner, which
seemed a kind gesture, so I thought nothing of it. In reality,
you brought him food as an excuse to move him to the iso-
lated bench on the far side of the plaza, away from the party.
During the party you got the idea to use the afghan because
you and Kevin had examined it earlier. This is another fact
Marcus mentioned that didn't mean anything at first. So the
second time you visited Marcus, you moved him, fed him, and

completed his inebriation with a hot toddy. Now you were set for the proper timing. Later, you used the cake as an excuse to leave the party again. If anyone asked, you were bringing Marcus dessert."

"It wasn't as if I had a well-thought-out plan," Liam said. "Cutting that bloody piece of cake was the trickiest bit, truth be told, because if Mrs. O'Brien had seen me at it, she'd have whipped up a song and endless toasts. But I managed it and mingled my way out the door and clapped backs with a few revelers near the lane and then went on my way."

"I'm surprised no one commented."

"Every year it's the same chaos with these parties. Everyone knows I get annoyed with so much bother and might wander into another pub for a break. Or sneak out the back door for fresh air. And even Mrs. O'Brien can't be everywhere at once with that prying nose of hers. I wasn't acting furtive, you know. I'm not that daft. Besides, the party was in full broil by then."

Merrit returned the smile that upended his lips. Then recalled why, after all, she was here and dropped her gaze to the fireplace. "You felt safe enough when you wrapped the afghan around yourself, except that it was too short so you needed Marcus's silly shoes. Oh, just Marcus, anyone would think, if they noticed at all. Most people look right past him, don't they?"

Liam grunted agreement.

"In fact, when Mrs. O'Brien said she saw Marcus lurching about on the plaza, she saw you."

"Maybe that bloody woman *is* everywhere at once."

"From there, you sauntered over to Internet Café. On your return trip to Marcus you ditched the afghan, it being bloody"—she hesitated at his squint, but he didn't deny it so she continued—"but why take the cake away after returning Marcus his shoes?"

"Because I realized my fingerprints were on that plate and also the dinner plate and the glass I'd left earlier. I threw them away on my way back to the party." He mused a moment. "I suppose this consideration caused me to forget to tie his shoes."

Merrit sank her head into the impression of Kevin's upper back in the chair cushion. She still cradled the little black box in her hands. Firelight brushed it with a touch of Van Gogh's orange. She kept picturing her mom's tears on the day she died.

"If my only goal in 1975 was to preserve my relationship with Julia," Liam said, "then so it goes now with Kevin. He'd never forgive me, not so much for causing and then covering up Adrienne's death, but for abandoning Kate only to turn around and adopt him. And he'd know me for a fraud too. I didn't adopt him because I longed to be a father but for reasons that only made sense in the moment. His world of hurt rammed into my world of hurt, and the decision chose me."

"I understand what you're saying, but surely—"

"I lost Julia, didn't I? The way she looked at me for the last time on the plaza still haunts me. So much pain and so much disillusionment. I refuse to cause the same for Kevin. Once in a lifetime is enough. I couldn't—can't—risk it. I know Kevin too well. He's a man of convictions, which means that when his truth shatters, he shatters. He's put his faith in me—too much faith—and his belief in me, in my goodness, wouldn't survive the reality of who I am. In other words, this time around I wasn't going to lose another relationship to the vagaries of chance—and by the thinnest of circumstances, I've succeeded."

"Vagaries of chance?"

"That I should happen to receive a letter that propelled me into Lonnie's shop to confirm Andrew's death. That Lonnie was just the type to be intrigued. That Lonnie happened to have a computer whiz at his side." He tapped his teacup a little too hard against its saucer. "More senseless than a headless chicken to go to Lonnie's shop, but I couldn't think what else to do to avoid Kevin's questions. He was already too curious about the bloody letter. I tried to forget the letter, believe me, I did. But it clawed at me for weeks until I finally had to know if Andrew McCallum died as he'd planned."

He grimaced into his teacup. "A little whiskey? I'm in need."

She waved him down and trotted into the kitchen. "To the right of the sink," he called. She found the liquor cabinet easily enough. Reaching for the bottle, she peered through the window above the sink toward a tidy little building with the same green trim as Liam's house. Kevin appeared in one of its lit windows and then disappeared only to reappear in another. He sat down and hunched over an object Merrit couldn't make out. Kevin still might interrupt them at any moment. She didn't relish facing him in his own territory. The hospital was bad enough.

Back in front of the fire, Merrit handed Liam the bottle. He poured a shot into his tea while Merrit held her cup out for a slosh. He continued talking as if she hadn't left the room, telling her that on the day of the party Lonnie had threatened to go to Kevin with the information about Adrienne Meehan.

"I hadn't heard that name said aloud in thirty-three years. Imagine my shock. I had paid him his €500 because Kevin didn't need to know about sisters and start rooting around in my past. All annoying enough, but then Lonnie demanded €1,000 because he'd landed on Adrienne's death. Would he have told Kevin about her death? Maybe not. But then maybe. I couldn't have that, but I didn't start the evening with anything in mind either. Marcus had mentioned you were Lonnie's date, so I watched out for you with interest. Noticed you well before you knocked my presents over. That was a precious moment, by the way. Quite the entertainment." He yawned back in an almost laugh before continuing. "It wasn't until

Lonnie whispered in my ear about you that I knew he had you under his thumb also."

"What did he say?"

"He reminded me that we had an appointment later that evening, and mentioned that by the way, you had also paid him for my sins. Unfortunately, that's when the ball really dropped for the little sod. If he could get money out of you for that reason, he'd have no qualms going to Kevin if the mood struck him. I had to take back control. It didn't help that seeing you on Lonnie's arm rekindled memories of Julia on Andrew's even down to Lonnie's smug and self-entitled smirk." Liam's face settled into an expression of wry self-deprecation. "Like a fool, I fancied I could rescue you from Lonnie's grasp as I couldn't your mother from Andrew's."

He paused. Firelight bronzed his skin, colored in his wrinkles.

"So," Merrit said.

"So, yes, I made do with what was on hand. Unfortunately, the first thing that popped into my head was your afghan. The next thing, the knife. I took Marcus his dinner as you said. I needed him passed out so I could borrow the afghan." He waved a hand. "You guessed the rest."

Merrit held out her cup for another tipple, thinking about Kevin in his studio, possibly unaware of the extent of Liam's love. "About Kevin—"

"Yes, Kevin. This conversation must come back to him. He was four years old when I visited the orphanage a few days after the festival ended."

Merrit almost stopped his recitation because she'd only meant to ask him what time he expected Kevin in for dinner. Instead, she sipped and tried to be OK with her Goldilocks presence in Kevin's chair.

"I had a mind to satisfy myself that baby Kate was safely tucked away," Liam said. "That's all."

He was lost in words now, back to the day he met Kevin. Melancholic envy jabbed at Merrit, the taste of it sour in her mouth. Ridiculous to hope that some of their closeness might rub off on her and that she might have a reason to stay longer. Theirs was a whole bond not readily cut into bite-size pieces for donation to the stray on their doorstep.

"Sometimes," Liam said, "I think about the small miracles that can occur in our darkest moments. Are they only coincidences? Or are they destiny? There I sat in the waiting room with a couple who waved their completed paperwork and raved about the cutest mite they'd ever seen. He was the sunniest most affectionate little boy and ran to them when they visited. I sat there mired in my misery while they flipped through an orphanage album. If I'd only taken the album when they'd pressed it on me, if I'd only pulled it from their grasp and cooed over the pictures of Kevin, they'd never have continued flipping and thus landed on the photo of the newest arrival. Kate." His expression turned sour. "Get her now before she's snapped up!"

He tossed doctored tea into the fireplace and the fire hissed. "They called in a nun to discuss Kate while another nun led me to the nursery to view her. She looked healthier than ever, and, believe me, I was glad for that. I was hardly there two minutes and already on my way out when the couple barreled in with ferocious expressions like they wanted to rip Kate from my arms."

Merrit held her breath, and Kevin the man came into focus with his curious mixture of reticence and pugnacious loyalty. Liam glanced at her and nodded.

"Right you are. They nearly trampled over Kevin in their haste to get to Kate. To them, he no longer existed. His lost look as they passed him by, it about broke my heart again. This too was my fault."

"You were there in the perfect moment for both of you."

"Maybe so." Liam grabbed his knees in a tight grip. "You Merrit, can allow me peaceful times with Kevin. Or not. If you want me all to yourself all you have to do is explain the story behind his adoption."

She shook her head, confused and feeling the whiskey now. The more she shook her head, the more he nodded by contrast until at last he said, "Come now, this is a grand opportunity."

"For what?" Merrit angled herself in the chair so that she faced him. "You vowed you'd never let yourself be railroaded again so why give me power over your relationship with Kevin? It doesn't make sense, especially because I could turn you into the Garda. They'd figure out your part in Lonnie's death."

"As if I care about them. I have nothing to lose except Kevin." His gaze turned inward. "Rest assured that I have a reason for everything I say."

"Oh, please, what a crock of Irish shite."

"So it would seem, but that doesn't change the fact that you're now in a position—like Kate was—to get what you want out of me."

Merrit swallowed the last of her whiskey. Her yearning must be transparent, leaking out of her like a needy, despicable creature that would trade on Liam's vulnerability and Kevin's finely tuned sensibilities.

"No," she said. "I'm in no position to judge you. Try granting power to someone who likes it—someone more like you."

Or someone more like Kate, she didn't say, but once again he seemed to know her thoughts because he said, "Less like me is better, I think."

The fire sizzled and behind her a grandfather clock ticked Merrit forward in time whether or not she cared to go. Kate. One hard-starting bite of air, no cutie-fying her name. Kate, who died in eerie mimic of her mother. A cranky rumbling sound approached the house, interrupting Merrit's next question.

"Ah," Liam said, "that would be Danny."

Merrit rose. "I'd better go."

"No, stay. There's no going back now."

Merrit lowered herself onto the chair, woozy from the whiskey. In a way, she was glad for the interruption. Her brain was so full of Liam's words they were about to dribble out her ears.

· 45 ·

The peaceful view along the track that ended at Kevin's cottage did nothing to ease the tension from Danny's shoulders. Before he left home, Ellen hadn't defended herself against her lapse in judgment except to say that she couldn't cope. All those agonizing minutes while he shoved clothes and toiletries into the cardboard box, she had fluttered about in a panic. Finally, he'd rounded on Ellen with, "You must start coping. I can't do this anymore."

"What about the children?"

"I'm not abandoning them, only gifting you the martyrdom you desire."

As he'd pushed the box onto the porch, she'd called out with hoarse words that she must have rehearsed for two years. "Beth was my fault. I forgot to warn Marcus she'd taken to climbing the playhouse and reaching for the clouds." For a moment, just a moment, he'd hesitated until she blurted, "Now I suppose you'll divorce me."

Martyrdom complete.

But at least he knew why Kevin disappeared for a while during the party. Fragile Emma.

Danny heaved himself and the box out of the ticking car. He dragged his belongings up the steps to Liam's front door, and from long habit knocked three times before entering. Here he was about to beg a room from a man he would soon be arresting, all because Ellen's observations about the night of the party had finally lit a bulb for Danny. His hands still shook from the force of his shock, which he'd barely managed to hide from Ellen.

"What's that then, bricks?" Liam said.

Danny turned from his struggle with the box to see none other than Merrit Chase, flushed and cradling her inhaler. Of course she'd found her way to Liam's house. This was what she did: appear. Anywhere. Everywhere. And, worse still, by the looks of her, she'd solved the mystery of Lonnie the Lovely. Knowledge peeked out from behind her worried blinks while Liam relaxed with a smile aimed in Danny's direction. A near-empty whiskey bottle sat at his feet. Damn the man. And damn Clarkson for being correct about Danny's lack of objectivity.

Danny pulled the scribbled party timeline out of his pocket and placed it on Liam's armrest. "Tell me I'm wrong."

Liam ticked down the page with a finger. "Bloody hell if he hasn't connected a different set of dots and come to the same verdict as you, Merrit. Fascinating."

"Glad I amuse you." Danny grabbed back the timeline. "Does Kevin know she's here?"

"No."

"I'll visit him then. You two are turning my stomach about now."

A minute later Danny arrived at Kevin's studio with beers in hand, wondering how to break the news about Liam to Kevin.

Danny cleared his throat. "Two things. I'll be taking over Liam's guest room for a while." He hurried on before Kevin sidetracked him with sympathy. "But I actually came to—"

Kevin defrocked his bottle with a quick jerk. "What's that then?

Danny realized he didn't have the heart to talk about Liam right now, not with Kevin looking at him with good-natured expectancy. "I came to warn you that Merrit has arrived."

"Nice way to ruin my mood." Kevin set his beer aside. He brushed wood dust off his jeans with more force than necessary, then let his hands go limp on his thighs. "Right then. Your broken marriage and my broken I-don't-know-what. Cheers to us."

Merrit picked up the tea tray and let the last glimmers of day guide her footsteps out of the living room and toward the kitchen sink above which the window offered a view of purple shadows settling across pastures, along stone walls, and within thorny briars. Kevin's lit studio stood out as the exception to the peaceful glow over the countryside. Inside the studio, Danny and Kevin appeared clear as actors on stage. With similar part-mocking grimaces, they clinked their beer bottles together.

Kevin and Danny were indeed like brothers. She, the interloper, wanted to yell at them, to tell them they were all three on the same side and trying their best to figure out how to orbit around Liam. Instead, her lungs tightened. So far, despite everything, her conversation with Liam had gone well. Too well. And now Danny had arrived with his conclusions and his convictions and his sense of duty. She could steer clear of Kevin for a while longer, but not Danny. Danny, who knew the truth about Liam.

She waited, watching, as Kevin began wiping down his woodworking wheel. He raised a hand in goodbye, shaking his head at the same time. A moment later Danny appeared outside the studio. Merrit stepped outside and lowered herself onto a step where the last magenta sun strokes must outline her, but Danny concentrated on navigating the tussocks. He flicked a few strands of hair off his forehead with an oddly graceful gesture. He squared his shoulders, which were broad enough, but let them slump again as he shook his head. A realization startled Merrit. Danny's presence held some sway, and as he approached, she acknowledged that the possibility of staying awhile longer attracted her all the more with Danny in the vicinity. Even if he didn't much like her. Even if he was married.

"I suppose you want to have it out with me now, Detective Sergeant," Merrit said just loud enough to wrest Danny's gaze from the ground. "Sure sounded like it when you arrived."

He dropped down beside her with an exhausted-sounding grunt. "You're a sorry piece of work. Let's leave it at that for now."

His leg started to dance in place, causing the step to vibrate beneath their feet.

"Your boss, your men, do they know? About Liam?" she said.

His leg stopped. "No."

Merrit smiled into the dark. Thank goodness.

"Let me rephrase that. Not yet."

Just like that, Merrit's relief disappeared. "You have to tell them?"

And just like that, Danny's tone hardened. "What do you think? You act as if Liam's guilt doesn't bother you."

"I've had a few days to get my head around it, that's all."

"Bloody fecking hell." Danny massaged his temples, shaking his head. "This is Liam we're talking about. He barely gets around without that cane of his. He's family. And when Kevin finds out—"

"So you may not arrest Liam, after all?"

"He did kill someone."

Danny reached into his jacket pocket. With a flick, the scrap of paper landed on Merrit's lap. She tilted it toward the kitchen window for light. Gurgling water and clanking tea ware signaled Liam's presence a few feet away.

"That's my wife's writing. She was there that night unbeknownst to me. While keeping an eye on me, she managed to be my star witness to events at the party. Liam conveniently forgot to mention that he brought Marcus dinner, and that later he did see the cake up close."

"He brought Marcus a piece of cake, so, yes—"

"But I didn't know that until now, did I? In fact, the beauty of it is that when I read my wife's notes, I remembered an offhand remark Liam made right there in his kitchen. He said it himself. He didn't try Mrs. O'Brien's cake, didn't venture near it for fear that she'd force everyone to sing 'happy birthday,' and he detests white cake in any case. He slipped up. He shouldn't have known it was white cake under the chocolate frosting if he never saw the cake up close. So he had the knife in hand later than he was willing to admit"—he tapped the paper scrap that Merrit still held—"and everyone except my wife spying on me near the window was too oblivious to notice."

Merrit pictured the cake on its table, in a corner, near a window. With back to the room, no one inside the pub would have seen what implement he used to cut the cake. He said he'd had to make do with what was in front of him, and so he had. No one gave him much thought precisely because he was a fixture his fellow Lisfenorans took for granted.

"Lonnie's blackmail wasn't why he died, not really," Merrit said. "Liam's motivation for Lonnie was rooted in the past, not the present."

"Yes, the final, irrovocable fact of the matter that both you and Ivan chose to keep to yourselves. Adrienne Meehan. There she was on the page in your mom's journal, alive and well shagging Liam—or so it read to me—but then here was Kate, the angry orphan. So, what happened to her mum?" He paused, staring into a somewhere-else place for a moment. "I have a vague memory of the body that turned up in 1980 and daring Kevin to spend the night out at Kilmoon. For as long as I can remember, Our Lady has enjoyed her haunted reputation. However, I didn't connect that old story—Kilmoon unburying her dead—until after I read my wife's observations about Liam. Suddenly, he was a suspect because of that bloody piece of cake. Why would he lie about it? From there, it was nothing to reinterpret the last entry in your mother's notebook, eh?"

Merrit nodded.

Danny held out his hand for the paper scrap. "I wager a trace will reveal no sign of Adrienne since 1975. Northern Ireland was a nightmare back then. Too easy to be lost."

Merrit folded the timeline and handed it back to Danny. He'd connected his set of dots quite well indeed. As for Lonnie's blackmail, he knew enough about the business of the orphanage—Kate's drop-off, Kevin's adoption—to understand what Lonnie was truly holding over Liam's head: Kevin's peace of mind.

Inside the studio, unsuspecting Kevin placed a bowl on a shelf that already held a potpourri of wooden items. He disappeared from view, taking the light with him.

Danny pulled Merrit up by the elbow and waved her ahead of him into the kitchen. "You'd best go."

Liam had decided to fix the evening meal himself as evidenced by the smell of cooking tomatoes. Chicken strips simmered in the sauce while Liam chopped mushrooms and tossed them into the pan. "Only potatoes to pour this mess onto, I'm afraid. Merrit, join us?"

"I'd better hold off on the family dinners for now. But I'll see you tomorrow, right?"

Liam stopped chopping. The knife blade glinted. "Oh yes."

· 46 ·

Well before dawn, Kevin eased himself into Liam's house and tiptoed past his bedroom. A hitch in Liam's snores caught Kevin with hand on the study's doorknob. The grandfather clock gonged once for the half hour, and Liam's breath resumed its sleep pattern. The knob slipped under Kevin's moist grip. Still locked, this door, which wasn't Liam's usual way.

Kevin's palms itched with the need to know why Liam had started locking this door. Something irksome stank the air, to be sure, and Kevin hadn't liked the hushed conversation he spied between Danny and Merrit last night, loitering there on the back porch. Somehow, they'd found a common ground, and Kevin had a feeling they weren't about to share it with him.

Kevin set his ear against the guest room door across the hall. Danny snuffled in his sleep.

The study door beckoned him again. Liam had apparently forgotten that as the contractor for the house, Kevin could intrude at will. This memory lapse worried Kevin. It could be the mental fog of old age, but more likely Liam was distracted for less benign reasons.

He steadied his hand and inserted the master key in the lock. Liam's sanctum was almost laughable in its masculinity, right down to the print of hunting dogs leading a merry band of steeplechasers. Kevin entered often enough to borrow a book but until now had never breeched Liam's trust. He parted the curtains, already noting this amiss. Liam never bothered closing them. Upon turning to sight along the moonlit stream, he caught a second anomaly. On a desk otherwise empty of gadgetry—no pencil sharpener, no calculator, nothing but a leather blotter and matching pen holder—sat a fancy laptop computer. A bead of disquiet settled in Kevin's throat. He could have sworn that Liam was computer-phobic.

Saying a prayer of forgiveness for which Father Dooley would be proud, he pressed the power button. The computer whirred through its start-up routine and then spoke to Kevin through a personalized password request. *Hello, Milady, you know what to enter in the spaces below.*

After a long pause, Kevin wrenched open the first desk drawer, and—God forgive him for this transgression also— those were his hands exercising their unspeakable need to find a sales receipt. Could be Ivan had needed the money and sold Liam the machine straight out of his workroom. Could be. Kevin didn't recognize the absurdity of his search for a receipt until his hands landed on the last thing he'd expected to find. A knife.

"Ah Christ," he whispered into the dark, realizing there must be more to discover.

· 47 ·

Merrit sat in her usual spot on the plaza, missing Marcus. Around her, Liam's petitioners mingled and waited their turns while Liam spoke to a grandmotherly type who smiled at something Liam said.

The sun had shifted position since her first days in Lisfenora. Twilight already softened the edges of the shops. Merrit tucked her sunglasses into her purse, which was now so heavy that the straps left dents in her shoulder. Time to clean house, she thought, and pulled the freakish thing onto her lap.

She'd just pulled out a wadded baggage claim ticket when she caught sight of Ivan ducking and weaving toward her. Poor Ivan. He was doomed to turn into an anxious little-old-lady man in need of chamomile tea blends.

Ivan arrived and stood before her, stepping from foot to foot. He'd cut his hair so short that he look scalped. "Danny came to see me this morning."

Merrit, who had started to pull crumpled receipts out of her purse, paused at his tone. She knew it well enough and always pictured a weasel in a coyote disguise, not so wily but pretending at it.

"There might be a problem, I am not sure." Ivan cleared his throat. "Danny is still questioning. He could still ruin my life."

Indeed, what about Danny? All day long, she'd been expecting the Garda to arrive and cart Liam off.

"After I saw Kate dead," Ivan said, "I told Danny that before the party I heard her arguing with Lonnie about money, but that is not true. I do not know who he was talking to. He was on the phone. Could be to you."

Merrit gathered a mound of purse garbage onto her lap and crushed it into a ball the size of a grapefruit. She lobbed it into the garbage can sitting next to the bench. Now that Ivan's hair was short, Merrit noticed his stretched and reddened right earlobe. Ivan yanked on it. "Danny is persecuting me," he said.

Merrit had a better theory. Maybe Danny was still conflicted about Liam and couldn't help pursuing the possibility of another truth, any truth at all.

"He will want to know why I lied and that is more obstruction. But it is obvious I fibbed because I wanted this business finished. No more inquiries, no more risk. Kate was the best candidate for killer, that was my thinking, and it was too perfect an opportunity. That is why I said I heard her arguing with Lonnie."

"He'd probably leave you alone if you stopped acting squirrely all the time."

"But I cannot help it. I cannot leave Ireland. I have to save my love."

Merrit halted in the midst of pulling out a tangled length of yarn. Ivan. In love. In secret love at that. No wonder he was twitchy. This had to be about one of the O'Brien daughters with their ridiculous names. "The youngest one, Constanza?"

"How did you know? Does everyone know? No one can know yet until we are ready to tell Mr. O'Brien. For now we act friendly with each other, nothing more." Ivan squirmed. "But that is not the point. Why can Danny not believe that Kate killed Lonnie and leave me alone?"

Beyond Ivan and the layers of people behind him, Liam stood up after dismissing the grandmotherly woman with a smile and a shoulder squeeze.

"I'm driving him home today," Merrit said.

She didn't mention that an information booth volunteer had found her in the crowd and asked her for this surprising favor on Kevin's behalf. Perhaps he was starting to come around. She could hope at least.

"So I should not worry, you think?" Ivan said. "That Danny still questions?"

"Go on, Ivan, be happy."

"You are the one to say that to me, absurd."

She waved him away with a nod to acknowledge that they could both use a little practice on that front.

· 48 ·

Our Lady of the Kilmoon nestled in her pasture with the Celtic standing stone her guardian. She extended her shadow over grave markers and minded her business in the genteel way of a bustled and high-bosomed matriarch of old, fanning herself with the breeze, dabbing herself with sea-scented rain. She neither turned away nor embraced visitors who passed over her threshold. When they departed, as they usually did, the fecund remains of the dead became hers to brood over once again.

Scudding clouds eclipsed the sun, and their shadows passed over Kilmoon like distress sullying an otherwise placid expression. Or so Kevin thought as he perched on a low stone ledge that formed part of Our Lady's inner wall. The red glow within his closed eyelids faded then brightened then faded with cloud movement. Though sad for all that had gone wrong, he also felt at peace with his decision and the rough emotional waves to come as a result. It couldn't be helped, change was change, and he'd done his best to avoid it for the past thirty-seven years.

He opened his eyes to the small wilderness Our Lady clutched to her bosom. The engravings upon the grave markers benefited from her shelter, and Kevin easily read the names and dates of those who'd died after the church grounds fell out of use for everything but burial services. Chattering wheatears darted from their roosts in the walls, calling to one another with staccato chirps. Human murmurs rose over the walls causing a flurry of twitters and sudden flights into nooks and crannies. Americans, by the sound, and a few moments after Kevin made out their accents, their faces appeared in one of the windows.

"How quaint," said the woman. "Oh, hi there, are we bothering you?"

The couple stooped hand-in-hand through a narrow doorway that marked the front of the church. They sported identical outfits that consisted of hiking boots, khaki walking shorts, and fleece pullovers. Kevin suppressed a groan. Liam had matched them. The fledgling pairs always looked as if he had injected them with a happiness elixir that caused their skin to glow.

The woman pulled the man along with her toward Kevin. "We couldn't help but stop. This is such a great site."

"So it is," Kevin said.

"I bet you hate tourists busting in on your quiet spots."

In truth, these refugees from an outdoor clothing catalog were a fine distraction. It was almost divine the way this reminder of Liam's good works displayed itself for Kevin's bittersweet perusal.

"We're here for the festival. I guess that's pretty obvious." The woman's laugh flew over the walls. "The matchmaker brought us together last night at the Pied Pig Pub. He's great. I really love him."

Ridiculous woman to speak of love as if she'd popped off her catalog photo and straight into a bad movie. A robin landed on a windowsill and puffed out its red breast. One of Liam's favorite birds—a symbol for new beginnings. Kevin leaned back and closed his eyes. The couple gushed on for a few minutes before departing. Birdsong and grass rustles took over once again, and sometime later—he couldn't be sure, perhaps he'd dozed—a shadow less transient than a cloud darkened his inner sky.

Emma stood before him in white trainers and one of her vintage dresses. She pointed toward a cat that had slunk out from behind one of the grave markers. "He's frightfully thin, poor thing. Not much of a hunter."

Her voice shook as if a cog that connected her vocal cords to her tear ducts had loosened. He didn't comment on this or the bruised skin beneath her eyes or her twitching eyelid. On some level, he still knew her. He could have predicted that she'd drop to the ground and with slow movements pull a sandwich out of the picnic basket she'd brought with her. The scrawny tabby inched forward with tail high. Emma clicked low in her throat and tore turkey bits out of the sandwich.

Kevin found himself staring at the back of Emma's neck. He'd never noticed the purplish birthmark just below her hairline or the way the vertebrae stuck out like fragile possibilities. He blamed himself for her current condition, of course he did, and he accepted that he always would.

A few moments later the cat was wolfing down turkey and almost choking over its purrs. "His tag says *Burt*," Emma said. "Someone loved him once." She picked up the cat and turkey and sat next to Kevin. She settled the cat on the ledge beside her. Her elbow brushed Kevin's arm as she leaned over to pull out another sandwich. "Would Liam take on a cat?"

"How many do you have now?"

"Three."

Kevin bit into the sandwich she handed him. Roast beef. The cat started to nose over Emma's lap. Kevin relinquished half the beef, and the cat settled back into purring gobbles. Liam with a cat. Might be just the thing.

Emma handed him a cranberry-apple juice, his favorite, and

he made much of opening it and drinking, unsure what to say now that the moment was upon him. "I think he'd accept a cat. But you will have to deliver it to Liam yourself."

Emma rolled the cat up into her arms and flipped him over for a look between his legs. She handled him with confidence, but Burt arched his back in an effort to return to his lunch. She set him down. "Burt is a girl. I'm sure the poor mite will need a de-worming and flea bath. I have a cat-care booklet I can give Liam, though I'm sure he's owned a cat or two in his life." She turned away from petting Burt. Her gaze held a thousand unsaids. "Hasn't he?"

Kevin almost laughed. Given what he now knew about Liam, a simple fact about pet ownership seemed ridiculous by comparison. "No worries, he'll take good care of any cat you gift him."

"You're in on this too."

He reached over Emma, inhaling the scent of jasmine, and scratched under the cat's ears. "You tell him I was with you when you found Burtene. He'll understand."

Kevin finished his sandwich, savoring the horseradish that Emma mixed into the mustard. He could never get enough of her sandwiches.

"Kev." She placed fingers on his wrist. "What about me?"

Kevin cursed timing and circumstance. If he'd been ready for her last year none of this would have happened. None. He couldn't say what he suspected was the truth. They'd likely never be together again. He'd allowed himself to hope, but now he must put an end to that also.

Tears dripped down Emma's cheeks. She delved into the basket and pulled out home-baked chocolate biscuits. They chewed for a while, while the cat lounged in a contented sprawl and washed her face with dainty paw swipes. The sun settled itself atop a wall, and the chill started as it slid out of view.

"What about Liam?" she said.

"I'm sure Merrit Chase will look after him."

"Oh, her." Emma leaned into him, then caught herself and pulled away. "What about money?"

"I've enough saved up, and I can land construction or wood work anywhere." A small surge of freedom startled him. He thought about the notebook filled with Julia Chase's erratic entries, and her descriptions of her future husband, Andrew. "And I suspect that Merrit has money should Liam need help."

"What about your business?"

"A fellow contractor has been giving me hassle to join our businesses together. He'll take over my projects and my men, and we'll see how he makes out."

"Does Liam know?"

"He will soon enough."

"You have all the answers," she said.

Now Kevin did laugh.

Kilmoon was well into shadow when they split ways. Emma placed Burtene in the picnic basket with tears trailing her cheeks. Her eyes skittered, never landing on him. "I hope it will be OK for you."

Still polite, even now. "And I hope it will be OK for you too."

Only after her Volkswagen chugged out of auditory range and bird calls quieted for the night did Kevin gather up their rubbish. A moist chill off the Atlantic had descended, crisp and clean. Autumn in the air, season for change, this September in particular.

He turned back for a last look at the church. Limestone glowed in pinks, and the secrets Our Lady shared with Liam remained safe. He bowed to her in goodbye. The banking sun slid into a thick wall of clouds on the horizon, and Our Lady bowed back behind a descending curtain of nightfall.

On the lane in front of the church, Kevin patted his truck canopy and gazed in the side window at his neatly packed belongings that included the wood turning table and Liam's cast. Goodbye, Mistress Kilmoon.

Liam Donellan's journal

Back then, I couldn't help thinking that Kilmoon Church at night exuded an unquiet air quite different from daylight hours. I fancied spirits cavorting through the grasses and whispers light as rustling leaves following me as I wound through the grave markers. Unfortunately, these days the spirit whispers have felt too real so I haven't returned except by day. And now these hours are ruined too. Perhaps I fear what the age-old rocks could say about my old-age bones . . .

That last evening with Adrienne, the church walls looked porous indeed. Solid yet not, all but crumbling in the damp. Weathered and crackled old limestone still to last longer than I, longer than Adrienne, and, now, these many years later, longer than Kate.

· 49 ·

Merrit hissed in frustration and ducked into the bowels of the kitchen cabinetry. She almost missed the front door's wheeze and indecipherable grumbles from the living room where Liam rested on his easy chair. A moment later Danny entered the kitchen, opened the dishwasher, and pulled out a clean pot. "Extra storage. They hand wash."

Taking over, he littered the counter with sandwich makings and got the canned soup going. Merrit retreated like the awkward outsider she was. Stretching for a conversational opener, she mentioned that she'd seen Ivan that afternoon, and that he was just as stressed as ever.

Danny continued slicing the Swiss cheese. "That's because he knows that I know he lied about overhearing an argument between Lonnie and Kate. He's still too slippery for my liking." The knife bit into the chopping board with a decided thump. "Telephone records are a wonderful thing."

Of course, telephone records. Much good arguing with Lonnie had done Merrit anyhow.

Danny left to fetch Liam while Merrit poured soup into bowls and finished the sandwiches. When they returned, Liam slipped past Danny to peer out the window toward Kevin's unlit studio. When he turned around a frown line bisected the skin between his eyebrows.

The men sat down. Still standing, Merrit bit into ham and cheese on wheat bread, and managed to swallow.

Danny stirred his soup restlessly. "I need to ask some questions. Then you two can return to where you left off last night."

"As you wish, Danny-boy, as you wish," Liam said.

"Why did you cut off Lonnie's braid?"

Good question, Merrit thought.

"A pair of scissors were in the desk," Liam said. "I held them through the afghan and snipped, that's all. I also scattered the money about the room. Only an ass would take the braid but not the cash." He sipped a spoonful of soup. "Kate was surprised to see Marcus enter Internet Café the night of the party and even more surprised to see him turn into me when I discarded the afghan afterward. I was sorry to do that, by the way, but I'd gotten blood on it."

"You thought it all out," Danny said.

"If you only knew how wrong you are. For example, my shoes. What to do with them? I had to tuck them into my waistband, which was awkward at best. And then on the return trip from Lonnie's shop, anyone could have noticed that I suddenly gained a stone in the gut because I needed a place to store *Marcus's* shoes after I set aside the afghan. I regretted borrowing Marcus's shoes, but the afghan was too short. That Kate, prowling as usual, of course she noticed it all. And of course she legged it into the café to see what I'd been up to. Even *I* said a prayer over Lonnie's body, but I'll wager she danced a jig knowing she had yet more to use against me, not to mention a perfect opportunity to complicate Merrit's life with an inhaler she'd stolen out of Merrit's purse that very day." He nodded at Merrit. "Eh?"

"Yes, at the tea house while I was in the bathroom," she said. "How did you know?"

"We talked." He stirred his soup and let the spoon clank against the bowl. "Just before she died."

Merrit swallowed another bite of sandwich. It felt like sandpaper sliding down her throat. Kate and her, they weren't so different, both of them daughters with broken childhoods, daughters who had followed their mothers' footsteps in search of something from Liam. She pushed the soup and sandwich away, sick with the realization that despite her best efforts, she had never come to terms with her desire for a sense of place missing since her mom's death, a true home.

But she could salvage something. Maybe. If Kevin let her. If Liam stayed out of jail.

"I'm not hungry either." Liam arched his back with a grunt. "Kate wanted me all to herself."

"Why?" Danny said.

"Because I owed her, of course. She told me quite the tale about her adoptive family. Seems Kate's younger sister, the miracle birth child, had severe asthma. Kate sat through many a doctor's appointment while her sister was tested. She even learned the name of the drug used—something starting with *M*."

"Methcholine," Merrit said.

She told them about Kate's visit to the hospital, where she confessed to the not-quite-sleeping Merrit that she'd stolen two inhalers, not one, out of Merrit's purse, and latched onto the idea of using Methcholine to screw with Merrit. "I didn't notice that the new inhaler was an Irish model. Since the placebos don't have labels, they look the same to me. She wanted to give me a scare, but I don't think she'd have minded if I'd died."

"Probably not," Liam said. "Kate told me she had a medical contact through her website design work. Apparently, she was quite good despite specializing in websites for the kinky set. I didn't ask how she coaxed a doctor out of a test inhaler." He grimaced. "I'm certain of her persuasiveness. In that, she was like me in my youth. She went on down to Limerick to pick up a new inhaler and later slipped it into your purse by way of one of our local lads."

A phantom ache reminded Merrit of the teenager who had practically broken her big toe when he bumped into her.

"What else did Kate tell you?" Danny asked Liam.

"She was the one to plant the afghan in Mrs. Sheedy's rubbish bin, also to implicate Merrit. You want to know how?"

This was crazy. Beyond crazy. The way Liam circled around the Kate topic without landing on her death. Yet, Merrit couldn't help nodding like a child before a storyteller.

"If you tilt the bin on edge and pull the chain so that it tightens against one side of the lid and loosens on the other—you need to be quite strong, obviously—you can lift the lid on the loose side. Kate had seen a few of the pub workers do it to mess about with Mrs. Sheedy."

Merrit didn't care about the garbage can. It was beside the point, a sideshow to the main event. She opened her mouth and closed it again, taking her cue from Danny, who merely stared off into space as if he were listening to a dull radio program. Silence reigned for a full minute.

"Our Lady of the Kilmoon." Liam repeated the words three times, each time in a softer voice. "She had her own designs. First the mother, then the daughter. Our Lady misses protecting families within her boundaries. She wanted the Meehans."

"Liam," Danny said.

"I'd like tea."

More silence as Danny prepared tea and heated up scones. "Here," he said a few minutes later. And then, "Your cane left a perfect circle of a bruise on Kate's chest."

Liam spoke with a hazy tone. "This time around, I thought to help Our Lady, yes."

"You—what?" Merrit said.

"She wasn't about to send a falling rock to my rescue, so I felled Kate toward her. It helped that Kate had a sprained ankle. I'd seen her limping around. That's how I got the idea. I suggested we meet so we could talk things out, and what better place than Kilmoon? Fitting, I thought."

Merrit leaned against the counter, her lungs beginning to cramp. "It was a defensive push. Tell me her death was an accident like her mother's."

Liam cut his scone in half and layered each half with red currant jam. Danny yanked out scone innards while muttering "Jesus oh Jesus fucking hell" under his breath.

"You pushed her with the cane, that's all," she tried again. "I saw her. Her shoe heel broke. She tripped. How were you to know she'd fall against a gravestone?"

"Providence looked out for me, but it was a decided aim. I had to wait her out though." Remorse entered Liam's voice. "She didn't die immediately. She looked so much like her mother. I talked to her, you know. I explained my actions, and I thought I heard her say I was probably right."

"Right about what?" Merrit asked.

"My instincts, which I know to be right anyhow."

Danny had by now buried his face in his hands. "Jesus, Liam, you make it sound like Kate was a sacrificial lamb."

"In a way, she was."

Danny raised his head with a wild stare. "For what? Tell me, sacrificed for what?"

"For the life I want to leave behind. I'm nonnegotiable when it comes to that, and when it comes to Kevin's well-being."

"You planted Lonnie's braid on her," Danny said.

"Poetic, I thought. Leave the braid in the same vein she left the inhaler at Lonnie's crime scene. We like to spread the blame around, don't we? I wanted Lonnie's case closed with no further investigation, so I did what I could in that regard, including breaking off one of Kate's heels so her death appeared accidental."

Danny groaned.

"I need to know why," Merrit said. "All to protect Kevin from your past?"

"Not all, no. Part of my motivation will become clear to you later with perspective and a little knowledge I'm unwilling to divulge at the moment."

Merrit breathed into her hands. Even when he told the truth, Liam didn't tell the whole truth. What the hell, ultimately, was he trying to accomplish?

Liam squinted toward the window. "Where is that Kevin? It's not like him not to call."

· 50 ·

Kevin drove toward the westernmost end of Connemara, land of shaggy ponies, lonely valleys, and pale mountains. A faint purple smudge of day's end colored the horizon, and his high beams spotlighted bumpy asphalt right before it passed under his tires. He sped up and felt the road stretch its miles out behind him, ever lengthening the distance between the known and the unknown.

On a hilly rise he caught the lights of Clare across Galway Bay. Lisfenora lay beyond a bend of coast, south, its glow hidden by a craggy shoreline and limestone plateaus. Too fast, the narrow coast road folded back on itself and Clare blinked out, leaving Kevin to his nomadic journey. And maybe even to his outlaw journey if the Garda decided they wanted him for breaking and entering. The thought thrilled him even as nerves sent his fingers rat-a-tatting against the steering wheel. Liam must be worrying by now.

He'd left Lisfenora with Emma's pain a lip gloss smear across his cheek. Now orphanage memories hovered like specters. The rustling wool, flickering candles, and echoing sorrow within a hall that led to rooms with crayon art on the walls. The area earmarked for the children had smelled like wood shavings from sharpened pencils and chalk dust flurries caught in sunshine. But Kevin still couldn't picture the couple who had almost adopted him. Of them he felt only a yearning for something lost. Now he knew that they'd adopted Kate instead.

Father Dooley's haunting question also remained close at hand: what scares you so? The answer hid within another orphanage moment. Kevin had stared up at a giant man with hair on fire and a white thing on his arm. He'd almost hid behind Sister Ignatius rather than risk venturing close to this stranger with sad eyes. He hadn't trusted his good luck, had lost faith that he wouldn't be traded in for a better model.

A better model. Kevin dropped a hand to the envelope that sat on the passenger seat. He held it pressed against the steering wheel with his thumbs and considered the name penned across the front. *Merrit*. He turned it over. His repeated tinkering had loosened the flap. He slipped his finger under the flap, ripping it open a little more, and tossed the letter aside once again. Not yet. He still wasn't ready to read the truths Liam had selected for her.

The clank of newly formed ice cubes startled Merrit. The refrigerator hummed, and a few more ice cubes fell out of the ice maker. The discordant sound seemed fitting somehow. Liam had excused himself to change for that evening's pub event, leaving Merrit and Danny to sit in silence. Danny still stared off into space. He eased a crumbled mess of scone into his mouth and chewed. Slowly. He looked like he was about to vomit, but he swallowed.

"Liam didn't seem so guilty until now," Merrit said. "Would you agree with that statement?"

"Tell me how that flight of fancy works."

"Adrienne Meehan's death was an accident, and Liam showed poor—rather, selfish—judgment in covering it up, but OK, let's grant him immunity because that was over thirty years ago and he was torn up with love over my mom."

"And Lonnie?"

"Seeing Lonnie at the party with me brought up all of Liam's old feelings of impotency because of Andrew, and I personally think he snapped a little, the past and present coming together that way."

"His defense would be what—mental impairment?" Danny didn't sound convinced. "OK, let's grant him immunity again."

"Then there's Kate."

"Yes, Kate."

"So what do we do?" she asked.

"There's no *we*. There's only me and—fucking hell—I can't let it go."

Liam reappeared resplendent as ever in his velvet jacket. "There's something to be said for reaching the end of a life. When you're down to congratulating yourself for waking up at all, what becomes important is how you leave your legacy. I've always preferred having my way, and Kate was fast becoming the sore spot on what I'd otherwise imagined as a peaceful tumble toward death. She'd have instigated a mess of a controversy with the festival and with you, Merrit. And I'll not have Kevin despising me at my bedside either."

He stood there, leaning against the door with fortitude squaring his shoulders and acceptance clearing his gaze of self-pity. No more revelations, Merrit pleaded silently.

"Lung cancer," Liam said, "and I've refused treatment. I smoked for years and that coupled with mixing it up in smoky pubs took its toll."

"No!" Merrit said. "You can't do that. That's not supposed to happen."

She clapped a hand over her mouth just in time to stop a sob from shaking itself free. Liam gentled the same smile at her that he bestowed on his petitioners. His expression said everything, and in that moment she understood the secret to his matchmaking success. He exuded compassion and love—could it be love?—yes, love of humanity in general, an acceptance of foibles and weaknesses in their myriad forms, and an innate awareness of those before him. She'd heard it said that he was charmed, and now she believed it. This man of immense paradox disoriented her, one moment nonchalantly describing Kate's death and the next saying to her, "You're stronger than you know, Merrit. I'd stake my peace on that. Andrew, me, who are we to the person you're becoming? We're nobodies. I know Julia would be proud to see you now."

Merrit ground her hands into her eyes but couldn't stem the tears. Charmed indeed, saying the one thing that would undo her. Cutting to the crux of her longing. And now, after Liam dies, there'd be no one around to be proud of her.

Merrit knelt on the floor, scrabbling for the purse she'd flung aside when she'd set about preparing dinner. Inside, her inhaler waited. She'd thought she was getting better, but her body had something else to say about it. Don't forget me, it said. You've got a ways to go yet, it said. Merrit pulled out the inhaler, gasping, sobbing, and inhaled a spray of the odious nothingness. Another squirt, and her panic subsided to a manageable level.

"I'm sorry you're ill," Danny was saying. "Have you gone in for a second opinion?"

"No need," Liam said. "It's the end of a long life."

Merrit caught her breath and wiped tears off her cheeks. Though Liam relied on the cane, though she'd caught him pinching his lips as if battling an internal demon, he didn't look sickly. She recalled Andrew and how for the longest time he managed to elude the appearance of illness even while the malignant feeding frenzy spread from his liver. Surely she could talk Liam into chemotherapy.

"Kevin was right all along when he complained that you weren't up for the festival this year," Danny said.

Liam's gaze flickered toward the darkened studio. "Until the balance goes the other way I will proceed as usual." He pulled on a gold watch fob and checked the time. "Let's give Kevin a few more minutes, then I'll drive myself. Don't worry yourselves over me."

"I can take you," Merrit said.

"No need for that. I humor Kevin his worries, but how do you think I've been to doctors and back?"

Danny *hmm*'ed under his breath, and Merrit knew he left unsaid other recent excursions. To Kilmoon Church. To Internet Café.

"I'll have to drive you into the village," Danny said.

If Liam heard the sorrow in Danny's voice, he didn't let on. "Never mind that, I have something to show you. A final bad deed on my part."

"Please, no more," Merrit said.

"This is nothing by comparison, a mere blip."

They followed Liam into the living room. This couldn't be happening, Merrit thought. It couldn't. Here she was, finally receiving answers, and Liam was about to be hauled off to the Garda station. Worst of all, he was dying. Which changed everything. Now he really couldn't go to prison. Not if she could help it.

After fetching a key from under his easy-chair cushion, Liam led the way down a hallway lined with bedrooms. "I'll be bedridden soon enough and best to have a new activity to keep me occupied. Danny, don't you piss yourself dry."

Liam pushed open a door with a flourish. Merrit saw nothing unusual about the room. An impressive hardcover book collection with not a lurid cover jacket in sight drew her gaze first. It took her a moment to realize that Danny had gestured toward the desk with a muttered *bloody hell*. Liam entered ahead of them and picked up a journal that had been lying on top of a laptop computer. He flipped through the pages until an envelope landed on the floor. Merrit recognized her mom's creamy stationery with Andrew's hateful letter tucked inside.

Liam hugged the journal to his chest and sagged onto the desk chair. "He's gone."

Two steps and Danny was stooped beside him. Merrit remained in the doorway, frightened by Liam's sudden pallor. She found herself staring at what had to be Kate's laptop while Danny spoke to Liam in a reassuring undertone, his role as Garda officer forgotten for the moment. Merrit ventured closer to hear Liam respond, "I store my journal in the bottom drawer. Leaving it out like that was Kevin's message to me." A sound like a sad and plaintive saxophone cry shook his shoulders. "All my efforts, for shite. He'll have read the letter Andrew sent me before he died. The mystery letter Kevin's been curious about ever since it arrived. And the journal too. He knows the truth about his adoption and Kate's mother. He must despise me now."

Danny strode past Merrit, back toward the living room. "Where's your mobile?"

Merrit steadied herself and ventured closer still. What a colossal idiot to think she could knock on Liam's door with her presumptuous list of solutions about the deaths, with her self-involved little storyboard about how it would all go once she'd gotten to know Liam. She chewed her lip, anguished by the sight of Liam's slack lips. So suddenly an enfeebled man come undone by yet another aspect of this affair he couldn't control: his son's love for him, a love burdened enough to propel Kevin out of sight rather than face Liam's catastrophic defects.

Merrit pulled up an antique wing chair, sat, and held Liam's bad hand with its knotty scar tissue and thickened knuckles. "You don't know for sure that he's gone."

"I'd tucked a letter to you into the journal. It's gone, so he is too." He grabbed her wrist with his good hand. "It must have been too much, a locked door after my oddness and events of these weeks. I never thought he'd use his master key, didn't remember it until now, in fact."

Danny reentered, phone in hand. "Tell Kevin the truth about your health. He'll return straightaway then."

"I'll not have him returning for that reason." Liam shoved the phone away. "The worst part is that he took the knife too. So now he really knows."

"What knife?" Danny said.

"The inlaid knife, you know, the one he made me." Liam shook his head in a confused manner. "It's past my appointed time at the pub."

Merrit pushed herself from Liam's side and grabbed the phone from Danny, who stared at Liam as if stricken cold by a medusa. Liam bent over an open drawer and tossed papers onto the floor. "Maybe it's still here."

"The knife's in evidence," Danny said.

Danny stooped to gather up the papers, but Liam swatted his hands aside and continued yanking out the contents of the drawer.

Merrit stepped away and dialed the phone. "Kevin, this is Merrit. There's something Liam ought to tell you in person. Something that makes all the difference. So come home." She added on a sigh, "Liam doesn't need me. He needs you."

She turned to see Danny shutting the drawer, to hear Liam say, "The second inlaid knife. Identical they were."

· 51 ·

From Galway City heading west, Route 336 became Route 340 became Route 341 in curves that followed the coast and outlined small bays. The inland route would have dropped him at Connemara's tip by now, but, Kevin reminded himself, he was onto something new. No more flying straight from one task to another. No hurry, no worry.

His mobile rang. It took every ounce of his self-discipline to ignore it. The mobile's tiny monitor stared up at him from the cup holder, the only artificial light for miles. A few flicks of his thumb and he erased the message left from Liam's number. He didn't need to hear it to know that he was being summoned home.

He couldn't return knowing what he now did. Deeper still, he couldn't return because reading Liam's journal had forced Kevin to admit that he, Kevin, needed to grow up. It sickened him that Liam had felt compelled to engage in one senseless act after another to protect Kevin from the truth of his adoption, Adrienne Meehan, the whole fucking mess. Christ, talk about remorse, talk about his, Kevin's, uselessness as a human being, talk about pain like a body blow. He would always be the fragile, bereft orphaned boy in Liam's eyes.

He eased the truck onto a dirt pullout and rolled down the window. A gust of salty air cooled his cheeks. He picked up the letter addressed to Merrit, congratulating himself for two seconds of hesitation before flaying the envelope.

Merrit, my dear,

Here I sit mostly staring into flames on this evening after my final visit to Kilmoon Church. I don't plan on visiting her again. Apologies for not seeking you out these past weeks. I have my peculiar ways, and in this case they most certainly apply to you. I wished to observe you from afar, and when the proverbial shite hit the proverbial fan, I used the opportunity to catch a glimmer of your coping mechanisms. You do have highly attuned skills, which is an invaluable trait and one I demand of my successor.

You read correctly: successor. (Ah, Kevin thought, the crux of everything: his legacy.) *And, you ask yourself—for I understand you this much—why not Kate, whose coping mechanisms were honed indeed? Here's the difference I discerned: You coped in a way inclusive to those around you— Marcus, for example—while Kate coped with no one but herself in mind. That you befriended Marcus told me almost all I needed to know about you. That Kate pretended to befriend Lonnie, more than enough about her. Also, unlike you, she yearned for power over others, starting with me.*

I watched you, watched Kate, and decided on you. That's it. Nothing more, nothing less.

All might have gone differently for Kate if she hadn't believed that becoming matchmaker was her right of entitlement in exchange for keeping my secrets from the public, and most especially from Kevin. Another devil's bargain like that with Andrew? I think not. As flexible as my morals may be,

I would never pass down my title to the unfit. This was not an option. She'd have made the worst kind of matchmaker because she resented others' happiness.

Her death, I'm afraid, was inevitable once I understood that she'd never let it go . . .

· 52 ·

Merrit watched as Danny dragged over a wing chair identical to the one Merrit sat on and positioned himself directly in front of Liam. "What second knife?"

Liam's bad hand tensed beneath Merrit's. Rather than answer, he gazed past them toward the hallway. In the living room, something knocked against a wall. A floorboard creaked, and then a high-pitched yowl echoed through the house, followed by a murmuring voice.

"Kevin, thank Christ," Danny said and strode out of the room.

Liam waved Merrit's helping hand away and stood on his own. He glanced around the room, at the laptop, at the papers strewn around the desk. "No, not Kevin."

Merrit escorted Liam to the living room, where a slight woman in a baggy dress kneeled under the dining room table. An empty cat carrier stood by the front door, and a thin tabby crouched under the table.

"Liam," the woman said, her voice ragged and clogged with tears. "This cat is meant to be yours. Kevin said it might be just the thing."

Liam straightened and some of the misery lines on his face

disappeared. He spoke to the woman in the same inviting tone that Merrit imagined he used with his petitioners. "The cat is fine where it is, Emma. Come on out of there."

So this was Kevin's ex. She wasn't what Merrit had expected. Emma looked like she was about to disappear into air molecules any second—and that she wouldn't mind if she did.

Emma scooted out from under the table and used the table edge to pull herself to her feet. She wrapped her arms around her torso, and in that movement, Merrit recognized her from the night of the party. She'd almost bumped into Emma as she wrestled her way through the crowd outside the pub, and now that Merrit thought about it, Emma had given Merrit a strange look before calling out to someone—Danny's wife presumably—and brushing past. She'd hugged a baggy cardigan sweater around herself just like she stood now.

"I saw you," Merrit said. "That night."

The woman fastened her gaze onto Merrit. Her short hair accentuated her boniness except where her face was red and swollen from incessant crying. Merrit stepped back involuntarily as emotion turned Emma's face a darker shade of red. Then, out of nowhere, Emma stood before Merrit, and Merrit was so struck by the despair leeching out of her that she didn't duck when Emma's clawing hands yanked her head back by the hair. Merrit's neck bones cracked. Emma wailed as if her soul were about to shatter into a million jagged pieces. A moment later, Danny pried Emma off her and stepped back with Emma pressed against his chest in a reverse bear hug.

"Are you OK?" Danny asked.

Merrit nodded, more startled than scared.

Emma squirmed. Her expression flitted between desperation and anger, sadness and indignation, so fast Merrit felt herself whirling too. "I saw the way Kevin looked at you at the party, and you looked at him," Emma said. "You hoping to grab him up, to use Lonnie to make him jealous. And now because of you, Kevin is gone. Without me."

Merrit opened her mouth, but Liam raised his hand. His tone remained calm, as if he were talking to an erratic child. "You know that doesn't make sense. Besides which, none of that matters. It's all over. You can relax."

Just like that, under his spell, the tension drained from her body. Liam nodded to Danny to let Emma go. Emma stumbled forward and clutched Liam's outstretched arms. "I'm so tired. I'd like to sleep for forever."

"We've talked about this before. Not forever. But a nap might be good. Over here on Kevin's chair."

"It smells like him. Like the wood in his studio."

Emma waited, placid, while Liam walked to a tall wardrobe, opened it, and lifted a blanket off a high shelf. He spread the blanket over her lap. Emma collapsed into sleep. It happened fast and with a vague smile as she snuggled into Kevin's chair.

Merrit's lungs were fine for once, but her skull throbbed. She lingered a moment in the living room after the men returned to Liam's study. Marcus had told Merrit about the rape, but he hadn't mentioned that Emma was still on the edge of a nervous breakdown a year later. One of her arms had flopped onto the armrest. Shiny scars lined her wrist.

Back in the study, Liam's show of strength had faded. He appeared fibrous around the edges like he'd gone spongy all of a sudden.

"Since the rape she's been erratic like you saw," he said. "Usually she takes her emotions out on herself though. I've been helping her as best as I can."

Danny frowned. "What are you on about?"

"I'm on about the second bloody knife is what. You two thought you'd connected all the dots, but did I ever admit to killing Lonnie? Did I?"

"You didn't—?" Danny said.

"No, I did not. You remember, I mentioned that when per-fecting a technique, Kevin's likely to work something dozens of times until he gets it right. For a while, Kevin carved knife handles—this was before the wood turning—and I don't know how many flawed handles he tossed aside until he got one right. And when he did, he made a second one, identical, that he gave to Emma."

Merrit watched Liam, who lied so well. So well indeed. Only maybe he was finally telling the truth. She'd just remem-bered something about the sweater that Emma had clutched to herself on the night of the party. A ratty thing, an old man's cardigan. The next morning with Lonnie lying dead in his office, Ivan had expected to find his sweater hanging in his workroom. Emma must have grabbed it up to hide the blood.

Liam leaned back in his chair with his head drooped against his chest. His voice sounded weary enough for an early burial. "I was supposed to meet Lonnie at midnight to give him my €1,000, but I was late. Emma had accomplished the feat by the time I arrived."

Danny paced the length of the room. "Are you out of your mind?"

"Indeed not. The moment I saw the knife in Lonnie with me carrying its duplicate in my pocket, I knew. After the rape, Emma used to carry that knife with her everywhere, said she felt protected with a piece of Kevin at her side."

"So you're saying the knife in evidence is Emma's knife, and the one that was in your drawer—?"

"Yes, Kevin's, the one I used to open gifts. You can see why I needed to hide it from Kevin."

Danny's voice rose. "Holy Mary—Liam, dammit, are you listening to me?—this can't go on. You can't always protect Kevin from the tough stuff. Did you think Kevin wouldn't find his knife at some point and realize you'd lied to protect him from Emma's guilt? What were you thinking?"

"Just that—protect Kevin from yet another penance in which he would blame himself for her mental troubles. I thought, I'm dying anyhow, let this be my knife, lost during the party. I used the afghan to wipe her knife clean of fingerprints, which is why the afghan ended up with blood on it." He aimed a wan smile into his lap. "Once again I thought I'd handled the mess, which seems to be my folly."

"Now the mess is on me." Danny stopped pacing. "I'll call the pub to announce your absence due to"—his eyes flickered over Liam's slouched form—"fatigue. Then I'll be on my way with Emma." He stooped closer. "You understand I must take her in? She needs psychiatric help at the very least."

"Kevin would probably agree with that assessment."

"And after Emma, I have to come back for you, by Christ."

Merrit had been listening quietly, massaging her sore head. She dropped her hand, her chest tensing. "After all this? He'll be a prisoner inside his body soon enough."

"Kate was bloody well premeditated. You think I can ignore that? You think Liam doesn't deserve the consequences before he kicks off?"

Merrit stood her ground, too aware that Danny would never understand her perspective. There was no way to explain how her own darkness got mixed up with empathy for Liam.

"Kevin's gone," she said. "That's the only consequence that matters to him. He's punished enough, besides which he won't survive a trial without Kevin at his side. You'll be sending him to the grave that much sooner."

"Maybe that's as it should be." Danny leaned over the desk on balled fists. His knuckles turned white against the dark-grained wood. "Don't you go thinking this is easy because it's not."

"There's nothing your Irish justice system can do to him

now—what would be the point?" She hesitated, hating herself, but knowing that if there was ever a time to use what she now realized was her one skill—her instincts about people, what Marcus meant when he'd pointed out her raised eyebrow—it was now. "You could care less about justice for Kate, and we both know it. But you're not immune to a little selfishness by way of professional recognition and a sex life with your wife. Happily ever after with your promotion in place. That's what this is all about."

"You—bitch." The words ground out between clenched teeth, almost against Danny's will, it seemed to Merrit. She blinked back tears, knowing she'd get over all this with Danny but never all this with Liam if she didn't help him the only way she could.

"How long do you have?" Merrit said to Liam, who roused himself to shrug a hope to see next summer. Then she addressed the bright spots on Danny's cheeks because she couldn't bear the sparks coming out of his eyes. "He'll be dead before the system finishes its process if he's well enough for trial in the first place. And then what will you have but your empty marriage and the wondrous satisfaction of knowing you obeyed the rules of your profession? Not to mention the end of your friendship with Kevin."

Oddly enough, an icy calm appeared to be slow boiling over Danny's features.

"If anyone's counting on you to be true," she continued, "it's not your boss or your wife or me, but Kevin. Just Kevin. But, whatever, it's your choice what you want to lose sleep over, not turning Liam in like a good little cop or betraying Kevin's trust. You know he'll never forgive you no matter what Liam's done and what Kevin can't face right now."

"Enough," Danny said.

Merrit forced herself to go on. Her fingernails bit into her palms with the effort. "But, you can still be a hero by bringing in Emma—Kevin won't begrudge that I'm sure—and maybe bringing in Emma for Lonnie's death will be enough to get you in good with your boss and your wife. And Kate? I'll bet the sprained ankle and high heels will trump the bruise on her chest. Easy enough to see that she tripped—"

"Enough!"

Danny pushed himself away from the desk. He stood with relaxed shoulders but hands fisted at his sides. He perused the book shelves with dazed interest, as if seeing them for the first time. Air hissed in Merrit's ears, the silence was so complete.

Danny ambled to the closest set of shelves and skipped his fingers over the jackets. He picked one at random. "Have you read this one yet, Liam?" The book landed on the rug with a muffled thud. "What about this one?" Another thud. "Catch up on your sickbed reading with this?" Another thud.

He began like a leaf caught in a slow spin. One book flew through the air, then the next; then the next and next; then the next next next until he accelerated into an inevitable sucking maw that only he understood. A fury of books streaked across the room in every direction, millions of words, some of which must convey emotions Danny couldn't express himself. Merrit hunkered down with Liam to wait out Danny's meltdown, silent except for cracking spines, ripping covers, and thuds against the walls. Several minutes later, the noise wound down to one final thud.

Merrit sat up with Liam, who appeared unfazed by the book carcasses that surrounded them. Danny stood as before with arms at his sides but now with sweaty brow and heaving chest. He searched Merrit's face. "Congratulations, you accomplished your purpose, which makes you little better than Lonnie or Kate—or Liam for that matter. You are quite good, quite good indeed."

Emma appeared in the doorway, blinking sleepily. "What's this ruckus?"

Danny welcomed the distraction from his disgust with himself, with Merrit, with this whole sorry shit storm. The sooner he left with Emma, the better for all of them.

Emma leaned against the doorjamb with her bitten nails and rounded shoulders, eyeing the tossed books with a wary expression. Hard to imagine her with enough pent-up rage to plunge a knife into Lonnie.

"I'm sorry. About before." She glanced at Merrit then back at the books. "You startled me is all."

"That's OK," Merrit said. "I understand."

Danny couldn't help noticing that, like Liam, Merrit used her voice to good effect. Almost seductive the way it had lulled Danny while at the same time jabbing him to the core with its blunt words. Now she spoke to Emma with the same intimate quality.

"I can see how it must have looked at the party, and how confused you must have been. But believe me, you misinterpreted what you saw."

Before Merrit could interfere further, Danny approached and laid a hand on Emma's shoulder. "Emma Foley, you're not obliged to say anything unless you wish to do so, but anything that you do say will be taken down in writing and may be given in evidence."

Emma slipped out from under his hand. "You think *I* killed Lonnie?"

· 53 ·

Danny's head felt like it was about to spin off his neck and rocket through the roof, never to be seen again. Perhaps he'd be better off without it at this point.

"Right then," he said as Emma brushed past him. "Would someone mind telling me what the hell is going on now?"

For once Merrit kept her mouth shut. She observed Emma as she sat next to Liam and shook her head vehemently against Liam's shoulder.

"I didn't do it." Emma's voice was muffled against Liam's velvet coat. "On my honor I didn't tell the Garda anything, not even about talking to Kevin outside the party. I haven't said a word to anyone. It was Kevin. I'm so sorry."

"You are mistaken," Liam said in what amounted to an order, an order issued with a note of distress, but still an order.

Yes, she had to be mistaken. Emma wasn't reliable. She couldn't be if she believed she saw Kevin showing interest in Merrit. "Tell us what happened," Danny said.

Emma sat up and haltingly related how beside herself she was the night of the party. "I'd already spoken to Kevin just as the party was starting, but our conversation left me sad. I wanted to—oh, I don't know—but I didn't leave. It was like I wanted to torture myself on the year anniversary, or prove something to myself. Either way, it was easy enough to watch the party through the windows for a while. Earlier I'd seen Lonnie with his date—Merrit—and Kevin looking too interested. I decided to wade into the party again to distract Kevin from Merrit. I was jealous, and I was mad and sad all over again about that piece of shit, Lonnie. It was just a bad night, OK? I should have stayed home in the first place. Should have known better."

"What time was this?" Danny said.

"Between ten and ten thirty."

"That early? You're sure?"

"Yes. I went around so I could enter through the back door— less crowded that way—when who should I see but the shit himself, Lonnie, leaving Internet Café with some leggy creature, pleased with himself as usual. Gave me the sick, it did, but I wasn't about to do anything. He said goodbye to the leggy creature and then he saw me, and I don't think he liked me noticing them together. He dragged me into the café and closed the door behind us, probably just to tell me off, but, oh, you should have seen me then, stark raving. He'd touched me, and that was the end of my sanity for a few minutes, waving the knife Kevin gave me around like a lunatic. But Lonnie only laughed and slapped the knife away. He thought the whole thing was hysterical, me, undone like that. I felt like a bloody freak, a humiliated bloody freak."

"What about the sweater you were wearing?" Merrit said.

"That? Lonnie had ripped my dress. He tossed the jumper at me like it was so much trash and so was I."

"You left your knife in Internet Café?" Danny said.

Emma nodded. "I felt worse about that than the rest, and I wanted to talk to Kevin so badly that I ached. But by then I was in no fit state to brave the party. Your wife was kind enough to get someone to fetch Kevin for me. I told him what happened but that I'd get his knife back, that he shouldn't worry about it. He was livid at first. We actually passed a nice few moments after I calmed him down. At least, I assumed I'd calmed him down. Then the next day news about Lonnie came out—my poor Kevin."

She started to cry again.

"Listen to me," Danny said.

Emma glanced at him.

"Kevin didn't kill Lonnie. I never thought he did, and I don't think so now."

"Are you sure?"

"I'm sure." Danny pulled his timeline out of his pocket, pondering the new fact: the knife was accessible earlier in the evening than he'd previously thought. "But now I'm back to ground zero."

· 54 ·

Kilmoon Church greeted Danny with moon-shiny stones and the quietude of the dead. He'd left Liam's house with one backward glance at Merrit, the woman who had flayed him pink side out, and one question. The original question: who the bloody hell had offed Lonnie?

Perhaps Kilmoon safeguarded the answer as she had the answers to both Adrienne Meehan's and Kate Meehan's deaths. He could hope anyhow.

He tilted his head back, felt the Atlantic winds circling him like banshees, felt for Kevin out in the wind too—lost to them for now—and felt for his wife, most of all his wife, who'd avoided the freewheeling winds since wee Beth's death.

He must accomplish one fecking thing. One—fecking—thing. He hadn't prayed in years but gave it a try now. "Lady Kilmoon, you mighty bitch, grant me insight."

He thought about his revised timeline and Emma's knife forgotten in Lonnie's shop, ripe for the sticking. Truth was, Lisfenora was full of characters who'd have liked to stick Lonnie. Even Marcus. Could he discount Marcus? Lonnie had been causing Marcus grief for months, after all, wanting to drive him out of the plaza.

Danny shook his head. No. Not Marcus. Ivan crept into his

head as he had throughout the investigation. From Ivan his thoughts wandered. He stared at Kilmoon's blackened-window eye sockets. What are you trying to tell me, bitch? You love your secrets.

Love. It always seemed to come down to love. True love, tortured love, unrequited love, match-made love, it didn't matter. Love.

He sat up. "Thank you, bitch."

A t the Grand Arms Hotel, Danny descended the stairs from the lobby into the pub, and thus, into Lonnie's wake. The low-raftered ceiling trapped conversations so that they sounded louder than they were. In the corner, a Celtic string band played ballads. Wall sconces designed to look like lanterns cast orange shadows over the guests, most of whom had been at Liam's party.

In her usual proprietary manner, Mrs. O'Brien stood at the bottom of the steps next to a sign that stated "Private." She shooed a couple of tourists back up the stairs.

"My condolences," Danny said.

Mrs. O'Brien took her time sipping from a glass of white wine. "I see that Marcus is off the plaza at long last. Good of you to do that at least. Go on then."

Danny nodded, reminding himself to smile as he slipped passed her. He edged along the walls and scanned the subdued crowd. The drinking had just begun. The jigs and the singing and the toasting would come later. He fingered the timeline in his jacket pocket. Along with the new fact about the knife's accessibility, an old fact had bobbed up with new significance.

He must do right by Lonnie's death, even if the truth brought down the hounds of hell on his sorry carcass. Two of those hounds stood in the corner of the room next to a memorial collection of bouquets, trinkets, and cards.

Clarkson held his whiskey glass up against Mr. O'Brien's, and they drank. O'Brien wore a black armband and a weary expression. Danny had nothing against the man. In fact, he was a decent sort who, unfortunately, had to contend with the rest of his family on a daily basis. Deep lines etched the sides of his mouth, and they deepened when he nodded a welcome toward Danny. Clarkson merely raised his eyebrows.

The cloying scent of calla lilies and gladioli tickled his throat. He offered his condolences and greeted his superior.

"This one here believed in Kevin Donellan's innocence all along," Clarkson said, his voice looser than usual. He swigged back more whiskey. "By shit he was right."

"Good to have the final answer at last," O'Brien said.

"Sir?" Danny said.

"Old Benjy the Bagger couldn't find conclusive signs of anything but an accidental fall for Kate Meehan. And Lonnie's braid under her body says it all. Cheers." Clarkson drank again.

"But what about the bruise on her chest?" Danny said.

"Inconclusive of anything. Seemed accident prone if her ankle had anything to do with it."

Merrit with her dead-on, bloody instincts had sized up reality just as Benjy had, and it was all too convenient for everyone, even for Danny if truth be told. Unfortunately, Lonnie's braid wouldn't be so easy to explain away when Danny officially absolved Kate of Lonnie's death. Hold that thought. A fresh wave of disgust washed over him. The braid *would* be easy to explain away. Merrit would be only too glad to confirm that Kate had snuck into the crime scene after Lonnie's death to steal the folder and while she was at it, snip the braid and throw the money around. Eloquent and believable she would be, he was sure. Liam would be off the hook again.

Clarkson and O'Brien continued their conversation where they'd left off when Danny appeared. Golf. Danny scanned the lantern-lit crowd again, stopping at Ivan. Dour and twitchy as usual, he slouched at one of the tables near the musicians. He'd cut his hair and bought himself a decent shirt in readiness for his new life. Danny felt sorry for the poor bastard.

He could still leave. He'd done his duty to politics and social niceties. But no, he had to find a way to live with himself, even if he served up only one slice of the truth pie. He excused himself from Clarkson and O'Brien. Clarkson, in true Clarkson fashion told Danny he wasn't all the way off the hook yet. "I'll be watching you."

"I expect so, sir."

Ivan drooped when Danny sat down beside him. "You are sitting in Connie's chair," Ivan said.

"I thought I might be." Danny started to pull out the timeline, but stopped himself. He didn't have the sauce to fuck about with Ivan tonight. Best to get straight to the point. "What time were you supposed to meet Connie at Internet Café on the night of the party?"

Ivan grabbed his pint. With both hands he upended the glass and gulped it down. "You have to harass me still."

"It's a simple question with a simple answer."

Ivan's gaze darted around the room and locked onto something behind Danny. Not something, a someone named Connie O'Brien, who arrived with a plate of cold cuts. She'd pulled her hair back into a tight bun and hadn't bothered to disguise her pasty complexion with makeup. She placed the snacks on the table, pulled up a third chair, and sat down. She immediately placed a roll of ham in her mouth and chewed.

Ivan lowered his head into his hands.

"What time were you supposed to meet Ivan during the party?" Danny said.

Connie pulled the plate closer and bit into another piece of ham. "Midnight."

"Instead of Ivan, you found Lonnie."

She nodded and plucked a piece of turkey off the plate. Tears gathered in her eyes, but she blinked them away. Through the turkey, she said, "It wasn't Ivan's fault. He couldn't find me in the crowd, so I thought we were still on. The door was unlocked anyhow, so I went in."

Liam was supposed to have arrived at midnight to pay Lonnie his latest installment. Lonnie must have been surprised to see Connie. More than surprised, he must have been appalled.

"Who was he to judge me with all the tarts he'd shagged?" she said. "But he did, couldn't stand the thought of us, the hypocrite." She met Danny's gaze. "We all just want love, don't we?"

"Yes, we do."

Ivan moaned into his hands.

"You ever wonder why none of us O'Brien children have married?" Connie said. "Because of my dear sainted mother. She'd like to drive the halo off an angel. So now I finally find a man who can tolerate her, and what does Lonnie do? He threatens to send Ivan back to Minsk. He was my mother all over again. He was always the most like her. But he couldn't do that to me. I deserve love as much as anyone at the matchmaking festival."

Danny held out his hand. Connie held it as they stood up.

Ivan lifted his head. "I knew you would ruin my life."

"I'm sorry for it," Danny said.

"Can Ivan come as far as the Garda station?" Connie said.

He nodded, and the three of them slipped out the service entrance. Tomorrow was soon enough for the drama to begin.

The usual festival buoyancy met them when they reached the plaza. Undaunted by the crispy chill of autumn's start, tourists and locals alike congregated around the benches while others sauntered along with smiling voices. Hopeful dancers swung around in time to hopeful music. Their scarves flapped behind them in the breeze.

"I didn't mean to kill him," Connie said. "It was too much love coming out of me all at once. It was too painful, and I couldn't contain it. The knife was right there on Lonnie's desk."

In a sorry way, Danny understood. He and Ellen had once loved each other in the same all-consuming way. He pulled up his collar against an errant wind gust. The matchmaking festival banner snapped its clichéd insistence that love conquered all.

Tell that to Liam, Danny thought.

He propelled Connie and Ivan away from the plaza. Tomorrow Liam would once again work wonders for everyone but himself, as he had since the seventies. Maybe that was as it should be.

And tomorrow Danny would wake up in his lost friend's bachelor's bed. The decision to take over Kevin's cottage didn't distress him as much as he'd expected. And maybe that was as it should be too.

· 55 ·

Merrit as the next matchmaker. Un-bloody-believable. Or maybe not.

Kevin sat, staring at the letter, awestruck by Liam's machinations, his audacity and will, his perverted sense of justice, not to mention his altruistic loyalty to the lovelorn and his desire for his own brand of good. Kevin continued reading.

. . . This evening I told you a story of hatred, but I stopped before I got to the worst of the cruel gestures that I mentioned. This hatred of mine, it didn't ease upon Andrew's and Julia's departures. If anything, it evolved into a festering pain that led me to grab at the only connection available. I hired a security agency that specialized in everyday spying. I learned of Julia's pregnancy, and I did the math.

Soon after your birth I wrote Andrew a letter, and in this letter I fairly crowed my triumph over him. Over the years, I kept my pain alive by sending him the odd note. I'm sure Julia told Andrew thousands of times that your paternity didn't matter, but I kept his hatred alive with my letters. This is the sorrow of your life, because—who knows?—Andrew might have made a good father. Of the people whose deaths I caused, I bear not the guilt for them that I do for you, because I damaged you the most—and in yet one more way that I now describe to my everlasting shame.

Even thirteen years after your birth, I couldn't resist poking at Andrew again. Near your birthday I sent him another letter, which he must have shared with Julia. In this letter, I made it clear that I was keeping a long-distance eye on you, and that I would like to take on some of my paternal obligations, starting with phone calls. This was a threat, and he knew it. Through you, I hoped to reconnect to Julia.

I can only imagine Julia's turmoil when she found out. She worried for you mightily, and I'm dead certain that her distraction and exhaustion—that insomnia of hers, you know—led her over the traffic line. I only realized my dire mistake weeks later. She wrote pleading me to leave her family alone, to forget about you, to grant her a full night's rest at last. The letter was postmarked the day of her death.

I leave these awful truths to a posthumous letter because I want you around while I die. I enjoy the bits of Julia you don't know you possess. The way you pick at your cuticles when you're hard at thought and the way you stand with your feet splayed. Simple pleasures, in the end, after a complicated life. I'm a selfish man. Believe me, I know it.

Truly, there are two loves in my life, your mother and Kevin, and you as the next matchmaker are my testament to that love. For Julia, who'd have spun a pirouette in pride, and for Kevin, who deserves at long last an unencumbered path in which to find his peace. For this reason, though I regret my actions, at the same time, I do not.

In a way Andrew did my job for me, sending you here. With my cancer diagnosis, I had to start thinking about my legacy anyhow. Little did Andrew know that this talent of mine runs in the family (it's the family curse, in fact), which *means that I have the last say over him anyhow. The notion pleases me mightily.*

Remember, you're charmed for it.

Sincerely,
Liam Donellan

After reading the letter through once and only once, Kevin folded it in precise thirds and slipped it back into the envelope. Little did Merrit know that her new father was as manipulative as her old father. Liam needed an heir sooner than he'd anticipated, and now he had one. If Merrit wanted a loving father figure, she'd best stick with Marcus.

With infinite care he stored the letter in the glove compartment along with the knife that had never gone missing, both of which he'd found in Liam's desk drawer. Only then, when Liam's letter was out sight, did Kevin relax. He needn't feel beholden after all. Liam had other agendas besides protecting the bereft boy—who was not so bereft, who felt fine driving through his homeland, thank you very much.

Kevin leaned his heated face out the window to sniff at wind-torn ocean spray and wince against its sea-salt sting against his cheeks. Route 341 curved out of sight around bends both in front of him and behind, leaving him with the perception he was the only soul on the planet.

But he wasn't. He picked up his mobile and pressed a few buttons to go straight to voicemail. "I made a casserole before I left. It's in the freezer. Old troll."

He hung up. Restarted the engine. Rolled up the window. Nothing to it really, this life as a nomad. Just a series of little actions, one at a time. So next stop, food. The Atlantic's low rumble retreated into the direction from which he'd traveled thus far. He'd let the miles that ticked by on the odometer be his roots. He'd let the knife, the one that had tested his faith, be his reminder.

An hour after Danny left with Emma following on his heels, Liam passed the last book to Merrit, and she positioned it in line with the others. Neither had uttered so much as a sigh since Danny's departure. There was nothing to say. They'd have to pick up the pieces as they did the books: one at time, on their own.

Before leaving, Danny had turned for a last look at Merrit. "I'll take over Kevin's cottage instead of staying here. I imagine you'll be visiting Liam too often for my liking."

The message beneath his parting words pricked Merrit because he was right. She had no morals to stand on with him. She'd gotten what she wanted, after all—Liam for the time he had left. She didn't know if she could bear to watch Liam's skin turn into a gossamer skein through which his blood vessels would show, or watch while pound-by-pound his bones floated to the surface and ill-used muscles puddled onto the mattress. But she would. This would be her price for getting what she wanted.

"You may have broken my mom's heart," she said, "but I'm the one who caused her heart to stop altogether."

She wasn't sure why she'd said this, but she decided that Liam deserved to know that he wasn't the only guilty one when it came to her mom.

"The day she died I saw her slip a letter into an envelope that was addressed to a man. You, though I promptly forgot your name after my mom died. She seemed secretive about it, and me being the spoiled brat that I was, I goaded her about sleeping around with her horse trainer, with the next-door neighbor, with everyone. I called her the worst mom in the world. She stood there with tears streaming down her cheeks, taking it and taking it, as if she deserved to be beaten down with my words. Then she said she must hurry to the post office before it closed. I don't know what happened on the road, but I do know that she wouldn't have been driving half-blinded by tears if I had kept my mouth shut." Merrit paused. "The worst of it was that I only blew up at her because she'd refused to let me ride her horse that day. And now, given everything I've learned, I'm certain I didn't just hurt her, I devastated her."

When she raised her head from sightlessly scanning book titles, she found Liam watching her. "I insist we ban Mrs. O'Brien from signing on for any of my caretaking shifts," he said.

She smiled at his lame attempt to distract her. "I can help you through the rest of the festival. Carry your matchmaking book for you, take your notes. If you'd like."

Some of the opaque dullness lifted from his gaze. "Interesting idea."

"And I can move into the guest room. If you'd like."

"That might be helpful too." Liam rested a hand on each thigh and squeezed them as he straightened his spine. His gaze lingered on the mobile that sat too mute on the desk. He picked it up, pressed a button, listened. "Hovering magpie," he whispered, then let the phone drop to the floor. "I'm cold, Miss Merrit. Shall we rally the fire?"

She settled him before a small mountain of peat and a steady flame. Liam shifted his feet onto an ottoman, wiggled his toes toward the fireplace, and invited the prowling cat onto his lap. Merrit grabbed her shoulder bag from the kitchen. Despite purging it that afternoon, it sat bloated with fresh excess. She pulled out one skein of yarn after another for Liam's approval.

"That," he said, "the purple. And that, the cream."

Next, she pulled out her tape measure. "Longer than Marcus's afghan, correct?"

Liam nodded. "Ah, yes, I do like my feet covered."

After a while, Liam dozed and Merrit hoped the rhythmic click of her needles was his lullaby. She'd care for Liam, yes, and if his pain became intolerable and if he so desired, she'd see to the morphine once again—but this time in honor of her mom who'd have hated to see Liam subjected to unnatural corrosion.

As she knitted, she pictured the photograph of Kilmoon Church that had hung on the living room wall in California. The crumbling walls, the Celtic crosses, the soupy mist. Her mom's hell that Andrew had insisted she live down every day. Little did Merrit and Kevin—and Kate for that matter—know that they'd grown up under Kilmoon's corrosive shadow.

She glanced up to see Liam awake again. "What's that you're thinking about?" he said.

Liam didn't need to know that her mom had let Andrew get away with his cruelty because she'd never stopped loving Liam. This was the penance she'd thought she'd deserved. Kilmoon had haunted her from afar, no doubt infiltrating her dreams, causing her insomnia, ultimately leading her into oncoming traffic. At long last, Merrit understood the enigma that was her mom, and she was grateful for that.

"I'm wondering how long it will take me to finish this afghan, that's all," Merrit said.

He grunted his skepticism.

She smiled. "Hey, I can be enigmatic too."

"Like father, like daughter?"

"Or like mother."

"Just so." Liam settled back into his chair. "I'm glad you're here after all that."

He slipped into sleep again. After a while, Merrit set her knitting needles aside and reached inside her bag for the black box with squeaky hinges. She popped the box open and brushed her fingers across the earrings nestled within. Firelight glowed deep within the moonstones. Merrit slipped them on.

"I'm glad I'm here too," she said.

Acknowledgments

I began writing *Kilmoon* in 2002. It's been a long journey. Apologies if I've forgotten anyone who helped me along the way. All errors in the manuscript are my own.

Elizabeth George, thank you for your supportive comments during my first-ever writers workshop. Your words gave me hope and helped me persevere. Especially, thank you for the Elizabeth George Foundation and for *Two of the Deadliest*. What an honor.

Another Elizabeth: Elizabeth Udall, patron of the arts, for the Walden Fellowship. Peace be with you, wherever you are.

In Ireland, Detective Sergeant David Sheady and Sergeant-in-Charge Brian Howard answered my questions about the Garda Síochána. Raising a Guinness to you! Hope I kept it real through the many subsequent revisions. So much still to learn. Teresa Donnellan, thank you for hosting me and for answering my random questions about life in Ireland.

Thanks to Chris Ginocchio (medical), Dallas Finn Calvert (equestrian), and Laura S. Trice (Russian) for your specialized knowledge.

So many supportive and wonderful writers provided feedback and moral support and good advice and writing tips (in no particular order): Michael Bigham, Jeannie Burt, Evan Lewis, Kassandra Kelly, Becky Kjelstrom, Jackie Blain, Gigi Pandian, Tracy Burkholder, Wendy Gordon, Charlotte Rains

Dixon, Deborah Guyol, April Henry, Bill Cameron, and Ann Littlewood.

Drink-and-thinkers, you fab mystery writers—I'd never forget you: Angela Sanders, Cindy Brown, Holly Franko (editor extraordinaire!). And special thanks to another fab writer I'd never forget: Stacy Allen for your sweet, inspirational words over the years—you're a generous soul.

My Eugene shadow-spinning peeps (even though some of you don't live there): Christina Lay, Pamela Jean Herber, Cynthia Coate Ray, Cheryl Owen-Wilson, and dear Elizabeth Engstrom, for so much.

Also, I'd like to thank two literary agents for valuable manuscript feedback: Elizabeth Kracht and Jill Marsal.

Arlene Alber, Kara Alber, Nicole Sidlauskas—my family. Can you believe it? Thanks for not pooh-poohing this crazy endeavor that took hold of me.

Photo: Jim Titus

LISA ALBER received an Elizabeth George Foundation writing grant based on *Kilmoon* in addition to a Walden Fellowship. Her short story "Paddy O'Grady's Thigh" appeared in *Two of the Deadliest* (HarperCollins), an anthology edited by Elizabeth George. In addition, Lisa was nominated for a Pushcart Prize for the story "Eileen and the Rock." A Californian with a penchant for travel, animal advocacy, and photography, Lisa worked in international finance and book publishing before exchanging the corporate ladder for storytelling. She currently lives in the Pacific Northwest. *Kilmoon* is her first novel in the County Clare Mystery series.

Learn more about Lisa at www.lisaalber.com.

Made in the USA
San Bernardino, CA
23 February 2017